Alan Dunn was ~~...~~ ~~...~~ ~~...~~ ~~...~~ but lives on
the fringes of the L~~...~~ ~~...~~ published work,
the Ian St James Aw~~...~~ ~~...~~ *French Kisses*, has
been anthologised twice ~~...~~ ~~...~~ as been a work study officer,
hospital administrator, insurance salesman, company
secretary, folk musician and teacher of creative writing.
He enjoys running, cycling and collects models of jelly-
babies.

He is the author of four other novels including *Die Cast*
and *Payback*, available from Piatkus.

Also by Alan Dunn

Die-Cast
Payback

ICE COLD

Alan Dunn

PIATKUS

All the characters in this book are fictitious and any resemblance
to real persons, living or dead, is entirely coincidental.

Copyright © 2005 by Alan Dunn

First published in Great Britain in 2005 by
Judy Piatkus (Publishers) Ltd of
5 Windmill Street, London W1T 2JA
email: info@piatkus.co.uk

This edition published 2005

The moral right of the author has been asserted

A catalogue record for this book is available
from the British Library

ISBN 0 7499 3623 1

Set in Times by Palimpsest Book Production Limited,
Polmont, Stirlingshire

Printed and bound in Great Britain by Mackays Ltd,
Chatham, Kent

For the past three years I've been fortunate to have taught English at Nelson Thomlinson School in Wigton, Cumbria. As I write, I'm preparing to move to another school. This novel is therefore dedicated to the staff and students who have enriched my life, particularly the English and Music departments, the infamous Solway Stompers and the shy, retiring Sambandits. Neil Walker, Eva Cook, Andrew Walker, Tim Eyrl, Jim Richardson, Mike Graves, Emma Bryson and Celia Chamberlain have all played their parts in making my life both exciting and tiring. MC, TR, LP, JP and LD have kept me right when it would have been easy to go wrong. I must also (because they asked) mention Issy, Kate, the girly chorus and the Theatre Studies group who are all (especially Rushton and Sophie Bob) destined for great things.

My wife, Jan, has encouraged and supported me throughout my writing career; my sons, Mike and Pete, continue to make me feel young and old at the same time; Sophie, Tim and Amy make me smile. And I wouldn't have had the will to keep writing if it wasn't for Diana Tyler at MBA. Thank you, everyone.

CHAPTER ONE

Kim Bryden always was persuasive. Perhaps that's why she prospered in the Police Force, she could make others – significant others – see what she wanted, and why she wanted it. While I was bouncing my head repeatedly against the brick wall of police bureaucracy, she simply smiled and spoke softly; she was given the key, opened the door and passed through. And she made sure she locked the door behind her.

She's a self-centred, manipulative woman. I know this, I've argued with her often enough – she's even been close to arresting me a couple of times. Yet she's sitting opposite me in the restaurant of the best hotel in town, trying to sell me something. And I'm close to buying.

Even getting me there is a triumph for her. I don't like social occasions. I feel nervous when there are people around, especially now I no longer have the support alcohol once provided. Eating has always been a private matter for me. I can cope with a quiet table in the corner of a small bistro, just me and someone I want to be with, sharing each other. But this is different. This is overpowering luxury; this is a demonstration of influence and power; this is Kim saying, 'look at me, look at what I'm becoming, look at what I can do.' If we were in a film, the director would have my point-of-view shots way down low. Kim would tower over me, smiling at my discomfort, leaning back and making wide, expansive gestures. Every time there was a shot of me I'd be glancing up, shoulders closed, toying with my food. She's in charge and I resent her for not hiding the fact.

I shouldn't have come. If Jen had been around I wouldn't

even have considered it, but it's another week until her return. Kim knew that (it was the first thing she asked), so she's obviously preying on my weaknesses. I reassure myself that this isn't paranoia. If it were, then the concept of paranoia would be beyond me; at least I think that's how the argument goes. But on the other hand, if I am paranoid, should I be able to persuade myself that I'm not by using this very same logic? The debate is quickly beyond me.

'Quite a place, eh Billy?'

I look around, nod my head. If opulence was a perfume, the restaurant has given itself a complete body rub. This is no eau de cologne; this is the unadulterated, undiluted straight-from-the-bottle fragrance. The décor is cool and modern, with pale colours, wide gaps between tables and spotlights emphasising the space. The tables are solid and heavy, fine-grained, bleached timber inlaid with dark abstract lines of swirling marquetry. Stare at them for long enough and you get a migraine. The chairs match in content but not in form, each slightly different to the next. The floor is a dark wood, black as a lake, reflecting the lights in its deep layers of varnish.

In a distant corner dogged musicians are grimacing over their instruments. Piano, bass and drums are fighting over the fragments of a contemporary jazz tune, all discords and arrhythmic arguments. They pause briefly and, although the room is full, there's no applause, barely even acknowledgement in the form of glances in their direction. They quickly bend their dinner-jacketed, craftsman-like frames to the next piece of modernist wallpaper.

There are works of art on the walls, an eclectic mix of collages and wire-form sculptures, embroidery and fabric reliefs, splashes of orgasmic colour next to acres of anaemic, monochromatic canvas. Some could be the mutant offspring of portraits or landscapes, almost familiar; others are completely alien. They look obscure enough to be originals, no doubt expensive originals. The reason they don't dominate

2

the room is that the room itself is so large, and one wall, curving into the ceiling, is made of glass. I'm not sure how the architect managed it, but there are no internal reflections. Instead the view looks out to the river, to the bridges and the lights; the pale towers of flourmill become art gallery, the huge organic puffballs of concert hall and conference centre, the silent ribbons of late evening traffic. The room has been designed to impress, but instead I'm overpowered.

'I expect you're wondering why I invited you here, Billy.'

'No. You were quite clear on the phone. You mentioned, in the most subtle of ways, of course, that I owed you some favours. That's true, I can't deny it. But we could have met over lunch, or you could have come to the office. I could even have come to your place, though I must admit I get a little nervous when I have to visit the bunker.'

'Too many memories?'

'Too many policemen. I don't trust them. Jen's the same, hates the idea of going into hospital. She's an insider, she knows what doctors get up to.'

Kim shrugs, and I look at her closely for the first time. I'd noticed the clothes when we met in the bar – she was power-dressed to match the room in a two-piece suit and colour co-ordinated shoes. I thought she must have come straight from an important meeting because Kim's usual style is comfortable-seedy. So now I take more notice. She's wearing make-up, her hair is styled, she looks less tired than I've seen her for years. She's in her late forties, early fifties, and she's almost attractive. Then she leans forward, rests her chin on her fingertips, and she's suddenly the policewoman again.

'So finish what you were saying, Billy. Why are you here?'

I put down my knife and fork – they've hardly been used anyway. I force a smile to my face. There's the distant sound of a siren; it pierces the glass for a brief moment but has no place in here. Like me, like Kim when she's dressed as her human alter ego, it belongs in a different world.

3

'You haven't asked me out because you like my company. You want something from me, you said as much. It's not likely to be a straightforward favour – if you wanted an alarm system fitted to your house you would have just mentioned it on the phone. In fact, you would have got one of your flatfeet to make the call for you.'

'I see you haven't lost your cynicism, Billy. So go on, tell me more.'

I nod at her. 'Flash outfit.' She nods back; she knows it isn't meant as a compliment. I look to the tables on both sides. 'Flash place. Flash prices as well, I imagine, especially since there weren't actually any prices on the menu. It can't be that you're trying to impress me . . .'

'You don't impress that easily. OK, Billy, I get it, you're just a plain, down-to-earth ex-copper. I've heard it all before. So cut the entrée, get to the main course. Impress me with your incisive analysis of my motivation. Tell me why you're here.'

Perhaps I'm beginning to annoy her. I have this effect on people in authority, it took me years to develop and I'm pleased to see I haven't lost the talent. I must have raised my eyebrow in self-satisfaction. Kim sees it immediately.

'In your own time, of course,' she says, sitting back in her chair. Her smile is quite disarming. I can see why she's such a good policewoman.

'It can't be anything to do with work, police work, that is. Not official police work. I mean, some of my old colleagues have passed my name on to firms who want security installations, but anything done through the Police Authority these days is triplicated and committeed and tendered for and there's no way . . .' I tail off, I don't really know what she wants. But now it's a challenge, and I have to start thinking. I do this aloud – at least I won't have to explain my deduction methods to Kim. 'So it's not police business. It's not personal. What's left?'

Kim's doing her best to be inscrutable again, aware that I'm talking to myself, for myself.

4

'It's something to do with security – that's my field, that's where I'm an expert.'

Kim nods; it's as if she's paying me a double compliment, agreeing with my statement and with the direction of my thoughts. That's when the tumblers click. I remember something she said when our paths crossed last time; I remember her air of dissatisfaction, her obvious weariness. None of it is there now.

'Kim, how old are you?'

This time she *is* taken aback. She looks puzzled. 'You should never ask a lady . . .'

'You're no lady, Ms Bryden, you're police. And you know the rules, every question is deliberate and asked for a reason. So how old are you? And how long have you been in the Force?'

She shrugs. 'I joined from school, when I was eighteen. Thirty-one years ago.'

'Up for retirement soon?'

'Why should that be of interest to you, Mr Oliphant?'

The formality's deliberate and she's being defensive, I'm on the right track.

'Difficult, isn't it, when you've been police all your life. You find yourself getting tired, you can't keep up with the pace, the changes, the technology. Your colleagues aren't so much young as juvenile. You get to thinking it would be good to slow down a little; you realise you could – if you really wanted – retire early. You start counting down the days and then, suddenly, there's a huge empty space ahead of you. Some people panic. Some are relieved. Others think carefully, they consider options, they plan. Not me, Kim, I didn't have time for any of that. The police and I didn't part amicably. But you? You've had plenty of time. And no-one could accuse you of not thinking clearly. So when's the party? Have they asked you yet what you want as a present? Have you been taken off investigative duties because you're unlikely to be able to complete them?'

'Christmas,' Kim says. It's enough.

'Congratulations. But you can't want advice, that's not why you asked me out. I can't see you wanting to set up your own business, not like mine. I can't see you crawling through roof spaces, fitting cameras and alarms, getting dirty. You never were the type to get dirty.'

'No Billy, I'm not the dirty type. So what are the options?'

'The options? You're not the murder squad's golden girl any more . . .'

'Never was, Billy. I'm more like you than you think, more than you'll ever know.'

I'll go back to that comment some day – it might be worth investing a little time there. But for the moment I'm on a roll. 'Not police, not self-employed. So you're working for someone. You've got a reputation – come on, no false modesty – as a good investigative cop. Where does that lead? Security consultant for a national firm? Fraud investigation for an insurance company? Perhaps something international, even? But why talk to me? Information? If that's what you're after it can only be that you're working for one of the really big boys, not a local yokel; you're too polite to get information from a competitor and I wouldn't give it anyway.' I have to stop there, the line's run cold. I don't have enough from her to let me take the next step and I'm not really prepared to guess. 'Anyway, if I can help, you're welcome. But there was no need to go to all this trouble, Kim. I'd have been happier with a salad roll and a cup of tea.'

She reaches down to her handbag on the floor beside her seat. She brings out a card, puts it face down on the table just out of my reach, keeps one finger on top of it. 'Perhaps we're both too modest,' she says.

'Meaning?'

'You're the one searching for meanings. So tell me. After all, I'm giving you plenty of clues.'

'Singular, Kim, clue. One clue. I said you were too modest, you returned the compliment. Perhaps it's not information you want. But what's the alternative?' I already know – there is only one. If she's not pumping me for information then she's after some type of resource, and the only thing I own of any value is me. The thought makes me smile. 'You want me to come and work for you? But of course, I'm too modest to figure that out.'

Kim turns over the card, pushes it across to me. When I pick it up I can understand why we're dining out in such style. The card feels expensive, not embossed, but with slightly chamfered edges. It's pale cream in colour. Her name is printed on it, no address, just a telephone number, a mobile number and an email address. There's a title, 'Security Consultant'. Above that information, in a similar bold, minimalist typeface, is the single word 'Amalgam'.

I put the card down in the same place, in the middle of the table. 'Doesn't look as if you'll be relying on your pension to keep you in spending money, then.'

'They made me an offer I couldn't refuse.'

'"They"? Who exactly are "they"?' I haven't heard of Amalgam before, and there's nothing to suggest that they're a limited company or a partnership, regional, national or even international. And I must admit I'm curious.

'Amalgam is a private company. Quite a good name, coined by the MD; it means a mixture of metals, silver or gold with mercury. Good image, isn't it? Mercury's sometimes called quicksilver. Value and speed combined? Anyway, Amalgam owns this hotel, half a dozen others in Britain, about two hundred world-wide, concentrated in the US and Europe. It's also a holding company with interests in the leisure industry, particularly resort complexes in Spain, Italy and around the Mediterranean – quite exclusive places, expensive, high quality. And it's expanding through acquisition and new build.'

'And you come in . . .?'

Kim can see I'm curious – I'm leaning forward, elbows on the table – she can read the signs easily enough. What she doesn't know is the focus of my curiosity. It's obvious that she's invited me out for this meal because she wants either me or my knowledge (call it expertise, I'm not as modest as Kim thinks) and she assumes that I'm interested in working with her or for her. I don't want to disappoint her, but I have no intention of ever working for anyone except myself. I can be a difficult person to be with, to live with; there are times when I wonder why Jen stays with me, and I'm desperate to have her back just so I can make sure she still wants me. But at least I recognise that I can be a problem. Kim knew me when I was in the force, when I had to work to the rules, had to do as I was told. Under those circumstances I was restrained to the point of docility (though some of my ex-colleagues would no doubt disagree with that statement) and my private life suffered as a consequence. The anarchist within me was only allowed to surface outside work. All those TV programmes you see about 'wild' policemen who are tolerated by their partners, their bosses, their work-mates, they're all fiction. Lies. In the British police you work to the rules or you don't work at all. It's the same in any organisation, and I can't believe that Amalgam will be any different. So I'm not curious about the prospect of working for them. But I am curious about the company themselves and how they latched onto Kim. I'm also keen to know whether she's approaching me with her bosses' knowledge, whether the decision to ask me to work with her is hers or theirs. Exactly what power does she have? Might she be of use to me? I can be an opportunistic parasite as much as the next man. Kim's taking her time, thinking how much she can tell me, how much she wants me to know. There are times when she reminds me of me.

Eventually she decides to speak. 'There's not really a lot to say, Billy. I got to know one or two of the directors about a year ago, when this place was about to open. They knew I was about to retire, they felt there was an opportunity for me to work for them, and they came up with an attractive package. But it soon became clear – we all acknowledged the fact – that I'd need help. I can't manage all the work myself. I need someone who's good in the field. And I thought you might be interested.'

I feed her the right line. 'Exactly what is "the work"?'

I can tell by the way her speech quickens that she's rehearsed this part. 'It's largely divided into two sections. Any new build, I get involved at the planning stage, talking to architects, researching the best way of overcoming security problems. I haven't actually taken over yet, but I'll have a team working for me, mostly ex-cops, quite a few experienced in working abroad. As a team, we can cope with that. But when we acquire an existing property there's usually a substantial upgrading involved – nothing less than five star is acceptable. I have to survey properties, check on local factors, set up the specifications and mechanics of the security system and provide a local manager I can trust. That's the part of the job I need help with – we're expanding at such a rate I won't be able to keep up. I've already had to take leave to do a survey in Italy because there was no-one else available. And that's where you come in. You could start on the backlog quickly. You'd need very little training. And it would be a permanent job. Salaried, but with a bonus and share options. You'd be earning ten times as much as you are at the moment.'

Kim is efficient. She'll have checked my income, found my tax returns. She'll have added on a small amount for cash jobs. She'll have figured out I make about thirty thousand profit each year. So this job is worth around three hundred thousand. I sit back again, this is a ridiculously large amount and it's suddenly tempting. My confidence, my control, both have disappeared.

'If you've done your research, that's a lot of money.' I believe, in times of stress, in being direct.

'I've done my research. You're worth it if you do the job properly.'

9

I have to stop myself laughing. There's always a catch. 'That's worrying, Kim, the word "properly". You know I'm the type who enjoys being unorthodox. I don't like rules. "Doing the job properly" suggests there's a certain way of doing it. A path to follow. I don't walk on paths. I'm more in favour of the freedom to roam, in other people's gardens, down private lanes, over gates, cutting barbed-wire fences. I'm a natural trespasser.'

Kim has anticipated my objections. 'That's the type of person I want. That's the type of person my bosses want.' She leans closer. 'We need someone who can bend the rules, someone who isn't afraid to try the unusual approach. You can do it, Billy. I can go up to three hundred and sixty thou.' She pauses to let the figure sink in. It does so like a good whisky, smooth and melting and dangerous and very, very tempting. I thought I was stronger than this.

'There are some drawbacks, of course. You'll be out of the country a lot, but that'll be no hardship; all accommodation paid for, top-class hotels. And on that money, Jen could stop working and go with you. We could even arrange to make you an off-shore company, keep your taxes low.'

It's too much to think about all at once, too much to think about by myself. I need Jen's opinion. I need something down on paper, something I can show to people, something to remind me that I haven't just dreamed this up. 'Make me a formal written offer,' I say, and I barely recognise my own thin voice. I feel sick though I've hardly touched the food on my plate. I take a sip of water. 'Then I'll think about it, talk it over with Jen. I'll get back to you.'

Kim shakes her head from side to side. 'You underestimate me,' she says, removes an envelope from her bag and hands it to me. It has my name on it, the same typeface as was on Kim's card. I don't even bother to open it, simply file it in my jacket pocket.

'My bosses would like to meet you,' she adds.

'So you're going to fly me out to . . .?' I imagine they'll

be in London, but it's conceivable that they might be based in New York or on the continent, perhaps even a tax haven in the West Indies.

'They're already here,' Kim says, 'at least most of them are. Some will arrive later tonight.'

'They're here? Surely they wouldn't come just on the off-chance that—'

'No, Billy, you're good but you're not that good. It's the anniversary of the hotel opening and they're celebrating. And they have –' she leans even closer ' – a weekend of entertainment planned. Did you see the posters in the entrance hall?'

I noticed many things as I walked into the hotel: the luxury of the surroundings, the desperate-to-please smiles on the receptionists' faces, the expensive emptiness of the three-storey lobby, the vast acreage of glass and the innumerable light fittings with not a single bulb flickering or out. But no posters. I shake my head, admit my guilt.

'They were rather discreet. But they were advertising the weekend's speciality, a murder mystery event. Very popular as well.'

'Isn't that a little downmarket? I mean, I can't imagine the Savoy doing this.'

'You're probably right, but the organiser knows one of the directors. In fact, the whole board is here to join in, on a semi-detached basis. It builds teamwork, apparently, gets people to recognise each other's strengths and weaknesses. That's why they're here. And they've agreed to put some time aside to meet you. Ten o'clock tomorrow morning?'

I shake my head. This is too much, too fast. 'I need to think about it,' I say.

'That's understandable. Ring me any time before nine to let me know whether you're coming or not. Do you want a dessert?'

'No. No, I think I'd better go home. I should get in touch with Jen, if I can.'

'Coffee?'

'No thanks.'

'Yes, it keeps me awake all night if I drink it after lunch. Come on then, I'll see you to your car. Then I'll deliver my report and hope to hear from you.' We rise to our feet and she leads me across the room. The maitre d' bows slightly as if he knows her, but she ignores him. 'Are you in the car park?' she asks, pointing to the lift doors.

'No. I came straight from work. I wasn't sure if the van would fit under the barrier.'

Kim gives me a playful punch that's too blokey, it's out of place in our relationship. 'You're going to find it difficult reconciling your new lifestyle with your old values,' she says, 'there'll be no need to run vans, Billy.'

It's as if she already knows the answer. She knows I'll come to meet the directors of Amalgam; we'll talk to each other; I'll wear my only dark suit and try to impress; they'll offer me the job. It's been carefully planned; the runes have been read, the bones cast, the stars and planets consulted. The future is already known, determined by the presence of money. I'd be mad not to accept the offer.

But there's always been some doubt about my sanity.

CHAPTER TWO

We step outside. The main entrance is away from the river, it opens onto a narrow strip of land, lawned and flower-bedded, flagpoles erect at regular intervals. There's a large sign announcing the name of the hotel, smaller ones advising people to keep off the grass. Beyond is the road, then a warehouse in the process of gentrification. Behind the warehouse rise steep slopes clad with steps and the walls of derelict houses, overgrown with nettles. They won't stay that way. Property prices are rising; this area between the river and the city is a brownfield site. I've seen the plans, photographs of scale models in glass cases unveiled in a blaze of publicity. Within a year the steep bank will be plugged with the foundations of apartments and offices, subsidised by the local authority and government. Someone will be making a lot of money.

Kim catches me gazing upwards. 'Amalgam owns that as well. Came as part of the package. No-one else imagined that anything much could be done with it. But they did. They're clever and they're ambitious.' She looks directly at me and I begin to feel uncomfortable under her gaze. 'When they see something they want, they go for it.'

'Look,' I say, 'there's no need to escort me all the way to the van. It's quite a pleasant evening, so I might take a stroll along the river. Thinking's a luxury, I don't normally have much time for it.'

Kim opens her mouth to reply, but the words I hear aren't hers.

'Bryden, you bastard! Been in to collect your next bribe?'

There are three people standing on the pavement beside the hotel sign; one of them, a young man, starts striding stiff-legged towards us, waving a placard. It's too dark to read what it says, but even in daylight the haste of his movement would have left any message blurred and incoherent.

'Bryden! Can you hear me?' His voice is harsh, loud, jagged, and I step towards him, ready to kick or punch if necessary.

'It's OK, Billy,' Kim's hand is at my shoulder, pulling me back, 'I know him.' She reaches into her bag again, speaks rapid words into a standard issue radio. 'Bryden here, main entrance, Riverside Hotel, assistance required, one car.' She looks at the man again. He's so close I can see his wide eyes, long hair; he's holding the placard as if he's going to hit Kim with it. 'Could be urgent,' she adds, 'over.'

'Terry,' she says, her voice firm and clear, 'this'll do you no good at all. Put it down and let's talk. You talk, I'll listen. I promise.'

He stops in front of her, glances at me but decides I'm irrelevant. He doesn't lower the placard and pole but holds it still, ready for action. I can read it now, block capitals yelling: 'THE REAL MURDER MYSTERY – WHAT HAPPENED TO ANNA?'

'Talk to you? I'll bloody well talk to you, Bryden. It's a year now, a year, and what have you done? Nothing. What have you found out? Nothing. Who've you charged? No-one.' He's lowered his voice only a little and the rage of his words is making him spit. 'You've been sitting on your fat backside, planning your retirement. And what're you gonna do? Work for this lot! Talk about a bloody conspiracy. How much are they paying you to keep quiet, eh? What've they promised you?'

'Terry, we've been through all this before, I've already told you . . .'

'Told me? You've told me nothing I didn't already know. Jesus Christ, Bryden, Anna was murdered! And what have you done about it? Nothing.' I think he's about to start again on his question and answer sequence, but he suddenly changes tack. 'And what are *they* doing now?' He jerks a thumb towards the hotel. 'A year, exactly a year, Bryden. And they're having a fucking murder weekend!' He lifts the wooden pole high and I step towards him, but before I can do anything he drops it, crumples to the ground. He's crying, and I can make out only a few of his words. He repeats 'murder' and 'Anna', but each word is elongated with ragged inhalations, punctuated by sniffs and sobs.

There's a flash of blue neon along the quayside, an angry orange-striped prowler spins towards us and squeals to a halt. The occupants are out and running – after all, it's one of their own in danger. Kim holds the palms of her hands out towards them, waves them to a walk.

'It's OK, Terry,' she says, and her voice is sugared, calming, 'it's OK. Come on, I said I'd listen. Let's get in the back of the car, you can tell me everything.' She bends down, gently helps the man to his feet. Then she looks at me. 'Sorry, Billy, I'll explain tomorrow. Ten o'clock, I'll meet you in reception.' It's a matter-of-fact statement, she's confirming an appointment, not asking if I'll be there. And then she's helping the young man, Terry, into the back of the car, waving the uniforms away, climbing in after him. I stand for a little while like any curious bystander, but there's little else I can do. I walk away, across the grass – I can't resist breaking rules – towards my van.

I'm feeling for the keys in my pocket when a voice turns me round. 'Excuse me, are you a police officer as well?' It's a polite voice belonging to a small grandmother of a woman who should be dressed in a bright bell-like dress, waving a wand with sparkles of light coming out of it, promising that I *should* go to the ball. Instead of a magic wand she's clutching the arm of an even older man. Both are wrapped in coats and scarves. Both wear glasses. They seem helpless, someone should make models of them and sell them as Christmas presents.

'No,' I say softly, 'I'm not a policeman. Is there a problem?'

They look at each other. I'm not a policeman, they've never met me before, but I'm asking them if they have a problem. I'm implying that I may be able to help if they do have a problem. The message passes between them, decades of speaking without words have taught them what a look means, a touch, a raise of the eyebrows or a flare of the nostrils. They appear reconciled to some loss. The man is shaking slightly, though it isn't cold. The woman pushes his spectacles up his nose. Once they were young.

'Terry is our son-in-law,' the woman says.

'Was,' the man interjects, 'he *was* our son-in-law.'

'No, dear, he still is. Some bonds . . . can't be broken.' She forces each carefully considered word through lips clenched tight, as if frightened that her meaning will be misinterpreted.

'Is he going to be arrested?' the man asks.

All three of us peer at the police car. The figures in the rear are still talking; there's no sign of any argument.

'I don't think he'll be arrested,' I reply, 'he seems to have calmed down.'

'Will it be alright if we wait for him?' It's the woman talking again, but her attention is focused on her husband. She seems more worried about him than Terry.

'I'm sure it'll be OK,' I say. 'Why don't we go into the hotel and sit . . .'

'Oh no, they wouldn't let *us* in there, would they, dear? We're definitely non gratis in that place.' She seems rather proud of the notion and of the vitriol in her voice.

'My van's parked just down the road. We could sit in there if you want. Until Terry's ready to go. You both look as if you could do with a sit down.'

They look at each other again. 'That's very kind of you, Mr . . .?'

'Oliphant. Billy Oliphant.'

'Would you mind taking my husband's other arm? He's

16

not used to being out so late, and he's not as fit as he used to be.' I do as I'm asked, steer them both towards the van as the woman continues her suddenly liberated chatter. 'He's eighty-four years old. I'm much younger, I'm sixty-nine. I'm his second wife, you see. We married after his first wife died. Are you married, Mr Oliphant?'

'Not now.'

'Shame, you seem like a very pleasant young man. A bit like Terry. I hope he'll be alright. He shouldn't have done it, shouted at the Chief Inspector like that. It was meant to be a silent protest, a sort of vigil. We were hoping that the TV would be here, or the radio, or even the newspapers. We sent out a press release. But there's been no-one. No-one at all. It's as if nobody cares.'

The woman isn't as old, as doddering, as innocent as she appears to be. She knows Kim's precise rank, Chief Inspector. She was taking part in some sort of protest, she was expecting some type of publicity. And Terry was talking about a murder. So I'm keen to find out more as I open the door of the van. I help her in first and she shuffles across into the middle seat. It's more of an effort to push her husband up beside her, not because of his weight (I can feel his arm through his coat, there's no flesh on it) but because he's so immobile. But she encourages him and tugs at his coat and between us we manage the job. I hurry round to my side but before I can even sit down the questions begin.

'My goodness, Mr Oliphant, it says on your van you're a security firm.'

'That's right, I . . .'

'I've read about businesses like yours – you're a sort of private detective, aren't you?'

'No, not quite, I do other things as . . .'

'So you do detective work some of the time?'

'Well, yes, but . . .'

'Are you expensive?'

17

I can see where this is going. 'Yes,' I reply quickly. It has the desired effect. The woman is quiet.

'Do you mind if I ask *you* a few questions?' My question is gentle, polite. The woman looks at her husband. He gives a nod, if I hadn't been watching carefully I wouldn't have seen it. I take it as a yes, go straight on. 'You know who I am, but I'm not quite sure who you are. Terry's parents-in-law, but that doesn't mean a lot to me. And who's Anna?'

To my surprise it's the man who begins to answer my questions. His voice is calm but, like his body, frail. 'I'm Charles Robertson. This is my wife, Emily. Terry Wilder –' he pauses momentarily before emphasising the next word '– *is* our son-in-law. Just about a year ago . . .'

'Almost exactly a year,' Emily Robertson pushes in.

'A year ago,' her husband continues, 'Annabelle – our daughter, Terry's wife – was found dead at the hotel.'

'And you think it was murder?' I shouldn't interrupt, but I can see Kim getting out of the police car.

'No, Mr Oliphant, we *know* it was murder. Her body was found in a walk-in freezer. She was naked. She was tied up. She was gagged.' He's silent for a while. 'And she was pregnant.' Emily Robertson reaches across, touches her husband gently on the knee. He puts his hand on hers, keeps it there.

'The hotel wasn't fully open at the time. There was a skeleton staff, just enough to cope with the special guests, the directors of the company owning the hotel. A year's passed, but the police haven't been able to find the person responsible. No arrest, not even a suspect. Chief Inspector Bryden was the officer in charge. And now we hear she's retiring to work for the company she was meant to be investigating.'

I have to make a point. 'She would be investigating the murder, not the company, Mr Robertson.'

'It comes to the same thing, Mr Oliphant. The hotel wasn't open to the public, the doors were locked, the security systems were installed and working. No-one came in, no-one

18

went out, the security videotapes confirm that. This much the police told us. So there aren't many suspects, we aren't stupid, we can work that out. But the police still can't find the murderer.'

'And that's not all,' Mrs Robertson adds, 'it's far worse than that. Poor Annabelle, killed like that exactly a year ago. So what do they do? They hold a murder weekend. That's terrible, it's disgusting. And *they're* back again, the directors, to gloat. They're only interested in making money. So we – Charles and I, and Terry – we decided to protest. We live near London, but we booked into the hotel; we were going to make a real fuss, but they recognised us when we turned up. They wouldn't let us have our rooms. So we had to change our plans, do our protest outside instead. But you saw it, Mr Oliphant. No-one cares. No-one's interested.'

Terry Wilder and Kim are standing outside the police car now. They're still talking but, as I watch, Kim holds out her hand. Terry looks at it, looks at her, then turns away. He strides across the lawn, scoops up his placard. His head is down, he doesn't care where he's going. Kim and the two policemen watch him cross the road. I can see him in the wing mirror, he's standing alone, looking around. I presume he's searching for his parents-in-law. When he can't find them he slouches deeper into his coat, pushes his hands into his pockets.

'We'd better go and get him,' says Charles Robertson, reaching for the door handle.

I call him back. 'Wait just a minute, until the police go.' I'm not sure why I should offer such advice. Perhaps it's because I'm naturally secretive and I don't want the police to connect me with the Robertsons and Wilder. It could be that I don't want to jeopardise the chance of working for Amalgam; after all, a new security consultant shouldn't be taking sides against the company. That thought is, in itself, worrying. Am I taking sides? Am I even considering taking sides? Are there sides to take? The truth is, I know too little about what actually happened a year ago. But I'll have the opportunity to find out when I go to meet the directors next day. That's a decision made, and it surprises me at first. My neutrality has been overcome. But my whirling, nebulous thoughts coalesce around this small point, and I realise why I've made this decision. It's because I have a picture in my mind of a young pregnant woman being bound and gagged and left to die alone.

I can't help but preface my words with a sigh. 'I'll see what I can do. See what I can find out. No promises, mind, just a little digging here and there.'

No-one should die like that. No-one.

CHAPTER THREE

I could go home. No, 'home' is the wrong word. I could go back to the flat, more of a bedsit really, where I sleep. It has the essentials. There's a fridge-freezer and a cooker, a bed, a television. There are books, unread, on cheap bookshelves. There's a single bed, a desk with a computer squatting on it. Jen insisted that I buy it, just before she left, so that I could send and receive emails. She's the only one who communicates with me like that, but I prefer to write letters, longhand, with real ink and a fountain pen. So she sends me emails and I send a perfunctory reply, but then I conjure letters into words on paper, sign the last page (there are always at least three of them, writing on one side only) then seal them into an envelope. I write Jen's latest address on the front in block capitals. The trip to the post office is as much a part of the ceremony – it's a physical sending of something I've thought about and created rather than the instantaneous transmission of pinpricks of electricity.

There are two photographs sharing space on the bedside table. One is of Jen, the other of Kirsty who, thankfully, resembles her mother. Both women are smiling at me, only a few years between them. They seem to get along with each other and Kirsty is in regular contact with Jen; at least, that's what Jen's emails tell me.

Somehow, on this autumn night, the flat doesn't seem a good place to be. I'd practically moved out when Jen told me she was going away for a sabbatical; a year in Canada. Medics can do this, they provide a universal service, their coin is valued throughout the world. At first we both thought

I was going with her, but we were worried – no, that's not true, I was worried, Jen simply humoured me – that it wouldn't have worked. There were the usual excuses, I'm good at excuses: we hadn't known each other long enough, I didn't know what I'd be able to do, the business was beginning to take off. So we reconciled each other to a year apart, promised to write in our various ways. There were no declarations of undying love; we'd barely begun to find out about each other. But in a way the letters and emails provided us with an excuse to ask questions and give honest replies undiluted by proximity. I'd always felt unsure of my own ability to love, the scars of a failed marriage still hurt. And Jen was younger than me, intelligent, good-looking (her description of herself as a 'bayb' – a big-arsed young black – was so obviously self-deprecation that it almost caused me to fall out with her) and the opportunities for liaisons abroad would have been many. Neither of us said anything specific about our relationship; there was no 'I'll wait for you,' or 'I'll understand if you . . .' but implied thoughts are often stronger than those openly expressed. And so after a year, with a week to go until Jen's return, both of us are still declaring how much we're looking forward to seeing each other again.

Jen decided to keep paying for her room while she was away; I promised to visit regularly, to air the rooms, vacuum the floors, flush the toilet and run the shower. It helped that the room was in a house owned by Rak, a good friend of mine. It was cheap, access was no problem, and when I felt low I could go there, spend the night, imagine she was in bed with me. There were other advantages as well. Rak is good company, her insults usually chafe the edges of depression away. And she's an expert in computers.

It's the logical place to go. I want more information on Annabelle Wilder and Rak will be able to find it far more easily, more quickly than I could ever do. I could ring ahead to warn her I'm on my way, but she might be busy, she might have gone out, she might have an excuse for me not to come.

The city's quiet, it's realised that summer is over. Brown-husked leaves have been asked by a polite breeze to dance in the shadows of garden and park. Streetlights are glowing warm. Behind glimmering windows, in the depths of wardrobes and cupboards, sweaters and overcoats are waking from their summer hibernation. It's a short journey through this self-satisfied suburbia to Rak's house, one of a row of stately terrace houses now the refuge of university students. I like the area, it's alive, expanding, youthful. Pubs spill bright onto the streets, shops stay open late. Perhaps my feel- ings suggest that I'm trying to regain my own youth. Is that why Jen is so attractive to me?

I abolish these thoughts as I search for a parking space – can students be so affluent? There are so many cars. The air is cooling as I hurry the distance to Rak's door; she doesn't go to bed early but it's Friday night and she could be on her way out. I ring the bell with her name on, I can almost hear her asthmatic panting as she hustles herself to the door. It swings open quickly.

'Billy Oliphant!' Her face is broad, round, laughing. 'You must be after something. A night of wild sexual passion?' Rak is almost as wide as she is tall. For as long as I've known her she's dressed herself in what seems to be coloured sack- cloth. This evening is no exception, her skirt is a mixture of rich reds and browns, a Scandinavian cardigan struggles to cover a blue silk blouse, there's a Paisley cravat at neck. I asked her once why she chose such colours. She told me that they reflected her colourful inner self; that they drew attention away from the body hiding beneath them; that they weren't a threat to other women and so allowed her to, as she said, 'catch them before they even know they're being tickled'; but most of all, they hid food and alcohol stains more easily than monochromatic clothes. I tend to believe the last of these – Rak doesn't live in hygienic surroundings.

I lean forward to hug her. She's carrying a glass in one hand, ice chinking at the rim, while in the other is a limp piece of pizza. She holds both at arm's length as if I'm going to steal them from her.

'Yeah, I'm after something. But it's not food or drink, or sex.'

She extricates herself from my grasp. 'Good, 'cos I've none spare; good, 'cos it's too expensive; and good, 'cos I don't fancy you. Come on, you'd better come in, I've got my reputation to think of.' She pulls me into the hallway and slams the door behind me.

'And what reputation is that?'

'Lesbian icon. I mean, a man coming into my house? And embracing me? Good God, what'll the neighbours say?' She leads me down the dark hallway, past the entrance to her bedroom and into what was once a dining room. This is her office. The rest of the house is let off as bedsits; Jen's is at the front on the next floor up.

'Let's get the small talk out of the way, Billy. I had an email from Jen yesterday; she's looking forward to seeing you and no doubt you're feeling the same. I saw Kirsty, oh, a week ago, she popped in to see me at work so I know she's well. Tea? Still milk and no sugar – no, sit down, I'll get it.' She wanders through into the kitchen, talking more loudly to make up for the distance. 'I'm OK, pissed off with the daily grind as usual, the Council doesn't recognise talent when they see it; but they get so annoyed when I point out their mistakes, it's worth working for the pleasure that brings alone. Biscuit? Something to eat? No, you said it wasn't that, so it must be information you're after.' She waddles back into the room and hands me a mug containing a teabag, boiling water, milk and a spoon. 'I'm sorry to rush you but I've a date in an hour's time.' She looks at her watch. 'Fifty minutes, actually. So what're you after?'

I explain the evening's events; as I'm talking Rak's already typing into her computer.

'Let's try the local rag first, background info only. About

a year ago? And the girl's name was Annabelle Wilder? It's bound to have been on the front page, let's see . . .'

I pull my chair round behind her, newspaper pages are flicking past my eyes. I can see only the headlines but Rak seems to be reading far more than me.

'Sure it was a year ago?' she asks. 'There's nothing on the front pages at all, morning or evening papers. There's nothing I can see that was so hugely important it would keep a murder off the front page. And you say she was found in a deep-freeze?'

'That's what I've been told. But the police wouldn't neces- sarily release details of the way she was killed, they'd just get hoax calls, even copycat crime. So it would probably just have been something about a body being found in a hotel and the police treating the death as suspicious.'

Rak sighs. 'Couldn't you just get information from your new best friend Kim Bryden? It would save us a lot of time.'

'I don't think Kim would like me to investigate a death where her employers are so heavily implicated. I don't really want her to know what I'm doing. Not yet.'

'OK, there's probably something in the press but it's buried too deeply to be of value. Let's have a look here instead.'

She taps a different website into the computer, I can't read the name. 'This is sometimes a bit lurid but it can give some good stuff as well.' The screen flashes and a banner appears: 'Unsolved Crimes'. 'It's a spin-off from a site in the USA; anyone can send stuff, mostly concerned relatives. But I've heard that the police sometimes contribute information, perhaps if they're stuck for a lead, or even if they want to release infor- mation unofficially, and I know they trawl sites like this. Sometimes there are links to other sites as well, so it's a handy place to know.' She's talking fast. It could be that she's intrigued by my story and wants to help. It could be that she wants rid of me. I'm already scribbling the name of the site on a piece of paper from Rak's untidy desk, and I don't even bother asking why she should know about this website.

'Hm, we're getting quite professional.' She points at the screen. 'Look, there's a search facility, that's new since I was last here. What was the girl's name?'

'Annabelle Wilder.'

'Sounds like a fifties film star. OK, let's see what we've got. Something, certainly.'

Another reason I like letting Rak do the footslogging, the spadework, is that her computer and her hands work far faster than mine. A headline appears on the screen in front of me, 'The Body in the Freezer'. Below it there's a photograph of a girl, clearly taken on some type of walking expedition. She's wearing shorts and heavy boots, a sleeveless vest; she's standing beside a rucksack and there are rugged brown hills in the background beneath a summer sky. She's an attractive girl with short brown hair and she's standing with one leg raised, her foot on a small rock, one hand on her hip. She's looking straight at the camera, eyebrows raised, a half smile on her lips. It's as if she's saying, 'Do you *really* want to take a photograph now?' And yet behind her apparent naivete there's a self-assurance, a knowledge that the camera will find something good to say about her because it always does.

'Pretty little thing,' says Rak. 'Bet she was a bit of a madam.'

'What makes you say that?'

Rak seems affronted that she has to explain herself to me. 'I know about women, Billy. She's got an air about her. Her hip's jutted forward, head on one side. She's giving him the come on. They probably screwed right there, as soon as he put the camera away.'

'Rak, how can you . . .?'

'Intuition? Come on, Billy, it's what we all do. We try to fit something new into a pattern. She looks like a girl I once knew – two different girls, actually – who would stand in that way, had looks like that. They were both floozies. Actually, one was more tart than floozy. Both great fun, but very aware of themselves. Knew what they wanted.'

I look at the girl again. Rak's continuum of flooziness seems to run as far as 'tart' in one direction, 'bit of a madam' in the other. If she's right about fitting people into pre-defined categories, then I must reserve judgement; Annabelle looks self-confident to me, but that's as far as it goes. If she reminds me of anyone at all then that person is Kirsty, my daughter, and I don't want to go any further in that direction. I put the thoughts to one side, concentrate on the words beneath the photograph. They re-tell the Robertsons' story with one or two extra details. Annabelle was thirty-one years old when she died, she was born in Essex, she'd been married for two months. She was about to start working in the hotel behind the bar, but was found dead in the walk-in freezer, naked, bound and gagged.

The report isn't unbiased when it moves beyond the facts. It states that the hotel hadn't officially opened, that there were a few people staying there from the company owning the hotel, that the security system was up and running and that there was therefore a limited number of people who could have committed the crime. That is, in shortened form, exactly what the Robertsons told me; it could, for all I know, have been written by them. But then it goes on to decry the police's lack of success in finding a suspect, it names Kim Bryden as the lead investigating officer and suggests that she's been bribed to bury the case because of her impending employment by the hotel group. It also, in a final paragraph directed at Kim herself, explains that such a statement is, if untrue, libellous; it adds that the article has been sent to the local press and to Kim herself; and it concludes by saying that the writer has not been threatened with court by anyone.

Rak has been reading alongside me. 'Lots of hot air, nothing of substance,' she says dismissively. 'But on the other hand, the police don't seem to have come up with much, not after a year's investigation. But then, they don't tend to let the public know how well they're doing, the direction they're heading. Do they?'

Her question is genuine; she expects me to know the answer. 'That depends,' I tell her, 'on how things are going. If the investigation's going nowhere they might release information. If they know where they're heading, what they're doing, they might keep things to themselves.'

'So it looks as if they might have a suspect?'

'Or they're trying to bury the case.'

'Billy! Come on, you'll destroy my trust in the boys in blue. Tell me it's not true, tell me Tinkerbelle can live if I'll only believe in fairies, tell me that if I think the police are infallible, they will be!'

I ignore her sarcasm, speak my thoughts aloud. 'I'll have to ask Kim. She'll know, it's her case. Or it was her case. But she won't tell me, she'll just say it's still active. So how can I persuade her to let me know what the police know?'

'Use your natural good humour, your native charm and wit?'

'They haven't been much use to me in the past, Rak.'

'Yeah, I know, but they're about due for some success now, eh? And let's face it, there's no way Kim Bryden's going to tell you anything about this case that you don't already know. So you might as well try the long shot. Dance naked in front of her. Fasten a black bow tie to your willie and conduct Beethoven's Ninth with it. Offer her your body at a discount rate.'

'Thanks, Rak. I can always count on you to make useful suggestions.'

She looks deliberately at her watch. 'Anything else I can help you with? It's just that my date'll be arriving soon and . . .'

'No, there's nothing else. At least, not yet. But I might just need to ring you over the weekend. Will you be at home?'

'No plans at the moment. Of course, that might change if I do well enough tonight. But even then, it's not that far from the bed to the computer so . . . yeah, I'll be around.'

'Good.' I realise I haven't drunk my tea and sip it gently, but it's lukewarm and thick enough to tar a boat.

'You staying here tonight?' Rak asks.

'No, I need to think about this case. If I stay here I'll spend too much time thinking of Jen.'

'Ah, true love in its purest form.'

'So thanks, but I'll go home. The austerity aids concentration.' I rise to my feet and Rak escorts me to the door. As she opens it a girl walks past the house, double-checks then returns. 'Rak,' she says, 'is that you?' She's young and good-looking and not at all the type of person I'd expect to find attracted to Rak. When I glance over my shoulder at Rak I find her wearing her broadest smile; she seems genuinely pleased to see her date. That's when I realise how wrong my preconceptions have been. Rak has never been anything but kind, protective even, to me and to Jen. She's always been there to help me whenever I've asked. Why, then, should I assign her and her relationships to the strange, the ugly even? Why did I think that her date would be a middle-aged woman, untidily dressed, no make-up? Why did I allow my prejudices to dictate the type of person she ought to be dating? I smile to myself.

'Something tickled you, Billy?' Rak asks.

'No. Nothing important. Have a good time, both of you.'

The girl brushes past me; she smells sweet. She seems a pleasant young girl, happy to see Rak. And that's what's brought a smile of appreciation, of encouragement to my lips. I'm no beauty. I'm going bald, I'm in my forties, under-height and overweight. I have problems with commitment, I'm divorced, I'm an ex-cop. I've been a compulsive gambler, I don't drink because I'm frightened I might come to depend on alcohol again. I worry a lot, I worry about worrying. I've a superiority/inferiority complex which, combined with an obsessive-compulsive neurosis, seems specifically designed to infuriate any profession beginning with the prefix 'psych-'. I'm not kind, like Rak. Yet Jen says she loves me. There's hope for all of us if people like me and Rak can find others who care about us. That makes me feel good, it makes me – for a brief moment – feel that the human race is going in the right direction after all. I wave goodbye and turn into the street.

I should have heard the sound of wheels rattling over the pavement but my mind is elsewhere. A skateboard hits me hard on the shin, the bulk of its owner knocks me to the ground. As I rise to my knees, winded, I expect to be met with apologies and offers of assistance. Instead the youth pedals a safe distance away from me where a friend, similarly dressed in baggy clothes, is waiting. Both of them turn round and begin to laugh.

'Watch where you're going, slap-head!' one of them yells.

'You little . . .' I begin, but the breath has been knocked out of me.

'Fuck off, wanker,' shouts the second, matching the call with the appropriate gesture. The first flashes a V-sign as they wheel away round the corner.

If the human race is going in the right direction, heading along the narrow path to righteous reward, then I can only hope that those two are diverted down a side road with a very large pothole leading straight down to hell.

CHAPTER FOUR

I'm wearing a suit. This is unusual, and I've brought with me my more casual clothes in a brief case. It was to have contained all my background information on the case of Annabelle Wilder, but I've found nothing to add to what Rak discovered the previous night. I've come early, hoping that Mr and Mrs Robertson will be outside the hotel. There are questions I need to ask them, I'd like to know a little more about Annabelle. I look around as I pay the taxi driver but there's no sign of them. It's after nine so the rush-hour traffic has declined, a lycra-clad cyclist is hurrying past, but the only other person I can see is a beggar crouched in the doorway of a disused warehouse a few hundred yards down the street. I have several choices: I can go into the hotel early and wait, have a cup of tea; I can go for a short walk along the riverfront; I can even announce my presence and see if the Amalgam directors will see me early.

The decision is taken from me. I hear my name being called. The beggar is on his feet, waving at me, looking around nervously. I walk towards him and he shrinks back into the doorway. As I get closer I see that my first impression was wrong. He's wearing a thick coat to protect him from the overnight cold, his sleeping bag is resting on a roll-up mattress, he has a vacuum flask by his side and a mug of steaming liquid in his hand.

'Hello, Terry,' I say, 'were you waiting for me?'

'What makes you say that?' He's defensive straightaway.

'No placards, no protests. You're out of the way here, so the hotel can't complain about your presence. But you can see everything that happens, who's coming, who's going. You're hardly likely to want to talk to Kim Bryden again – this time you would be arrested. And the Amalgam directors are already inside. So that leaves me.'

Terry looks as if he's spent the whole night on the street. His hair is unkempt, the stubble on his chin suggests he hasn't shaved for several days and there are shadows under his eyes. The eyes themselves are wide, wild; he seems on the verge of madness.

'My parents-in-law . . . They said you'd offered to help. I didn't believe them, why should you help us? The police haven't helped. Why should you? A year, a whole year, and they've got nothing.' He isn't looking at me, his eyes are darting from side to side, as if he's expecting to be attacked. 'I wanted to break in, to get some real publicity. I would have as well, but Emily and Charles said it would be stupid, I'd just get locked up. So I said I'd wait, to see if you appeared.'

'And I have.'

'For all the good it'll do. I mean, who were you with when we first saw you?' For a moment he summons the courage to look me in the eyes, but that moment is brief. He stares at his feet, his voice becomes a mumble. 'You were with Kim Bryden, that's who. You're probably in her pocket, and she's in *their* pocket, so you'll go in and you'll find nothing. It doesn't matter to me, I don't expect anything from you anyway, but you should have seen Emily and Charles last night. They actually believed you might be able to do something.' He shakes his head. If I was in his position I'd feel the same way, I wouldn't trust me. 'And even if you do want to help, what can you do? It's *their* territory, *their* hotel, they've got the police on *their* side. I saw your van, Mr Oliphant. You're not a detective, you install burglar alarms. And you're going to find out who murdered Annabelle? Yeah, course you are.'

I'm not angry at what is obviously intended as an insult.

32

I've said I would help and so set myself up as a target, Terry's simply taking the opportunity to let fire.

'OK,' I tell him, 'I'm either useless or have no intention of being useful. You say that's your opinion, and if it is, you're entitled to it, I accept that. But you're still here. And you were here for most of last night. So perhaps part of you thinks I might just be able to come up with the goods?'

He snorts, 'I'll let you know when the pigs do their fly-past.'

'You can do more than that. You can tell me about Annabelle.'

He seems surprised at the request. 'You mean you don't know?'

'I know what your parents-in-law told me last night. Other than that, nothing. A friend did a quick internet search last night, came up with nothing. That, in itself, is unusual. So I'm extra curious. When I go to meet the directors of Amalgam I don't want to be unarmed. So tell me about her.'

'You're going to meet the directors? How the hell did you manage that?'

I could find an appropriate lie, but there seems little point. How can he trust me if I don't tell him the truth? 'They want to offer me a job. Kim Bryden's assistant. She chose me. They want to meet me, to approve me. To discuss wages, a contract.'

I don't often see a person really speechless. Silence is usually a time for someone to gather thoughts, to think of questions, to pursue an argument, even to digest a complex piece of information. But Terry wants to speak, he's desperate to say something, yet his words can't escape. His mouth is open, his eyes are wide. He hurls his mug to the ground but it's plastic – it doesn't break, it merely bounces out into the road. His fists clench and I take a small step backwards, ready to run. He stares at me, then turns, beats his fists against the door, kicks at it. The staccato rhythm increases at first, then slowly subsides in force and tempo. When he turns round he's grinning.

'You said you were going to help, and I was almost ready to believe you,' he says. 'What a stupid fuckin' idiot I am.'

'I'm not going to take the job,' I explain. 'I couldn't work for anyone else. If they knew me, really knew me, they wouldn't want to employ me anyway.'

Terry shakes his head in disbelief. 'Oh great, that's even better. You're going to go in there, start asking questions about Annabelle, and tell them you don't want to work for them? I was going to go home, get some kip, but I think I'd better hang around. Then I can try to catch you when you come out of those revolving doors so fast you'll think you're heading for orbit.'

I'm trying to remain patient. 'I said I wasn't taking the job. I didn't say I was going to tell them that.'

He lets the information filter through. 'OK, then. So how are you going to persuade them to let you investigate Anna's murder?'

'I'll improvise.' Terry's eyes rise to heaven. I can see why he isn't impressed, I don't even impress myself. He begins to turn away, I reach out my hand to touch him and he recoils from my potential touch. It's as if we have impenetrable force fields surrounding us, making physical contact impossible. At least I have his attention again. 'If it's all you understand, Terry, I'll talk in clichés. Are you listening? Because I know I may not be much, but I'm the best you've got. I'm all you've got.'

Who needs to hit someone when words can have the same effect? He leans against the door, lets his head fall back then allows his body to slide down until his hands are resting on his knees, backside on heels. His eyes are closed.

'So tell me about Annabelle.'

He begins to talk, his voice slow and easy, as if he's told the same story before. 'Anna and I met about eighteen months ago. I was working in London, as a chef, she was a waitress

34

in the same hotel. We hit it off straight away.' He's smiling to himself at the memory. 'She moved in with me inside a week. We just seemed right for each other. She was older than me, five years, but it didn't seem to matter. And she was good for me, she gave me self-confidence. I wasn't really happy in London; I was only there to get some experience.' He looks up at me, as if he's worried that I might not believe what he's going to say. 'I'm a good chef, Mr Oliphant, I've got potential, lots of people said so. But I was lost in London, it was too big. Anna told me I was good, she kept on telling me. She had faith in me, she helped me when things got bad, when I felt down. Then a job came up here, at the Riverside, Anna found it. She suggested I apply – she knew I was born here, knew I wanted to come home. We talked it over; I said I wanted her to come with me if I got the job. And I did. So we moved.' He looks up at me. 'Anna helped me write the letter, she was good at things like that.'

He reaches into the depths of his coat, brings out a credit card holder, hands it to me. When I flick it open there are several photographs inside. The first is the same one Rak discovered the previous evening, Annabelle walking in the hills. The second is of Annabelle and Terry in a photo-booth behaving as two people do in such a place, pulling faces, happy together; her hair seems darker against the pale back-ground of the booth wall, but even the harsh light can't hide her beauty. She seems, if anything, more aware of it, more confident.

The third photograph has been cut from a larger crowd scene, probably at a party. Annabelle is wearing a low-cut evening dress and there are dislocated arms around her shoul-ders. The fourth and last is a contact print of a formal portrait, taken some time before the others. Annabelle looks in her late teens, her hair is light, almost blonde, and she's looking at the camera over her bare shoulder. All the photographs have Annabelle's smile in common, her heart-shaped face, her happy good looks.

'Can I keep these?' I ask softly, holding out the pictures in front of me. 'Just until I can get some copies made?'

Terry nods, gestures to me to put the photographs away. 'When I asked her to marry me, I thought she'd laugh. I was drunk, not falling over, just enough to give me some Dutch courage. She said yes. She was so beautiful, I don't know what she saw in me. It was a registry office, no family, just a couple from the hotel as best man and bridesmaid.' His hands become more animated. 'We hardly knew anyone else, we didn't go out much, we were working different shifts so sometimes we didn't see each other for a few days, but it didn't matter. We just needed each other. And then we moved up here, found a flat, things seemed to be going well. Almost straightaway she managed to get a job in the bar, right here. Everything seemed to be going right. She was due to start when the place opened properly; she was working some-where else until the place was fully opened. She said she liked it up here. We had it all sorted out, we'd save some money, get our own place, start a family.' His voice cracks. 'And then she was killed.'

'How old are you, Terry?'

He seems surprised at the question. 'Twenty-six.'

'And Annabelle's parents didn't come to the wedding?'

'No. We arranged it quickly and she said they wouldn't want to come. In fact, she said they'd fallen out with her. She didn't say why.'

'And you didn't ask?'

He becomes defensive. 'No. I didn't feel the need. If she'd wanted me to know she would have told me. She *would* have told me. Some day. You see, Mr Oliphant, we trusted each other.' He's building walls; there are places he doesn't want me to visit.

'So presumably you contacted Mr and Mrs Robertson after Annabelle died?'

He's becoming animated, fingers dancing, as if I've accused him of a crime. 'No, I didn't know where they lived.

36

I looked through her stuff but there was nothing with their address on it. They found out about it, I assume the police told them. They contacted me. I was . . . I didn't cope very well. Still aren't, I suppose. They moved in for a while, took over. They looked after me. I couldn't work – haven't been able to since then, as a matter of fact.' He holds out his hand – it's shaking. 'That's nerves, I don't drink, I'm not taking drugs. It's difficult.' He's holding back tears. 'I see her face everywhere.'

'It's OK, Terry. I understand.' I'm not saying that just to calm him down. I can imagine how I would feel if anything happened to Jen. He doesn't object to my outstretched hand on his shoulder, he just inhales deeply.

'The police asked lots of questions, that was when I realised I knew hardly anything about Anna. When Emily and Charles arrived it was like . . . it gave me the opportunity to fill in all the things about Anna I'd never got round to finding out. What she was like as a child, as a teenager. The things she liked doing. Her pets. What she was like at school. The music she liked, all that sort of thing. And I could tell her parents what she was like as well, how beautiful she was, how thoughtful.' He holds out his hand towards me again, separates his fingers so I can see the ring on his wedding finger. 'She bought me this. I know it doesn't look much, but it's special because it's from her. It came with her love.' The ring seems to be made of inexpensive, dull silver, one of those intertwined Celtic designs, several bands joined together.

'It's beautiful,' I tell him.

'She didn't tell me she was pregnant. Probably didn't know – we weren't trying for children, not yet. And she always was . . . irregular.' He seems a little embarrassed.

'Did Annabelle's parents mention why they fell out with her?'

'Sort of. That is, they didn't say exactly.' He forces a wry smile to his lips, leans towards me as if telling a secret. 'But

I gather it was something to do with pot – they found her smoking it and said she shouldn't, not in the house at least. But she kept on doing it, something like that. So they told her to leave, didn't think she would, but she did. She could be like that. Impulsive.' He smiles at some secret memory.

'Was she working at the hotel in London before you arrived there?'

'Yes, she'd been there for a few months.'

'And before that?'

'Same type of thing. She told me she'd moved around a lot, from job to job. She'd save some money then she'd leave, blow it all, bum around Europe a bit, find another job, start again.'

'So she travelled?'

'Yeah, she spent some time in Spain, Greece. Bar work, you know the type of thing. And then she did the long tour back, through Europe. She showed me some photographs once. Made me quite jealous, really, topless sunbathing and all that, always surrounded by a crowd of blokes. But like she said, that was her past. If she wanted to do that again, she could, any time. But she didn't. She wanted to be with me.'

We're silent for a while, lost in our own similar thoughts. Terry pulls me away from a dream of Jen and back to reality. 'So now what?'

'Now I go and ask more questions, think about motivation, confront people. I get friendly with some, awkward with others, nasty to a few. I aggravate people, make myself unpopular. Fitting burglar alarms is far, far easier.'

'Why are you doing this, then? Why help us?'

It's a genuine enough question, one that demands a considered, careful response. It would be easy to show the trite side of my nature, to say that I'm Robin Hood in disguise, the Lone Ranger reborn, Batman without the mask. I'm on the side of the little man, fighting to bring the evil conglomerate to justice, to expose those who've done wrong, to uphold the right of the law. That wouldn't be true; if it was, then I'd be doing this all the time instead of treating it as a sort of sideline. My impending sainthood would allow me to give money to all the charities whose junk mail I throw unopened into the bin; I could spend nights working for the Samaritans, sell poppies in November, be one of Santa's elves at the North Pole. I can't pretend to be that good, I can't even pretend to be good at all – I've hurt too many people in too many ways. But it's not a craving for absolution that makes we want to do this, nor do I consider it an intellectual exercise, a wish to solve the unsolvable crime. If I can define a reason – and I'm not sure I can, not at the moment – then it's not altruism but selfishness that has driven me to intervene in this case. It's the thought that one day someone might be considering whether or not to help me and, if I can demonstrate that in the past I've been willing to help others in the same way, the spinning coin might just fall in my favour. It's not much of a reason. It's not even mathematically sound. But it's the best I can do.

'I don't know yet that I'm helping,' I tell Terry. 'All I've done is say I'll ask a few questions. And as for why – well, I've got a free weekend.'

OK, I'll admit it, I can't resist a platitude, but Terry isn't listening anyway. During my thinking he's taken a mobile phone from his pocket and is talking softly into the mouthpiece. 'Yeah. Yes, he's here. He's just been asking some questions. Yes, he still says he'll help. OK. Yes, I'll go home now. Bye.' He closes the phone. 'That was Emily; she and Charles are staying at my house. They're going back home this afternoon. She says thank you and good luck.'

I nod my own thanks. 'You'd better let me have your home and mobile phone numbers, in case I need to ask you or your parents-in-law any questions.' As he writes down the numbers I make some quick notes on what he's told me. 'I'll keep in touch,' I tell him, turn to go, but he calls my name and that pulls me back.

'Thank you.' He holds out his hand awkwardly; I join it with mine, we shake hands gravely. I turn away again and, even as I cross the road, he's packing his blanket and mattress away, ready to go home to a bed too large to sleep in.

CHAPTER FIVE

Despite the diversion of talking to Terry, I'm still early. I walk through the reception area and peer into the dining room.

One of the few things I can remember from school physics lessons is watching smoke particles exhibit Brownian motion; battered on all sides by molecules, the particles would move around their little light-box until they were spread equidistant from their neighbours. I've found that the distribution of hotel guests at breakfast normally obeys a similar rule: individuals (or couples acting as individuals) will never occupy a table where someone else is sitting unless all other tables are full. The first to arrive establishes squatter's rights, either by concentrating on eating or spreading newspaper over that part of the table unoccupied by his own cutlery and plates. There are, of course, exceptions to Oliphant's hypothesis: the lonely, the garrulous, the mentally disturbed, all of them will deliberately seek out company. And there's a corollary which states that those attending residential conferences of any type will be either rigid adherents (scowling at those who seek to disturb them, even bringing spare clothing to occupy vacant seats) or heretics determined to disprove the conjecture. There's no halfway house, no continuum of indecision.

Breakfast this morning is obviously dominated by exuberant extroverts, with only two tables containing suited singletons; the rest are overflowing with casual, talkative, pastel-shirted, grey-haired, bespectacled people, a SAGA holiday made flesh. Some tables have even been pushed together so that discussion and argument can be carried out more easily.

'Murder mystery weekends,' says a familiar voice behind me, 'attract a certain type of person.'

'Clichés and stereotypes so early, Kim?' I respond without turning round.

'Sad but true, Billy. It's a gentle pastime that suits those who like their melodrama served lukewarm and without too many surprises.'

'Really? I thought that surprises were the whole point. You know, solving the mystery, finding the murderer. After all, it would be rather an anticlimax if everyone figured out by lunchtime that the butler did it.'

Kim is suddenly jovial friendliness. 'Come on, Billy, I'll treat you to coffee and explain what's going on. You haven't been to one of these murder weekends before, have you?'

'I've been too involved with the real thing.' I follow her to the bar. 'And I'll have a weak tea, if you don't mind.'

It's as if Kim's trying to keep away from the subject of me working for Amalgam. She's pleased I've turned up, doesn't want to push me too hard in case I behave in my own stereotypical manner and leave abruptly. So she tells me the rules of murder mystery weekends. Apparently there aren't many. Guests are divided into groups of about a dozen, each group has its own murder to solve. It's essentially role-play, improvisation following written guidelines; each person is a character, they're thrown together in some artificial circumstance. They're given cards telling them who they are, and, by discussion and the gradual release of further information, they find out who they like (usually no-one) and who they dislike (everyone, it increases the number of suspects and motivation for the crime). One of the characters is then murdered, the others have to find out who did it and why. This takes a day – there's a coach tour of the city and surrounding countryside in the afternoon – and then the groups reform and solve another murder the next day.

'Just like real life,' I say.

'Cynic. They're enjoying themselves. It gets them thinking, they meet new people.'

'I suppose you're right.'

'Keeps them off the streets as well.'

'The city's a safer place with them closeted in here.'

Kim sips her coffee, black and strong. My tea is weak, no milk, no sugar. It's nothing more than hot water in a flimsy disguise, but I drink it to be sociable. I'm working my way through my vices, gradually discarding them all. Alcohol was the first to go, then gambling. Coffee, salt, sugar. Jen's advising me on my diet – she says she wants me fit and well. Sometimes she seems to worry that I'm much older than her. Jen. One more week and she'll be back.

'You seem happy,' Kim says.

'It's just that I feel safe with all these amateur detectives around here.'

Kim smiles. She's probably happier than I am, she's in control, it looks as if she's getting what she wants. I'm here to see her bosses; it looks as if I'm prepared to work for her. It's time to spoil things.

'What happened last night,' I ask, 'with that man? It looked as if he was going to attack you but . . . You managed to calm him down.'

'Perks of the job, Billy, you know that. I've been too high profile in the force, people recognise me. He had a chip on his shoulder, I helped him take it off. He was OK.'

'Big chip?'

'Big enough to weigh him down. But once I told him . . .'

'So exactly what was his problem? I mean, you seemed to know him quite well? I assume it was to do with one of your cases?' My voice rises in artificial question at the end of each sentence, I sound like an Australian soap actor.

There's a pause before Kim talks, she's wondering whether she should tell me anything. Should she tell me the truth?

43

Should it be a version of the truth? Should she lie? Should she refuse to say anything? She glances at her watch. 'It's a long story, Billy, quite a complicated case. There isn't really enough time . . .'

'Terry Wilder thinks you're not working hard enough to find out who murdered his wife Annabelle. She was found dead inside a walk-in freezer here, at this hotel, a year ago. There, you can assume I know the background. Now fill me in on the details.'

Kim's surprised, her mouth opens, eyebrows dance up behind her fringe. I take advantage of the silence. 'And he thinks there's a conflict of interest between you investigating the murder and starting work for Amalgam, which just happens to own the hotel. He figures it might be a good way of buying you off.'

'Billy, what the hell . . .?'

I decide to push all the way. 'And at the time of the murder there weren't many people on the premises, an impenetrable security system, and so far no arrests, not even any suspects as far as Terry knows. It's a bit like a murder mystery weekend, eh Kim? A locked room murder. Except the guests here solve two murders in twenty-four hours, but you can't solve one in a whole year.'

That might be going too far. Kim looks as if she's going to erupt. There are the tell-tale signs, storm clouds above the mountain, trembling in the foothills, a deep rumbling noise from her molten core; but she breathes deeply, brings herself under control. She takes a deep drink of water from a glass at the table; it cools the lava within. 'This is some type of test,' she says. 'You're trying to make me angry. You're wondering what I'm really like to work with. You want to know whether you can actually work with me.' She gives a little laugh and shakes her head coquettishly; the gesture looks learned, as if someone has told her it's a way of winning arguments, disarming opponents. It's strangely out of place on her middle-aged, police-hardened face, even though it's painted more than I've noticed in the past. She's taking her new job seriously, and her new employers have invested some money in her appearance. I'm almost looking forward to meeting them.

'It's not a test,' I tell her, 'it's my curiosity.'

'Billy, it amounts to the same thing in the end. You spoke to Terry last night . . .'

'His parents-in-law, actually.'

'Ah, the redoubtable Mrs and Mr Robertson.' There's no affection in her voice.

'And Terry this morning.'

'It makes no difference, Billy. You see, I can't tell you anything because the case hasn't been closed. But it's no secret that I'm not working on it any longer. So there's no conflict of interest, no conspiracy.'

'No suspect?'

'Lots of suspects, always have been. And yes, everyone in the hotel that night is, or was initially, a suspect. But there's nothing concrete to tie them to the murder. And the people you've been speaking to, the Robertsons and Terry Wilder, they're not exactly disinterested parties, are they? They're dissatisfied with the way the investigation's gone, but is that dissatisfaction justified? You haven't considered that, have you?' She leans forward in triumph, eyes wide, voice sharp as a politician's finger. For a moment I believe she's on the point of ripping off her mask of calm, but her training has been good. She takes a deep breath, leans back in her seat, waits for me to speak.

'So you haven't spoken to your new bosses about this at all?'

'Billy, there's nothing to hide! I was on the case to start with. That's when I met my, as you so delicately put it, "new employers". I wasn't gentle with them. I was thorough, I was efficient. I was even effective, as far as was possible. I got to know them and they got to know me. They knew I was close to retirement, they liked the way I worked, they offered me a job, I accepted. I asked to be taken off the case. That's as far as it goes.'

She hasn't actually answered my question, but I can always ask it again later, ask different people. And I've touched a tender spot, found an itchy little scar that hasn't healed yet. Perhaps it's her pride that's been wounded, the fact that she didn't solve the case. Perhaps, at the back of her mind, there's a suspicion that she was enticed into working for Amalgam, not because she was good, but because it would remove her from a murder enquiry when she was getting close to an unpalatable truth. I reserve judgement for the moment; I need more facts, more information.

'So you can't tell me anything else about the murder?'

'Not "can't" Billy, "won't". It's not my case and it's not your case.' She stops abruptly, works her way back to the script. 'But I'm still glad you're here, I'm pleased you've decided to take the job.'

'Oh, I haven't. Not yet, that is. I've some questions I want to ask, I need to see how Amalgam works, how the directors work. But I've no doubt they'll do all they can to help me. To reassure me.'

I can see that Kim is angry. She could threaten me, warn me, tell me the invitation to work with her has been withdrawn. That she does none of these is worrying. She's trying desperately hard to stay in control, she doesn't want to lose her temper. 'I feel sure,' she says evenly, deliberately, 'that the directors will do everything possible to assure you of their good intentions in all they do and have done.' She rises to her feet. 'But I would ask you, advise you, not to do anything silly. They're important people, powerful people. I hope you're not planning on embarrassing them.' She leans over me. 'Or embarrassing me.'

'If I was, I wouldn't tell you. You have to trust me, Kim. Isn't that fun? Don't you just love depending on someone who's proved how undependable he is?'

Kim leans closer, her voice a whisper. 'Billy, I'm tempted

to tell you to piss off right now. The only thing stopping me is the fact that it would give you so much satisfaction. Oh, and the fact that I do, truthfully, believe you'd be bloody good in this job. See, I can pay you compliments even when greatly tempted to do the opposite.' She glances at her watch. 'But you won't even get to ask any questions if you don't get a move on, so shift your arse now.'

I climb to attention. 'In which direction would you like my arse to move? Don't tell me, the penthouse suite?'

'Where else?'

I follow her out of the bar and into the lift. Groups of mystery detectives are emerging from the restaurant, they crowd in after us, almost suffocating us with their enthusiasm. They're firing questions at each other, squinting at scribbled notes and crib-sheets held up close to their eyes.

'Motivation, there's got to be motivation . . .'

'Could he really have run round the outside of the building while everyone else was going through the inside from the library . . .?'

'No, I'm a film director, not a producer, it might be important . . .'

'She could have more than one lover . . .'

'An injection of potassium chloride, or is it chlorate, that's meant to be untraceable but deadly . . .'

'It was a snake through a vent, that would have been so easy to figure out these days, but Holmes didn't have the advantages . . .'

'You beat me up, that's what it says here, you swine . . .'

They decant slowly over three or four floors, still talking. 'Murder's never been so popular,' Kim says wearily as the doors shut out the last monologue, 'everyone thinks he can be a detective. And this way there's no violence, no unpleasantness, no body fluids to mop up. Witnesses give all the information they have to, no more and no less, without any pressure. Suspects don't turn nasty and attack you. Best thing of all is that the guests pay a lot of money for the pleasure of solving a puzzle that's literally incredible, and for playing implausible roles.' She seems keen not to talk about the questions I want to ask the board. They could, after all, be about the terms of contract. They could be about the job description. But she knows that if *she* suggests I limit myself to talking about those subjects, I'll do the opposite and mention Annabelle Wilder. She's trying to persuade herself I was pumping her for information merely from curiosity, and I'm quite happy to fall in with her, to restrict my own comments to the mundane.

'I wish real police work had been as easy as it is for these people,' I tell her. 'I might have stayed on.'

'I seem to remember your leaving wasn't really your choice, Billy. And anyway, if it had been easy you would have found a way of making it difficult, a way to fight against the system. You're a born rebel.'

'Is that a character fault or a positive side of my individuality?'

'Both,' Kim announces as the lift glides to a halt.

Each of the previous floors has been the same as the others, only the lift's voice has made the outlook any different. This time, however, the doors open onto a wide, airy space, the bright light makes me blink, makes me want to sneeze. I close my watering eyes until the desire passes, step forward into the sunlight. This floor, the top floor, has been modelled in an entirely different way to those beneath whose orthodox rectangular rooms were the essential building blocks of hotel design. Each room had a window looking out over the river or onto the road paralleling the hotel, and the windows were all visible from below. But up here on the top floor, the architect has taken a flat roof and built four different suites. From where I'm standing I can see a part of each of them through five tall plate-glass windows, four heavy wooden doors between them. The apartments share certain features: I can see curtained floor-length windows with balconies and patios outside; each patio area has tall green palms in heavy pots anchored to the floor, furled parasols and wooden tables in case it should ever be warm enough to step outside. But when I take a step forward and my viewpoint changes it becomes apparent that each apartment is a different shape. One is circular, the second angular, the third has a viewing platform built on top of it. The area between them, the flat roof where I would have expected to see a myriad of television aerials and air-conditioning units, outlet pipes and stainless steel ducts, is plain and bare and green with well-kept grass. Evergreen shrubs and flower beds coloured with autumn blooms relieve the monotony. There are, however, no doors from the landing onto the sward. Trespassers or accidental visitors from lower floors would have to gain access to the apartments themselves before they could reach the roof garden.

'It's quite something,' Kim announces as if the statement is a fact.

'I've seen better displays of ostentatious wealth.'

'Billy, come on. If people are willing to pay for the rooms, why shouldn't they have access to the gardens?'

'Couldn't they have put in a door so the merely wealthy from down below could admire the views, instead of keeping it for the obscenely rich?'

'I didn't take you for a socialist, Billy?'

'That's why you'll be first against the wall when the revolution comes. But seriously, Kim, it's a bit tasteless. There's a lack of subtlety here – someone's trying too hard; someone wants to impress too much. It's too – ' I search for the word '– faultless. That's it, it's like a photograph for a beautiful homes magazine. It looks as if it's just been cleaned, as if the kids have been sent out for the day. Too much gloss, not enough substance.'

'If you don't like it, just say so.' Either Kim's sense of humour is improving or has disappeared entirely, but there's no time to test further. She's stepped forward and is about to knock at one of the doors. Above it there's a CCTV camera with a red light shining at me. The other three doors are similarly decorated.

'Do the cameras have screens inside the apartments or in a central control room?' I've been so involved in making fun of the hotel I've forgotten my promise to Terry and the Robertsons. It's time to get back on course.

Kim lowers her hand without knocking on the door, she seems pleased that I'm asking questions about security rather than mocking her employers. 'In this instance, both,' she replies. 'There's a small LCD viewer on the back of the door and the image is transmitted to central security as well.'

'And is that duplicated on every floor?'

'No, there's a camera at the end of each corridor, one in each lift and on each landing, one inside and outside each entrance or exit, several in the dining room and bar. In fact there's no part of the building that can't be seen by camera. Except inside the bedrooms, of course.'

'Of course. But that's a lot of screens for a guard to watch.'

'Each camera's motion and infra-red sensitive, so it only comes on when the sensor tells it to. And then everything's recorded, just in case the guard misses it. Switches off after a suitable time lag which can be programmed into each camera. It's good stuff, Billy, state of the art.'

The hardware is certainly impressive, the cameras are expensive German imports, high-quality lenses and electrics; I couldn't afford to use them. 'So no-one gets in or out without security knowing about it?'

'In, out or around, Billy. An intruder could be tracked through the whole building.'

'Kitchens as well? Behind the bars? Maintenance and house care rooms? Storage cupboards? Toilets? Delivery areas?'

'Everywhere, Billy. Obviously not inside the toilets, but at the entrance. Everyone who goes to the loo can be counted in and counted out.'

'Fort Knox comes to town.'

As if urged on by the homophone Kim applies her knuckles to the door. The wood is thick, but I can hear someone beyond talking loudly, as if desperate to continue a conversation despite an ever-increasing distance to the other party.

'If security's so good, how come you haven't found out yet who murdered Annabelle Wilder? Nothing showed up on the cameras?' I've timed the questions well. Kim's face hardens and she's about to shout at me or swear when the door begins to swing open. A tall round-faced man in a lounge suit is beaming down at her and she manages to rearrange her features into a smile in a fraction of a second. I find myself wishing I could congratulate her on her feat – such control over the plasticity of muscle and skin should be applauded. But Kim would probably consider this further aggravation on my part and I do still value my life.

'Kim,' says the man, 'great to see you.' He shakes her hand, pulls her into the entrance hall by moving deftly to one side and placing his left hand in the small of her back; it's almost like dancing. He turns to face me. 'And you must be Mr Oliphant. We've heard so much about you.' He takes my hand in his paw, shakes it with practised manly ease. 'We're really pleased you could make it. Do come inside. I'm Trevor Rawlings, Finance Director.' He's quite old beneath the grey-black hair, in his mid-fifties I'd guess. He shepherds me after Kim and into the conference room, office, whatever passes in expensive hotel suites as a place of work. The murmur of conversation subsides and I quickly realise how a tin of beans feels when it's passed over a supermarket bar-code reader. Laser eyes are examining me from every angle; no matter which way I turn I can't escape them, they're all around me. Kim is off to one side, smiling, enjoying my discomfort; she's been through the same.

I stare back at my silent inquisitors, trying to put them in a hierarchy. The man on the sofa has removed his jacket; he's wearing a white shirt and plain blue silk tie. His legs

51

are crossed to reveal dark socks. Everything about him is understated, from his neat, well-groomed grey hair to his mirror-polished black shoes. He could be any age between forty and seventy. He returns my gaze without changing his expression of controlled neutrality, ready to move to a smile or frown with minimum use of his facial muscles. I need to remember who's who so I christen him Mr Smooth.

I now have the chance to examine Rawlings more closely. He's moved close to Mr Smooth – he's tall and large, rounder than he seemed when letting me in, certainly portly enough to make even a tailored suit look untidy. He's pink-cheeked, balding and holding a thick report in one hand. He's picked up a report or other similar document, and is underlining something with a pencil, demonstrating an important point to his neighbour. I can just see columns of figures – perhaps he was discussing company accounts. He becomes, for the sake of consistency, even though I know his real name, Mr Cashbag.

There's a table in front of a lace-curtained window which is covered with a crisp-folded white linen cloth, decked with cups, saucers and chromed pots of tea and coffee. The woman standing beside it seems almost amused by the silence or by me. Short dark hair, red lips, trouser-suited, she's almost as tall as me without wearing high heels. There's no jewellery on her left hand. She's sinking sugar cubes into her coffee–cup. I count them, one . . . two . . . three . . . four. She, then, can be Miss Sweet.

My enjoyment with this new game is almost brought to a halt as I meet the scowl of the next member of the team. His hair and beard are both razor short, he's wearing an earring, and his suit, though still formally dark, is different enough in its style and cut to make him seem flamboyant. He doesn't blink, puts his head on one side, and stares; when I mimic him, he turns his head away and becomes Mr Poseur.

I run through my cast of characters again. There's Smooth, Cashbag, Sweet and Poseur. That leaves one more, another

52

woman. She's wearing a wedding ring, an engagement ring, and numerous other rings on every finger of both hands. Her ears and neck are similarly hung with precious metals. Her hair is curled and died blonde, her clothes shout 'designer label'; if I looked beneath her fringe I'd probably find the words 'high maintenance' tattooed on her forehead. She's Mrs Bling.

The naming has taken no more than a few seconds, its purpose is simply to attach a label to each individual, to make them memorable so I can fill in their real names and characters when I have time. Of course, there are problems associated with assigning names like this to people. The fake identity can sometimes dominate the real personality to the point of excluding it entirely. Mr Poseur might be shy with strangers, Miss Sweet could be unpleasant, Mrs Bling could buy all her clothes and adornments in charity shops. But my first impressions are normally good, and I feel that Mr Smooth is undoubtedly the leader of this little group of capitalists. I'm smugly, silently proud of myself when he rises to his feet and proves me right.

'Mr Oliphant, good to see you. I'm Michael King, Managing Director of Amalgam.' His voice is deep and reassuringly doctorish, dry and firm. 'Please allow me to introduce my colleagues. Heather Cookson, Publicity; Carol Parker, Sales.'

Bling and Sweet nod their heads in that order.

'You've already met Trevor Rawlings, Finance –' Cashbag, nearest to me, shakes my hand '– and Liam Sanderson, Research and Development.' Poseur's acknowledgement could easily be a sneer.

'Please, Mr Oliphant, do sit down.' King gestures at an armchair behind me and I lower myself obediently into its arms. 'Tea, coffee?' he asks, 'or if you'd prefer fruit-juice or something stronger I'm sure we could find it for you?' I shake my head. The directors settle themselves around me in an inquisitive semicircle; Kim Bryden sits beside the beverage table, furthest away from me.

'It's good of you to come at such short notice,' King continues. 'Kim has explained the job, the salary, the commitment we require. I appreciate that you may have questions – that's why we're all here, to provide you with answers.'

'And to ask questions of your own?' I'm sure there must be some curiosity amongst them, after all, no firm is so wealthy that it can spend three hundred grand a year on someone without wanting to know something about him.

Rawlings-Cashbag leans forward. 'We may have some questions, Mr Oliphant, but you wouldn't be here unless you'd already passed through a vigorous vetting process.' He reaches down to the side of his seat and produces a paper wallet. He holds it out to me, beyond my reach, but the words on the cover are large and I'm familiar enough with the pattern of my own name. He puts the folder down again, looks across at Kim Bryden.

'Kim has vouched for you, although initially this was in somewhat guarded terms. She pointed out that you have had some problems in the past. We checked. They do seem to have been in the past. You don't drink any more, do you Mr Oliphant?'

'Nothing stronger than herbal tea.'

Carol Parker's smile is humourless. 'Given up gambling as well?' she asks.

'You bet.' I can't resist the obvious.

'And you're in a stable relationship?' she continues.

'Even better, I'm in several.'

Kim is shaking her head in despair, but King sniggers and the rest take it as a sign that they too are allowed the luxury of smiling.

'I'll be honest with you, Mr Oliphant –' King has the floor again '– you seem ideal for the job. You aren't fazed by authority, you're determined to get to the root cause of problems, you are – in everything you do – your own man. We'd like to have you on board.'

I've had experience of over-enthusiastic employers in the

past. Kim and I crossed swords on a case when a client took me on precisely because she thought I was washed up, a five-star failure, one round in the chamber and that guaranteed to misfire. But Amalgam are in a different league, they have a public image and they wouldn't want to be associated with failure in any way. So although I'm suspicious about their motives, the hairs on the back of my neck aren't warning me of any danger. No, the problem is that I've found a cause that conflicts with my best, possibly my only, chance of earning a fortune. This is no time to develop a conscience, but I do begin to feel a smug self-satisfaction, both in the value placed on me and in the new-found morals which will allow me to turn the job down. This spurs me on, forces me to be honest. I decide to ask the questions I ought to ask, though in a necessarily opaque manner.

'You aren't all here simply to meet me, to offer me a job, are you?'

King speaks on behalf of his colleagues. 'No. No, it wouldn't be true to say that your presence here warrants the entire board of directors making a special visit. Some of us would have come to see you, or invited you down to London, had it not been for our annual bonding session.'

'Which is?'

'The murder mystery weekend.' He rushes on to explain. 'Yes, I know it seems a little lowbrow, perhaps even – to someone in your particular business, Mr Oliphant – macabre. I first came across the game three years ago, at a charity fund-raiser, and I was amazed at the way it worked. I thought it an ideal way of team-building and letting off steam together, a chance to do something both informal yet intellectually rigorous. We've introduced it throughout the company, at all levels, and it's brought very good results in employee morale. And that's why we're really here.'

'And you do this frequently?'

'Once a year for the past three years. Our first venture was in London, in one of our hotels there. Second was in the Bahamas but the location didn't seem conducive to murder. So last year we decided on the rugged north as a venue, this hotel was newly built, and it was so successful we decided to return.'

I nod my head as if I to appreciate the advantages the city can offer, even when compared to the Bahamas.

'You don't seem very impressed by our devotion to the game, Mr Oliphant.' Sanderson the poseur has decided to go on the attack. 'You probably think it's strange for us to find enjoyment in a game built around murder. With your intimate knowledge of the subject, that is.' He simpers, rocks forward then back in his loafers.

'Were you all here a year ago?'

'I missed it,' says Heather Cookson, light flashing from her jewellery, 'prior engagement.'

'And was the murder solved?'

'Oh yes,' says Rawlings proudly, 'not one, not two, but three murders. We were really on the ball that weekend!'

'We are quite good at it, Mr Oliphant,' King adds, 'in fact our problem now is that we can't find basic plots and scripts that are challenging enough.'

It may be King's addiction to this game that's driving them all, but there are nods and sounds of assent from all of them. So I decide it's time. Now is the moment.

'I might be able to help you there,' I say. 'I can give you a murder to solve that needs careful thought. Consideration. Questioning of a high calibre.' I can see Kim out of the corner of my eyes – she's shaking her head slowly; I take it as a warning, which I decide to ignore. Even if it had been an order, I would still ignore it.

'This is a game, Oliphant,' says Sanderson, suspicious, 'there are certain rules we follow. Would you follow the rules?'

'It seems that one of the reasons you want to employ me is that I don't follow rules, I do things my own way. So I'm not going to promise anything. But I know about these games

56

you play.' I look around the room, look at each in turn, not to intimidate or embarrass, more to show that I can't be intimidated by their numbers, their money, their – with some of them at least – antagonism. 'I'll follow the basic principles,' I tell them. 'One of you will be the murderer, the others will ask questions, listen to answers, find clues.'

'Sounds familiar,' says Heather Cookson.

'But we're used to things being done in a certain way – this might be a complete waste of . . .'

'Liam Sanderson, you're not turning into a killjoy, are you?' The interruption comes from Carol Parker who's leaning over him, dripping honey and promises from her deep voice. But he's not taking the bait, he backs away from her a little.

'No,' he says warily, 'I enjoy these games, you know I do. But . . .'

'No buts, Liam, I'm all for something different, something a little nitty-gritty, something like real life. It is based on real life, isn't it, Mr Oliphant?'

'Yes, Miss Parker, it certainly is.'

Sanderson is still sulking, his angry pout pointed straight at me. King is eyeing me up carefully, he's wondering what I'm going to say, whether I'm about to subvert the plans for his weekend. And in the corner Kim is staring hard at the carpet, absolving herself of all responsibility for my actions.

'Do you want to play, then?' I ask.

King looks round at his fellow directors; only Liam Sanderson turns his head away. 'We'll play,' he says quietly.

'Good. In that case, I'll need a room for the weekend.'

'Why's that?' asks Carol Parker. 'I thought you lived locally.'

'I do. But I want to be here with you. I have a role to play as well.'

'Really? That'll make things more interesting, are you good at acting?'

57

'No, I'm afraid not. I can only ever be myself. But that doesn't matter, not for what we're going to do.'

'Heather,' says King, 'can you arrange a room for our master of misrule, please.' He turns his attention back to me. 'Is there anything else you need, Mr Oliphant? It might be better to know now, rather than interrupt matters once we get into the swing of things.'

'Nothing I can think of, Mr King, except for your collective co-operation. I think you'll find that the whole thing is tailored to your own personalities. How far and fast we progress depends on you. But I'll explain it later. Now then, do you normally play your game in one of the conference rooms downstairs, like the other groups?'

'Good God no, we don't want to be associating with *hoi-polloi*.' His lips are parted, I can see his teeth, but I'd hesitate to describe the look on his face as a smile, or the tone of his voice as humorous. 'We have the use of all the penthouse suites, and tend to work from this room. It should be large enough, even when our partners join us.'

'Your partners?'

'Wives, husbands, lovers, this is a social weekend, Mr Oliphant, so we're encouraged to bring our partners along. It does make matters more interesting, I assure you. That won't be a problem, will it?'

'Not at all, Mr King. Should we say back here at eleven? That gives me just under an hour to get ready.'

'Excellent. May I tell everyone that dress is informal? Now that business has been concluded and you're a member of the team?'

'Informality is my middle name, Mr King. But I'd like to point out that I haven't said yet whether I would be taking the job or not. The reason is, I don't know you and the rest of the board well enough. That's one of the reasons I've proposed this addition to your activities, so I can get to find out more about you. But by the time you're ready to leave I'll give you my answer.' I rise to my feet feeling that I'm controlling matters fairly well. If King is surprised by my statement he doesn't show it; he merely nods then holds out his hand to me. We shake. Then Heather Cookson's at my side – she's been speaking on the phone and left the room momentarily.

'Your room is on the floor below – here's the key.' She gives me a plastic card. 'If you need anything just charge it. Do you have any luggage to bring up?'

I pat my briefcase. 'I travel light.'

'In that case,' King says, 'We'll see you at eleven.' He turns away and moves towards Kim, presumably keen to know what I'm up to. But I want her first.

'Kim,' I call over the polite gentility of boardroom conversation, 'I need to talk to you urgently. Would you mind coming down with me? It'll only take a few minutes.'

Kim looks at King, then at me, back to King. He nods his permission and she follows me out of the door. She opens her mouth to speak as soon as the door closes behind us, but I shake my head, raise my finger to my lips; it's almost pleasant, treating her like a naughty schoolgirl. But she's silent while we're waiting for the lift, silent in it, silent as we walk down the corridor to my room. I usher her in before me and she remains silent as she lowers herself into a seat beside the window.

'Now you're sulking,' I tell her.

'No, Billy, not sulking. Wondering what you're up to. Considering whether there are grounds for having you sectioned under the Mental Health Act. Thinking that I was a fool for inviting you along here in the first place. Surprised at the way you're behaving, embarrassed for you, worried what my bosses will think about me because it was me who suggested you could work for them. Angry.'

'Not curious?'

'Only in the sense that I think something bad is going to happen and I'd rather know about it in advance. But I doubt you'll tell me.'

59

'On the contrary, Kim, I'll tell you everything I know, which isn't much. And you won't be pleased. But you can help me.'

'Can? Perhaps. Will? Not the way I feel at the moment, which is completely and utterly pissed off with you, Billy. Why did I even think we could work together? Why did I try to persuade King he should offer you a job? Why . . .?'

'Because I'm sexy as hell and you're after my body? No, I don't think so. Because I'm good at what I do? That's nearer to the mark – that's the reason I was offered this job in the first place. So trust your instincts, Kim. Trust me. And help me.'

She shakes her head, twitches aside the curtain and glances out of the window as if she's waiting for something to happen outside. 'Nothing's unconditional, Billy. Tell me what you're after. Tell me what you're up to.'

This is the next hurdle to leap, the next obstacle to overcome. Getting Kim's help will be difficult. Saying that I want to investigate Annabelle Wilder's murder carries with it the implication that Kim hasn't done her job properly. That might even be the truth – she could have been bought off by Amalgam. If that's so, then pursuing the case might even be dangerous for me. But I can't imagine Kim taking bribes, I can't even imagine she would allow her interest in Amalgam to distract her from her investigations. The only conclusion is that it must be a tough case. So what am I hoping to achieve in a weekend when the Force has come up with nothing after a year? When I put it like that, my decision to help Terry Wilder and his parents-in-law is silly, based on vanity rather than sympathy. Logic dictates that I should pack up and go home.

I have a magical talent for transmuting my enthusiasm into despair in a matter of seconds. Like some wild-eyed thaumaturge, I'm able to distil the word 'can't' from the air I breathe. Being aware of this allows me to anticipate my descent into despondency, and I can hide my melancholy from those around me. But this is nothing more than treating the symptoms – the disease itself remains. If Kim hadn't been sitting there I might have just packed up and gone home, lied to Terry, told him I couldn't find anything. But she's a physical object and I have to negotiate with her, bargain with her, armed only with the vestiges of my pride. 'You're good,' I tell myself, 'you can do this.' But I don't believe my lies.

'OK,' I say, drawing a deep breath, 'this is what I'm up to. I'm going to go back upstairs and tell your friends, your employers, that together we're investigating a murder. For the sake of brevity let's call it "Ice Cold". That could be because the trail's gone cold, but it's not, it's because the body of a young woman was found . . .'

'. . . in a walk-in deep freeze, and the answer's no, Billy, no.' Her voice is far calmer than it should be. 'I'm not going to jeopardise my future career, my security, my happiness even, because you listened to a jumped-up aggravating little sod with a grudge against me.'

I remember those silly lessons I had when I was a policeman, the ones where an actor explained how body language can be used to bend others to your will. I adopt an open pose, legs apart, hands outstretched, I radiate peace. 'Kim, don't take it personally. Look at it from my point of view, a neutral point of view. There's a limited number of suspects, the hotel was locked and barred, but you've got nothing and we're a year down the line. And I don't want you to physically help with this, I just want information. How far has the case progressed? Do you have a prime suspect? Just tell me what you know, that's all.'

'Christ, Billy, don't you think I've tried!' she snaps at me. 'You're not the only one with feelings, sympathies, sorrows. But I can't help you.' She holds out her hand, index finger jabbing at me. 'First, I was taken off the case as soon as it was clear there could be a conflict of interests. Before I was even offered the job, as soon as there was a mention of the possibility, I was onto the boss straightaway. That was six months ago. I've kept well away since then.' Another finger joins the first. 'Second, everyone had a cast-iron alibi until they went to bed, and all movement after that could be traced by CCTV.' Another finger joins the first two. 'Third, Annabelle Wilder didn't die from being stripped, tied and locked in a freezer, she died from carbon monoxide poisoning, the autopsy told us that much. Her dead body was put into the freezer so we couldn't accurately determine the time of death. Fourth,' her whole hand is performing karate chops at me now, 'there's no CCTV footage of anyone carrying anything as big as a body into the freezer, but the system was up and running throughout the weekend.' She sits back, takes a deep breath.

'I'm glad you ran out of fingers,' I tell her.

'Don't make jokes, Billy. I don't like it when murder cases are unsolved. I don't like it when, as with this case, every-thing's in place to make solving a crime easy but we still can't do it. I don't like feeling helpless, and I don't like the feeling that someone's laughing at me.'

'Kim, that someone is upstairs playing games.'

'No, Billy, there's that little rule you're forgetting, "inno-cent until proven guilty". There's no proof, no motive. There's no evidence.'

Despite Kim's statement that she wouldn't help me, her comments are proving surprisingly useful. I wonder how much further she'll be willing to go.

'So you don't know when Annabelle was killed. When was the body found, then?'

'Sunday, mid-morning. Terry Wilder came in at six-thirty to get breakfasts ready. He opened the freezer straightaway – apparently there was some pastry he needed to defrost for the evening meal.'

'It was Terry found his wife's body?'

'Yeah. We closed the place down. There was nothing, Billy, nothing. We don't know how the body got in there, or who put it there. No-one came into the building, no-one went out.'

'Who was the last to use the freezer, before the body was put in there?'

'Terry Wilder. He put the pastry in there the previous night. Billy, we've been through it all and we haven't been able to find out a thing.'

I glance at my watch – another half hour before I have to be back upstairs. 'Are you going to help me on this, Kim?'

She's beginning to get angry. 'Help? I've already told you as much as I know, more than I should have. I'm not prepared to side with you against those people upstairs if that's what you mean. And anyway, as soon as you tell them what you're doing they'll kick you out.'

'OK, let's leave it like this. You won't hinder me and, if I can get King's say-so, you'll give me any back-up I need. You don't have to be pro-active. Just do as I ask you. And I want this to be a surprise, so don't tell them what I'm planning.'

'Jesus Christ, Billy, no!'

'If King says it's OK, if I can get him on my side, he'll let me have you anyway. But I'd rather you offered than have him force you.'

She rises to her feet, her anger at its peak now. 'Can't you get it through your thick skull? He won't let you take this any further. And even if he did, how are you, by yourself, going to solve a murder in one weekend when the Police Force hasn't been able to do it in a year?'

It may not be deliberate, but she's playing on my weakness again – my defeatism could easily swamp me.

'I won't be working by myself,' I tell her. 'After all, they said it. They're experts in solving murders now, two or three in a weekend. So I'll let them solve it. It'll be easy for them. All I have to do is guide them in the right direction.'

She says nothing but she doesn't move. Her lips are set in a thin line of defiance, but I can read her – she's not going to tell King my plans.

'All I need is a quick shower and to make a phone call or

two. It would help if I can shout a question or two through from the shower. Would that be OK?'

'Billy, there'll soon be another murder around here, but there'll be no mystery, I'll admit to killing you out of sheer annoyance.'

I step into the bathroom. 'I'll take that as a yes, then.'

CHAPTER SIX

When I step out of the bathroom I find that Kim has been busy. She hands me a sheet of paper on which she's written down the answers to the questions I've been shouting at her. I read the sheet carefully.

A year ago four of the directors were staying at the hotel: Managing Director King, Financial Director Rawlings, Carol Parker, Sales, and Liam Sanderson, Research and Development. All four are here again, this time with Heather Cookson and her husband, and Rawlings and Sanderson have both brought their partners.

I'd also asked who else was in the hotel during the weekend. Kim's scribble adds a few more names, the reason they were in the hotel, and any extra information she feels would be interesting. Terry Wilder was the only chef at work over the weekend, and had left at ten-thirty on the Saturday night after doing advance preparation of the next day's meals. He'd put some pastry in the freezer immediately before leaving, and it was Terry who'd found the body next morning at six-thirty. A waitress, Lisa MacDonald, had served the meal and cleared away. She'd worked a split shift on the Saturday, seven in the morning to eleven, six in the evening to ten. The only others in the hotel had been the security guards: Mike Beechey had started his twelve-hour shift at eight in the evening.

'At least seven suspects,' I say aloud, more to myself than Kim.

'Not quite,' she replies, not realising my speech was intended as a soliloquy. 'Lisa MacDonald helped tidy up after the directors had finished their evening meal. That meant she and Terry putting some items away in the freezer just before she left at ten when, they say, there was no body there.'

'Could they be lying? Working together for some reason?'

'She's got no criminal record, sound family background, no reason to lie. But anything's possible.'

'So the body must have been put in the freezer before six-thirty on Sunday, and after ten-thirty on the Saturday.'

Kim gets to her feet. 'That's one way of looking at things. But we know a little bit about the time of death as well.' She's speaking wearily, explaining the obvious to someone who might not understand the painstaking explorations necessary to come up with such detailed information. 'Her core body temperature when she was found was the same as that of the freezer. She'd been in there at least four hours, depending on the degree of cooling that took place immediately after death.' She's almost at the door.

'Hold on,' I say, 'tell me that again. I didn't quite . . .'

She stops and turns, her suspicions obviously correct – I can't understand simple English. She begins again, annoyingly slowly. 'If she'd been killed at, say, five in the morning and put straight into the freezer, her core body temperature . . .'

'The temperature deep inside her body?'

'Yes, it would still have been slightly higher than the freezer temperature when she was found, or rather, when the duty doctor did his examination, which was about seven-thirty am. It wouldn't have had time to cool fully. But she could have been killed, her body allowed to cool, and then been frozen. There are too many variables, the only certainty is that she couldn't have been killed after, say, three o'clock Sunday morning.'

'What about her movements on the Saturday? Who was the last person to see her alive?'

Kim comes away from the door, resigned to further questions and determined to make her boredom as overt as possible. She leans against the wall. 'Terry left her in bed when he came to work, says it must have been about five forty-five am on the Saturday morning. He . . .'

'Does he have any criminal record?'

She diverts to answer me. 'Minor indiscretions in his youth. Nicking cars, he was always a follower, never a leader. Thick as pig shit, so I'd give him the benefit of the doubt. I don't think he had anything to do with it. We never treated him as a real suspect.'

'He wasn't worried when his wife was away all night?'

'She was meant to be away, working nights at another hotel. When the Riverside opened fully she was going to come and work here; probably Terry managed to put a word in for her. I forget the name of the place she was waitressing, helping behind the bar, whatever – it's somewhere up beside the park. Not quite a flophouse but pretty close to it.'

'And her movements?'

'She was due to start work at six that Saturday evening, but she didn't appear. Rang in just before she was due to start, said she was going to be late. It didn't worry them much when she didn't appear, she wasn't very reliable, she'd missed shifts before. They managed to get someone else in.'

'I suppose you checked all these things out?' There's no need for Kim to reply – it wasn't really a question. She's a professional, she wouldn't be telling me this unless it was a cast-iron certainty. But she adds more information just to prove she's been trying. 'Phone records show the call came from her mobile at five fifty-seven.'

'That's quite a narrow window, eh? Nine hours, six in the evening to three the following morning. I don't suppose you know anything about her movements between those hours? Or beforehand – what did she do during the day? Did she make any other calls on her mobile?'

'No calls, Billy, no-one saw her; we drew nothing. Somehow she made her way from her house to the deep-freeze, from life to death, without anyone catching sight of her. And the hotel CCTV records show no-one moving in the kitchen from the time Terry Wilder left until the time he returned. Can I go now?' Her hand's reaching towards the door.

'Just one more thing, Kim. You said she died of carbon monoxide poisoning, but she was tied up in the freezer. So you're taking the line that she was tied up, left in a car or some enclosed place, and the gas introduced until she was dead? Then she was brought here?'

'Yeah, that's about it.'

'But why?'

'Enough, Billy. There are people upstairs who are far more interested in playing games than I am. Go and see them.' She's out before I can say anything, though I'm not too worried. I'd rather let her cool down a little and use her again than push too hard now and risk permanent alienation. And there's a lot for me to digest. I've another fifteen minutes before I'm due back upstairs, so I lie on the bed to gather my thoughts.

Terry Wilder told me someone from Amalgam murdered his wife, and I was eager to believe that was the case. It made things easy, gave me a limited range of suspects. It was like an old-fashioned detective story – eliminate the suspects, check the motives, eventually I'd end up with only one possible solution, one murderer. Now it's not so easy. Anyone could have killed Annabelle Wilder. But why bring her dead body to the hotel? And how did it get into the freezer without anyone seeing it? Why the freezer, why not an empty room, a cupboard, a bin outside in the yard? There must have been some degree of collusion, some contact with one of the people staying in the hotel.

Any problem, particularly a murder, can be approached from several different directions. One way is to begin with the body and use forensic evidence to connect it with an individual, the murderer. Sounds easy, rarely worked in the past, but becoming a viable option now with the use of DNA records. It does rely, however, on the murderer leaving a DNA sample, having a criminal record, and having a matching sample on that record. I can only assume that nothing has been found in that direction.

Another option is to consider motivation. Who would have wanted to kill Annabelle Wilder and why? So that's where I have to go next – find out what I can on Annabelle herself and on those in the hotel. Rak's the person to help. I call but her phone's on divert – she must have had an exceptionally successful night with her new friend – so I leave the names of those Amalgam directors present a year before and ask her to dig the dirt.

There's time for one more call, and Terry Wilder answers the phone quickly. I identify myself, push straight on. 'Terry,' I say, 'you didn't actually tell me everything about the murder, did you? You mentioned the freezer, the body, but you didn't say that the post mortem showed death by carbon monoxide poisoning. That changes things. Widens the possibilities, wouldn't you say?'

Terry's silent.

'You still there?'

'I'm here.'

'Terry, don't play with me, please. I hate being made a fool of. I hate that feeling of not knowing things, I get butter-flies – it's a bit like sitting an exam and finding you don't understand any of the questions. So is there anything else I should know?'

He sounds suitably contrite. 'I'm sorry. I was going to tell you but I thought you . . . I thought you wouldn't take the job on. I thought you'd say what you said just before, about there being too many suspects. I thought you wouldn't give me enough time to explain. It doesn't really alter things, Mr Oliphant, even if Anna was killed somewhere else, someone must have brought her into the hotel. And to do that, whoever it was had to have help from someone inside. And an accomplice is just as guilty as the murderer.'

'Yes, Terry, but why? Why bring the body into the hotel? Why not just dump it?' I don't expect an answer and Terry doesn't disappoint me by giving one. I decide to make him do some work for me – if I'm giving up my time for him then he can do the same for me. 'Look, I may need to jog some memories. You've given me some photographs of Annabelle, do you have any more?'

'Yeah, somewhere around the place. She had an album, I was looking at it the other night. It's on the shelves right here.'

'Good, if it's an album I want the whole thing.'

'Why?' It's a reasonable question.

'I want to get to know her. I want close-ups, some long shots as well to give an idea of her height and body shape. And if you can think of anything else that might help, anything that gives me an idea of the type of person she was, scribble it down for me. Put everything in an envelope with my name on, leave it at reception. Don't do anything else, no protests, no aggravation, don't muddy the water. Understand?'

'Yeah.' His voice sounds surly.

'Good. Don't forget, anything else that might help. And I want it within an hour.' I disconnect quickly before he can object. There seems little else I can do beyond confront the directors, and I'm not looking forward to doing that. I remember Terry's prediction that I'll be thrown out. I have a vision of myself lying on the lawn outside the hotel, two big doormen dusting their hands, the contents of my brief-case scattered around me. I look at my reflection in the mirror above the dressing table. 'Another fine mess you've gotten me into,' I say, and the me in the mirror looks back at me with bemused innocence.

CHAPTER SEVEN

There are more people waiting for me than I expected. My seat, the seat to which Heather Cookson shows me, is placed directly opposite the sofa. An adversarial semicircle of other chairs surrounds me, though only one is occupied. Carol Parker has changed her clothes – she's casual now, jeans, a scoop-necked T-shirt tucked in at the waist. She's slimmer than she looked in her power suit, though still as tall.

'So you've got a little game lined up for us?' She's making conversation, sounds a little embarrassed that my presence is being ignored.

'I'm not sure if it's a game or not.'

'Not a game? Something serious, then? Or perhaps a little more light-hearted than a game. Do we have to dress up? Sometimes we do. One evening the murder was committed in a theatre and we all had to dress up as characters from the play. It was a made-up play, of course, so the characters were clichés. You know the thing: vicar, tart-with-a-heart, jealous husband, mistress, young wife, lusty lover. I was a nymphomaniac nun.' She shakes her head as if amazed that she could ever have played such a part. 'Things like that only really work with copious amounts of alcohol.'

'I wouldn't really know about that, Miss Parker, I've never been to one.'

'Please, call me Carol, we're almost workmates.' She grins, leans forward. 'Where was I? Oh yes, murders. I was just saying, wine or grass, you need one or both to get rid of inhibitions, then the evening goes with a bit of a swing. People can really get into their roles.' She pulls her chair a

71

little further forward. 'So what have you got for us today?' she whispers conspiratorially, 'Will we need to play parts?'

'I think you could get by just being yourselves.'

'Oh, how disappointing. And what about you, Billy – you don't mind if I call you Billy, do you – do you get to play?'

She's close now; I can smell her perfume. Her eyes are wide, the pupils dilated as if she's had too much to drink. But there's no smell of alcohol on her breath and she doesn't seem uncoordinated. I lean a little closer to her in return. 'I suppose I do have a part to play,' I whisper back. 'It's not a very exciting part. I get to play the puzzled detective who relies on everybody else at the scene to give or get information that helps solve the crime.'

'And the crime's always solved,' she says disappointedly. 'That's the trouble with these things. Too far-fetched and the crime's always solved. Real life just isn't like that.' She leans back in her seat, pushes the front legs off the ground and stretches. Her right hand comes close to striking her boss's nose.

'You won't get promotion that way,' Mike King grins, 'assaulting the MD.' He manoeuvres himself into his place opposite me; he's taken off his tie and his jacket but his shirt-sleeves are still rolled down and cuff-linked. His top button is undone but he looks uncomfortable, as if he's trying hard to be something he isn't. His first romper suit was probably pinstriped. The lighthouse gleam of his smile washes over me as he slides into his seat.

'Very well, everyone,' King announces, 'Mr Oliphant has returned and I feel we ought to begin.'

Heads turn, mouths are opened and eyebrows raised in apparent surprise to find me there, as if I've materialised without having walked past them five minutes before. There's a slow stroll to find seats.

'Now then,' King continues, his eyes roving the room, 'I don't need to remind you that Mr Oliphant has promised us an entertainment which, based on our knowledge of his expertise and experiences, we've been anticipating with some relish.' His gaze focuses on me. 'You'll find some faces new to you, Mr Oliphant. On your left, next to Trevor, is his wife Natasha.' Natasha Rawlings is as small as her husband is large, as delicate and pale as he's florid. She looks fragile beneath lidded, princess eyes. They're probably the same age, but it's as if they're symbiotically linked and he's living and thriving on her energy. As he grows bigger and fatter, so she'll shrink away to nothingness.

'To your right, behind the sofa, is Ben Worrall.' Worrall is a young man, tall and thin, perhaps in his late twenties. He raises his hand in what might be a salute, might be an apology for his inability to reach me and shake my hand. He mouths a friendly 'Hiya', turns his head and the light is reflected directly into my eyes from his two silver earrings. He doesn't seem quite right for the company, and I'm just about to start wondering who he is, who he's connected to, when I notice Liam Sanderson in front of him. Ben's hand is resting on the back of the sofa, Sanderson reaches back with his own hand to touch it briefly. That's his little sign saying 'My property.'

'And last of all, sitting beside you on your right, is Gary Cookson, Heather's husband.' Gary and Heather are a matched pair. If I detect a trace of tiredness in his eyes it's because he's weighed down with chains and rings of gold and a heavy watch. I notice that some of my audience have pens and paper at the ready; Gary Cookson has a mini computer, his hand is already raised, stylus poised ready to write down my every word.

'Introductions complete, then. Over to you, Mr Oliphant.'

I haven't thought how I'll introduce this most delicate of subjects. 'You're all suspects in a murder investigation' might be taking the art of directness to an extreme. But there seems no way of being delicate, of dancing round the subject. They're expecting a game, and I'm about to suggest that one of them was involved in killing an innocent girl, a pregnant girl. They'll probably throw me out. But I might also get a reaction from one of them.

'Mr Oliphant?' King's voice pulls me back. 'We're ready. We're waiting.'

'I'm sorry. This could be quite a complicated matter and I'm not sure I'll be able to explain it properly. But let's just say that I'm open to questions at any time, from anyone.' The faces surrounding me seem interested, keen, helpful even. I wonder how long they'll remain that way. I take a deep breath, begin my speech.

'Let's begin at the beginning. Some of this may seem familiar to some of you. You're all guests at a luxury hotel . . .'

'Sounds good to me,' says Gary Cookson.

'. . . and, to make the investigation easier, you can all play yourselves.'

'Typecast again,' says Carol Parker.

'Like you were as a sex-mad nun?' says Trevor Rawlings. Carol sticks out her tongue at him.

'Do you play a part?' asks Liam Sanderson with icy politeness.

'I play a detective. A hard-pressed detective who has to come up with a result before the weekend's over. A detective who thinks he might know what happened but has no hard evidence.'

Liam Sanderson offers an opinion, ' "Thinks" and "might" seems more like guesswork than detection. Perhaps the detective you're playing isn't very good at his job.'

'Perhaps you're right, Mr Sanderson. Or it might be that he's waiting for the criminal to make a mistake, incriminate himself by something he does. Or even something he says.'

'Or she,' says Heather Cookson laconically, 'the murderer could be a woman.'

'Almost guaranteed,' adds her husband, ' "The female of the species is more deadly than the male." Kipling. Only poet I've ever been able to understand.'

While he's talking I'm trying to remember exactly what I

said. I'm sure I've only mentioned the word "criminal", yet Heather Cookson definitely said "murderer". It might be that she's assuming that the crime to be investigated will be a murder. I'm nearly sure that these games do normally involve a character being killed. But I don't like being anticipated.

'Go on, Billy, we're all trembling with expectation,' Carol Parker encourages me.

'You're guests in a hotel. No-one can get in, and a body's found . . .'

'How can no-one get in?' asks Trevor Rawlings.

'It doesn't really matter.'

'Oh, but it does. I'm not an artistic person. I need concrete facts to help me get into this role-playing business; I need to imagine myself into my part. So I need to know why no-one can get in – after all, most hotels welcome people coming in, we certainly do. So why can no-one get in?'

I'm beginning to lose my patience. 'It's a hotel on a small island. There's been a storm, trees have blown down blocking every road. It's been snowing for a week, so there's no way through to the hotel.'

'It's very posh,' adds Heather Cookson, 'exclusive even, there's a security fence surrounding it. Electrified. With barbed wire on top.'

Carol Parker takes over the baton. 'Ferocious dogs are patrolling the grounds . . .'

'No, it's besieged by werewolves,' Natasha Rawlings continues excitedly, her pale face coming to life, 'they've eaten all the staff and . . .'

A nudge from her husband silences her, he sucks the energy from her and her head slumps onto her chest. I can imagine him threatening to remove her batteries if she speaks out again.

'It's a locked room murder,' announces Mike King, 'that's all Mr Oliphant is saying. Is that right?'

'Thank you. Yes, that's right. A murder has been committed

and there is a finite number of suspects.' I look around the room. 'One of you has killed someone.'

No-one flinches. No-one turns away from my gaze. True, one or two people aren't looking at me, but it's surprising that those watching should all be willing to eye-wrestle with me.

'Go on, then,' says King again, beginning to show his magisterial impatience. 'And can I suggest that we keep the interruptions and questions and comments until Mr Oliphant has finished or we'll be here all day.'

I can hear the faint rumble of bridge traffic crossing the river, a train, a starling chortling outside the window. For a brief moment I'm the centre of the world.

'A young woman has been murdered,' I say softly. 'She's in her early thirties, outgoing, attractive. Her body has been found inside the hotel. I'm not sure of the time of death, for one simple reason. Her body was placed inside the hotel's walk-in freezer . . .'

'That's enough!' Trevor Rawlings explodes to his feet. 'Just what do you think you're on about? Are you trying to make fools of us all? Get out, get out now before I have you . . .'

'Trevor, please sit down.' King's voice is almost a whisper. 'I did ask for no interruptions.'

'But he's talking about . . .'

'I know what he's talking about. We all know what he's talking about, even those who weren't here a year ago are aware of the incident. But I think we should let Mr Oliphant go on.'

'Why? Christ, Mike, why the hell should we . . .?'

'Trevor. Once again, please sit down.'

The authority in his master's voice forces Rawlings back into his seat. His wife looks at him, pats him on the hand. He pulls his hand away.

King opens his hands in my direction. 'You have the floor, Mr Oliphant. No, let me use a theatrical metaphor instead.

You're centre stage. However, centre stage is a dangerous place to be. There's a trapdoor beneath your feet. And I am a stage manager with my finger on the button that operates that trapdoor. Is there a landing mat beneath it? We may find out very soon. Please, do go on.'

I decide to begin again. 'You are guests in a hotel. The hotel is locked, secure, not yet open to the public. No-one can get in without being noticed by the security guard and the CCTV cameras. No-one can get out without setting off alarms at emergency exits or being seen by the security guard. We have, in effect, a locked room. Yet a body is found in a walk-in freezer. It's the body of a young woman. But a post-mortem examination shows that the woman did not freeze to death. She died from carbon monoxide poisoning. And she was pregnant.

'The body was not in the freezer at ten-thirty pm – two witnesses confirm that fact. The body was in the freezer at six-thirty the next morning. Given the nature of this particular closed room, one of those present at this hotel a year ago was involved in the murder of Annabelle Wilder.'

People are looking at each other. Conversations are beginning.

'Why on earth is he . . .'

'You weren't here, it was the . . .'

'Not again, we've already been through this . . .'

'We ought to get him out now . . .'

'Ring Kim. It's her fault . . .'

I can see King about to pass judgement. His finger is reaching for the trapdoor button.

'I haven't finished yet.' My voice manages to silence the talking, halt all movement. I have the spotlight on me again. 'You've offered me a job here. It's a good job, a fascinating job. The package involves a salary far in excess of what I normally earn. I assume that you're willing to offer me this much money because you believe I'm good. If so, then consider the following.'

They're listening again, listening carefully.

'What type of employee would I be if I ignored an essential part of my job? Would you really consider me worth my substantial salary if you heard that I knew of some wrongdoing in one of your establishments, yet chose to ignore it? And what if that act was not mere forgetfulness, or rudeness to a customer, or losing some valuable property, but the worst possible crime, murder? If I chose not to investigate a crime in one of your hotels, you would – justifiably in my opinion – fire me immediately.'

'You're twisting words,' Rawlings shouts again, 'there's already been a full investigation!'

'An investigation leading nowhere. No arrests, no suspects.'

'Gentlemen, please, let me speak.' King is conciliatory again, smoothing the troubled waters. When he talks, his words are directed at me. 'Yes, there was a murder investigation a year ago. All of us present at the time were questioned, have been questioned since. Our evidence is on record, no charges have been made against us. We've helped the police at every juncture. Do you really believe that Kim Bryden would have come to work for us if she believed that we'd had anything to do with the girl's murder? And as you said, she was killed elsewhere. How can one of us have been responsible? We were all locked in the hotel.'

'It's taken the police a year to get nowhere,' Liam Sanderson adds, 'yet you want to solve the whole thing in a weekend? If you're that good we should be paying you double what we've offered.'

I resist the temptation to tell him that I'll take up his offer of increased pay – he's already antagonistic enough. 'I may be that good, but that isn't the point. If you want me to work for you, you have to trust me. And, of course, I have to trust you. I want to investigate a murder that took place in your hotel. You, as responsible directors of a responsible company, have to allow me to do so. I need to interview witnesses and

78

suspects. You, as the same responsible people you were in the last sentence, have to agree that that is the only logical way to proceed. The fact that you are the witnesses and suspects is irrelevant. You've suggested, threatened even, to have me thrown out of the hotel. I won't even give you the opportunity of doing that. If you don't allow me to investigate this murder, give me the whole weekend to do so, and co-operate as witnesses in giving full interviews, then I shall simply refuse your offer of a job and leave immediately.'

'Sounds like a reasonable argument to me,' says Carol Parker, 'I don't mind being asked questions again. I've got nothing to hide.'

Rawlings is bellowing again, 'It's a specious argument; he's just playing with words. We should kick him out.'

I rise to my feet. 'Thank you for listening, ladies and gentlemen. I see that you need to have a serious discussion on this matter. I'll give you an hour – that should be long enough to explain more fully to those not present a year ago exactly what I've been talking about, and to come to a decision about whether to allow me to investigate further. If you're in any doubt, please consider the following. The good publicity you will get from allowing me to pursue this matter could, if organised properly, be of huge benefit. A board of directors that puts itself under investigation is a rare thing. And if, as you say, you are innocent, then you have nothing to worry about. I'll call back in an hour.'

I head for the door. My shirt is wet beneath my arms and I need to relax, to still the adrenaline flow and calm my fast-beating heart. I'm quite pleased with myself – my argument may have been specious, but it sounded good. And I've tried; I can tell Terry Wilder and Charles and Emily Robertson that I tried. Just as I reach for the handle I hear my name being called.

'Billy. Mr Oliphant, come back.'

It's Mike King. And for the first time he's called me 'Billy' instead of 'Mr Oliphant'. That in itself is worrying, annoying

79

even. I like to make people work for the privilege of using my first name.

'Mr King?'

'We've made a decision. I could tell by looking at people how they felt – a majority feels you should carry out a full investigation. But we leave on Sunday evening, straight after an early dinner. You have until then. A little over a day.'

It's too quick a decision, there's no consensus, there's been no discussion – it's simply King's decision. But it shows where the power is in the company. I offer a polite thank you.

King is almost ingratiating, 'We'll do all we can to co-operate.'

'I'm pleased. But I need to think, gather information from other sources. Perhaps you can start without me.'

'Certainly. What would you like us to do?'

'Those who were here a year ago can write out a statement confirming what they were doing for the whole weekend. You've been questioned by the police on several occasions, so you should all be able to remember what you said with a fair degree of accuracy. Those who weren't here a year ago can cross-question those who were, check that alibis and times you were together are accurate, look for inaccuracies. That will probably do until I get back. Then I'd like to start asking questions.'

'Very well, I'll see that happens.'

'And there is one other thing. You said it was a majority decision to allow me in. I would have preferred a unanimous vote, but there are hidden advantages to everything. Please let me know who voted against me. I might want to interview them first.'

CHAPTER EIGHT

I'd like to rest for a while. I'd like to lie down, gather my thoughts, think carefully about what happens next. I'd even like to have some time to congratulate myself for persuading these people to allow me to investigate them further. I knew they would, one way or another. In the same way that the possibility of good publicity swayed them, I was prepared to threaten them with bad publicity. I had the offer of a job, in writing, tucked away in my pocket. How would they have explained my reluctance to take up that offer when I wished to investigate a year-old murder and they refused to give me even a day of their time? They would have given way, reluctantly, and then they would have been as obstructive as possible. Now, for a while at least, some of them will be working on my side. But there's no time for telling myself how clever I am. There's no time to think of the questions I'll have to ask them, no time to worry about the impossibility of solving this crime in the meagre few hours I've been given. If I do either of these I'll give up in despair. Instead I fall back on the essential part of all investigations, gathering evidence.

My first call is downstairs to reception to collect the photographs Terry Wilder is meant to have delivered. There's a plain brown envelope, bulky, and it feels as if there's an album inside. While I'm there I explain that I need to speak to the security guard who was on duty when Annabelle Wilder's body was discovered. The receptionist is a young girl; decision making is beyond her and she summons the duty manager. I repeat my request, suggesting that he phone

Mr King if there's a problem with my access to the guard or any other member of staff, or any part of the building. The duty manager disappears for a while then returns with an ingratiating smile to inform me that Mick Beechey's due to start work at eight. I thank him unenthusiastically then return to my room. It's almost one o'clock and I've some phone calls to make.

Rak's first. She picks up the phone on the second ring, threatens to put it down again as soon as she realises it's me. 'Christ, Billy, you saw Fiona last night, she's bloody gorgeous and she's asleep in my bed while I'm piddling around trying to find info for you. She'll wake up soon, wonder where I am and I'll be back in bed with her before you can say Amalgam. And I'll stay there till she goes, then I'll catch up with my sleep, then – and only then – I'll do what I can to help you. OK?'

'What does she do, Rak?'

'What does she do? Christ, Billy, what does she not do! I have never . . .'

'No, I don't want to know about your sordid sex life. What does she do for a living?'

'Why?'

'Just curious.'

'You're wasting valuable computer access time. Oh, what the hell, she's a computer analyst, she's doing post-grad work at the university. There, now you know, we've got something in common apart from lust. Does that satisfy you?'

'Go and wake her up, tell her I want to speak to her.'

'What? Are you mad?'

'Wake her up. I want to tell her what I'm doing. She knows about computers, she might be able to help you. You've always got a spare laptop, she can use that. You'll work twice as fast.'

'You're joking. You are joking, aren't you Billy? Anyway, I'm not waking her up – you can't speak to her.'

I wait. I can hear Rak's asthmatic wheezing down the

phone. It's the old game of chicken, whoever speaks first loses. Except I've got nothing to lose – if Rak puts the phone down I have no less than when I telephoned her.

'You still there, Billy?' she whispers.

'You know this,' I say softly. 'If you let me speak to her, if you let me explain what I'm doing, why I'm doing it, she'll want to help. So will you tell her, or will I tell her?'

There's silence again, a long silence. Then a single word, a yelled 'Bastard!' before the phone is disconnected. She'll soon be at work.

Next is Sly. Saturday afternoon, so he'll be at home with the kids while Paula's out with her sister. Weekend shopping is their religion, the town centre their place of worship. I don't mind wrecking Rak's day, but Sly's different – he has family and obligations. And Paula might snap my arms off if I lure him away when he's already promised the rest of the weekend to her.

'Hello, who is it?' It's a young voice, a child's voice.

'Is that Joanna? Or Tim? This is Uncle Billy.'

'It's Gav,' comes the slightly disappointed reply. I'm not very good with kids' voices.

'Can't be Gav,' I say quickly, 'I heard he was always out on a Saturday, but I can't remember which team he's signed for. Man U? Chelsea? Leeds?'

'Leeds?' The voice is recognisably older now, 'I couldn't play for Leeds. Rubbish team, Leeds. Worst team in the league. Ought to kick them out. Anybody who supports Leeds is sad, that's what I say, and . . .'

I can hear a voice in the background getting louder; there's a sound of high-pitched laughter and a delighted scream.

'It could only be you, boss, turning a man's own children against him.' Sly's voice is round with a Yorkshire burr. 'Ringing on a Saturday as well, must be important. What can I do for you?'

I can hear Gav. 'Is he coming to see us?' he's shouting. Even with Sly's hand over the mouthpiece, the response is audible. 'I don't know, I can't hear for the noise you're making.'

'I need a favour,' I say, 'a big favour. And you're allowed to say no. In fact, if I was you, I'd definitely say no. So I'm not really sure why I'm ringing you. Ah well, it's nice talking to you, I'd better go.'

'Just tell me, boss,' Sly says wearily. 'You don't have to go through this act every time you want me to do something a little . . . well, something a little unusual. You wouldn't ask me if you didn't need help. So the answer's yes.'

'You'll probably need assistance. I thought Norm . . .'

'Not available. He's away in London for a dirty weekend.'

Norm is in his sixties, grey-haired and pot-bellied, me in two decades. His wife died a few years back and he hasn't really shown any interest in women since. His passion is cars, they recognise his love and return it in manifold ways. But he isn't a ladies' man. 'A dirty weekend? I didn't know he was seeing anyone, he never told me . . .'

'No, boss, literally a dirty weekend. Some mechanics' get-together, drooling over car engines, taking gearboxes to bits. So it's me alone, I'm afraid. Tell me what you need doing.'

'OK. But don't forget, you're allowed to say . . .'

'Boss!'

'I'll tell you!' I leave a pause just long enough to guarantee his attention. 'I want you to break into the Riverside Hotel.'

'Any particular room?' I've known Sly for a long time, he's a damn good electrician, he can build walls or knock them down, he's strong and big, he's honest, and he's the ideal person to have with you if there's even the hint of danger. I use him as a sub-contractor when I've too much work. I'd trust him with my life. The trouble is, he'd pay me the same compliment, and I'm not really worthy of such faith. Plus, he's got a beautiful wife and four gorgeous kids. I'm dealing with a murderer here and I don't want Sly to get hurt.

'I need to know how good the security is,' I tell him, 'I might be doing some work for the owners. So if you can get down here for eight we'll have a look round, talk to the security guard, look at the plans if I can find them. Then you can go away, come back some time in the early hours – you can decide when – and try to get in. That should be a good test. It's not strictly legal, even if the guard does know about it.'

'I'll be there, boss.'

'Thanks, Sly.'

'But it'll cost you. Jen's back next week, the kids have been emailing her and she's been sending them pictures. Paula wants the two of you to come out here for dinner first chance you get. I'll give you two whole days in bed together, our place on the night of the third day. You'll need feeding by then.'

'Sly, Gav might be listening.' I feel a flush of embarrassment.

'He is, and he says you're too old, you won't even last a day and a half. But I think he figures Jen likes him anyway, so he's next in line if you make a mess of this one.'

'Tell him he's precocious. And tell Paula we'll be there.'

'And I won't make a mess of this one,' I tell myself.

The telephone's warm against my ear, I put it down for a moment and tear open the padded envelope left by Terry Wilder. Inside is the promised album and a piece of lined paper. The writing on it is immature, improperly formed; it straggles blindly across the page at all angles, there are no paragraphs, no full stops. I have to squint at the page in an attempt to read it, to understand it.

Deer billy olifant, i tryd to think of things to say about Anna that was difrent that mite help u, but i carnt think of things eksept wot i said b4, i reely luvd her and she reely luvd me she sed it lots of times, when we moovd i sed id luk afta her and she sed

sheel luk afta me we cud hav owa own place not just
a hows to liv in but a restront as wel sheed be the
won in frunt and id be in the kitchen and weed mayk
lowds of muny and i sed it costs 2 much but she sed
no weel hav it 1 day soon, u see she reely luvd me
that's y I hav to no hwo did this
    Yor frend Terry Wilder.

I read it through three times, twice to make sure I understand it, the third time because I want to make sure I
remember how much Terry loved his wife. If it gets tough
when I get upstairs I want to be able to remember these
misspelled, clumsy words, they might just remind me that
someone there must be lying.

I lay the letter aside, open the album. It's old fashioned,
the prints held in place with self-adhesive triangles at each
corner, a sheet of tissue between each page. I turn the first
page and photographs slide out of the back. I push them
together, concentrating on the early images of a dark-haired
baby held proudly by a middle-aged woman, recognisably
Emily Robertson. She said she was sixty-nine; Annabelle
would have been thirty-two, that would make her thirty-seven
when the baby was born. Charles, an old fifty-two year old
then, is standing proudly behind.

Further images show the baby becoming a little girl,
growing up in what seems to have been a respectable, white-
collar, professional background. The photographs have been
carefully selected from what must have been a far larger
collection – there's no more than one of each situation. Here's
Annabelle in a dress, brown hair ribboned, surrounded by
other little girls in a semi-detached garden at a birthday party.
Next to it are a slightly older Annabelle and grey-haired
Emily digging on a sunny beach. Annabelle's first day at
secondary school is recorded, neat in white socks and grey
skirt, white blouse and blue tie. And everywhere she's
smiling.

I flick forward through a short life. Annabelle grows from a pretty girl to a good-looking teenager, shy in her swimming costume. She's less coy in a bikini, hair bleached by the sun, attracting an admiring glance from an anonymous youth caught at the edge of a foreign snapshot. That's when I realise that this isn't Annabelle's album. There's too much of her, it's about her, not from her. I turn again to the front, to the very first page. More prints drop onto the bed, their corners have loosened or they were never fixed in the first place; I ignore them. Inside the front cover, written in faded silver ink on the black page, is a simple message; to Annabelle with love on your sixteenth birthday, love from Mum and Dad.

They chose the photographs. This is their version of her life, neatly summarised, in evenly measured chronological order. And then it stops. One person has made this album, the prints have been placed by the same hand, and the last is of a poised, self-confident young woman sitting on a garden wall. She's wearing tight jeans and a T-shirt, a silly, floppy hat on the back of her head, and she's pointing at the camera as if to protest that she's not ready. After that there are empty pages. Although more photographs are jammed into them, between them, none have made a home there. It's as if they don't belong.

I put the album aside, turn instead to the photographs on the bed. The first is of Annabelle at a party, an older Annabelle, red-eyed from the flash, bottle in one hand, cigarette between two fingers of the other. Another is of a group of young people, poorly focused boys and girls, on a broken-backed sofa, cans in their hands, rabbit-ears behind two heads; Annabelle could be one of them, but it's difficult to tell. A third, in black and white, shows a solitary coated figure on a wintry beach; she's gazing moodily out at an expanse of flat, wind-blown sand. Yet another is of Annabelle pretending fear, looking down at the familiar avenues and boulevards of Paris stretched out below her in a stock Eiffel Tower view.

There are strange photographs. A hand blocks half the frame, on that day she must have been in a bad mood. There's a terraced house, tall, white and broad, balconies on each floor decked with well-trimmed potted plants, front door a glossy black. There's no-one there to wave or smile at the camera, nothing special about the view. Another black and white print could be of a naked body – there's the texture and folds of flesh in close up, dark spots of what could be freckles, a faint sheen of down caught by an angled spotlight. Annabelle smiles and laughs and frowns at me; I see her in right and left profile, full face, looking over her shoulder. I see her in Paris and (probably from her tour of Europe) Barcelona, Berlin, Prague and Amsterdam. She's been to New York; she's worn an evening gown to visit a film premiere (the venue is clearly Leicester Square); she's urged a horse on to win at Ascot, if the ridiculous hat is anything to go by. She's kept two photographs taken within moments of each other – a front and back view of her posing topless, a minuscule thong her only protection against nudity. It could be anywhere on the Mediterranean, perhaps the Côte d'Azur – there are no high-rise hotels in the background, only a ribbon of well-spaced villas with blue-tinged mountains beyond.

If the album was a view of Annabelle from outside, her parents' view, then the collection now spread out over my bed is of her from the inside, the photographs she wanted to keep. Yet there's no cohesion, nothing to say 'this is me'. If this is Annabelle as she wanted to be seen, her memories of herself and others, then she's a person of too many personalities and, at the same time, no personality. She's blonde and brunette, temptress and housewife; she poses here and she's natural there. At least the album has a focus, even if it's on her, not of her. But here? There's something wrong. There are other people, but not the same people. Very few faces appear on more than one photograph, no-one on more than three. And there's no likeness of Terry, no modern images of Emily or Charles.

I've another ten minutes before I'm due upstairs. I ring Terry's home again, although it's not him I need to speak to this time. I play a game as I wait for an answer. It's Terry's house, but his parents-in-law are staying. If one of them answers the phone, this investigation will go well. I don't bother considering odds or alternatives. I feel Fate is on my side.

'Hello, this is Emily Robertson speaking. How may I help you?' The language is precise, the pronunciation from a kinder, less-troubled age. It's the formally dressed voice of a BBC presenter, like the one my grandmother employed when she first used her new bakelite telephone.

'Hello, it's Billy Oliphant here.'

'Mr Oliphant. How good to hear from you. How are you?'

'I'm well. Mrs Robertson, I've some questions . . .'

'Please, call me Emily.'

'Emily. Can I ask . . .?'

'May I call you Billy? I feel as if I know you quite well already.'

This could take all night. I inhale deeply and refuse to allow a full stop to complete my sentence until I've finished. 'Emily, Terry brought me some photographs of Annabelle; I've looked through them but they're puzzling; there are very few people cropping up in more than one snapshot and that suggests she moved around a lot, perhaps didn't have many friends, and I was wondering if that was the case?' I can hear Emily breathing but there are no words. Could I have gone too fast for her? 'And it's rather strange that there are no photographs of Terry.' Another pause. Another silence. 'And, apart from her early days at home, there are no photographs of you or Charles.' This time I do hear something. At first I imagine it's sniffing, Emily must have a cold. But each sniff is followed by an intake of breath. Emily's crying.

Even as I listen the sobbing gets deeper, more protracted. There's some muffled talking, then the crying moves away.

'Mr Oliphant,' says a deeper voice, more controlled but recognisably weaker. 'It's Charles Robertson here.'

'Is Mrs Robertson OK?'

'She'll be alright in a minute or two.' He speaks slowly, as if he's spending time choosing his words.

'I'm sorry, I was asking her some questions about Annabelle and . . .'

'She gets upset easily. I was listening on the extension and heard what you asked Emily. We weren't aware that Terry had brought you some photographs, though we were aware that Terry had them. We're very familiar with them. They were – I'm not sure if you'll understand this – they were a great comfort to us when we heard that Annabelle was dead. You see, we hadn't seen Annabelle for quite a few years. We didn't even know when she died – it was a month afterwards that the police traced us. By that time there'd been a post mortem, a funeral, a burial service. We were put in touch with Terry. He was surprised to hear from us, but he told us the story, we came up to see him and . . . well, we keep on coming back – it's a sort of connection with Annabelle. We stay here with Terry and he looks after us. He's a very kind young man. Strange, we didn't even know we had a son-in-law.'

I sit down on the bed. I feel guilty for having to ask questions. There's pain in Charles Robertson's voice. I'm meant to be helping him, not hurting him. But I have to go on.

'The photographs in the album, they seem to go up to round about Annabelle's sixteenth birthday, then they stop. Did something happen?'

It's Emily's voice answers. 'I'll tell him, Charles,' she says, voice weaker than before but edged with determination. 'You're right, Billy, there was something. Annabelle changed. She was our only child, she came late in life to both of us; perhaps we spoiled her. The album you have, it was our birthday present to her on her sixteenth birthday. You can see the sort of life we had, middle-class suburbia and all that. I suppose Annabelle rebelled against it.'

Charles takes over again. 'It wasn't a sudden change, nothing we could blame specifically like – oh, I don't know – a new friend leading her astray. But from the age of fourteen she just wasn't the girl we knew so well.'

'Thought we knew well, dear. It was little things at first. Staying out too late. Doing less well at school than expected, not handing homework in on time. You know the type of thing, Billy.'

I think of Kirsty, my own daughter, safely past the turmoil of adolescence. I was no help to her anyway, never at home, out of my head half the time. I missed part of her growing up; I missed part of *her*. Yet even Annabelle, with all the love she received from two doting parents, seems to have lost out somewhere. What did Emily say? 'You know the type of thing.' It wasn't a question, yet it demanded a response. And if I was to tell the truth, it would be that I don't know because, if it did happen, if Kirsty did ever fight against her upbringing in any way, I missed it. But I must say something.

'Yes, Emily, I know. These things happen. You do your best but – well, eventually you have to loosen the reins a little. And you can't tell what might happen when you do that.'

'I'm not blaming her, you understand. There was a good reason for it. But . . . It's rather complicated, Billy, and I feel a little uneasy talking about Annabelle over the phone like this. It's almost as if I'm betraying her. Oh, I know it's not really, and you must think me a silly old woman, but we – Charles and I – must share the blame in this.'

Charles butts in. 'It's quite complicated, Mr Oliphant. Would it be possible for us to come down and see you? We've tickets booked for the train later on, but we could talk in your van again; the hotel isn't too far from the station. We may be able to give you information which helps you understand a little more about Annabelle.'

The Robertsons' need may be to help, or it may be to pass

on information. It's more likely, however, that they simply need to talk to someone about Annabelle. I could find myself playing the role of priest-confessor, spending time – wasting time – giving absolution when I should be investigating, asking questions. I decide to tell them it would be better if they didn't come.

'I'm just about to start questioning the Amalgam directors,' I say, trying to impress upon them that I'm likely to be very busy. I'm hoping they'll change their minds without me having to put too much pressure on them.

'Oh, that's wonderful, Billy . . .' 'Well done, Mr Oliphant, I don't know how you managed to persuade them . . .'

Annabelle Wilder has been in my mind. She's the reason why I decided to carry out these investigations. I'm beginning to create a composite image of her, an image made up of the photographs I've seen. But even that is overlaid with a picture I can only imagine, a thought of her body – dead, perhaps still with a vestige of life left in it – bound and gagged and thrown into a freezer like a side of meat. I'm not confident in my ability to do anything about this, I've been given a little over a day to solve a crime that took place a year ago and has already been thoroughly investigated by the police. But I'm trying, I'm trying for Annabelle's sake. And that's where I've gone wrong.

Annabelle won't benefit from what I'm doing. She's beyond help. If I'm honest – and I try to be honest – I'm doing this for me as well, to show the directors that money can't buy everything. I'm doing it to show that I have a degree of independence they should know about but haven't allowed for. But the people who should be uppermost in my mind are Charles and Emily. Terry's an angry young man, but he has a life ahead of him. In that life he can nurture his memories of Annabelle, perhaps find someone else to love as much as he loved her. Charles and Emily had only one daughter. Something happened in their relationship with her – in some way they feel themselves to blame. They're the ones I should be helping, and if they need to talk, I should be prepared to listen to them.

'Yes, Mr Oliphant, you're about to start talking to the directors?' Charles Robertson reminds me.

'I'm sorry, Mr Robertson, a thought just occurred to me. Yes, please, do come down. The reception staff will let you in this time, I'll make sure of that. I'll leave a message asking them to let me know when you get here. I'll tell them to take you into the coffee lounge and look after you. If there's anything at all you feel can be useful to me, I'd be very grateful.'

'Thank you, Billy. We'll come straight down.'

It's worth complicating matters just to hear the smile in Emily's voice.

CHAPTER NINE

I'm ready to go upstairs. No, 'ready' isn't the right word. I don't know what I'm going to say, don't know what I'm going to do. Perhaps that's why I press the lift button marked 'G' and step out into reception. I walk slowly out of the hotel, straight across the grassed lawn and across the road. Then I turn round. The hotel is the same monolith it was when I last looked, four-square to the road. I can't see any of the penthouse suites from down here. I walk along the pavement to my right, upriver. The hotel car park has been glued onto its western extremity at right angles to the hotel itself, entry to which is by means of a spiral of concrete which curves three stories up and gives access to spaces below ground as well.

I cross back again, dodging the traffic. The steep bank at my back gets closer to the river, leaving only enough room for the road, a riverside path and cycle track. I continue my circumnavigation of the hotel. The river, now on my right, washes its way slowly down to the sea. It's grey, heavy with dull reflections of the far bank and the bridges high above. Gulls screech and swoop for detritus best left unidentified. A small boat, red funnel rescuing it from anonymity, chugs against the current. I can remember days like this from my youth, calm autumn Saturdays when it was easy to notice that a swaggering, raucous gull had only one yellow-green leg, that someone in the boat had a blue jacket and was waving at me. I wave back. I'm not nostalgic. The past holds no fascination for me; I have no desire to be young again. I know that days like this always resurface infrequently enough to make them special, often enough to make them recognisable. That's why I enjoy the moment, the stroll beside the river, using my senses. The rest of the weekend won't be easy. I should enjoy myself while I have the chance.

On my left I can see the ranked colours of cars at their stations, half-hidden, half-revealed by alternate blocks of brick and wrought iron. Below it a fenced area with a tall gate hides a multitude of wheeled bins and several doors with signs above them proclaiming 'boiler-house', 'store-house' and 'fire-exit – keep clear'. On the wall above these are a camera and floodlight.

The rooms on the river side of the hotel have a more pleasant view than those on the land side. Their windows are high above the tall curved glass of the dining room, the timbered veranda and solid dark-wood chairs that extend the bar out into the open air. Four or five steps lead down to the river-side path and I pause to look up them and beyond. My attention is turned inward again – I'm wondering how anyone could get into the hotel other than through the front doors. Here again there are lights, many embedded in the decking, some high on the walls, others on short poles between waist and head height. Perhaps in summer or warm autumn evenings it would be possible to enter the hotel from this area, but not a year ago when the only guests were the Amalgam directors. All doors would have been locked, all furniture stored away. And the ubiquitous cameras would then, as now, glare down, their cyclops eyes missing nothing, angled to catch all.

I keep walking. At the east end of the building is an enclosed staircase, a fire escape with an exit at its base, no doubt alarmed inside but with light and camera outside as well. The next building along is a car dealership, another new building filled with lights and reflections from polished metal. I think they're Japanese cars, though these days I'm unfamiliar with logos. A pavement leads between the two buildings and I'm soon at the front again, standing once more facing the main entrance. The building seems secure, well guarded and well watched. Yet a year ago, someone managed to bring a body into the building without anyone noticing, without any cameras seeing the passage, without any alarms being sounded. So there must be another way in. If there is, Sly will find it. He must find it.

The staff are becoming used to my wandering about the building, no-one says anything as I go back in. Heads are raised in case a greeting is necessary, but I'm there on sufferance and the smile of welcome becomes an acknowledgement of my presence, no more. The lift speeds me to the top floor and I press the button to allow access to the board of Amalgam. I feel nervous, try telling myself that this is simply an investigation, I've done it hundreds of times before. It doesn't work, of course. I've a group of people who are mostly antagonistic, at best neutral. They would be considered important people by many, not least themselves. And they're used to telling people what to do. Pleasantness will be useless, they're used to that. A straightforward refusal to bow to their recalcitrance, a determination to be nastier than they could ever be, could be my best weapons. Yet in the boardroom, even more so than downstairs, I'm there on sufferance. The ball belongs to them, and if they decide to take it away, the game is over.

I press the doorbell. It's answered by Gary Cookson. 'Mr Oliphant,' he says pleasantly, 'we were just beginning to get worried, you're a touch late.' I push past him, though he appears not to notice my rudeness, and into the main room where the tables have been moved into the centre. Cookson follows behind like an eager lapdog. 'I rang your room, then reception, they told me you were examining the outside of the building. Getting to know the place, I assume.' People are scattered around, in easy chairs, one or two at the table with pads of paper in front of them.

'OK then,' I say in my best schoolmasterly voice, 'let's get going. Please take your seats.' I sit down at the head of the table. It's probably the seat King assumed would be his, but he's one of the first to sit down, further along to my right, and he shows no sign of umbrage. As the others drift slowly in I offer an audible sigh of impatience. Liam Sanderson and Trevor Rawlings are the last to arrive, they receive my glare.

I count round the table. Carol Parker's sitting on my right, next to her the Cooksons are in whispered conversation. King is nodding at something Natasha Rawlings is saying. Even as I look round, Trevor Rawlings and Liam Sanderson are edging into their seats.

'We seem to be one short,' I announce.

'Ben's not well,' says Sanderson, 'he's lying down. He's probably just tired, needs a rest. He's had a hard couple of days.'

Carol Parker sniggers and turns it into a cough. Sanderson glares at her and she raises her eyebrows at him.

'We'll start without him, I can always see him later. First of all, can I have your statements. Only from those who were here a year ago and were questioned by the police.' Sheets of handwritten A4 make their way up to my end of the table. 'And can I ask those of you who weren't here, what have you managed to find out about the events of a year ago?'

There's silence, not unexpected.

'Carol,' I say, turning to my right, 'I don't suppose you'd care to summarise what these papers will say?'

She seems embarrassed by the attention, turns to face me, shuffles her papers in front of her then begins to read. 'Well, I don't think I can add anything much to what you already know. There was a body put into the freezer. We don't know how it got there. Everyone was together until about two in the morning.'

'So all those here have substantiated each other's alibis. Handy. And after two? No alibis at all.' I decide to leave that for the moment. 'The murdered girl was called Annabelle

Wilder, she was married to an employee here. Her maiden name was Robertson. Did any of you ever meet her?'

This time there's a chorus of 'no's, a communal shaking of heads.

'Next question. How did she die?'

'We all know what the autopsy uncovered,' says King. 'She died of carbon monoxide poisoning. Her body was placed in the freezer after her death.'

'That's possibly the case, but I'd like . . .'

'I think you'll find,' says Rawlings slowly, 'that the word you're looking for is "definitely". We don't know how, but the girl's body was placed in the freezer after her death. That's what the coroner said.'

It's difficult persuading intelligent people that they could be wrong, particularly when you know they're right. I've found that the best way is to go for the big lie from the beginning. So I do. 'Please don't interrupt me,' I say to Rawlings, turning to speak to the table as a whole. 'The coroner's report stated that there was a high concentration of carboxy-haemoglobin in Annabelle Wilder's blood. This is normally due to the inhalation of carbon monoxide and its reaction with red blood cells, it reduces the cells' ability to transport oxygen around the body. It does not invariably result in death, dependent upon the amount of carbon monoxide inhaled. It can, initially, lead to unconsciousness. If the sufferer is then removed from the source of carbon monoxide, he or she can recover. Annabelle Wilder may have been alive – close to death, but still alive – when she was placed in the freezer.'

There are no worried faces looking back at me. If I'd hoped for a reaction (and I hadn't, not this early in the investigation) I'd be disappointed.

'Mr Oliphant,' says Gary Cookson, chewing on his stylus, 'I think you may have missed something here.' He peers at me earnestly. 'If the girl had still been alive, then her body would have been warm and, on being placed in the freezer, the alarm would have gone off. It didn't. So she must have been dead.'

'Gary,' whispers his wife, 'it doesn't matter whether she was dead or not, it's still a horrible thing to think about.' She accuses me with a stare. 'To talk about.'

'I'm aware of the alarm system,' I reply. 'There are ways of circumventing that. Disconnection. Cloaking the body with wet blankets, depositing it in a cold bath, anything to lower the temperature artificially. Don't assume that anything you've been told about the previous investigation is correct. Now then, please tell me what you did on the evening in question. Miss Parker, would you start.'

'I'd love to. We were playing a game, a murder game, I can't quite remember who won . . .'

'I did,' says Trevor Rawlings, triumph in his voice.

'Yes, I think you did,' continues Carol Parker. 'We were having dinner up here, the table was cleared, and then we played other games, cards, charades. It was all quite civilised. We stayed up late, until about two.'

The phone rings. Everyone looks at it. 'Gary,' I say, 'would you mind getting that?' Gary Cookson is used to doing as he's told, forgets it's me giving orders and rises to his feet. It's a short stride to the phone. He speaks only one word, 'Hello,' then holds the phone out to me. 'It's for you,' he says, surprise in his voice.

I listen to the receptionist telling me that Charles and Emily Robertson are waiting for me, decide to give no reply – it adds to the drama of the situation – then put down the phone. All eyes are on me. 'I'm sorry,' I say, 'I need to talk to someone. I hope I won't be too long. When I return I'd like to go over your statements. You see, one of you must be lying.' I look around them all, give each a few seconds of the Oliphant glare. It's never worked in the past and I've no reason to imagine it might start working now, but it makes me feel good, makes me feel in control. 'Given the circumstances, the death of a young lady in a locked building, a limited range of suspects all of whom are present in this room. Given that information, I can come to no other conclusion. One of you is lying.'

That's when I make my exit. When I'm too old for this I might just consider taking up amateur dramatics.

CHAPTER TEN

I make my way down to the riverside terrace where Charles and Emily are waiting for me. Even as I enter the lounge, they're looking round anxiously. They're still wearing their outdoor coats, as if they're expecting to be ejected at any moment. Two small suitcases are on the floor at their feet. Emily sees me first, she nudges Charles and points; her face seems, for a brief moment, free of care. I've seen that look before, in a court room. The jury had just returned a 'guilty' verdict on a murder suspect, and the victim's wife had shared the same look of relief as Emily's wearing. So too, I remember, had the murderer. There'd been an outcome, a conclusion, some degree of finality. Emily and Charles don't have this yet, their relief is simply that someone is doing something to help them. I sit down at their table. They have tea and biscuits in front of them, but there's no liquid in their cups.

'You got here quickly,' I say, 'thank you.'

'It's because we have something important to tell you, Mr Oliphant.' Charles has been elected first speaker. 'It's not that we've been trying to hide anything from you, simply that we haven't been – probably still aren't – aware of what might be important to you.' He pauses, I feel I ought to be saying something, so I make encouraging, affirmative noises, nod my head.

'Do go on, Charles,' says Emily.

'Yes. Where was I? Oh yes, we aren't sure what might be important. So we thought we'd better tell you face to face, so you can, as it were, channel us in the right direction.'

'And you were going to tell me ...?' I've a feeling this conversation might last a long time, I pour tea into the two cups and pass them out to the Robertsons.

'About Annabelle. You see, we loved her dearly, but – you may already have guessed this, or perhaps Terry told you – we didn't get on well.'

I can understand that. I've argued with my own daughter, sometimes just cross words, two opinionated people finding that their opinions would never coincide. But there was once, just after Sara and I split up, when things went beyond that. I can't even remember how old Kirsty was, but the day was cold and I was running out of things to do with her, places to take her. We'd exhausted most of the possibilities: cinema, ten-pin bowling, ice-skating, all the familiar haunts where desperate dads (not allowed into the family home, unwilling or unable to take offspring to cold, depressing flats) and exasperated kids (just wanting life to be normal again) fret and tear at Sunday afternoons. I thought we'd go to the park, tempted Kirsty with a ride on the boats, but it was late autumn and they'd been taken off the water. We peered into the boat-house, I lifted her up so she could press her nose against the dusty windowpane. She hurried round the corner, found the bottom of an ill-fitting door, and began to pull at it. The fingertips of her gloves – blue and white, woollen, strange how that recollection stays – were grey with scrabbling at the spider-webbed wood. 'Break in,' she kept on saying, 'break in and we can steal a boat.' I told her we couldn't. 'Yes,' she said, 'break the door down.' Then she stared at me. 'You're good at breaking things.'

She must have recognised that she'd hurt me, I wasn't very good at hiding my feelings then. So she ran away. I chased her. She managed to scrabble beneath a hedge where I couldn't follow. So she sat hunched, alternating her tears with cries of 'I hate you, Daddy, I hate you.' I crouched down, tried to get to her. The earth was muddy, the knees of my trousers were stained with black which eventually

102

dried – again my memory recalls the colour – a dark, funereal grey. The hedge's discarded twigs sewed my hands to the ground. It began to rain from vast, mournful skies, and with it the wind's final autumn litany of blood-red leaves threw themselves in front of me.

'I'm sorry,' I repeated into the gaps between Kirsty's words and tears, but it didn't help. I wanted to say that I loved her, no matter what she said or did, and that I always would love her. But I didn't. I couldn't, not then; it would have been wrong, a reaction, something to tempt her out of her hiding place. So we stayed where we were, sharing our misery. After a while she came out. She held out her hand to me. 'You're wet,' she said, 'I think we'd better go home.' There was no resolution.

Thoughts can be instantaneous, memories – which are, after all, no more than ordered recollections of thoughts – are almost as brief. I haven't relived my memory sequentially – it was all there at once. Charles and Emily haven't seen me in a trance; I haven't disappeared for a few minutes. I feel a need to tell them I understand, but what words can express that sympathy? I make do with a gesture. I reach out and touch Charles's hand. That contact, flesh on flesh, seems to focus his attention.

'Annabelle was our only child. She was so loved, not spoiled, Mr Oliphant, just loved. Emily and I married late. We desperately wanted children but we thought we might be too old. Then . . . Annabelle arrived. We . . . on reflection, we may have kept her on too tight a rein. Not deliberately, you understand, but it was as if the years had played tricks on us; we were from a different generation. There were times when I took her out in her pram or her pushchair and people would tell me I had a beautiful granddaughter. And I didn't blame them, I couldn't. You see, at times I did feel too old. Out of touch.' He shakes his head, unable to go on. His memories are too painful. They had no happy ending.

Emily leans in front of him, making sure he's alright. She

has a handkerchief in her grasp but he waves it away, the same gesture indicates that it's her turn to talk.

'It wasn't inevitable that she would turn against us. In fact I'm not sure she did, it was more of a drift in a different direction to that we would have preferred. She started wearing make-up, she was . . .yes, she was aware she was attractive. She had her first . . . that is, she became a woman when she was ten.' There's a slight blush on Emily's face. Embarrassment? Pride? 'After that there were always boys calling, boys on the phone. Then she started going out a lot, staying out too late, staying overnight with friends. We always checked, of course, that she'd been invited, that the girl's parents would be there. She resented that, but we weren't about to change. We did it because we were worried about her, because we cared about her. Because we loved her.'

'Did you tell her that?' It's a question that has to be asked, I've asked it of myself often enough and the answer always shames me.

It takes a long time for Emily to reply. 'No. No, not in so many words. Not then.'

Charles takes over, 'We didn't think we needed to, it was obvious to us. She was our whole life. But she couldn't see that. And we didn't realise that she didn't understand.'

'She was having problems at school; all the teachers said she had great potential but she wasn't working. She was behind in her course work; nothing we could say or do seemed to help. In fact it made it worse; we had rows; she said she felt suffocated by us. She said we didn't trust her, and I suppose that was true. But when we told her she'd done nothing to earn our trust, she just exploded. Then she came up with an idea. She wanted a sixteenth birthday party, and she wanted us to move out for the night. She said we should go into London, see a show, have a meal, enjoy ourselves. The way she said it, it was a sort of test. If we said no it would mean we didn't trust her, even though she was almost an adult. She didn't stamp her feet, she didn't threaten us with sulks or tantrums, she just asked if it would be possible. Then she was silent. She said she'd let us think about it. She went out of the room.'

Charles leans forward. 'She knew, of course. She knew we'd have to say yes. She could be a devious little madam.' His statement is flat, bland, like a calling card edged in black.

'I can't remember what we went to see. *Cats*, I think.'

'I never did like Lloyd Weber. Or T S Eliot,' Charles says. 'Too deliberately obscure.'

'She said not to come back too early, certainly not before midday next day. But it was a Sunday, it was raining, we had nothing else to do. It was eleven-thirty when we got back. The house was quiet, in fact it was immaculate. It was as if nothing had happened, as if no-one had been there.'

'That's because no-one had been there,' Charles says. He reaches forward again, but this time it's to dip a biscuit into his tea. His hand trembles slightly. 'We checked with the neighbours. They hadn't heard a thing. She hadn't had a party at all.' He folds the biscuit into his mouth.

They're like a double act, each taking up the conversation as the other stops. Their prompts are the familiarity of years. 'We went upstairs. Her door was closed, we knocked, there was no answer. We went in. The bed hadn't been slept in. She'd taken everything that was hers. Her wardrobe was empty, she'd taken all her clothes, her stereo and CDs, her television and video. Some of her books, some soft toys, they were all gone, and her building society account book, and her passport. She had a big jar which had once had jelly babies in it, then she kept silver coins in it. That was gone.' She takes a drink of tea and I notice that her hand is shaking as well. With Charles, the tremor is permanent, age-induced; Emily's is prompted by her emotions.

'Take your time,' I say, 'this can't be easy.'

'We've never told anyone else this before,' Emily hurries

105

on, 'we thought we'd better tell you but I had no idea it would be so difficult. She was so young, so innocent.'

Charles takes his turn. 'I checked our bedroom. I always kept some money there in my bedside drawers, well hidden, of course. It was still there, all of it, over a thousand pounds. And there was a note from Annabelle.' He sits back, fishes in his jacket. He has to check both inside pockets before finding it, then he hands me a piece of fading, purple paper. It has deeper purple hearts around the outside, and is held together with pieces of sellotape as if it's been handled too frequently, folded and refolded many times. The paper isn't lined, but the writing is neat, small, cursive, formed in straight lines as if a template has been used beneath. I begin to read; the sentence construction is mature, impressive. It's too good for a sixteen year old, unless it's been honed to perfection over weeks and months. It shows how long Annabelle must have been planning her escape.

Dear Mum and Dad,

I knew you'd look in the drawer. I knew you didn't trust me. Perhaps I haven't given you grounds for trusting me. But you'll find I've taken nothing that isn't mine, nothing that wasn't a present from you. I'm grateful for what you've given me over the years, not only the material possessions, but the unconditional love which has surrounded me at all times. Please remember, the reason I am who I am is because of you.

I think we ought to get out of each other's way for a while, and I can't see any way of moving forward unless I leave. If I stay, we'll start hating each other, and I don't think I can stand that. So I've made the decision to go.

I've been thinking about this for some time. I've arranged somewhere to live, I've found a job. Please don't come looking for me. You can tell the police if

*you want, show them this letter. They'll tell you
there's nothing they can do, I'm old enough to take
care of myself. And anyway, their time's better spent
looking for criminals.*

   *I'm not pregnant, I'm not in any trouble, I'm not a
drug addict. Don't worry about me. When I'm settled
I'll get in touch with you to let you know I'm okay.
Just think of it as me going off to university, but three
years too early. I've also enrolled myself in a college
course, so I'm taking care of my education as well.*

   I do love you and always will,
   Annabelle.

I hand the letter back to Charles. The sun is dancing on
the river outside, bright crescents of light in every ripple. All
three of us sit back in our seats.

I find that hotels are usually comforting places. That is,
after all, their raison d'etre. It's certainly warm and the music
in the background is soothing without being distracting.
During our conversation waiters have approached us twice,
but I've waved them away. We could move onto huge sofas
in front of a fire, we could take newspapers from a rack on
the wall, we could even – a notice on the wall tells us – play
cards or Scrabble. We're the most important people in the
room. For a brief moment all seems well. It's been painful
for Emily and Charles, but they've given me some useful
background information and may even have gained some
benefit from talking openly.

'There's more,' Emily says, and the air seems suddenly
chilled. Her eyes are filmed with tears. 'We told the police,
but Annabelle was right, there was nothing they could do.
We heard nothing from her, despite her promises. Then one
evening, about six months after she left, there was a knock
on the door. It was the police. They had Annabelle with them.

'She was thin, she had bags under her eyes, her hair was
unwashed, greasy. Her clothes seemed dirty. She wouldn't

look at me, she just stared at the ground. The police had to support her, almost carry her into the house. They brought her into the living room, sat her in a chair. She looked so small, so very small. She just sat there, hands on her knees. I noticed her nails – they were bitten and lined with black.

'She wouldn't speak. The police encouraged her, but we had to rely on them to tell us what had happened. We thought she must have gone off to London but she hadn't, she was in some little town in Hampshire, Alton. She'd been working in a book shop that belonged to the parents of a girl she'd met at a rock concert. They'd let her have a bedsit above the shop; she'd changed her name, everyone knew her as Stacey Richards. By all accounts she was getting on quite well, she worked in a pub some nights to boost her income – said she was nineteen, I suppose she looked it as well – and people seemed to like her. Then one of the regulars in the pub asked her to babysit.

'She did. When the couple got back, they arranged a taxi to bring her home. Next day the police called and arrested her. They said she'd stolen something from the house where she was babysitting, a valuable necklace. She denied it, so they took her away and questioned her. That was when they found out things weren't as they seemed – they couldn't trace "Stacey Richards" with the birth date Annabelle gave them, and she wouldn't tell them who she really was. After keeping her locked up overnight, next day she wouldn't speak at all. They got a doctor in, he thought she might be in danger of self-harm, but she wouldn't take any medication. They decided to send her to a mental hospital for her own good – section her, I think the term is – but they had to wait for a while to get the paperwork done. While they were doing that she was locked in her cell. She started hurting herself, so they put her in a straitjacket. I didn't know they still did that, Mr Oliphant.' There's pain in her eyes and her voice; Charles is gripping the arms of his chair and shaking his head from side to side.

'She was in hospital for almost a week, Mr Oliphant. Then the police came back to get her, to release her. The people who had accused Annabelle of theft had found the necklace. Apparently the husband had found it lying on his wife's dressing table a few days before and had put it away somewhere safe. Then he'd forgotten about it. It was his wife who'd found it again. When the police told Annabelle this, she gave them our address. She told them her name. She said she wanted to go home.'

Charles Robertson is pointing at me. 'They never even said sorry, Mr Oliphant. The people who accused Annabelle of theft, accused her wrongly, but they didn't say sorry. Didn't get in touch with us.'

'Did you contact them?'

'No, we didn't know them, we were just pleased to have Annabelle back. The police left, we washed her, put her to bed, sat with her. We were both there, one on each side of the bed. She reached out and took both our hands, said, "I'm glad I'm home again. Thank you for loving me." Then she went to sleep. Woke up again a day later. She wasn't quite her old self, of course, but she was willing to talk and she occasionally smiled.' He too smiles at the memory.

'Can you excuse me a second,' I say, 'it probably isn't important but I need to make a phone call.' I head for reception leaving Charles pouring another cup of dark tea into his cup while Emily gazes out of the window. I can't help but feel sorry for them, and worried. If I do manage to come up with anything (I shy away from saying the word "solve") then what will it mean for them? Their purpose in life is finding their daughter's murderer. What will they do if that purpose is taken away?

The reception staff are getting used to me. One of them, a young girl called – according to her name badge – Jodie, even manages a smile. She rises to her feet, comes to stand beside one of several large vases filled with dark red, sweet-perfumed roses. That's how luxurious the hotel is, the contents of each vase must have cost in excess of a hundred pounds. 'Can I help you, Mr Oliphant?' she asks.

'Phone?' The scent of the flowers is cloying.

She motions to one of several small cubicles opposite. 'Number one,' she says, 'I'll put the line through now.'

I'm not used to such pleasantness. Has King passed the word on, told them to be co-operative? I go in. The chair is comfortable, there's a small table with paper and pens, directories, a list of important local numbers. But I've no need of them, I know who I want to speak to. I wait for the phone to be picked up.

'Rak? Yes, it's me, can you check this for me? Got a pen? Good, here we go. Alton, Hampshire, about fifteen years ago, a young girl called Stacey Richards accused of theft but released before the case got to court, no evidence offered. There might be something in the local press, I need anything you can get. And how's the hunt going for other information?' I enjoy putting Rak under pressure, she's so easy to bait but always manages to come up with the goods. But this time her voice sounds weary, that's unusual. And she doesn't insult me, that's even more unusual.

'There's next to nothing, boss, and that's very strange. The *way* I look, the *places* I look, there's always something. But Annabelle Wilder is a non-person. Same for Robertson. What makes you think you'll be any luckier with Stacey Richards?'

'A hunch? Because I trust the people who've been talking to me? Because I'm clutching at straws? Perm any three from three. Oh, and this Richards girl worked in a bookshop, there can't be that many bookshops in that part of Hampshire. You could always give them a ring, see if they remember her.'

'Sounds like a long shot to me. I'll see what I can do, get back to you.'

'I need something, Rak. Anything.' I put the phone down, go back to the Robertsons. They may have more to tell me.

The lounge is filling up. It must be a communal tea break for the murder mystery groups, there's a hubbub of excitement swimming from table to table. Shoals of grey-haired people raise their heads as I walk in, decide I'm not with them and therefore not worth looking at. Others around me are more favoured, encouraged to tables, tables made larger by being dragged together into small islands throughout the room. Charles and Emily look frightened by their enthusiasm.

'Do you want to go somewhere more quiet?' I ask them, sliding back into my seat.

'No thank you, Billy,' says Emily, 'it's quite reassuring when you get used to it. All these people working together. And anyway, there's not much more to tell. You see, Annabelle seemed to get better very quickly.'

'Too quickly,' says Charles.

'We looked after her as best we could, took her to see the doctor. He referred her to a psychologist and a psychiatrist, who agreed she'd had – still did have – chronic, deep-seated depression. She went back to see them once or twice, then she felt she didn't need them any more. Of course, they couldn't do anything about that. And we couldn't when she moved away again, about a year later. She told us this time, we helped her find a flat and set up a standing order into her bank. She rang us once a week, then that became once a fortnight. Then it stopped. We rang her but there was no answer. We went to see her but she wasn't there. She'd closed her bank account. It was as if we were too close, as if we were the walls and the ceiling of the room that made her claustrophobic. That time she was away for three years. There was a pattern – she'd come back when the depression returned, stay until she felt better, then go again. She would never talk about where she'd been, what she'd been doing, who she'd been with. It was as if her time with us was for gathering herself together, finding herself again. Because every time she was away she came back as someone different. It wasn't just her getting older, reacting to things that happened to her. I'm sure it was a conscious decision, as if she was dissatisfied with the person she'd become and wanted

111

to change herself.' She nods her head firmly, confirming her thoughts. 'Yes, every time she was someone different.'

That seems a curious way of talking about your daughter. 'What do you mean,' I ask, 'in what way was she "someone different"?'

'Oh, little things. She'd change her hairstyle or colour. Once she had her nose pierced. Or her clothes were different, you know, as if her character had changed. And the way she walked, or sat, or looked at you, they changed as well. But despite this, despite the changes, nothing had changed.' Her smile is wry when she looks straight at me. 'I'm not making much sense, am I? I'm just a silly old woman. But the thing was, she was the same Annabelle we'd always known, the Annabelle we loved. We couldn't turn her away, could we?'

'No, you couldn't turn her away.' If it had been my daughter, I couldn't have turned her away.

'She knew how much she was hurting us – she knew, but she couldn't help herself. There was no-one else. She once said she found it easy to make friends, but her friendships were so very fragile, and she seemed to have the knack of breaking them just as easily.'

Charles Robertson is shakily building cubes of brown sugar into a wall on his plate. It's a proper wall, not just a pile of cubes; each small piece overlaps the next by half and there are buttresses at right angles to add support. Without warning he brings his spoon hard down against them. They scatter over the plate, over the table, over the floor. His voice is hard, sad. 'The last time we saw her alive was almost two years before she died. When the police came to tell us she was dead, we thought they were just bringing her home again.'

We're silent again. There's little any of us can add. The Robertsons know nothing of Annabelle's movements except when she came back to them. They'd been her bolt hole, her refuge, her safe house. And with them, she was constant. But Emily's phrase stays with me, a splinter in my mind. She said Annabelle used to rebuild herself in a different way, re-invent herself, change her personality. I can understand that, I've felt like that myself sometimes. If only I could be anyone other than me, all the problems I had would disappear. If I could be like a snake, slough off my skin and replace it with one bright and shining and new, then the me within that skin would be just as refreshed. I'd feel like a new person. It didn't work, of course, and when I'd described it to Jen she suggested it sounded like schizophrenia by proxy; a desire to be a different person couldn't be real schizophrenia because schizophrenics were by definition paranoid and in-capable of recognising their illness. I, on the other hand, merely wished to be schizoid. At least I think that was her argument, I couldn't understand it then and I didn't want to understand it now. But I can appreciate the dissatisfaction Annabelle must have felt with herself and her life if she kept trying to change it. It doesn't help me unravel the knotted cord of her death, or even understand why the strands were knotted in the first place. It does, however, make me even more determined to untie it.

'I have to go now,' I tell the Robertsons, 'I've to deal with the small matter of interviewing the Amalgam directors and their partners. Do you want me to call a taxi to take you to the station?'

'If you don't mind,' says Emily, 'We'd like to sit here for a moment longer.'

'It's a sort of silent memorial to our daughter,' Charles explains. 'It's fitting that we should be here, where her body was found, a year after she died.'

'We should have brought flowers,' Emily adds. 'We could have scattered them outside. On the river perhaps.'

I can do so little to help them, but this, at least, is within my powers. I hurry back to reception.

'Mr Oliphant,' says Jodie again, she's clearly been dele-gated to deal with me, 'how can I help you?'

'Charge these to Mr King,' I reply. I reach for the nearest

vase, pull it towards me. It's heavier than I anticipated, there must be a considerable amount of water within.

'Certainly, Mr Oliphant,' says Jodie, 'would you like a hand with them? We could empty the vase. Is it just the flowers you want?'

This is taking service to extremes. She points to a cleaner's cupboard; between us we manoeuvre the vase through the door and pour the water into a sink.

'I just want to wish you good luck,' whispers the girl. 'I read about what happened a year ago and I think it's terrible that the hotel is running this crime weekend thing.'

'Thank you,' I reply.

'And if there's anything I can do to help . . .'

I look at my watch. I've been away from the directors for too long. 'There is, if you don't mind. There's a couple sitting in the lounge, an old couple, by themselves. You'll recognise them – they don't look as if they belong. They're the parents of the murdered girl. Would you take these flowers to them and help them out to the riverside walk. They might want to throw the flowers into the river, one at a time. As a sort of memorial. They're a bit frail and I'm worried about them. Could you help them?'

Jodie smiles sweetly back at me. 'All part of the Amalgam Hotels service, Mr Oliphant.'

As I make my way back to the lift I reflect happily on the fact that somewhere some diligent English teacher is passing on to his or her pupils the gentle art of irony.

CHAPTER ELEVEN

Lifts must qualify as the most uninteresting places in which to spend any length of time. At least men's urinals have adverts or graffiti to occupy the minimal time spent there, but lifts have only a range of buttons. This lift is worse than most, with several small mirrors, one in each of the walls. I presume it's to allow occupants the opportunity to check make-up or hair before stepping out to that important meeting or dinner date. To me, however, the mirrors are an accusation. Wherever I look I find one of them staring at me with my own tired eyes. I should be familiar with my own face by now, I've watched it grow ungracefully old in the past four decades. But today – could the lighting be more harsh than I'm used to – it seems even less attractive than usual.

My forehead is, I'll admit, high. That's a euphemism, an alternative phrase I used to use jokingly when I was in my twenties. These days I prefer the more precisely Anglo-Saxon 'bald'. My baldness, however, was at one time countered by the darkness of my remaining hair and the smooth skin of my face. The man staring back at me from the mirrors is grey-haired with a sallow complexion, he looks as if he didn't shave properly this morning. He has lines on his forehead, cracks at the corner of his eyes, bags beneath them. The eyes themselves, I seem to remember, sometimes have a puppy-like enthusiasm about them, a willingness to laugh at or with their owner. There's no sign of that today – they're hangdog, devoid of humour. I look like a football manager about to meet his board after five successive losing games, a teacher due to spend Friday last period with his second bottom set, a man going to confess an affair to his wife.

I bend closer to one of the mirrors. My eyebrows are growing bushy, hair is sprouting from my ears and nose, my pores are cavernous. I'm getting old. I've spent too many years in this lift. Next time I'll attack the stairs instead, that will improve my fitness and give me extra thinking time rather than indulging in self-pity.

I get out at my floor as I need to get the photographs to take upstairs. Even as I approach the door I can hear the phone ringing but I have no enthusiasm for answering. It can only be King or, more likely, lapdog Gary Cookson asking where I am, summoning me to the Star Chamber. I take my time opening the door and even glare at the phone, but it keeps ringing. I have no option but to pick up the handset.

'Hello,' I say, trying to convey in that word the fatigue I genuinely feel.

'Hiya, misery-guts, this is your favourite superhero, none other than the webslinger herself, hurling herself from building to building using only the elastic from her over-large knickers to stop her plunging to her doom.'

The voice is familiar. 'Rak? What the hell are you talking about?'

'What? Oh, yeah, quite a sentence, wasn't it. And filled with cross-cultural media references that probably slipped by your preoccupied mind. But I'll translate for you. This . . . is . . . Rak. Rak . . . is . . . good. Rak . . . find . . . what . . . you . . . want.'

An exuberant Rak is probably the most infuriating individual on the planet. Her self-esteem, never very low anyway, rises to inestimable heights. It's no good reminding her about Icarus, she merely counters with the fact that she always has a parachute. With a motor. And wings. If only her good humour was infectious rather than irritating.

'Tell me then,' I say.

'What's it worth?'

I don't want to play games with her, and if she was in the room with me she'd realise that. But Rak isn't good at reading voices. I decide to go for the blunt rather than the subtle. 'Rak, tell me what you've found or I'll come round and kick your bloody arse so hard your intestines will drop out of your nose.'

There's silence for a few seconds.

'You're not in a good mood, are you?'

It's my turn to stay quiet.

'OK, I get it, not the time for jokes or wit. So pin back your ears. Got a pen, Billy?' She doesn't wait for an answer. 'Here's the news for *your* region. Fifteen odd years ago the little old local weekly press of Alton, Hampshire had no news whatever on an Annabelle Robertson or a Stacey Richards. I didn't really want to search every column inch, not for the year either side which would be a reasonable margin of error. But it did have an advert with the address and phone number of a bookshop. I rang the number and it's still a bookshop.' She stops; I'm sure it's deliberate.

'And?'

The prompt is all she needs. 'And the owner has been there for only three years.'

'Shit!'

'But she gave me the number of the previous owner who'd owned the place for over twenty years. Bingo!'

'And what did she say?'

'She remembered Stacey Richards. She remembered the theft accusation. She was quite contrite, really, apparently she and everyone else in the town thought Stacey/Annabelle was to blame for the theft. She was babysitting for someone who was a pillar of local society, or so it seemed at the time. By the time the case was dropped Stacey had disappeared and, of course, no-one knew how to get in touch with her.' Rak's voice gets lower in tone, the volume decreases. 'But this, Billy, is the most important thing. You see . . .'

*

I don't enjoy being sent naked into the conference chamber, so Rak's information is valuable. It is, however, the only piece of clothing I possess. As I gather together the photographs, shuffle them into a rough order, I consider how I might wear my garment. It isn't large enough to cover my entire body; I couldn't even wrap it around my waist. It's as substantial as a fig leaf, a pocket handkerchief, a thong fresh from Brazilian beaches. The thought of me dressed in any of these is either amusing or disgusting, I can't decide which, and it forces me to reconsider my metaphors. It is, I eventually decide, like that disposable paper underwear briefly fashionable about twenty years ago. I can use it only once, there's a chance it may be ineffective, but it's all I have. Despite my misgivings, for the first time I enter the directors' conference room with a degree of enthusiasm.

They're beginning to get bored. The television in the corner is switched on and four empty chairs are watching a football match without enthusiasm. Carol Parker, Liam Sanderson, Ben Worrall and Natasha Rawlings are playing cards. King is reading some work-related document, half-glasses perched imperiously on his nose. He looks up as I enter then returns quickly to his spreadsheets or report. Gary Cookson, having let me in, is hovering aimlessly at my side. I make an announcement, loud as a railway tannoy but much, much easier to hear. 'All hard at work thinking about murder? I'm pleased to see you co-operating so fully.'

King looks up with mock weariness on his face, he's been practising for this moment. 'Mr Oliphant, we've had a discussion during your last absence – their frequency and duration are a little excessive, they do rather tend to lower our estimation of your abilities – and have come to the reluctant conclusion that we must withdraw our offer of employment.' He rises to his feet without pausing. 'We will, of course, make a generous payment to reflect the time and energy – albeit badly used – that you have used and, ah, expended over the past day. But . . .'

Now is the moment. Trevor Rawlings and Heather Cookson have drifted into the room to watch the ritual slaughter; all eyes are focused on me. I milk the moment, then begin. 'Mr King, your erudition knows no bounds. I can't compete with such classical phrasing, such an elegant syntax, such a ridiculous desire to wander round the boundaries of a sentence without getting to a conclusion. So let me counter this with my own language. Sit down and shut up.'

There is silence for a moment. It lasts longer than expected but I'm no longer the centre of attention, King has come under the gaze of his fellow directors.

'How dare you . . .' he begins, but I'm ready.

'Which of the words don't you understand, Mr King? I really can't think of anything more blunt, more simple.'

'You . . . You bastard!'

'My mother, bless her soul, always told me that swearing was a sign of poor vocabulary and poorer intellect.' I wait a few seconds for the bluster to reach boiling point, turn down the gas before it can overflow. 'She didn't really say that, it's a cliché a little like those you're using, King. Now then, I have something important to say and I'd rather have you paying attention so I don't have to repeat it for those of you a little slow on the uptake. So take your seats, ladies and gentlemen.'

They do as they're told. This isn't really surprising – I've managed to overcome the leader of the pack, if only for a short while, and the others aren't sure enough of themselves to fight on their own. They may discover that resilience soon, however, so I push on.

'When I left you last I suggested that one, perhaps more of you, were liars. You objected to this both individually and as a group.' There are nodding heads around the table. 'Very well. I will demonstrate that one of you is a liar. Now that may not be too difficult, given that you're all directors of a thriving company. Fast-lane capitalism and lying often do go hand in hand. So I'll make it even more difficult for myself. I'll link one, perhaps two of you, directly with the murdered girl. If I can't do so then I'll leave immediately. If I can, then you co-operate more fully with my investigations than you have done in the past. Agreed?'

King begins to shake his head, he's about to start another of his peregrinations through the fields of verbosity.

'Be quiet, King. You might be the person I'm talking about here.'

His mouth opens wide but no words come out. Trevor Rawlings reaches across to offer a manly pat on his shoulder, the gesture is intended as both comfort and promise, a 'calm down, we'll get him later' moment.

'Let's go then.' I turn my attention to the Director of Finance. 'Rawlings, would you mind going to sit beside your wife.'

For once he's truculent, but he does as he's told willingly and doesn't even seem to mind my over-formal use of his surname only.

'Thank you. Now then, have you or your wife ever met Annabelle Wilder?'

'No,' he says, nudging his wife so that she too gives the same answer.

'Very well. Please will you look at this photograph. Oh, and don't show anyone else please, not yet.' I slide the photograph of Annabelle at age sixteen, face down, across the table.

He glances at it for a moment. 'It's a snapshot of a girl,' he says. 'Could be anyone. Don't recognise her at all.' He hands the photograph to his wife. She studies it with a little more detail; it takes her longer to come up with the same answer.

'Can I ask you both to cast your minds back fifteen years. I believe you used to live in Alton, Hampshire. Was it a pleasant place?'

'I don't see what that has to do with . . .'

'It's a perfectly innocent question, Rawlings. Let's assume it was a pleasant place for commuting to London. Big house. And the job you had then – you were an MD, I believe, merchant banker – paid you very well. You had a car, a chauffeur, someone to look after the little Rawlingses. Yes?'

'Yes.' Rawlings has no help from his wife. She's still staring at the photograph.

'Why did you leave that job, Rawlings?' I leave the question to hang in mid-air.

'I . . . I wanted another challenge, a different type of challenge. I had other posts, non-executive directorships. They kept me busy for a while. Then Mike invited me to join Amalgam. I've been there for, oh, about twelve years now.'

'So you weren't asked to leave because of your drinking problems?'

The response is quick. 'I don't drink, Oliphant.'

'That tense worries me, Trevor. Present tense. Not past. Not "I've never had a drink problem". But let's just leave that for a while.' I reshuffle the single piece of paper that passes as my notes. 'You had a nanny to look after the little ones but, like all nannies, she sometimes needed time off.' I smile at the table, some of them are looking at Rawlings with suspicion. This is going well. 'And one evening it happened. Nanny off, dinner invitation . . . Damn! But there was a solution. Get one of the local girls in as a makeshift. And that's what you did, isn't it?'

Rawlings snatches back the photograph from his wife. 'Alright,' he says, not quite a shout but heading there, 'we did get a girl in to babysit one night. And this . . . I suppose this could be her.'

'I think it is, dear,' says Natasha Rawlings, 'I thought I recognised her, but you were so sure it wasn't. But then you were a little squiffy that night, even before we . . .' She holds her hand to her mouth. 'Oh dear. Have I said something I oughtn't?'

Rawlings can't see his wife's face, but I can. When she

takes her hand away from her mouth there's a trace of a smirk there, a streak of rebelliousness, a smile of self-satisfaction. It was a soft blow, but it was effective, it was in the right place.

'Annabelle Wilder was the girl you hired that night. Annabelle was the girl you kept waiting until four in the morning. What else did she have to put up with? When you took her into the library to pay her, did you suggest that she might earn a little more by performing an additional service?' I have no grounds for making any such suggestion, but it seems to fit with the character so I press on through the build-up of Rawlings' bluster. 'That doesn't really concern me, Rawlings, what does is that you accused her, only a few hours later, of stealing a necklace from your wife's dressing table.'

'It was a mistake, I . . .'

'The police arrested her at six o'clock in the morning, a ridiculously early hour, but you were, after all, a prominent member of the community. And she was a young, sixteen-year-old shop girl.'

'But . . .'

This is the time. I rise to my feet, lean across the table in Rawlings' direction. 'And what had really happened to the necklace, Rawlings? You'd put it away in a "safe" place. Trouble was, you were drunk when you did it and you'd not only forgotten where you'd put it, you'd forgotten you'd moved it at all. It was only by accident that it was dis-covered, and that was by your wife.'

'Mr Oliphant,' King says soothingly, and I note that I've been graced once again with the appellation 'Mr'. 'This happened fifteen years ago, I fail to see what bearing this has . . .'

'Annabelle Wilder was kept locked in a police cell.' I keep my voice calm. 'She was strip-searched. She had no-one to turn to. She'd fallen out with her parents. And so she retreated. She retreated into herself. She wouldn't, couldn't speak. She was sent away to a mental hospital, locked in a padded cell, tied up in a straitjacket. She was, let me remind you, sixteen. And how long was she kept like this, Rawlings?'

His head is down, but his wife is looking at me. She seems able to speak on his behalf. 'I think it was four or five days later I found the necklace. Perhaps a week. Of course, I told the police immediately. I had no idea the poor girl was locked away for so long, poor thing.'

'Such a shame,' choruses Heather Cookson.

'You contacted the girl, of course. Apologised. Made some effort to repair the wrong you'd done?' I quite enjoy the theatrical pause, I raise my eyebrows in a mock-innocent question. 'You mean you didn't even think of it, Rawlings? A touch selfish, don't you think?'

'She was only a local girl,' Rawlings growls, 'I had other things to worry about at the time.'

'I see. You had things to worry about. Like your drinking and losing your job. And she was only a local girl, and therefore by definition less important than you.'

'Now hold on, Mr Oliphant.' This time King rises to his feet. 'Nothing you've told us can be defended by Trevor. He was in the wrong.' He pats Rawlings on the shoulder. 'But this happened fifteen years ago. I fail to see its relevance to your current investigation; there's no connection at all.'

I push back my chair, begin to circle the table. 'None of you admitted knowing Annabelle Wilder. It now appears that at least two of you did. That's a reason for investigating further. A normal girl, a sixteen-year-old girl, was so affected by what happened to her that it triggered an episode of clinical depression which recurred at intervals for the whole of her life. Yet you appear to show no remorse.'

'I couldn't help it,' says Rawlings, 'and anyway, she was probably a lunatic in waiting. It would have happened to her sometime, somewhere.'

'Is arrogance an essential part of working for this company, Rawlings?' He looks as if he's going to reply. He looks as if he's going to pick up the table and throw it at me. But he won't. 'A year ago, Annabelle Wilder had just succeeded in getting a job at this very hotel. Why? That's a reason for investigating further. If she had a specific reason for working here, working for you, then that's certainly relevant to the case. I believe there are other connections to be made. That's why, with your co-operation or without, I intend investigating the matter further. And my threat – yes, it was a threat – to involve the press still stands. Only now I have something concrete to offer them.'

'I think we should let him go on.' It's Heather Cookson who speaks out.

'I agree, it's a damn sight more interesting than playing silly games.' Carol Parker too appears to be on my side. Rawlings is about to interject but she keeps talking, 'Come on, Trevor, we all know you had problems with the booze. Now you don't. Yes, an apology would have been a good thing. A human thing. But you can't go back now and put it right.'

'He could at least say he wished he had,' mutters Natasha Rawlings. 'I wish I had. I didn't even think of it. What a terrible person I must have been.'

'You had your own problems,' says Heather Cookson, making it clear that those problems began with Trevor Rawlings and aren't yet over. It appears that I've mined a vein of female resentment against Rawlings; womanly solidarity is to the fore.

'I must point out,' Rawlings interjects, 'that since Heather wasn't here a year ago, she isn't exactly putting *her* reputation at risk by agreeing to this farrago of an investigation. This poor excuse for an amateur detective is wasting our time and trying our patience.' He pushes back his seat, nods at King and leaves the room.

'Even if you tell me you love me, I'm still not going,' I say. King stares at me. I stare back at him. He's wondering whether he should go as well. He's wondering if the others

124

will still be willing to co-operate if he isn't there. The trouble is, if he goes, he'll never find out. 'Your move, Mikey,' I tell him.

'I'm beginning to dislike you, Oliphant. I have no wish to see my fellow directors subjected to attacks and allegations that are either unfounded or irrelevant to this "investigation". But I'm also aware that, if I go, I won't be able to defend myself, or Trevor for that matter, from your gross calumny.'

'He means "false accusations" ladies and gentlemen,' I point out. 'Of course, I'm only telling you that to show that *I* know what it means, not because I think *you* don't know.'

King continues as if I haven't said a word. 'So I shall stay to defend the reputations of those who are unwilling or unable to do so for themselves.'

'Thank you. Now I'd like to begin asking a few questions, privately. Is there a room I can use?'

'There's a separate office,' Carol Parker says, 'you can use that.' She looks across at the frowning King. 'If that's alright, of course?' King waves her on.

'That should do nicely,' I say. 'Perhaps I could start with Mr and Mrs Cookson?'

They're about to leave the room, but turn when I mention their names and the ceiling spotlights reflect in their gold chains. They seem surprised at being the first to be called, but follow me into the small office.

'Sit down, please,' I say. There's a two-seater sofa and two armchairs around a coffee table, a desk and some more formal seating at the window end of the room, a tall wooden cupboard filled with books, both novels and works of reference. I take an armchair; the Cooksons sit close on the sofa.

'I thought I'd see you first,' I say, 'precisely because you weren't here a year ago. This is purely to satisfy my own curiosity, you understand, but King seems to run this board very tightly. Why was it you couldn't attend the meeting?'

Heather Cookson smiles broadly. 'Normally we would

have had to come. You're right, Mike doesn't like people missing meetings. But our daughter had an accident the night before we were due to leave and we had to take her to hospital.'

'Oh dear. Nothing serious, I hope.'

'She fell, split her lip. It needed a couple of stitches, she had to stay in overnight, then she had an anaesthetic next day and it was evening until she was discharged. Looking back it seems such a minor thing, but at the time . . . Do you have children, Mr Oliphant?'

I nod proudly. 'I've a daughter. Late teens now, but I know how you feel. It's one of the worst feelings there is, knowing your child's in pain but being unable to help her.' I can show sympathy, but beneath it is the guilt of knowing that Kirsty's pain wasn't physical, and a large part of it was caused by me. 'But your daughter must be quite a bit younger than mine.'

'She was four then,' Gary Cookson picks up the story, 'I suppose we could have managed with just one of us staying but, well, we share looking after her. And we were both worried.'

'I can imagine.' There seems little else I can ask. It's a little too early to spring the big question on them, 'Do you think that any of your colleagues could have murdered Annabelle Wilder?' Their role is obviously minimal. I'm about to thank them and dismiss them, but Gary Cookson has other ideas. He reaches into his jacket pocket and brings out a small wallet.

'This is Donna. It means "gift".' He hands several photographs to me and sits back, the stereotypical doting father.

'Gary, Mr Oliphant is too busy to look at photos.' It's clear that she doesn't mean it. What she means is 'look at our daughter and rejoice'. So I flick through the half dozen snapshots of child at birthday, child on swing, child in bridesmaid's dress and so on, making the regular cooing noises demanded on such occasions. In my clumsiness, as I look at the last photograph, I manage to drop them on the floor. 'Whoops,' I say, scoop them up and bundle them together, hand them back with a smile. 'Pretty girl,' I say, rising to my feet in my standard dismissal gesture.

'We think so,' they concur. 'And if we can be of any further help, just let us know.'

'Nothing very difficult, I'm afraid. Would you mind asking Carol Parker to pop in.' We smile at each other ingratiatingly and I resume my seat. Carol Parker slides into the room and throws herself onto the sofa.

'I was wondering when you'd ask me to come up and see you.' Her voice is low and tinged with an appalling American accent; her eyebrows dance.

'Goodness, what beautiful diamonds,' I feed her, determined to show that I recognise the reference.

'Goodness had nothing to do with it, dearie.' She returns to her normal accent, middle England, middle class. 'Sorry, it's this detective business. Brings out the worst in me. But it's good to meet someone who can recognise my Mae West impersonation.'

'Shouldn't it have been Lauren Bacall? That's more detective genre than Mae West.'

'Detective, film noir, who cares. And I'm certainly no femme fatale, Mr Oliphant. So how can I help you?'

It's almost pleasant to listen to her. After the cloying Cooksons and the aggressive King, the argumentative (and arguing) Rawlingses, she seems almost normal. But normality can hide unpleasantness and I have questions to ask regardless of whether I might like my respondent. I force myself to become the professional again, lift up my pen and leave it poised over the paper on the coffee table. 'I need to ask you about your movements a year ago,' I say, 'but first . . .' I put down my pen and paper, lean back in the chair. 'Tell me about the Cooksons.'

'The Cooksons?' she seems surprised at the question.

'I know they weren't here last year so this doesn't really

involve them, but . . . I've spent ten minutes listening to them talking about their daughter. They seem . . .'

'Over-protective? Monomaniacal? Clichés on legs? Mr and Mrs Medallion Man?' She giggles. 'No, I shouldn't, they're too easy a target. And they're always there, sitting beside each other, in each other's pockets. In fact Heather often slips her hand into Gary's back pocket. Do you know why?' She doesn't wait for me to answer. 'It's because that's where the string is.' This time a response is demanded.

'What string?' I say dutifully.

'The string that curves under his arse. The string that's tied firmly and tightly around his balls and his dick.'

'Speaking metaphorically, of course?'

'Well, I haven't actually had a look myself, but he does wear tight trousers sometimes, and I'd swear his visible panty line is augmented by some string-like material. Of course, she didn't always keep him on such a tight leash.' She hurries past what might have been a joke. 'Heather was always at work, she's an ambitious woman, a real high earner. Good at investments, she must earn as much as King. Had to, because while she was working away, Gary was like a drone, flitting from flower to flower, pollinating here, pollinating there.'

I decide I won't point out that the female workers pollinate flowers, while the male drones only wish to impregnate the queen. Perhaps bees aren't Carol Parker's strongpoint, while gossip obviously is.

'So what made him change?'

Carol is determined to make the moment last. She climbs to her feet and walks over to the cupboard. She's kicked off her high heels, her T-shirt and jeans add to her normality. 'Drink?' she asks. 'Mid-afternoon isn't really too early.'

'I don't,' I answer, 'unless there's something soft. Fruit juice?'

She comes back with two glasses, orange juice for me and a warm mellow liquid for her. If it's whisky, and if it's un-diluted, it's a very large measure.

'Now then, Gary Cookson. Bit of a ladies' man, or so I heard. Didn't have to work, though I think Heather bankrolled one or two failed ventures. He spent a while organising parties – I went to one, rather wild even for my debauched tastes. I don't know why Heather put up with him, but she doted on him. She wanted a child, apparently.'

'Did you know her well?' It's important to consider the source of any information. Primary's best, secondary's acceptable if it confirms primary. Any further away than that and it becomes hearsay, so I want to get back to Carol Parker as primary source.

'Not at the time, she told me later. Some drunken girls' night out, I expect. I can't recall exactly where or when. Anyway, five years ago, things changed. They decided to adopt, must have been something wrong with one of them. They found Donna and Gary became the doting parent. He's a house-father, though they do have an au-pair as well. Male, funnily enough. I don't think Heather would trust Gary with a nubile young Swede. And that's it.'

'Nothing sinister, then.'

'No. Why, should there be?'

'Only if you're a suspicious person like me.'

We seem to have exhausted the potential of this avenue. I raise my glass in thanks, climb to my feet and walk across to the window. It's beginning to get dark, the lights are blooming on the bridges and along the waterfront. The river is copying the streetlights into its deep, slow water, memorising their shape and texture but failing to perfect the reproduction. Spots of cool white become drawling hyphens of yellow, neon blue almost disappears, amber shifts to light green. A breeze confuses the palette, and on the south bank the bare-branched trees (ready for an early Christmas, over-decorated with firefly candles) echo the agitation.

I love this city. That doesn't mean I'd never leave. On the contrary, if the opportunity arose to move away, I'd go. It possesses all the vices associated with cities: it's sensual, it demands undivided attention, it dances and displays its beauty for all to see. It flaunts itself (entirely hermaphrodite, ungendered) until it captures its audience, then rejects them. It kicks with sharpened Saturday night stilettos, it fights with broken bottle knuckles, it spits and snarls and spurns its former lovers in the secure knowledge that the love is inbred, an addiction that can never be satisfied. Yes, I'd go if I had the chance. But I know I'd always come back, perhaps not to stay, but certainly to spend time, to reacquaint myself with the bridges, the castle, the station, the parks and the statues and the people I admire.

Carol comes to stand beside me. 'Bit of a hellhole,' she says. 'Best thing about it is the road leading south.'

'Yes,' I answer. Some secrets are best kept secret.

'So do you have any more questions?' It doesn't take her long to become bored with the view; she goes back to the cupboard and I can hear her pouring herself another drink.

I take my time replying. 'Yes, yes, there are always more questions.' When I turn round she's already back on the sofa, legs stretched out, black painted nails wriggling. She must have worn ill-fitting shoes in her youth as both little toes overlap the toe beside them. Her jeans are tight from ankle to waist, they seem a relic from the age of beatnik cool. There's a gap between belt and the bottom of her white cotton blouse, and although the skin is elegantly tanned, the flesh at her waist folds slightly with the pressure of her position. She doesn't seem to care about this, she's looking at me with her head tilted to one side, hair framing an untidy, uneven face. Her nose doesn't seem quite straight, yet this lack of symmetry doesn't detract from her attractiveness.

'Nobody can be this good,' she says.

'I'm sorry?'

'You. Knight in shining armour, riding to the rescue of those less fortunate than yourself. Robin Hood, taking from the rich to give to the poor; at least, trying to take our reputation and give it to . . .' her analogy breaks down '. . . give

130

it to somebody else who deserves it more. Or something like that.'

She'd been drinking before and the glass has been twice filled since she joined me. I decide I'd better press on before she's incapable of answering any questions.

'So tell me about yourself. How long have you been with Amalgam?'

She counts on her fingers, black-varnished like her toes. 'Let me see . . . yes, eight years now. I've been a director for three years.'

'Always in sales?'

'Always in sales.'

'And what does that involve? In a company that's primarily a chain of hotels.'

'And high-class, high-quality holiday resorts, don't forget that.' She swings round to face me; it looks as if she's going to demonstrate a sales pitch on me. 'It largely involves finding each hotel's characteristics and pushing it, marketing it. Of course, it's different with the resorts – that's longer term stays and you need different strategies for that. But we cope. In fact, we cope rather well.'

'Lots of foreign travel, then?'

She shakes her head from side to side in a 'could be yes, could be no' motion. 'I wish it was more. When I started, before I became a director, Amalgam was expanding in Europe. We mostly went for top-class individual hotels, not chains. Mike has a nose for quality product – in one month he bought five hotels. I had to go and visit them all, check them out, find out what their strong points were so we could promote them, find out their weak points so we could rectify them. I was new to the job, young, I had major responsibility for the first time. God, the places I visited – and we've still got those hotels: Amsterdam, I think that's my favourite; a Gaudi-esque place in Barcelona, I still don't know if it was designed by him; Berlin, post wall; Prague – have you ever been to Prague?' She doesn't wait for an answer which would

131

have been no anyway. 'You must go there, in spring. Beats Paris. Anyway, I must have done well, they made me a director. Less travel, more administration. But loads more money as well!' She grins impishly.

'So Amalgam's a good company to work for?'

'Oh yes.' She's relaxing again, stretches out once more on the sofa. 'But you've probably blown your chances of experiencing our generosity. Sorry and all that, I think you'd have been just the person for us. But you've got this knack of annoying the people you should be trying to impress.'

'You mean Mike King?'

'The very. The big boss. It's his idea, his company, his baby. They say he knows everyone's name at headquarters, all the way down to security and cleaning staff. He remembers birthdays, important anniversaries, when kids are born and parents die. I've seen him work a room, he's outstanding. A touch here, a smile there, a handshake. He's the biz.'

There seems little point in seeking a hostile angle from one so besotted. I change tack. 'Tell me about the night of the murder. You said . . .' I check through the sheets of notes I've made, the statements I've collected '. . . there were three others, King, Sanderson and Rawlings. You were playing cards until quite late. All three confirm that you went to bed about two, that no-one else was left. I don't suppose you have an alibi from two until three-thirty?'

'Mr Oliphant! If I did then it would mean I spent that time with Mike, Trevor or Liam. You can't be suggesting that, surely?'

I manage, without saying a word, to repeat the question by raising my eyebrows.

'Come on, Billy, please. Rawlings is, despite what he told you before, a drunk, Liam's as bent as they come, and Mike . . . Yeah, I could go for Mike, just to see if he's as smooth in bed as he is out of it. I could screw him at the drop of a . . . a pair of knickers.' She giggles. 'But he wouldn't go for me. Does that surprise you?'

'Nothing ever surprises me, Carol.' I'm lying, of course, some things do surprise me: the inherent good in most people, for example; the generosity of the poor; the beauty to be found in a scrapyard. But I can see why King would decline Carol Parker's advances. She's a cliché, she paints herself as the attractive woman with a voracious sexual appetite; it's apparent in the way she dresses, in the way she pours herself over the sofa, in the way she's looking at me.

'I'm sorry,' she says suddenly, 'I shouldn't have said that. It wasn't very professional of me.' She giggles again, sits up straight. 'I don't know what came over me. I'm not normally so open.'

'The alcohol?' I suggest.

'Yeah, could be.' She appears to be thinking. 'Booze affects different people in different ways. But perhaps you already know that, Billy.'

I don't want to answer that; I don't want to tell her anything about me, but my silence is itself a statement.

'You have a look about you, Billy, a look that says you've suffered in the past. Let's just leave it that we understand things. Like when Trevor admitted that he'd had a problem with booze in the past. We might have thought he was referring to the incident fifteen years ago. I happen to know that alcohol played a part in his past up to and including a year ago. And you can count Trevor out as a suspect for this girl's murder – he was smashed out of his mind that night and the rest of us had to drag him to his room. That might explain why *he* might appear a little reluctant to talk about an alibi.'

'Are you sure Rawlings was drunk? Could he have been pretending?'

'No, I don't think so. But I'm hardly going to tiptoe along to his room in the dead of night to check, am I. Besides, I was mortal as well.'

It's my turn to think for a while. I reach for the photographs of Annabelle, flick through them. I find the photos of Annabelle at the top of the Eiffel Tower, in front of the

Gaudi cathedral in Barcelona, outside the van Gogh museum in Amsterdam. All places Carol is supposed to have visited. 'Do you recognise this girl?' I ask, handing her the three snaps.

Carol looks at them carefully while I look at her, even more carefully. She stares at each in turn, then overlaps all three together. 'Pretty thing,' she says. 'Is this Annabelle Wilder?'

I can't believe that the police, in their investigations, haven't shown her a photograph of Annabelle before. She anticipates me, anticipates my question.

'The police had only two photographs, one was of her when she was much younger. The other was . . . The other was of the body. Not as it was found, at least I don't think so, but probably . . . Probably taken in the mortuary. It was just her head. Eyes closed. I don't know which is more shocking, seeing her dead or seeing her alive.' She hands me back the photographs and her fingers are trembling. There are tears in her eyes. She rubs them away. 'It's terrible, she's so young, so attractive. She looks so full of life in the photographs.' She seems on the point of controlling herself when her head falls to her chest and the sobbing becomes audible. Her body rocks to and fro.

There's a box of tissues on the table, I push them towards her. She takes one, blows her nose noisily; she takes another, wipes her eyes. It's like dealing with a child, or an adult pretending to be a child. Or, that part of my brain dealing with suspicious thoughts suggests, an adult who's trying to find out whether I might be sympathetic to women crying, and what my weaknesses may be. Being cynical makes life complicated.

'I'm sorry,' she says, 'it just came over me. She must have been about the same age as me.' She shrugs, forces a smile to her face. 'She even seems to have visited the same places as me. Might have been my sister.'

'And you don't recognise her? You haven't seen her with

any of the other directors, noticed her working in one of the group's hotels? Try thinking of her with different colour hair, different make-up.'

'I don't think so. She is . . . was . . . very attractive, I would have recognised her. But . . . no, I don't know her at all.'

There's nothing else I can think of to ask. We sit in silence for a while, caught in our own thoughts.

'Do you want me to ask anyone else to come in?'

'No. No, not yet, thank you.' Carol seems surprised. 'I need to write up my notes,' I explain, 'and I haven't decided who to listen to yet.'

'Well, I don't know if anyone here had anything to do with killing that girl, but if he did, I certainly hope you find him. And if you need any help, you know who to ask.'

'Thank you,' I say, not pointing out that a 'she' could be just as responsible as a 'he' in this, and nothing she's said has removed Carol from the list of suspects.

As soon as the door closes I pick up the phone, check the card on the desk and dial the number for reception. 'Hello,' I say, 'it's Billy Oliphant here, I just wanted . . .'

'Oh, Mr Oliphant, Jodie in reception here, I'm pleased it's you. I've just left a message on your phone in your room to say that Mr and Mrs Robertson have left. They seemed pleased they'd talked with you and they were overjoyed that you'd found the flowers for them.'

'That's why I was ringing, to find out if they were OK. Thank you for looking after them, Jodie.'

'It's a pleasure. They're a lovely old couple. Did you get your other message?'

'No, I haven't been back to my room. Who was it?'

'I'm not sure – it was a man but he didn't leave a name. It was only a few minutes ago. I said you probably weren't in your room but he could leave a message and he seemed pleased to do that. I can play it back to you now if you want?'

It could be Sly or Terry, it might even be Charles Robertson with some information he and Emily had forgotten. 'Yes please,' I tell Jodie, 'that would be helpful.'

'Just hold the line. If you want to call them back, press the CB button on your handset.'

There's a click and the sound of an unnatural, electronic echo. Then a deep voice. 'Oliphant,' it says, 'go home before you hurt anyone. Or I might just be forced to hurt you. Permanently.' The click repeats, the call is ended. I press call-back. After two rings the message I knew would be there tells me that the caller withheld his number. I ring Jodie back. 'It was nothing to worry about,' I tell her, 'just a death threat. Can you remember whether it was an external call?'

She takes the news in her stride. 'External. And it sounded like a land-line – mobiles always seem to have a peculiar tone to them. Apart from that . . . I can't really be of much help. Is there anything I can do?'

'No thanks.' I put the phone down. I ought to feel frightened, but I don't. Instead there's a strange exhilaration. A threat like that can only mean I'm heading in the right direction. I just wish I knew what direction that was.

CHAPTER TWELVE

I pick up the phone again, dial a familiar number. Rak answers quickly.

'More work, Billy? Or just checking up on me?'

I've two photographs in my hand. The first is a snapshot of Donna Cookson, the one I didn't pick up and hand back when I deliberately scattered the others to the floor. Behind it is one of the photographs of Annabelle as a child. Both girls are dressed in party frocks, smiling at the camera; no, they're both smiling for the camera, putting on a display. The smiles are identical; the posture of both girls is the same; the two photographs are separated by about twenty-five years, but they could be of the same person. Or of mother and daughter.

'You keep on telling me how wonderful you are,' I say to Rak, 'now I want you to prove it.'

'Again? Are you never satisfied.'

If Rak wasn't gay, I might consider marrying her for her sense of humour. It's the only one I've found which is as caustic as mine; the trouble is, hers is far quicker. On second thoughts, even if she was straight, I'd have to pass her by. I'd just be jealous when she beat me to the punchlines; I'm not good at being the straight feed. 'OK, wise guy, answer me this. How do I find out the true parents of an adopted child?'

'Simple answer, Billy. You don't. The system hardly helps those who were adopted to find their own birth parents. A stranger? No chance.'

Two pairs of eyes stare at me, taunt me. 'And if I wanted to find out by any means, illegal if necessary?'

'How the hell do I know, Billy? You're the one who's most experienced in the ways of the criminal. Find the child's birth certificate? Find the adoption papers? Anyway, why do you want to know?'

'A suspicion,' I tell her, 'someone talking to me from the past. I'm trying to make connections where none might exist. Could be clutching at straws.'

'Sounds desperate to me, Billy. But I honestly don't think there's anything I can do to help with this one.'

'That's OK. Like I said, it was a long shot. I'll have to work on it from a different direction. I might need you again, though. Are you going out tonight?'

'Quite the opposite, Billy, I'm planning on having a quiet night of passion right here. So don't go disturbing me.'

'And if I need to speak to you? When's the best time?'

I can hear the sigh down the phone, the exasperation. 'Billy, you're talking about women here. Two women. Haven't you heard of multiple orgasms? This isn't your "take it out, stick it in, jiggle it about and still time to watch the football" sex. This could last all night, all weekend, into next month, we might still be at it over Christmas if we didn't have to come up for air occasionally.'

An image appears unbidden in my mind; I abolish it swiftly. 'So anytime before nine and after ten?'

'After nine-thirty, probably.'

'Thanks, Rak. I owe you.'

I put down the phone quickly so I can't hear her reply – it's bound to be rude or over-specific in the rewards she expects from me.

The photographs are on the table in front of me. I remove the one of Donna Cookson, slip it into my pocket. I've never believed in coincidence. If two or more seemingly unconnected events do turn out to have some relationship to each other, then it's simply that the relationship was never recognised in the first place. If Donna Cookson is Annabelle's daughter then other questions arise, but that doesn't make

138

the original premise wrong. Yes, it's possible Annabelle became pregnant but couldn't – or didn't want to – look after the baby. But how did the Cooksons manage to adopt that specific child? And, taking it further, neither Heather nor Gary Cookson was present a year ago. So is it worth chasing up that flimsiest of possibilities, pursuing some nebulous and apparently unverifiable connection between Annabelle and the Cooksons? I must make a decision, quickly, and I do so. It's not worth the effort. So where do I go from here? None of the directors admitted knowing Annabelle by name, yet Rawlings had met her before when she used a different name. According to Carol Parker, the police had shown her only two photographs. So this wider range of photographs might jog a memory or two; Annabelle might be known to one or more of the directors under a different name. That, I decide, is the way forward. But what happens, whispers the cold voice of the little logical devil sitting on my left shoulder, if they recognise her but deny it? You'll be no further on.

They might own up, suggests the angel of optimism on my right shoulder.

When they've already denied knowing her? The devil laughs, jabs the heel of his pitchfork into my neck.

Rak was right, this is desperation. But I have little choice, I have no idea where else to go. I make my decision, spread the photographs across the table, then open the door.

Faces look up at me with urbane nonchalance, keen to show that they don't really care what I do next, who I question next, because there's nothing for me to find out. By now I'm beginning to have doubts myself, beginning to wonder whether the directors were involved in Annabelle's murder. And even if they were, what chance have I of uncovering information, evidence, clues, when the police have found nothing in the course of a whole year? Why am I bothering?

'Ah,' exclaims King, centring me in the crosshairs of his sarcasm, 'Mr Holmes returns.'

It's the wrong comment, the wrong tone. It gives me a

reason for bothering. 'Would all of you mind coming in?' I say with exaggerated politeness. 'I'd like you to look at some photographs.' I walk back into the room, wait for them to meander through the door. I'm aware that they're being deliberately slow to aggravate me, and I find it even more annoying that they're succeeding in their aim. I stand behind the table and face them. 'These are photographs of Annabelle Wilder, newly discovered. She may have used many different names, and as you can see by these photographs, she changed her appearance through the years. In her hairstyle and colour, her make-up, the type of clothes she wore. Please look carefully at these photographs. If you recognise the woman – then tell me.'

I take a step back and watch them as they pass in front of me. I see only a succession of masks. Each is painted with a studied, carefully rehearsed neutrality. Each examination is followed by a glance in my direction, a shake of the head, a raised eyebrow. Heather Cookson must notice the resemblance between her daughter – her adopted daughter – and Annabelle Wilder; she can't fail to see what I saw. Yet her eyes are as blank, as vacant, as Liam Sanderson's before her. That's when I realise they've been talking together – they've made a decision, a group decision, to withdraw their cooperation. King is the last to stand in front of me. He doesn't make a pretence of looking at the photographs. He turns to his colleagues, whether as a sign of his control over them, or as a gesture of thanks for their complicity, and gives a brief nod.

'Nothing I'm afraid, Mr Oliphant. Looks as if you've drawn another blank.'

'I commend you on the efficiency of your organisation, Mr King.'

He pretends innocence. 'You're not suggesting that we're telling lies, Mr Oliphant? All of us? Come come, as you said earlier, we're reputable businessmen and women with much to lose. Why would we lie to you?'

The phone rings, rescuing me from the possibility that the invective I intend releasing might culminate in me hitting the smug, smiling face in front of me. Everyone looks at the phone, no-one moves to pick it up.

'It's probably for me anyway,' I say to no-one in particular. The phone is nearest to Carol Parker, she moves slightly to let me past and the look on her face is almost apologetic. It might be worth asking her more questions, after I've dealt with the call.

'Mr Oliphant? It's Jodie, down in reception. I've a message for you. A man asked for you but said he wouldn't come in and wait. He didn't give his name, said it would be too difficult. He said he'd like to speak to you, about your current investigation, those were the exact words he used. He said he'd wait for you outside.'

'What did he look like?' I'm not expecting anyone, it's six o'clock, too early for Sly to appear.

'He had a parka jacket on, he kept his hood up. And he seemed to have a cold; he didn't take a handkerchief away from his mouth. He was wearing jeans, and those big boots.'

'Riggers?'

'Yes, I think that's what they're called.'

'And his voice? Was he local?'

'Difficult to say; it was deep. Like I said, it sounded as if he had a cold.'

'Think of the voice again, think of the man who called and left a message earlier. Were they similar? Could it have been the same man?'

She's quiet for a while; I don't want to hurry her. 'I'm not sure,' she says eventually, 'it's difficult to remember voices. It did sound as if he was trying to disguise his voice, but . . . no, I'm just not sure.'

'Where did he say he'd be?

'Outside. In the car park. Top floor. I'm sorry I couldn't get anything else out of him. I told him I'd pass the message on but you were very busy.'

'That's okay, Jodie, you did very well.' No-one has been showing any interest in my conversation, though everyone has been listening. 'I have to go,' I tell them, 'though I can guarantee I'll be back soon. And I haven't had the chance to speak to some of you yet. I'll begin with you, Mr King, as soon as I return.'

'Nothing could give me less pleasure, Mr Oliphant, I assure you.' His mouth drips acid as he unpeels his lips to reveal a second, extendable jaw. His tail is barbed, his blood undoubtedly acid, and his claws reach out to me as a warning of his intent to destroy me.

'Please look again at the photographs,' I say as I go, 'they may bring back some memories you've locked away somewhere. Perhaps recently. Perhaps intentionally.'

I hurry down to reception, wink at Jodie, make my way to the security office. The guard looks at me wide-eyed, as if he's just woken up, but this is a qualification for guards everywhere.

'Mick Beechey?' I ask, dredging his name from the vaults of memory. He nods guiltily as if he's stolen the name from someone else. 'Great. I need to talk to you later, but for the moment, could you give me a look at the car park, top floor?' I'm assuming that he's been told about me, that my licence to investigate hasn't yet been revoked by King. No, of course he won't do that. It would be too easy. It's far better to let me bumble along and fail miserably.

In what might just be an automatic reaction to authority, the guard glides his fingers over the computer keyboard in front of him. 'Car park,' he says to himself. There are six screens above his desk, each with a colour image. I can recognise the views of the front desk, the rear door and the dining room, several anonymous corridors and, on the last screen, a darker area filled with cars. 'Sub-ground,' says the guard, and the view changes. 'Ground . . . one . . . two . . . top.' On each level there are fewer and fewer cars, and on the top floor, open to the elements, there are only two cars, both close to the camera.

'Can you do a close-up?' I ask.

'Of what?'

'Oh, the far side. Just to see if there's anyone there.'

It's almost dark, and the camera is relying on the artificial light from the floods stationed along the wall. There are deep shadows stretching away from the cars, deep enough to hide someone if they lie down, but no-one is standing waiting.

'No-one I can see,' says the guard. 'You expecting someone?'

'Someone's expecting me. Can you keep on that view, I need to go up there, have a look around. And I'd prefer it if someone was watching me, just in case.'

'If I see anything,' the guard assures me, 'I'll be straight on the phone to the police.' He taps his side, there's a police issue truncheon in its leather holster resting against his hip. 'Then I'll be straight up there. Never had the chance to use this in anger.'

Somehow I don't feel reassured by this announcement. Mick Beechey is the smallest security guard I've seen, but this is the only offer of protection I've had. It might even be that the whole thing is a hoax; the cameras show no-one present on the top floor of the car park and there was no movement on any of the other levels. But I have to check. It could be Terry Wilder, it could be an anonymous informant. Or it could be my mystery adviser, the one who suggested, with threats of violence, that I cease my investigations.

'Look,' I say to the guard, 'I'm a little bit nervous about going up there by myself. I know you can't leave your post, but I'd feel much better if I had something to protect myself with. Is there any chance I could borrow your truncheon?'

The guard is unsure, his face falls. His hand reaches out and caresses the leather pouch, his fingers moving onto the smoothness of the hard plastic. He looks as if he's escaped from the opening scene of a homo-erotic movie. I feel I might have to tell him I'll look after it, I won't hurt it.

143

'Strictly against regulations,' he says, 'but I suppose it won't harm.' He unbuttons the holster, hands me the weapon. 'Do you know how to use it?' he asks.

'I've had some training,' I tell him truthfully, though it's a long time since I've handled one of these in anger. I feel its weight in my hand, grip the t-bar firmly, let the satisfying weight and length above it rest against my forearm. 'Thanks,' I say, hide it inside my jacket in case I alarm anyone on the way out, 'keep your eyes open.'

There's a corridor leads from reception along the front of the building to the ground floor of the car park. From there a lift rises or falls, and around its tower runs an enclosed staircase. I choose the stairs for my heart's sake and to hide from myself the suggestion that my increased pulse rate is due to nervousness rather than exertion. I tread the steps slowly, pause at each turn to sneak a glance around the next corner then, when I find no-one's there, look out of the window as I catch my breath. The conurbations on both sides of the river, town to the south, city to the north, are turning the cloudy skies pink. Each of the bridges is lit with its own character: fragile, modern silver white; sturdy iconic arch imprisoned by pale towers; dark stone solidity; comical red-green; modern concrete wash. Car lights beat a staccato rhythm on pillared green uprights and inflexible grey diamonds. A train passes along the upper deck of one bridge, gaudy windows London bound; and further away a yellow tram's passengers, more standing than sitting, read the adverts until the next stop. All the world, except for me, is going home.

The door at the top of the stairs is opposite the lift. It opens towards me, I pull at it gingerly and the cool night air takes the opportunity to sneak inside. I peer out. There are still two cars, both close to the door, both quiet, both empty. The white-lined tarmac is scuffed with tyre marks, lit brightly as a football pitch. I can see no-one. I step out into the evening.

'Hello!' I shout. There's no reply. I look up to where I think the camera will be, though the bright lights shining in my eyes make its exact position impossible to determine, and wave boldly. It's a gesture for my mystery caller, not Mick the security guard. If ever I wanted a gesture to have a sound, it's that one. I want it to say 'I'm being watched, don't try anything silly,' though I suspect it may signal 'I'm frightened as hell and I'm trying to persuade myself help is very close.' I take a few more steps out into the lights. It feels less like a car park, less like a football pitch, more like an amphitheatre. I listen for the sound of a door opening, the pad of lion's paws, the metallic complaint of gladiator's armour. But the only noise is that of distant traffic and the muted growl of a jet high above. I'm feeling nervous, despite the cool air I'm sweating. This isn't right. If the stranger wanted to give me information he could have done so outside the main entrance, across the road, even in the bar. Why here? My mind is persuading my legs that I'd be better off elsewhere. I'm moving backwards towards the doors when I hear the voice.

'Over here, Billy.'

It's a deep voice, not overly concerned with pronouncing its words clearly.

'Where are you?' I reply. I can see no-one. The voice appeared to come from my right, away from the hotel, where the car park is nearest to the river. 'Step forward into the light where I can see you.' I feel the reassuring hardness of the truncheon inside my jacket. My breath is steaming in front of me. I take another step back.

'No, you don't need to see me. All you need do is listen.' The voice is confident, in control.

I turn my head to pinpoint its exact position. 'I'm listening,' I say, trying to capture the same air of bravado, hoping he'll have far more to say than me. If he talks then I should be able to work out exactly where he is.

'Good. You don't seem to have paid any attention to my

145

first warning, Billy. This is the second one. There won't be a third. Go home. You're doing nothing to help Annabelle Wilder by being here. Quite the contrary, you're just going to upset a lot of people. So check out, go home, wait for your young lady friend to come back from Canada. Forget about Annabelle. Do I make myself understood?' His voice is low, soft, hypnotic. It has the dogged insistence of Bill Sikes, the weary potential for harm that comes with every evening soap's procession of hard men. It suggests that its owner is tired of hurting people but will continue to do so, simply because he can.

'I understand. And if I don't do as you . . . advise?'

'Don't let the thought enter your head, Billy. You aren't safe here.'

I ought to turn and go. The man with the voice seems to know what he's talking about, and what he's talking about is hurting me. He knows too much about me. He knows about Jen coming home. But what can he do to me? I have protection, I know how to use the truncheon, I was even quite good at it a few years ago. And I hate being threatened. I edge towards the voice. 'Who are you?'

'Someone who's been sent to warn you. And yes, I'll admit it, to frighten you.' There's a long pause. 'I think you'd better stop now. You're getting a little too close.'

I look back at the camera.

'The guard will see you walking slowly towards the edge of the car park, Billy. The camera's resolution is set to make the most of the bright lights. Even when I step forward, as I'm about to do, the camera won't see me. I'll stay in its blind spot. Do you want me to step forward, Billy?' There's a threat in the question, an implication that I won't want to see the owner of the voice. Or that, once seen, some form of physical retribution will be inevitable. But he doesn't know about my truncheon, my ability to use it.

The figure I see ahead of me is hooded, hands held low by its side. I can hear the crunch of metal shod boots on tarmac as he turns to one side, hugging the shade. I turn on the spot, ready to attack, ready to retaliate if I'm attacked. I'm on the balls of my feet, ready to move quickly, but my potential adversary seems relaxed. He's turned sideways to me, he's walking slowly. It's the walk of a hunter, casually circling its prey.

'Who are you?' I ask again.

'My name would mean nothing to you, Billy. Think of one for me, make one up. It doesn't really matter.'

'Do you play chess?' I ask him quickly.

He stops walking, considers the question. The pause tells me he's curious. 'Go on then.'

'I'll call you "Rook".'

'Why.' His response is swift; he doesn't want to play games.

'In chess there's a move where the king and the rook change places. That's why.'

There's another pause while he thinks. Then there's a noise, a noise that could be him laughing, and the brief movement of his shoulders which reinforces my opinion that he has a sense of humour. 'Very good, Billy. But I'm afraid it's common knowledge that the chairman and CEO of the group owning this hotel is called King. Are you suggesting that because I know this, there might be some connection between us? That I've been sent by him? I'll acknowledge that you're smart, quick with words, but it's hardly conclusive evidence. His lordship wouldn't be impressed.' He sniggers again. 'Not that this conversation will ever be reported in court.'

I edge towards him. 'It's a good name, though, isn't it. Rooks are carrion birds. Dirty, scruffy, they're bullies, always ganging up on others. Intelligent, yes. But not constructively so. Highly destructive, in fact. Noisy. Garrulous. I can't think of anyone who likes rooks. Eh, Rook?'

'It takes more than insults to annoy me, Billy. Now for the last time, are you going home?' He's on the move again, keeping to the shadows. That's when I realise he's cut off

147

my escape route. He's nearer to the door than I am, and there's a darker patch of shade where the lift tower occludes the nearest light. It's as if the shadow has been designed to hide some act of evil.

'I don't think I'll accept your offer,' I say. 'And I think I'll just stay here, out in the middle of the car park, in the bright light where you don't want to come. Does the bright light scare you? Does it make you wither and die? Is that what you are, a bloodsucker, a vampire, a leech? All mouth but no action?'

He laughs again, this time much louder. Then he stops, suddenly. His voice becomes lower, more menacing. 'There are different ways of frightening people, Billy. Can you watch over Jen all the time when she comes home? I know where you live, I know where she lives. I know all about you, I know about your friends. Rak and Sly and Norm, Kirsty even, they're in my file on you. And you were right, Rook is a good name. I don't work alone; there are others like me, almost indistinguishable from me. One or more of us can visit one of your friends any time, anywhere, when they're least expected.' He laughs to himself. 'When I tell them what you called me, called us, they'll appreciate it. And I suppose we do like carrion. Which is just as well, because you're dead meat, old son.'

I never move gracefully. I can't dance, there's no hint of elegance about the way I walk. But I can move fast when I want, when I have some purpose. And I'm never more purposeful than when people I love are threatened. He's only five paces away from me. I give no warning of my attack. I rush at him, pull the truncheon from beneath my jacket and raise it above my head to strike him. The blow, if it connected, might have broken his skull. But he too moves, slips to one side, and brings his own defence to bear. My weapon hits something hard, metallic, it glances to one side and my momentum forces me to follow it. I spin back, crouch down, truncheon ready to ward off a blow. Now I have my back to the light and Rook is a silhouette ahead of me.

'Size counts, d'y' know that, Billy,' he says. He's carrying a baseball bat easily in both hands, ready to protect himself. Then, as I watch, he moves his grip. Both hands are now on the handle; he's pointing the bat straight at me. 'And you were trying to goad me into attacking you?' He jabs at me; I knock the head of the bat to one side and lunge, but he's too far away from me. As the bat comes swinging back at me, I can see the long arc of its descent and have to throw myself back. I can feel the breeze of its passing.

'You seem to be stuck in the shadows,' he tells me. It's true, I'm retreating into an angle formed by the lift shaft wall and the metre-high balustrade surrounding the car park. The bat swings again, this time it's aimed at my midriff. I move my truncheon just in time, the bat hits it and I can feel the jarring vibration run into my hands and up my arm. The bat itself slides down the handle and hits the fleshy part of my thigh. I hear an exhalation of breath, my own, then the bat is coming at me again. This time it's aimed at my ankles. I leap into the air and it passes beneath me. If I had time I might be able to counter-attack, but the bat swings back again. This time it hits me on the arm. There's no crack of breaking bone, there wasn't enough force in it, but the pain is intense. He was aiming for my elbow; this time the blow is deflected upwards, over my head. I have no feeling in my right arm, I switch the truncheon across to my left. I'm breathing heavily, my useless arm limp by my side.

'First blood to me,' says Rook.

'No blood yet,' I rasp.

'There will be,' he counters, 'and it'll be yours.'

He clearly has the advantage over me. I need to get close to him or, if I can, beyond him into the welcoming yellow light. He's equally determined to prevent me doing this; every time I make a feint, he counters. But most of the time he contents himself with scoring points. He hits my arm again, this time directly on the elbow, and I'm aware that it's possible to feel greater pain than I thought possible. He swings again and this time the bat hits my leg, knocks me onto my back. I ward off an overhead blow with my truncheon and feel it spin out of my hand. I can taste blood in my mouth where I've bitten my tongue. I suspect he's playing with me, that he could hurt me far more than he is doing. He could be playing the cat, or he could sympathise with me; I suspect it's the former. I scramble to my feet; my truncheon is metres away to my right, closer to Rook than to me.

'D'y' know, it would be far easier, far quicker, if you'd just stay down.'

'Fuck off,' I whisper and throw myself at him. His bat whistles overhead, misses me. If he hadn't swung at me, I would have hit him in the midriff, knocked the wind out of him, knocked him to the floor and ended up on top of him. But he's half turned, moved away from me. My charge is too straight, too direct. I catch him with my shoulder, succeed in spinning him around, but am rewarded by myself falling headlong to the ground.

'Not quite, Billy,' he grunts. I try to rise to my feet – if I can just scrabble a little further forward I'll be in the light, the camera will see me, rescue will come. But Rook knows this and I feel an intense pain as the baseball bat hits me across the shoulders. I can't breathe, I can't think. A second blow hits me on the side of the knee, another in my side makes me curl up, retching. He's on the other side of me now, each strike of the bat driving me back into my corner. He doesn't want to kill me, not yet.

'Yes, come on little man, back where you started.'

I want to swear at him again, I want to kick out, but I have no voice, no eyes; I'm incapable of independent movement. Only the fall of the bat, and the pain it brings, exists in my world.

'Had enough yet?' His voice is hoarse now, he's breathing

heavily. I open my eyes to see him above me, his hood is off his head but I can see no details of his face. 'You should have gone when you had the chance. You see, you don't matter.' He reaches into a pocket, brings out a handkerchief, dabs at his face. 'I could probably kill you right here, right now, with this bat. But it would look suspicious. So what can I do with you? Has this been enough of a warning?'

I still can't speak, but I nod my head.

'Somehow I doubt it. Stand up.'

I crawl to the rail running round the building, slowly, waiting for the bat to prompt me, to hurry me. But it does nothing. I reach the point where ground and upright meet, haul myself with my one good hand onto my knees. My face is wet, though it isn't raining. I touch my head with my fingers, try to focus on them. They're red. I didn't even know he'd hit me on the head, I can feel no pain from any blow there.

'You must have cut yourself when you fell,' Rook says, giving me the answer. 'Come on, on your feet.'

I can feel some life edging back into my dead arm and leg, but I think I prefer the numbness. The pain isn't constant, it drives like a knife into every bone and muscle, then retreats and pierces my flesh again, and again. I groan.

'For Christ's sake shut up,' Rook says. 'Upright, stand upright.'

I do as I'm told, I have no choice.

'This was your choice, Billy, not mine. You could have gone away peacefully, but you decided to behave like a hero. I'm sorry it has to end this way.' He's standing now like a batsman, arms extended, close to the wall where I'm leaning. I can see what he's going to do. One strike, one single strike will suffice. He'll hit me on the side of the head, perhaps on the neck. That might kill me outright, but it doesn't really matter. If he times the blow properly, its force will carry me over the edge of the wall and sixty feet down to the ground. If he doesn't hit quite right I'll slump

151

onto the wall, but I'll be unconscious and he can push me over. The end result will be the same. And if he mistimes the blow completely, or if I manage to avoid being hit by sliding down the wall, he'll simply capitalise on the new target I represent and hit me while I lie there. He's a strong man, I know that much. He could then, if he wanted, hoist me over the rail. It's quite clever really, my injuries will be very similar to those sustained by falling to the ground. Severe bruising, broken neck, fractured limbs and skull. Even as I'm waiting for the death blow, I can appreciate a professional when I meet one.

I open my eyes to look at him. For the first time I see his face. He'd probably be described as handsome, his face is thin with prominent cheekbones. He has grey hair cut short and neat. He could be a mature model, the type that used to grace catalogues, standing in Y-fronts and pointing artistically at some distant viewpoint. And he's smiling at me with perfect teeth. His mouth forms the word 'Goodbye', his hands go back. That's when a scream tears at the air. It's not my scream – I'm incapable of attaining that pitch, that volume. Rook and I look in the same direction. There's a woman framed in the staircase door, arms spread wide in supplication. Rook looks back at me, lowers the bat. The whole point of knocking me over the wall has disappeared. He would have a witness now, it would be murder, not death by falling, be it misadventure or suicide. Of course, he could kill the witness as well. But two bodies on the same rooftop would be a coincidence too far. He has no choice. He nudges me in the stomach with the bat, hard enough take me down again to my knees. 'Another chance, Billy. D'y' know, not many people get that. Certainly not the ones I deal with. Take my advice, mate. Go home.'

He pulls his hood over his head again and marches towards the door, towards the woman. She scuttles sideways, not to the escape of the stairwell, but into the bright light of the car park. She waves frantically at the camera. Rook passes her by, bat slung over one shoulder. 'Too late, love,' he says. Then he's gone.

The woman watches him go then runs towards me. At first I don't recognise her. Then her face ceases to become a blur, her clothes materialise into the hotel uniform.

I manage to croak the word 'Jodie', before my eyes close again. I can remember no more.

CHAPTER THIRTEEN

I wake up in my hotel room, in my bed. My clothes have been removed. A man is standing over me with a syringe. Jodie is peering worriedly over his shoulder.

'Ah, Mr Oliphant. I'm Doctor O'Donnell. You seem to be in a bit of a state. What appears to have happened to you?'

I look over his shoulder. Jodie shakes her head; not a sign that she doesn't know anything, more a message to keep silent.

'I can't quite remember,' I slur.

'Hm. What *can* you remember?'

I shrug, but that turns into a wince of pain. I decide to go on the necessarily slow offensive. 'What happened? I certainly wasn't in bed.' Even talking hurts.

'I found you in the stairwell,' Jodie says, 'beside the car park. I think you must have fallen.'

'Does that sound plausible?' The doctor is tapping the syringe with his finger. 'This will help deal with the pain. There seem to be nothing but soft tissue injuries. I couldn't find any broken bones, but it's difficult to be certain when your patient is unconscious. Still, they'll check on that when you get to hospital.'

I begin to shake my head but stop before the muscles in my neck begin to move. Shaking my head will hurt. It'll hurt a lot. But I can't afford to go to hospital. I'm onto something – that's why I'm lying here with pain demons dancing in every muscle in my body.

'No,' I say, slowly, even my lips hurt, 'no, not hospital. I'm OK.'

The doctor's eyes open wide, his eyebrows scurry for shelter beneath his sideways-swept fringe. 'You're one of the least OK people in this hotel, and believe me, I've seen some of the old dears spending the weekend here. If they were any older I'd be testing them to see if they were zombies.' He sniggers; he clearly has a well-developed sense of his own humour. 'And if they were any less mobile, I'd be a market gardener.' I must look puzzled. 'They'd be like vegetables or plants?' he continues, 'I'd be looking after plants, so I'd be . . .'

'Are you trying to kill me off with your jokes?' I ask.

'It's no good trying to flatter me, Mr Oliphant, hospital's where you should be and hospital's where you'll go. Now I don't think you'll need an ambulance, Miss Richardson here will find you a taxi – you are most definitely not to drive yourself – just as soon as the painkillers start working, and they'll begin to kick in very soon. Miss Richardson also has an x-ray request card, and I've left a prescription for more painkillers should you need them when you return. Any questions?'

The doctor is as keen to leave as I am to see him go; he probably has ten more lives to organise within the next half hour. He'll step outside into the hall, make sure no-one's watching, then pull his red underpants over bright blue tights. I want him out. I need thinking time. So I mutter the magic words of dismissal, 'Thank you', and send him on his way.

As the door closes Jodie moves closer. 'The taxi's coming in half an hour,' she says, 'and I've arranged with the porter . . .'

'No taxi,' I whisper, 'no hospital. Painkillers, yes. Let me see the prescription.'

She brings the piece of paper closer, holds it out to me, then realises that I can barely move my arms. 'Sorry,' she says, 'it's for something called tramadol hydrochloride, fifty milligrams. One to two . . . I think it says "quids", but that can't be right.'

155

I'm beginning to control both my voice and my thought processes a little better. 'Not "quids",' I tell her, '"QDS". It means four times a day.' I'm remembering the books and magazines Jen would bring home, the ones on different drugs and their purposes, their side-effects. I'd read them to find out how much potential damage there was in taking cold relief potions. 'Tramadol, you say? That's quite powerful.'

'It says there could be dizziness or drowsiness.'

'Even more? Just what I need.'

'Don't you think you should go to hospital?'

The pain-killing injection is beginning to work. 'No, not hospital. Now tell me what you saw. I can remember going up to the car park, I can remember asking the security guard to watch out for me, I can remember being attacked. I think.' My eyes are closed, so I can't see Jodie's reaction. I hope it's one of sympathy, those pain demons have brought out their motorbikes, the ones with studs in their wheels, and they're riding them up and down my body.

'I didn't see much,' she replies. 'I wandered through to the guard's office, to see what you were up to. He was watching you, or rather, he was watching the top floor of the car park. He said you'd gone up there, he'd seen you go out through the door. And then he saw you standing there, just walking out of the light into the shadows, then coming back again. He thought it was strange, but there was no-one there with you, so he wasn't too worried. That's when I started watching.' I hear the sound of the chair being pulled close to my bed. 'Are you alright? Is there anything you need? A drink of water?' I can feel a warm, dry hand on my forehead. 'You're a little hot; would you like a cool flannel?'

'That would be wonderful.'

She goes away; I can hear water running in the bathroom. 'I've done a first-aid course,' she calls, 'I'm the duty first-aider when I'm on shift.'

I open my eyes as she comes back to the bedside. She really is young. 'Why did you come to find me?' I ask.

She beams down at me, folds the flannel over and holds it to my head. It's cold and I wince, but she fights me with the pressure of one hand. The coolness begins to penetrate the pain in my skull. 'I could see something was wrong,' she says. 'You were dancing in and out of the light. I mean, they aren't very good pictures. You were so small and the colours weren't very good. I was trying to think what you looked like; it was just like those martial arts people who do the funny movements. I was looking closely at the screen and I thought I saw someone else. Then I thought I saw you on the ground, but I wasn't sure. Anyway, you went into the shade and then you didn't come out again. I said the guard should go and see what was happening, but he said there was no-one else there, and you were probably on your way down. I thought there was something the matter. So I came to have a look.'

The words are simple, but they probably saved my life. 'I came to have a look.' If I was in trouble, as Jodie suspected, then she was coming up into the dark night, to the very place where that particular trouble was taking me apart with a baseball bat. She was coming into possible danger. This young girl, armed with nothing but a first-aid certificate, was coming to rescue me.

'I saw that man attacking you. I was going to come and help, but then I thought a scream might be the best thing of all – someone might hear, the guard might realise something was wrong. It didn't work, of course. No-one heard and the guard couldn't tell what I was doing. But at least it made the man run off.'

'Thank you,' I tell her. I reach out and touch her hand with mine. There's less pain than there was a few minutes ago.

'Anything to be of service,' she says quickly, then rushes into an explanation. 'Company motto, it's what we say when anyone thanks us.' She seems almost embarrassed. 'It's part of the script.'

'Pity it doesn't apply to the directors,' I whisper under my breath.

Perhaps my hearing has improved to make up for the dullness in all my other senses. Perhaps the comparative quiet makes unusual noises, unexpected noises, easier to hear. Whatever the reason, my ears pick up the slight brush of door on carpet, the faintest change in air pressure. The doctor must have left the door unlocked or ajar as there's no click of the lock. Despite my pain I push myself upright, unable to stop the groan as I do so. I try to push Jodie behind me, but succeed only in forcing her to her feet. The door is opening. It's opening wider. And then a high, wide, black face peers into the room.

'Hiya, boss,' says Sly.

'You stupid bastard, what the hell are you doing tiptoeing around like that?' I sink back onto the bed.

Sly steps into the room, looks around as if certain the words can't be directed at him. 'What'd I do?' he asks. 'They told me in reception you'd had an accident and weren't too good, though they wouldn't give me any details. The door was open, I didn't want to make a noise in case I disturbed you, so . . .' He stares at me. 'You're a bit bruised. Been in a fight? And shouldn't you cover yourself up, there's a lady present.'

That's when I realise that, when I heaved myself into a sitting position, the sheets slid from me. I can't remember being aware that I was naked, but my present situation undoubtedly confirms that to be the case. And Jodie has been so focused on this stranger – whom I obviously know – slipping into the room, that until Sly mentions it, she hasn't even noticed my nudity. 'It's alright,' she says, adding, as if it's an adequate explanation, 'I'm a first-aider, I'm used to . . . to things like this.'

I creep back under the covers. 'Jodie, this is Sly, trusted friend; Sly, this is Jodie, she helped me out with a little problem I had earlier but now she's going. Aren't you, Jodie.'

Jodie holds out her hand to Sly's vast paw but makes no attempt to leave. Why do women never do as I ask? Sly

158

shakes her hand then returns his glance to me. 'I might as well go too,' he says, 'looks as if I'm too late to help anyway. Got the case sown up yet?'

'What the hell are you talking about?' The pains in my body are becoming more bearable, I can feel them being replaced by aggravation.

'Well, you know how it is. You're working on a case, getting nowhere, then someone beats you up.' He glances at Jodie, trying to gauge her character, decides she's friendly. 'Someone kicks the shit out of you.' Sly bends closer still – he can see that my bruises are cultivated in a bed of scrapes and cuts. 'Or in this case, someone kills you then brings you back from the dead. Movie zombies look better than you do at the moment, boss. Anyway, that makes you mad; you get to thinking properly, you pull together a few clues and, bingo, the case is solved. What stage of the process are you on with at the moment, boss? Do you need me? I've a warm wife waiting for me at home.'

He's joking, of course. Jodie doesn't know him at all, but even she's beginning to believe he's joking. But I want rid of her; she's young, she seems to have attached herself to me, and this case shows every sign of becoming dangerous. I make a decision. 'I'm going to get dressed. I'll fill you in with what's happening at the same time. And I might need some help with getting my underpants on and putting my legs into my trousers.'

'In that case I'll go and get this prescription filled,' Jodie announces too quickly, 'I won't be long, bye.' She's gone before I can tell her not to come back. I groan, and it's not with the pain of aching limbs.

'You certainly pick them,' Sly grins. 'You're not going to get rid of that one easily.' He helps me into my clothes and listens to my rambling, punctuates it with nodding and yessing at intervals. Then, when I'm as dressed as I want to be, when I'm lying again on the bed with eyes closed in a vain attempt to stop the room spinning, he reports back what

I've told him. It's a good way of making me rethink what I know, what I suspect.

'Let's start at the beginning. Girl dead, probably murdered, cause of death carbon monoxide poisoning. Body found a year ago in hotel's walk-in freezer. Of those at the scene no-one admits anything to do with the girl. Security systems show no forced entry, no strangers present.'

'But the security system's no good. At least, not on the top floor of the car park. The cameras are ineffectual, resolution's poor. There's no sound.'

'I was coming to that, boss.' Sly seems aggrieved, offended that I might be challenging his memory. 'Your investigations show the girl was prone to change her name. At least one director, Rawlings, did know her. He was instrumental in causing her to have a mental breakdown; she could have been an embarrassment to him. But is that really motivation for murder? I haven't met him, but it sounds a bit extreme.'

'Agreed. But it does establish a link.'

'Agreed, but it might be immaterial; let's leave it for the moment. Now where was I? Oh yes, girl gets herself pregnant by unknown man. Baby taken from her, reasons unknown. Resemblance between girl and adopted daughter of – no, don't remind me – Cookson, yes, Heather and Gary Cookson.'

'More than a resemblance, Sly, far more. It could be the same person, but in photographs a generation apart.'

'OK, strong resemblance. Possible blood relationship. Question is, how to establish a connection? And even if there is a connection, what would the motivation be for murder?'

My mind is beginning to spin as fast as the room. 'If Annabelle Wilder was the mother, perhaps the Cooksons fostered the baby when she was in hospital. Then they adopted it. Moved away, lost touch. If Annabelle wanted to get in touch with the child, that might have embarrassed them.'

'Embarrassment boss? I sometimes get embarrassed at the

things you say and do, that doesn't mean I try to kill you. And that's on top of an "if" and a "perhaps". Rearrange the following in a well-known phrase or saying: "straws, at, clutching, you're".'

'OK, OK, I know it's flimsy, but it's the best I've got.'

Sly begins to pace the room. His tread is heavy, each step seems to make the walls vibrate and the ceiling shimmer; it's as if I'm in a small boat in a storm. I feel sick but don't have the energy to move myself. All I can do is listen to the waves of Sly's voice washing over me.

'Not quite the best you've got. You're on the right track with something because you were threatened. No-one is ever threatened or attacked like you were, unless there's a reason. So what was the reason?'

'I don't know! Christ, Sly, I just wish I could think straight, I feel as if my mind's full of scorpions.'

Sly looks at me. 'That's good,' he says, '"My mind is full of scorpions." I wish I'd said that. Did you think of it yourself?'

'How the hell do I know, it was just there! Forget it, forget possible connections and links; let's go onto things we can do, material things. Tell me about the security.'

Sly speaks confidently, sure of himself. 'The security's crap. Well, possibly crap, we aren't sure yet. But we suspect it of crapness, despite the fact that it's meant to be top quality.'

'If it's that bad on the roof, it might be that bad elsewhere in the building. I see a possible means of bringing a body into the building here.'

'So we chase it up. Check it. Audit it.' He stops walking. 'And we do all this in a day. Just you, me and your little friend.'

'Jodie's a kid, Sly, a nice girl. She'll bring my medication, finish her shift and go home.'

Sly laughs. His laugh sounds like an engine starting up, gathering speed, accelerating into the distance. It starts in the hotel basement and bursts through floors of concrete, it

161

breaks all the windows and winds itself round every steel support of every bridge on the river. He doesn't really own the laugh, he borrowed it from the pagan gods who once lived in earth and tree and river, in lightning bolt and thunder-cloud, and it still contains their power. Sly's laugh cheers me. Then he explains why he's laughing.

'Boss, you can't see people, can you? What I mean is, you can see their physical presence but nothing beyond that. She's not a kid, she's a young woman. And she fancies you – God knows why – she really fancies you. Or, if you find that difficult to believe, she's a crime groupie, she gets high on the idea that she might help bring criminals to justice. Either way, she'll be back, and she won't want to go, take my word for it.' His attempt at mimicking her voice is poor, turning into a high-pitched squeak. '"Is there anything else I can do to help, Mr Oliphant? Or can I call you Billy?" You wait and see, boss, just wait and see.'

'Sly, stop it. I can do without any more complications.' I don't have to speak loudly, he can see that he's gone too far. Or perhaps he can see I'm worried he might be right.

'Sorry,' he says contritely. He knows me well enough to change the subject quickly, 'So what're we gonna do?'

'You're going to break in, like I said on the phone.'

'Shouldn't be too difficult, given your experience on the roof.'

'That's why I make it difficult for you. You break in, you get into the kitchen without anyone seeing you. If you can do that, then you find out how far you can get through the rest of the hotel. Up to the penthouse would be perfect. And you'll need proof that you were there. Photographs of clocks, that would be good. Or, if you get as far as the top floor, introduce yourself to my friend Mr King.'

'Any particular starting point?'

'Top floor of the car park? The camera couldn't reach as far as the walls, even if there was a car parked there . . .'

Sly was brought up to believe it's rude to interrupt someone

162

else speaking, but even he's exasperated by the long delay. 'Yeah?' he says, 'come on, boss, finish your sentence.'

My words are slow and deliberate. 'If there was a car parked there, Sly, it couldn't be seen. Annabelle Wilder died of carbon monoxide poisoning. Source? A car hosepipe?'

'On the roof?' I can tell by his voice that Sly doesn't think it's likely. But there would have been few cars in the hotel on the weekend Annabelle was murdered, and they would have been parked underground, out of the weather. I'll need to check whether the top-floor cameras were used at all? Could a car drive into and out of the top floors without being seen? Questions, more questions, they're breeding around me, splitting like amoebae; one begets two begets four begets eight, reproduction gone wild. They double and redouble; I can see them covering the carpet, dulling its blue with their shimmering, pulsating slither and slide.

'What's the matter, boss?' Sly's voice pulls me round.

'Nothing,' I say, too quickly, 'why?'

'Oh, I was just worried. Worried why you were sweating so much, why you kept saying "no, no", why you were swaying backwards and forwards.'

I reach up to touch my forehead; it's wet. I move my head; the hair at the nape of my neck is soaking. 'Side-effects of my medication,' I explain, hoping it is that and not my body's reaction to some undiscovered internal injury. 'But it's worth it. I can move now; the pain's going.' I rotate through ninety degrees, lower my feet to the floor and stand up slowly. The room's rate of spin decreases slightly, and that on one axis only. The pain is less severe – before it felt as if my limbs had been ripped from my body; at least they've been sewn back on now, though I'm not sure all the nerve endings have been connected correctly.

'And what are you going to do while I'm breaking and entering?' I notice that Sly has moved a little closer to me; if I'd fallen, he'd have been able to catch me before I hit the floor.

163

'Stay here and rest, of course.'

'Liar.'

'OK. I might go and see Rak. I might go and see Terry Wilder. Perhaps both. I need to follow up some leads.'

Sly laughs, but there's concern in his voice. 'You can't drive, boss. You can barely walk, you're even having problems standing up straight. Who's going to take you? I could, but who'll do the legwork you've just mentioned? I can't see how . . .' He scratches his head in mock thoughtfulness. 'I know. You could ask your new best friend.'

I shake my head, which is a mistake. I have to reach out for the wall, hold myself upright with one trembling arm. 'No,' I say in as firm a voice as I can summon, 'not Jodie. She's already helped enough. I don't want to put her to any more trouble. And it might be dangerous. I can hardly look after myself, let alone . . .'

'Dangerous? Come on, boss, she'd be driving you to two houses then coming back. How's that dangerous?'

'She might not be able to drive.'

'Then she can go with you in a taxi. I don't want you left alone, and if she can't go with you, I'll have to.' He's stubborn. He's made up his mind. I can't see any alternative.

'How come you win arguments? You never used to.'

'I suppose I'm spending too much time around you.' He takes my elbow. 'Come on, old man, clue me in on anything else I need to know.' He leads me to the desk where the photographs are spread. 'Tell me about this girl, this Annabelle Wilder.'

The telling doesn't take long; I realise how little I know about her. He picks up each image as I explain, puts it down without comment. Some, of course, have no part to play. I pass the photograph of the flat to him without saying anything. There's nothing to say. But then he whistles in mock envy.

'What was that for?' I ask.

'Posh flat,' he replies.

'Looks an ordinary house to me.'

'You're going blind, boss. Look at the door, there are multiple address plates and bells. And there's a plate on the wall on the left, a road name. I can't quite read it, it's not all there. "Something G – O – N Place." And it looks like a Westminster crest. Not much there under a million. Per flat.'

I take the photograph back, look at it more closely. Sly's right. I pull the desk light closer, shine it directly at the image in front of me. I've been in the habit recently of trying on those cheap spectacles found in supermarkets. I've found them comfortable and – alarmingly – helpful in deciphering the smallest font on the eyesight test. I haven't bought any yet but I fear I'll have to. I reassure myself that I can't see details because my head is still swimming from the beating or the painkillers or my reaction to them. Or it may be that I'm trying to see things that aren't there. 'Can you see anything else?' I ask. 'In the windows, perhaps?'

Sly bends closer. 'Could be. In the ground floor flat. Two figures.'

I can see nothing.

'Could be a reflection. The photographer and someone else? But why take a photograph of a house? It's more likely to be a photograph of people inside, taken by someone who didn't realise that they wouldn't be seen clearly at that distance. Do you know who lives there?'

'No.'

'Pity.'

'Yeah. But it wouldn't take someone long . . .'

'. . . if they knew the exact address . . .'

'. . . to go along and have a look at the place . . .'

'. . . and find out who lives – or lived – there.'

'But we don't know anyone in London, except . . .'

We speak the word together. 'Norm!'

'He wouldn't do it,' I say.

'He would for you, boss. Ring him. It's not as if he's away with a woman, he's down there for some motor convention.

"Friends of the Fiesta" or "Maestro Magic" or something like that. He'd be pleased to have something to do.'

Any type of action, even if it's just asking others for help, is welcome, enervating, it's a far better pain-killer than any drug. It doesn't last as long, of course, but I do feel better. We'll be working on several different courses, three lines of investigation at once. The trouble is, I always have to remind myself of the downside of every course of action. It could be that we'll look busy, we'll actually be busy, we could even be working very efficiently. But that work could, at the same time, be highly ineffective. We won't know until we try it, move in our separate directions.

'I suppose we've got nothing to lose.' Even using that first person plural pronoun makes me feel good. 'I'll ring him.'

There's a polite knock on the door. Sly's there even as I'm thinking of moving, asking who it is before he opens the door. I can't hear the reply, but he turns the handle to allow Jodie to enter.

'I'll ring Norm,' Sly says, 'you negotiate terms of employment with your new minder.'

Jodie's path into the room curves around Sly's bulk, she's clearly wary of him. She begins talking to me but she's watching Sly at the same time. 'Here's your tablets,' she says handing me a packet from within a carrier bag, 'and I got you some energy drink as well, I thought you might need it.' Two bottles of orange-coloured liquid are placed on the bedside table. 'Jelly babies as well, they're almost pure sugar and can give you a boost if you need them. And some ibuprofen cream to rub on your muscles; I thought you might want to tackle your aches and pains from the outside as well as the inside.'

Sly, dialling Norm's mobile, is paying enough attention to be able to smile his knowing smile, the one that trumpets 'I told you so.'

'This is very kind of you,' I say, 'but there's no need to go to so much trouble.'

'"My aim is to please",' she says in a voice that is obviously a product of her training. 'And anyway, I'm off shift now. I've got nothing waiting at home except a night out with the girls, and they'll just want to go drinking.'

'Mature outlook,' Sly agrees, 'just what . . . Hello? Norm? Hiya, shortarse, how you doing?'

Jodie shrugs the interruption away. 'So if there's anything else I can do to help?'

'There is. I mean, there are.' I try to make my voice sound weary, as if circumstances are forcing me to do something I don't really want to do. In that way it's quite easy – I don't want a nosy, inexperienced young girl around me when there's a possibility of danger. On the other hand, Sly thinks I need someone to help me. While he's on the phone to Norm, only half listening to me, I can try to dissuade Jodie from helping. I've too many other things to worry about. 'Look, Jodie, I'll be honest with you. I need to do some investigative work.' Jodie's eyes widen in excitement, I have to speak quickly to calm her. 'It's boring, routine stuff, probably talking to some pretty rough, seedy characters. But Sly's worried about me collapsing, he thinks I need some help. Personally I think I can manage by myself . . .'

A sideways glance at Sly shows him frowning at me.

'. . . but I do feel a bit rough. So yes, there are two things you can do to help, but it's very limited help, that's all. Short term, one off.' I lower my voice. 'And when they're finished, or even sooner if I feel better, you go home, no arguing, that's a pre-condition. Of course, it doesn't matter if you say no, I can find someone else to help.' Sly's talking so he doesn't catch the lie. My voice is almost a whisper. 'And you've already been more than helpful. In fact, it's unfair of me to ask you. Look, Jodie, forget I've said anything, you'd better just go home and spend the evening . . .'

'Yes!' she says before I can finish; I might as well have kept my warnings, my unsubtle dissuasions, to myself. 'Just tell me what you want me to do!' She's like a child at

167

Christmas, wrapped in her dressing gown, tiptoeing into a room lit only by candles on a tree, presents stacked on the floor below. Her whole face beams. Her eyes widen, her shoulders lift, she looks as if she's about to perform a celebratory dance. I don't know if I can cope with such enthusiasm, but Sly's shaking his head at me to tell me I have no choice.

'Sit down.' I motion her to a chair. 'I said there were two things you can help with. This is the first. You see, Sly's going to test the security system here. I need to know who installed it; I need a plan of the building, I need a plan of the security system. Normally I'd be able to get things like this from the architect who designed the place, but it's a weekend, so there's no chance of that. Sometimes copies are kept on site. Do you know where they might be? And could you get a copy?'

She nods. 'There's a plan of the hotel on the wall in the manager's office. It's quite large. I suppose I could take it down. The security firm's called "Armaclad", they're a local firm. I've had to ring them a few times when the alarms have gone off for no apparent reason. But I haven't seen any separate plans of the alarms and cameras anywhere.'

'Does the duty manager stay in his office all the time he's on shift?'

'The day manager, yes.' She lowers her voice and bends closer, as if she's going to tell me a secret. 'He hides in there, so he can avoid work. He's never on the desk, never around when you want him. But when he's off, the assistant managers are far too busy doing the work he should have done, so it's empty most of the time. Like now.'

I suppose I could ask King for access to the office and the files and cupboards, but I doubt he'd let me. Besides, I don't want him to know my lines of investigation. 'Would you help me break in?'

'Break in?'

'Yes. Illegal entry. See if the information I want is hidden away.'

It doesn't take her long to reply, 'Yes,' she says, she can barely stay on her seat. 'When do you want to do it? I can create a diversion, you can break the door down, then . . .'

'Don't you have a key?'

'A key? Well, there's a key in reception, but . . .'

'That's what we need. Is it hidden or kept away from everyone?'

'Well, no, anyone can use it; it's in the key cabinet in the general office. I could just go in and take it.' She seems disappointed that there's no need for jemmies and hammers, breaking glass and splintering wood.

'That's what we do, then. We go in quietly.'

Her enthusiasm rekindles. 'What about the filing cabinet, the desk drawers, the cupboard? Won't we have to force them?'

I shake my head. 'Simple locks, Jodie. I could open them with a paper-clip. But I don't even need that – I never go out without a set of skeleton keys. I'll open them.'

'Oh. It's not quite like the movies, is it.'

'No, it's not like the movies.' I shift painfully on the bed. 'In the movies the hero's handsome and strong; he figures out what's happening. He gets into fights that should send him to hospital for a month, but he's up and about ten minutes later and raring to go again. He solves the crime, gets the girl, wins the prize; but that's not real life.' She looks as if she's going to interrupt, but this is my speech, my moment. 'Real life is people being hurt. Real life is murder, pain, devious criminals trying to hide the truth. Real life is a detective who doesn't really know what he's doing, a short, overweight, balding detective who relies on his friends to help him out. Real life is finding your way through a maze. It's banging your head against a brick wall and hoping you might knock a little bit of mortar out, then you can chip away at a brick, take it out and peep through at what's beyond. Life is . . .'

'Norm's up for it,' Sly announces triumphantly. 'He'll

need a copy of the photograph, but there's a computer in his hotel. I've got the email address, we can get Rak to send it through.'

'I can send emails from here,' Jodie says.'

'Good, that's your first job.' Sly's enjoying the responsibility he's assumed because of my infirmity. 'He's got a street guide, he'll look up the possibilities, find the place and see who the occupants are.'

'How will he do that?' I ask.

'God knows, boss, it's Norm we're talking about here. He'll probably knock on the door and ask.' From somewhere in his bass Yorkshire vowels he finds a caricature of Norm's estuary tenor twang. '"I've been arsked t' enquire 'ere t' see if you've any connection wiv a murder. Oh, an' what's yer name?" He'll be OK, he normally manages to come up with something through his devious ways.'

'Someone else working for me,' I explain to a bemused Jodie. 'But I said there were two things I needed. The second one is this. Sly doesn't feel I'm well enough to look after myself. I need to go out, to talk to someone.' I take a deep breath. I feel like an old lady asking for help to cross the road, like I need an escalator because I can't manage the stairs, like a child waiting to be lifted onto adult shoulders to see a passing celebrity. I hate being dependent on anyone. 'Like I said, I need a little help. Would you be willing to come with me? Just to stop me falling over and making a fool of myself. To ring for an ambulance if I collapse.'

'More likely an undertaker, the way you look.' Sly's whisper is meant to be heard.

'I'll do whatever I can,' Jodie says.

'I'll pay you, of course.'

'There's no need.'

'There is. You tell me you're willing to accept payment now, or you don't come.'

'OK, then, pay me!' She doesn't quite stamp her feet, but there's a latent talent for petulance in there. It's soon

170

submerged beneath her enthusiasm, however. 'So what do we do first?'

'Email the photograph and send it to Norm. Then we look for the plans, that'll let Sly have a chance of breaking and entering. Then the two of us go to see Terry Wilder. Sound OK to everyone?' There are no dissenters.

CHAPTER FOURTEEN

The email is easy, it takes Jodie only a minute or two to send from the empty, unlocked general office. The manager's office is immediately behind the reception desk which is staffed, at this time of the evening, by a young man, groomed and polished fresh from the cupboard where receptionists are stored when not in use. Jodie has prepared us, however, and we prepare to act out our roles. Jodie and I are the first to make our entrance, with her support I limp along the corridor. I'm obviously in need of assistance – there's no pretence involved on my part – and have to rest in one of the comfortable seats in the entrance lobby. Jodie pats me into place then wanders over to the desk.

'What're you doing here?' the receptionist asks. 'You're not on duty, are you?'

Jodie nods in my direction. 'Overtime. Mr Oliphant had a fall.' Her voice becomes a whisper. 'He needs a babysitter.'

Sly walks past us, goes into the toilet.

'We're just waiting for a taxi,' Jodie explains. 'Thought we'd better get down here early. Mr Oliphant can't move too fast at the moment. Is it still busy? It was sheer hell earlier?'

'Busy? Never stops. That's the trouble with having all these old buggers about; they're so demanding.' He leans towards Jodie, a smile on his face. I resist the proprietorial temptation to object. I tell myself it's his comment I dislike, not the attention he's paying to Jodie. I see Sly leave the toilet, he hurries across to the reception desk.

'Can I help you, sir?' the young man asks.

Sly is every inch the concerned guest. 'I certainly hope

so. There seems to be a leak in the gentlemen's toilet; there's water all over the floor.'

The young man's face falls. This is outside his experience. 'I'll telephone for the duty manager,' he says. 'I'm not meant to leave the desk unstaffed.'

'It's OK,' Jodie chips in, the young man has given her the cue as if he was reading the script. 'I'll fill in,' she says helpfully. 'It shouldn't take too long for you to see what the problem is.'

'It's quite a flood,' Sly insists. 'I just hope there's no permanent damage.'

'Thanks, Jodie, you're a star,' says the young man; he's round the desk and following Sly before I can even rise to my feet. Jodie's his mirror image, she takes his place and opens a wall-mounted box containing keys, selects the one that opens the manager's office. I hurry over, my muscles aching with each step, but I know that haste is important. Sly's plan is simple – he's dismantled the water valve in one of the toilets so that water will be overflowing onto the floor. As soon as the receptionist enters the toilet Sly will find some way of causing the door to lock behind them. He should be able to keep the young man occupied for at least ten minutes, but I might need longer. Jodie opens the door for me, I stagger inside and she follows me.

The office is spare, undernourished, functional but with no sense that it's ever been used. There's a desk facing the door, nestled beneath it a black leather chair, behind that a window. Against one wall is a tall grey metal cupboard, a matching filing cabinet in one corner. There's an empty table and four chairs. 'There's the plan,' says Jodie unnecessarily, 'on the wall. I'm not sure where other information might be kept, but try the cabinet first – there might be some sort of index on the files.'

'Jodie, I know all this, I know what to do and the order to do it; I'm an expert on breaking in. So please, you just keep watch outside. Whistle if anyone comes and I'll switch the light out. Pretend to be a hotel receptionist.' I don't hear her response, I'm already at the filing cabinet. It's locked so I leave it and turn to the desk; always attack the easy target first. There are three drawers, they all open. The two on the left are filled with the detritus of a tidy mind: all the pens, rulers, calculators and pencils, erasers and sharpeners, drawing pins and paperclips that might happily have played on the desk top have been thrown into the drawers to hide in the darkness. The larger drawer on the left contains several sizes of paper and envelopes, below these are two mildly pornographic magazines. I close them all, careful not to cut my finger on the flaps of veneer peeling away from the drawer edges.

Half bent over, realising it will be too painful to stand upright again, I hunch across to the steel cupboard and try the handle. It's locked. I swear to myself, not because it will be difficult to open, but because to do so will require some physical effort. I stand up, move round to the side of the cupboard, and push against the top corner. If it's cheap – and it looks cheap – then the two metal stays which shoot up and down from the door will engage with the frames by only a few millimetres. Pushing the cupboard frame out of true will disengage the stays and the doors will open. Opening the door this way is easier than searching for the right skeleton key. I push harder, reach for the handle, tug; the door remains closed. I mutter the magic words 'Open, you bastard,' and push again; still nothing. Playing with the lock could take two or three minutes so I decide to attack it once more. I heave at the corner, reach out at the same time and the door swings open. I realise I'm sweating heavily.

Inside there are four shelves. The bottom two contain box files, neatly labelled with letters. I pick one, open it. Inside are folders, each with a person's name on it. They're obviously personnel folders, I put them back. One of the other shelves contains a laptop computer and a printer; the top shelf is empty. There's nothing of interest. I close the cupboard by reversing the opening process, the stays spring into place and it's as if I've never been there.

There's no similar trick to be played on the filing cabinet – it's too squat, too heavy to bully into submission. I take my skeleton keys from my pocket. Watch any crime film and you'll see one of the characters using these. He flicks through a hundred or so, chooses one or two, three at the most. He fiddles about, the camera hangs on his expression of concentration; a bead of sweat forms on his forehead; threatening music plays in the background; and the door opens. This is how it really works. A single skeleton key can fit more than one lock because the interior of its bit is hollowed out. But there are too many styles and sizes of locks for a single key, so I need a set. I can narrow the choice for a simple lock down to about ten potential keys, but each key can fit in several ways. I can open a five-lever lock, like the one that keeps your house secure, within fifteen minutes or so. But a two-lever lock, like this one, can actually be more difficult. They're cheap to make, cheap to import, and there are hundreds of different makes. Easier to open, but more choices of key. I need time and patience, neither of which I have.

I select one, insert it in the lock, move it to and fro. I concentrate. I can feel a bead of sweat trickle down my forehead, roll down my nose. I blow it away. And the lock clicks open.

I don't bother protesting that it's too easy, just open the top drawer. Folders hang neatly, tabulated in a precise, legible hand. I flick through from the front, there's one labelled 'Armaclad'. Inside are invoices stapled to order forms, a catalogue, but no plans. I take all the documents, put them on the table behind me and close the drawer.

The next drawer contains other folders with company names; I close that quickly, move on to the next. There's no folder marked 'alarm system'; nothing under 'burglar alarms'. I keep looking, there's no folder for plans; then I discover what I want. 'Come to daddy,' I say, take out the concertina of card labelled 'security system'. It's empty.

I look in the bottom of the drawer in case the plans I expected to find have fallen through; they aren't there. Nor have they been misfiled in the adjacent folders. I search through another folder, and another, but there's nothing there. I close the drawer, lower myself gently into the chair and stare at the plan of the hotel on the wall. It's useless to me, there's insufficient detail. But the plans should be somewhere in the room – there's a folder for them. Perhaps they've been taken away because someone's using them. But who would be in the hotel at this time of the evening, working on the security system? I certainly haven't noticed anyone. And it's not as if security plans would be small – there'd be a separate sheet for each floor. There might also be a set of instructions for use, some explanation of how the system works, perhaps even the original bill of quantities.

The door opens. 'Everything alright?' Jodie asks. 'You've been in for more than ten minutes.'

'Out,' I growl, 'I'm thinking.'

She closes the door so quickly I'm surprised – I'm not used to colleagues doing as I ask first time. I sit back again, close my eyes. I've searched the room, there's nowhere else the plans could be. The assumption must be, therefore, that they aren't here. If they're kept in the hotel, they're kept elsewhere, despite this being the most logical place for them. After all, where would I keep plans if I managed the hotel? I'm neat, I'm obsessively tidy, just like the owner of this office. I'd want to put them away somewhere, not fold them in a cabinet where they'd be crumpled and misshapen. The ideal place would be one of those large desks with pigeon-holes beneath where the plans, properly rolled, could be stored and easily retrieved. But there's nowhere here like that and the top of the cupboard is empty. But . . .

I climb to my feet, go back to the filing cabinet. It's not quite in the corner, its rear jammed hard against the wall, but one side has been left a good six inches away from the right-angled return. I bend to see if there's anything there, reach my hand into the gap and bring out a cylinder of cardboard. It's quite heavy; I pull off the lid and peer inside. There are concentric curls of paper. I tug at the inside one and it spirals reluctantly out by a few inches. That's enough – I instantly recognise electrical diagrams. There are symbols to represent alarms and lights, sensors and circuits. I push the paper back, replace the lid, head for the door.

'Got it?' asks Jodie, staring at the cardboard tube.

'Yes,' I reply, 'I'll take it upstairs. You'd better go and rescue Sly and your friend.' Just carrying the plans soothes my aches. At last something's working, something's happening, something's moving. Within a minute or two Sly will have released the young man, he'll have repaired the leak, and he and Jodie will be on their way back upstairs. Something is taking its course.

CHAPTER FIFTEEN

The plans are spread out on table, bed and floor, held flat by bills of quantity and mobile phones, shoes and an ashtray. Some are overlapping others, some are hidden, waiting to reveal their secrets. Sly's looking from one to the other; every now and then he whistles, darts across to another plan and whistles again. Being less mobile I stay in one place. I've already looked at the invoices I brought with me, they're part of a series of bills for a maintenance contract including call-out fees; Armaclad makes more from this in a month than I do in a year. I've put jealousy behind me and I'm scouring the bills of quantity, the architect's specification for the security system.

'All high-quality stuff,' I say appreciatively. 'This system won't fall to bits easily.'

'High quality and overdone, I'd say.' Sly's impressed. 'There's a system here with far more than's necessary; it's ridiculously over-specified. And there seems to be a back-up in case the master system goes down. If I didn't know better I'd swear we were looking at plans to a bank or a palace. Or a prison.'

Jodie is perched beside the window munching a biscuit. 'You mean,' she says through a mouthful of shortbread crumbs, 'it's meant to be good?' She probably hasn't eaten since midday and it's now, I realise guiltily, almost eight pm.

'It's good,' Sly says.

'Every component is top of the range. Do you want me to send down for a sandwich or something?'

'No ta, I'm OK with this, honest. Can I ask a question?'

'Ask away,' I tell her.

'If it's so good, how come it breaks down, oh, at least twice a week. And during the summer it was more often, sometimes twice a day.'

Sly looks up. 'Shouldn't do that,' he says, 'not unless it's been installed wrongly. Which is possible, given how complicated the system is.' He returns to the plans. 'But the installation was in a new building, all the cabling should have been in and tested before final plaster skims and decoration. I suppose someone could have cut a cable or something, but that shouldn't be a reason for any recurrent breakdown.'

'Cowboy installers?' I suggest.

'New building, boss. It would have to be signed off by the architect, and with a spec like this he'd know if there was any poor workmanship. No, can't be that.'

Jodie chews on her biscuit. Sly's finger scrapes the lines of cable, follows them from room to room, floor to floor. I listen to their lives passing their quiet ways along random paths. Predetermined paths? Has it already been decided that I should have that thought at that moment? That I should tire of this temporary inaction and rise to my feet? One day I'll have time enough to waste on such thoughts, but not now.

'OK, you have to find out, Sly, if there's a problem with the system or the operators. Keep in touch. Jodie, you and I go to see Terry Wilder, see if Annabelle left anything at home that might be valuable. Norm's at work in London and I've got Rak searching the net for anything on Amalgam that might prove interesting. That means we're all busy. What more can I ask?'

'Let's go, then,' Jodie announces; when she picks up her coat I notice her cram more biscuits into her pocket. She's already at my side as I begin rising to my feet and tugs me gently the rest of the way. 'Come on, Grandad,' she says. I hear Sly's snigger turn into a cough.

By the time we get downstairs the taxi Jodie's ordered is waiting for us. The driver shakes his head and pulls his breath through unwilling lips when I tell him our destination, but a twenty-pound tip and the promise of a return fair, including waiting time, secure the deal. As we wind through the City's amber-glowed streets, Jodie finds it an opportune moment to ask me questions. They aren't limited to work. She finds out that I'm divorced, that I have a daughter only a year or two younger than she is, that I have a partner I haven't seen for almost a year now. She finds the last fact fascinating, difficult to understand.

I find in turn, because she volunteers the information, that she's been working at the hotel for a little over six months, that she left school at sixteen and has secretarial and computing qualifications. She lives with her mother, she doesn't have a boyfriend and her ambition is to manage a large hotel. Such trivialities keep us from dwelling on the man who attacked me and the possibility of him attempting to do so again. Given our destination she could ask – but doesn't – about Annabelle Wilder's death and the reason I'm investigating the case. I don't think she's lacking in curiosity, more that she doesn't want to dwell on matters still close to her. The death of a young woman in a hotel where she now works, when coupled with the police's lack of success in finding the murderer, could resonate with unpleasant potential for her.

Follow the river east towards the sea. First you'll find gentrified wharves and warehouses; people will pay to be close to the city centre with river views, even if the river is more often grey than blue and tinted with rainbow slicks of oil. Further east are the shipyards where skeletons of once proud cranes are now resting places for starlings and angels. The houses that striped the slopes down to the river, the houses that fed demands for steelmen and colliers and boiler-makers, have long gone. In places their graves are still rubbled and overgrown; elsewhere their replacements, slums of the future, have taken root. Keep going until the gulls' cries shout the proximity of sea and not landfill, but stop before you reach the elegant cliffside terraces and Victorian hotels. Turn into the warrened roads of an old council estate (giving thanks that the taxi driver knows his way), past photocopied houses and gardens with no grass, street-hungry lurchers and feral hedges, broken bollards and sullen streetlamps. Ignore the twelve-year-old girls become women, the laughing, pointing youths with tobaccoed fingers and razored hair, faces pierced with gold and anger. Tell yourself that what you're seeing isn't real, that it's a cliché, that people and places like this don't exist any more. Remind yourself that you should resist stereotypes. But don't get out of the taxi to chat or pass the time of day, don't ask if that was a stone hurled as you passed. Just watch and remain quiet and be pleased you can leave.

'Interesting place,' Jodie says. She's becoming adept at the deliberate understatement.

'It doesn't need much to make it better. Just proper investment in housing and healthcare and education and social services. Spread over decades. A few more pence on income tax. But of course, no sane politician's going to propose that because most of us are idealistic in public but selfish in private.'

Even as I say it I regret the sermonising, such speeches are best left to politicians. I look at Jodie staring out of the window; it looks as though she hasn't heard a word I've said, or she's chosen not to hear. But then she says quietly, 'I'd pay.'

'That's always the case, isn't it. The ones who want to help most are the ones who can least afford it.'

The driver slows the taxi to a halt, turns in his seat. 'I hope the party political broadcast's over, because we're here. And if you want to get back to town with four wheels and an engine, don't be too long.'

It's my turn to gaze gloomily out of the window. There's a row of white rendered houses with communal porches, their doors opening onto straight-through passages; stairs lead to upper floor flats, doors to those on the lower floor. Half the hallways are in darkness, half the streetlights aren't working, half the windows are boarded and graffitied.

'Come on,' says Jodie, 'let's do as the man says. I don't like this place.' Before I can move she's out of the car and holding my door open. I haul myself out of the seat, ignoring her helping hand. I've been sitting still for twenty minutes, that's enough time for my muscles to begin stiffening. I hope Terry's is a ground-floor flat, even one flight of stairs might be too much for my aches and pains.

A few numbers are scattered, seemingly at random, along the wall of terracing. I squint at them, unable to decipher them in the gloom.

'What number are you after?' Jodie asks. 'I'll find it.'

'Twenty-five.'

Receptionists' outfits aren't designed for running, but still she manages to break into a click-clacking shuffle along the uneven pavement. She stops and stares, moves on, stops again then hurries back. 'High numbers at this end,' she says, 'twenty-five must be further down. Come on.' She links arms with me and I feel the future wash over me. Yes, I'll get over this temporary inability to control my limbs, but it'll take longer than in the past. My recovery time is lengthening because I'm getting older. And one day I'll need help like this all the time. Grandsons or granddaughters will offer me an arm, slow their pace to match mine. They'll watch for uneven ground, make sure I'm wrapped up against the cold. They'll hold my arthritic hands, make fun of my baldness, laugh when I reminisce about my past. And I'll remember when I stood at the top of the hill of mortality and gazed down without a care. Now, I have cares.

Our progress is slow; I notice that the taxi has followed us, eager for company. Man and machine curve to avoid a carpet of broken glass that spills from path to road. And around us there's silence. Some windows are lit to tempt our eyes, there's a smell of chimneys and fires, an acrid after-taste in the mouth, but the only sounds are those we ourselves are creating. When a distant dog howls it could be a banshee, a creature from another planet, and I feel Jodie's grip on my arm tighten.

'We must be almost there,' she says, 'can't be far now. Yes, here we are.' She leads me down a concrete-slabbed path, long grass biting at its edges. 'What if no-one's in?' she asks.

'I've got my keys.'

'That's alright then. I suppose breaking and entering doesn't really count as a crime round here.'

The porch door is jammed open, leaning on drunken hinges. We go through. Number twenty-five is on the left, no number plate, just the figures scrawled in yellow paint on a regulation green-glossed door. I knock hard. We wait. There's no panel above the door to see whether a light's on inside and I can't hear the sound of movement. But then there's a voice. 'Who is it? Who's there?'

'Terry? Terry Wilder. It's Billy Oliphant here. Can we come in.'

There's a sliding metallic sound from inside, then the door opens a little, held in check by a security chain. A suspicious eye peers at me.

'There's somebody with you. Who is it?'

I usher Jodie forward; she smiles nervously at the gap between door and frame. 'I had an accident,' I explain. 'I need someone to help me around. Jodie's my minder.'

My sarcasm is lost on Terry. 'Is there anyone else with you?' he asks nervously, 'Anyone else hanging about?'

I look around me. 'No-one I can see, Terry.'

There's a pause; I can hear Terry thinking. And he makes his decision. 'I suppose you'd better come in, then.' The door closes again then opens, and Terry's standing there, welcoming us. I'd been worried that he and his home might confirm the stereotype of the estate, but he's untidy rather than dirty, his hair is ruffled rather than unwashed. The flat smells clean, the hall's painted pale yellow, there are clip-frames of miniature film posters at regular intervals. He catches me looking at them. 'Anna's,' he says. Doors to right and left lead, I presume, to bedroom or bathroom. At the end of the hall is a black and white photograph of Annabelle. She's sitting on a ruffled bed with her knees drawn up to hide her breasts, presumably naked. Behind her is an ornate, gilt-framed mirror and, to one side, a tall window with billowing net curtains. Through them can be seen a glimpse of steep rooftops punctuated by tall chimney-stacks and dark-slated attic windows. It's Paris, and a critic might feel that the room and the background are, perhaps, a cliché of that city. But, for me, Annabelle so dominates the photograph that little else but her matters. She's undoubtedly beautiful, but her head is on one side and her smile is wistful. 'Nothing can last,' she's saying, 'not me, not this room, not my happiness. They're all temporary.' She's reminding me that I'm looking at a photograph, the past, a time when she had the potential of so many futures.

'Is that her?' Jodie whispers to me.

Terry catches the words. 'That's her,' he says with pride. He ushers us into the living room. It's simply furnished, a small sofa and easy chairs; TV, video and DVD in one corner; stereo system in another. One wall is taken up by a window; on each of the other three is another framed photograph of Annabelle, though not by the same photographer. These are colour snaps, and there can be no doubt now that this is Paris: here she's on the Champs Elysee; there, staring at the camera from a wooden bench at the tip of the Île de la Cité; and sitting in a street café drinking coffee.

'She's beautiful,' says Jodie.

'Was,' Terry corrects her, 'she was beautiful. Have a seat, please. I'm sorry it took me so long to answer the door, but I was having a sleep. I can't sleep properly at night, so I doze when I can.' He looks at me expectantly, as if frightened to ask outright if I've found anything.

184

'We've made a connection,' I say, plunging straight in, 'between Annabelle and one of the Amalgam directors, but –' I have to hurry on, his excitement is too great ' – it was a long time ago and it's not really motivation for murder. We're on the right track, Terry. Someone's tried to put the frighteners on me, that's a sure sign we're close. So now I need to find out more about Annabelle. Those photographs you gave me were very helpful, but I need to know more. Did Annabelle have any other stuff – papers, documents, letters, anything that might tell us more about her? I've a feeling that the more we know about her, the more we'll know about her murderer.'

Terry sits back in his chair. He closes his eyes, as if he's trying to summon memories that might really be dreams; then he flicks them open again, bright, shining. 'It's funny,' he says, 'but Anna didn't really have a lot of things. Possessions, that is. When she died – no, when she was murdered – I got all her stuff together, put it on the bed. She had clothes, two bin bags of them. I gave them away, to one of the local charity shops. And she had a suitcase, really old, battered, and I put her other things in there. That's where her photographs were, the album, so I've had it out quite recently. There's no problem, you can look at them. But I don't think you'll find anything.' He looks up, and I can see how tired he is, how young he is. 'I'm sorry, I'm forgetting my manners. I'm going to make myself a cup of tea. Would you like one? It won't take long, and you'll need a little while to look through the case.'

Jodie and I nod. Terry goes out. I can hear the sound of cupboard doors opening and closing; after a short while he comes back into the room and places a suitcase on the floor in front of us. He holds his hands open, inviting us to look inside. Then he leaves to tend to his kettle and teapot.

Jodie can see that I'll have problems descending to the floor, so she leaves her seat, pushes the case toward me and kneels at my feet. 'It does look rather old,' she acknowledges.

'Or well used. I've a feeling Annabelle Wilder lived more from her suitcase than she did from any home.' The suitcase has travelled a great deal, but not widely. It doesn't have patches of material showing where stickers bearing her name and address might once have been. There's no last remnant of an airline flight, no baggage handler's barcode label. The material is brown and scuffed, two mock-leather bands stretching across its lid, the fake brass lacquer scraped away from its catches and hinges. There's no lock – either Annabelle considered the contents not valuable enough or she was aware that suitcase locks don't deter anyone who really wants to get in.

'Should we open it?' Jodie asks.

'That's why we're here. Would you mind doing the honours?'

Jodie presses the catches; only one of them springs open easily, the other releases its stay but the spring has broken, so it has to be lifted open. She folds back the lid in which a piece of lining material has been formed into a small pocket with an elasticated opening. I point at it and Jodie puts her hand inside. She shakes her head, 'Fluff, crumbs, nothing else.'

Whatever is in the main body of the case is covered with a piece of cotton material printed with a red and black pattern of lions and giraffes. Jodie takes it out, holds it up for me. It's about four to five feet square, fringed at all edges. 'Sarong,' she announces, in case I'm not familiar with the garment. She folds it again, puts it to one side.

'Just a minute,' I say, 'is there a label? Where does it come from?'

'Most high street stores, I'd think. But . . . yes, here we are. "Made in India." Doesn't mean she bought it there, though. I've got one a bit like this at home.'

'OK. Move on.'

186

Next out of the case is a large off-white teddy bear, its limbs a little misshapen as a result of being folded and squashed. Jodie hands it to me. One paw is labelled 'squeeze me', and I do so, but the batteries (if there are any) have run down. I turn it over and round but there's nothing attached to it, no message written on it.

'I've got some of those as well,' Jodie tells me, 'presents from boyfriends, mostly. I don't really like them; they're on a shelf opposite my bed. I imagine them staring at me, even coming to life when I'm asleep. Evil things, teddy bears.'

It doesn't look evil to me, just a little sad at being hidden away and neglected. 'Come on then, let's see what else there is.'

Jodie hands me a small wooden box. I open it to find a fountain pen inside. I unscrew it into its constituent parts; there's no cartridge inside, no trace of ink on the nib. I put it back together. 'Looks unused,' I decide, pass it back to Jodie. 'Next?'

This time it's a plastic bag. Jodie unwraps it, peeps inside and gingerly brings out several items of clothing. Seamed stockings, a white thong and suspender belt, a cap with a red cross emblazoned on it, a short dress or long blouse flared at the waist, again white. Put them all together and it's a sexy nurse's outfit.

'Don't tell me,' I say, 'you've got these at home as well?'

'Mr Oliphant! Of course not. I work in a hotel. Mine's a sexy waitress's outfit.' She looks at the blouse-dress, feels the fabric. 'It's not cheap stuff,' she says, 'not from a joke shop; take it away and wear it once.' She does the same with the garter belt. 'This is good too.' She feels the stockings, 'And these are silk. This little lot would cost a fortune, believe me.'

Not being an expert in the field I have to agree with her. I too examine each item, feel a blush rise as I realise she's watching me closely.

'I've brought some biscuits and things as well,' announces

Terry Wilder from the door. 'Home-made. They're quite good, even if I say so myself. I do them for the old lady next door. It's even got to the stage where she buys me the ingredients.' He puts a tray down on the coffee table beside the sofa; it's stacked with biscuits and cakes, serviettes folded neatly at their side. 'There's nothing in there that's anything to do with me,' he adds. 'I've looked through it, of course, and it got me thinking. Milk? Sugar?'

Jodie takes neither; I have milk.

'I could have been jealous. You see, I didn't know what was in the suitcase before I opened it. She never showed me. I knew it was there, of course, but I thought it was just a place to keep personal possessions, things she didn't want me to see. Things from her past. Sexy clothes, a cuddly toy, perhaps presents from previous boyfriends; you can see why she wouldn't want them on display. But they meant something to her. Cake or biscuit? Have both if you want.'

They both look delicious, so we accept both on our plates.

'That's why I couldn't throw them out. She kept them because they were important. And if they were important to her, they're important to me. So please, don't mind me, I've seen everything in there. Keep looking.'

So Jodie fishes more items from the suitcase. A strange green hat with ears and a bear's face embroidered across it; an anthology of poetry called *Wicked Women* with an inscription, 'To my very own wicked woman', but no accompanying signature; a hairbrush disguised as a microphone; an old record sleeve of the soundtrack to *The Sound of Music*. Alone or together, none of them give me any clues. I already knew that Annabelle Wilder had a complex personality, but these possessions just make her even more complicated. They aren't helping; they're making me more confused. And still Jodie, like a magician, pulls more rabbits from the magic hat.

'Two knives and forks with . . . yeah, good for her! They're from the Savoy. A piece of rock of some type. Hey, there's a photograph of you, Terry, in a photo booth. A school report book; that could be interesting.'

She hands it across. It has a red cover and inside is Annabelle's photograph at eleven and at sixteen, different degrees of innocence. The comments and grades seem to demonstrate a growing disenchantment with her formal education. As she grows older she's absent more often, her effort and attainment grades decline, her teachers' comments become more and more despairing. Only Art and English appear able to excite or attract her.

'Yes,' I say, 'it's interesting. But I need illumination. Anything else in there?'

There's an expensive scarf, an old-fashioned, unworn woollen sweater. In a jewellery box there's a cheap-looking ring and necklace with paste red stones.

'That's it,' Jodie tells us, 'nothing else.' She turns the empty suitcase upside down to prove it.

'Was any of that any use?' Terry asks.

'All of it,' I say, 'if I had enough time to look into it properly, have samples of material tested for, oh, blood, DNA, saliva. If we could find out where the bear was bought, for example, we might be able to find out who bought it for her. But there isn't enough time.'

'Well,' announces Jodie, 'at least we've been fed. I'm a bit of an expert on biscuits and I can tell you now, they were absolutely wonderful. And the cake! Marvellous.' Terry smiles, lowers his head in embarrassment. 'Perhaps I'd better take some for the taxi driver, if he's still waiting. Keep on his right side.'

'Is this all Annabelle's possessions?' I ask Terry. 'Nothing else anywhere, no letters or diaries, bills, receipts? No paper-work of any type?'

Terry shakes his head. 'The police took everything else away, but there wasn't that much of it anyway. I don't think there was anything important there.' He's holding the white bear in his lap, cradling it as he would a child. 'I just wish I could help in some way.'

'Could I have another look at the bear, please?' I take it from him, look closely at the mouth and the ears. There's a flap at the back covering the battery holder; I open both. 'Empty. You don't have any AA batteries in the house, do you?'

'Not that I know of . . . except for the radio, that takes AA batteries. Hold on.' He leaves the room, returns a moment later even as I'm hushing Jodie's questions about what's going on. He has with him a radio, opens the back and flips the batteries into his hand, gives them to me. 'It'll just have some silly message on it,' he says, 'a song or something.'

'No it won't. If you look closely, it's got a small speaker in its mouth. But it's also got a microphone in its ear. I think it's one of those toys where you could record your own messages and the bear would speak them back to you.' I fiddle the batteries into place.

'Won't the message have disappeared? With there being no batteries?' There's no enthusiasm in Terry's voice. I'm so concerned with finding out whether there's a message that it hasn't occurred to me that his point of view might be different. If there is a message, if Annabelle didn't delete it herself, it will be from Annabelle's former lover. Terry might not want to hear that voice.

'If there's a message, it'll still be there. This is all low-tech – it's not a microchip inside, it's a miniature tape recorder with a loop.' I take my hand away from the on-off switch. 'Do you want to hear this, Terry?'

Terry nods. 'If it helps you, it helps me. And I'd like to know who it is, or was. I know she had lovers before me, and anyway, it'll just be a voice, an anonymous voice. Go on, play it.'

I click the switch, sit the bear so it's facing forward, squeeze its paw. There's a hissing noise and then the tape begins to play. The bear begins to sing. The words are soft but clear. The voice is slightly out of tune. And it's a woman's voice.

'Rock-a-bye baby, taken away,
Into the gloom, locked far from the day.
Ice-cold the rain, and dark black the night,
But Mommy will love you, make it alright.
Mommy will find you, love you tonight.'

There's a slight pause, then the same voice begins to repeat: 'Mommy loves you, Mommy loves you, Mommy loves you.' It does this four complete times, halfway through the fifth the tape loops back into the song. I press the bear's hand to stop the message, hear the tape rewind.

'Was that Annabelle?' I ask Terry.

His 'Yes' is hesitant. I can understand why; the voice and the words are those of someone on the edge of losing control. If it's Annabelle, then, despite her grief, she took the time to think carefully about what she wanted to say, to write it down, to work on rhyme and rhythm. Such focus under stress would make me question her sanity. Can Terry admit that too? 'Are you sure?' I ask again.

'That was her. But it sounds . . . so far away. Not in distance, in time. And she doesn't sound right.' He giggles. 'She sounds as if she's acting in a bad horror film.'

'I don't think she was right, Terry. I think . . .' There's no way to say this easily. 'I think she may have had a baby and had it adopted.'

Terry shakes his head sadly, wistfully. 'If you're right,' he says, 'if you're really sure . . . well, she never mentioned it to me, she can't have known where it was because . . . she liked children. She was good with them; she was always stopping and looking at babies in prams, talking to them. I suppose that could've been because . . . But she didn't tell me she'd had a baby.' His voice dies to a whisper, any other thoughts are his own.

'Now what?' Jodie asks, almost as quiet as Terry.

'I don't know. What we've got tells us about Annabelle, but there's nothing to link her directly with anyone in

191

Amalgam. It's what's missing that's so infuriating; there's no paperwork of any type. You'd expect to find a bank statement or a few bills, national insurance card, passport, a doctor's prescription, appointment card. Something like that. Anything like that.'

I must sound demoralised, Terry wakes from his dream and pats my knee in sympathy. 'Anna used to keep our records,' he says, 'but I've already looked through them, there's nothing that goes back to before we met. Everything she brought with her was in that case.'

'A new life?' suggests Jodie. She takes the case, puts it on her lap, turns it in her hands. 'Perhaps she didn't want to bring anything from her past with her.'

'But she did,' I remind her, 'she brought photographs and toys, souvenirs and personal mementoes, all the unimportant things. So why nothing else?'

'The bear was important,' Jodie reminds me.

'So everything else was as well! Great, a suitcase full of cryptic clues. I don't have time for all this. I need answers.'

Each of us stares around the room, avoiding each other's gaze. Terry's still clutching the bear, my hands are tapping at my thighs, Jodie's still examining the suitcase. 'I've got a box at home where I keep things that are important to me,' she says. 'Silly things. A poem from a boyfriend. A special birthday card. A letter my gran sent me just before she died. But it's not hidden away; anyone could look at it when I was out. My mam, I mean, I trust her, but there some things I wouldn't want her to see. So . . .' She giggles, she's embarrassed. 'So I made a false top, in the lid, and I keep really private things there.' She opens the suitcase again, runs her hand round the lining without looking inside. 'Perhaps Annabelle did the same.'

Terry and I watch her. She's concentrating, her fingers reading; they slide across the satin of the base, then around the sides. They stop, then they move on, stop again, move again. They move up, onto the inside of the open lid, then into the pocket. They stop again, concentration becomes puzzlement. She puts the case on the floor at her feet and pushes her hand back into the pocket.

'What is it?' I ask.

'Stitching. Different to the rest, it feels as if it's been cut and sewn together again. And I'm sure I can feel something inside, something flat. Paper.' She pushes the case across to me; my own fingers confirm that there is indeed some uneven stitching and perhaps something beneath. It's right at the bottom of the pocket, too deep to let me see.

'Scissors,' Jodie says to Terry, 'do you have scissors?'

'To hell with scissors.' I grab a loose fold of material and pull. It comes away easily, not just the pocket but the whole of the lining. A piece of paper flutters heavily to the floor. I pick it up, unfold it. No-one asks anything. They wait for me to read it.

'It's a birth certificate. A baby girl, called Samantha Emily Robertson.'

'She chose her own mother's name,' Terry whispers.

'Born in London, Tower Hamlets. Annabelle's registered as the mother.'

'And the father?' Jodie's leaning towards me, urging me on.

'The father? Well, there's something of a problem there. There is a man's name.'

'Go on then. Who is it?'

'Gary Cookson. The same Gary Cookson who's Heather Cookson's husband, I assume. Heather Cookson who's a director of Amalgam.'

'Yes! So there's a connection!'

'No, no, hold on. Don't get excited. First of all, let's think of motivation for the murder. Neither of the Cooksons was present when Annabelle was killed.' I'm ignoring Jodie, more concerned with Terry. He's hunched and small, elbows and knees glued together, head in hands. He looks as if he doesn't want to know anything else, as if Annabelle had too many secrets.

'And there's something else?' Jodie asks. She thinks she's found something, so she's personally involved. She hasn't noticed Terry's silence.

'At the time the birth was registered, the father's name was left blank. It's been added afterwards. Several times.' I turn the certificate round so that Jodie and Terry can see it. The registrar's neat hand is in official black ink, neat curlicues embellishing the paper and lending it gravity, authority. Surrounding (but leaving blank) the box where the father's name ought to have been, a scrawl of red ink spreads like a cancer across the page. In places it's decipherable, the name is clear. Elsewhere the name has been overlaid, overwritten so often that the pen has pierced the paper and the ink is like matted blood from a wound.

'It all comes to nothing,' Terry mutters. 'In the end, everything comes to nothing.'

CHAPTER SIXTEEN

I check my watch before asking the taxi-driver to take us to Rak's. It's ten pm and I don't want to impose on her, but I need her help. There could be a lot happening over the next few hours, and I'd rather use her house as headquarters than my room at the hotel. I tell Jodie where we're going, describe Rak to her in terms that I hope won't scare her.

'Aren't you going to ring her to say we're coming?' she asks, sensibly.

'No. She might tell me it's not convenient.'

'But what if it isn't convenient?'

'If it isn't when we get there, it will be by the time we get in. I've a key, remember, to Jen's flat and therefore a key to the house. If Rak's in bed, if she's indisposed, we simply make as much noise as possible to get her up. If she's out, we use her computers until she comes back in. Don't worry, she's used to me behaving like this. If I started being thoughtful she'd think there was something wrong with me.'

The journey through the Saturday night traffic doesn't take long. It's too early for the cinemas and theatres to have thrown their customers out, and the first wave of pub-goers is already safely installed; they'll be joined by wave two, the out-of-towners, about midnight, and together they'll surge through the dizzy streets heading for the late-night clubs and discos, their minds focused on alcohol, sex and drugs. It's a normal city Saturday.

'Would you be out there,' I ask Jodie, 'if I hadn't hijacked you?'

'Not here,' she says disdainfully, 'not in town. This is

where the tarts and slags come. I think I've been down town twice on a Saturday, for hen nights, friend of a friend.' She wrinkles up her nose. 'I'm not a prude, but the things you see . . .'

We sit in silence, staring out of our respective windows. The driver's switching between radio channels: first we hear country-and-western music, a song of lost love and heart-break; that's replaced by something classical which is, in its turn, sent quickly on its way to be followed by a rock ballad, a rap, and some pulsating, repetitive dance track. A voice talks about possible strikes in the public sector. There's some modern jazz, a rhythmic drum-backed choral from some-where in Africa, a melodic guitar blues. He eventually settles for a local phone-in.

It seems appropriate that we should be travelling through a succession of similarly well-lit suburban streets lined with the same small family cars (nearside wheels hoisted onto cracked pavement slabs) protecting rows of identical well-clipped hedges and neatly-painted terraced houses. Beneath this apparent conformity the occupants, like the taxi-driver's music, will be wide-ranging. They'll be different ages and genders, they'll have different coloured skin and hair and eyes, they'll have different ambitions, achievements, loves and hates. No matter how homogeneous the group, scratch the surface and the idiosyncrasies will appear. It's the same with Amalgam's directors. They're all different, but what-ever motivates them is unique to the individual. They may seem to be playing as an ensemble, but they're nothing more than a group of soloists. I need to find out more about them, then I might be able to widen the cracks appearing in the collective façade of their uniformity.

Jodie interrupts my reverie. 'She was beautiful, wasn't she. Annabelle Wilder.'

'Yes. Yes, she was.' I think of the photograph on display in Terry's hall; it displayed an elegance not seen in amateur photography. It did indeed make Annabelle look beautiful.

'I wonder what she was really like.'

Jodie's thinking is a little too lateral for me at the moment. 'What do you mean?' I ask her.

'Well, we don't know much about her. Terry was in love with her, so what he says about her is a bit biased. The same with her mam and dad. Is there nobody else who's been able to talk about her? No friends?'

It doesn't take me long to answer, because I'm dealing, not with facts, but with my own opinion. 'I don't think she had any friends. I think she was the type of person who could love people intensely or . . .' I'm having problems finding the words.

'Hate them?' Jodie offers.

'No, I don't think so. Not hate, just . . . ignore. Not even acknowledge their existence. She could love one person at a time, and all her love went to that person. There was none left for any other relationship.'

'So you think she loved Terry?'

'Yes. At first I only hoped that was the case, but now I believe it. It was her who found him the job, wrote the letter for him, she moved up here with him; she was willing to work unpleasant shifts in sleazy hotels for him.' I think back to the first time I talked to Terry. 'He was clearly besotted with her; I think she recognised that and returned his love. She even bought him a ring. Not much of a ring, but . . .' I can see the ring in my mind. Intertwined celtic bands. Made of unpolished silver or some base metal. Pleasant to look at but hardly valuable. No, that's not true. It was valuable because it was given with love, it was, in Terry's own words, 'more valuable than gold' for that very reason.

'Are you alright, Billy?'

She loved him. She would have done anything for him. And they weren't Terry's words, they were Annabelle's words. 'More valuable than gold.'

'Billy. Billy, speak to me.' Jodie's voice pushes its way into my consciousness, her hand is shaking my shoulder. I look into her eyes. 'You were away,' she says, 'in a trance, I thought you'd lost . . .'

'Turn the taxi round,' I say to the driver, 'I need to go back, back to where we've just come from.'

He does as he's told without question, realising that he has some strange passengers but they're better than a carload of drunks determined to get to the downtown bars while cheap drinks are still on offer. Jodie too seems to accept my decision; the only questions she asks are with her eyebrows which dance momentarily upwards. She takes her hand from my shoulder, rests it demurely in her lap.

'I'll tell you when we get there,' I explain. 'I could be about to make a fool of myself.' Jodie weighs up the odds for and against and nods wisely to herself.

The journey back to Terry's house seems quick because of its familiarity. I'm out of the taxi before it stops, hobbling down the pathway, groaning softly with the pain that jars at every step. Jodie's beside me, easily keeping pace.

'It's time for some more tablets,' she says, 'as soon as you get into Terry's. I've got them with me. And you shouldn't be rushing around like this, you'll suffer for it in the morning.'

'Yes, Mum,' I reply, managing to squeeze the words from lips that are tight with suffering. I hurt all over, each small muscle and every joint tormenting me, though it's not bad enough to bring me to a complete halt. I find myself wishing perversely that I could be injured just a little more, sufficient to keep me in bed for a day or two. It would be an excuse to stop, to lie down and give in.

Jodie overtakes me and bangs on the door loud enough to wake every neighbour in the whole terrace, shouting 'Terry! It's Jodie!' She hits the door again with her fists. 'Oh, and Billy Oliphant's here as well!' she adds as an afterthought.

The door opens quickly this time, no chain, no questions. Perhaps Terry thinks we're being pursued or we're under attack; whatever the reason he ushers us inside, closes the

198

door behind us and guides us into the lounge. 'What's the matter?' he asks.

I sink into the supporting arms of the sofa, beckon him closer. 'Your ring,' I say, 'I need to look at it. You said Annabelle bought it for you. When?'

He pulls at the ring, it seems quite tight. 'I can't quite remember.'

'Before you got married? You're wearing it on your wedding finger but it's not a traditional wedding band. You said something about it when you first showed it to me. Can you remember? Can you remember what you told me? Can you remember what she said?' I'm desperate not to prompt him from my own memory – that's been wrong too often in the past. 'Come on, Terry, it might be important.'

He manages to unscrew the ring from his finger and hands it to me. 'It was after I got the job at the Riverside. Not long after we moved up here.'

There's a light on the table beside the sofa. I shuffle towards it and switch it on, adjust the head so it's pointing at my lap. 'Can you remember the exact occasion when she gave it to you?'

'I'm not sure, it's . . .' He sighs, perhaps in exasperation, perhaps at having to explain a moment that's very personal. 'She said it was a token of her love. She said she was sorry it wasn't a gold ring, but that it was more valuable than gold because it came with her love. She said I had to remember that. And it was . . . Yes, I can remember! It was the day *she* went for an interview at the Riverside.' He's more confident now, reliving the moment, the words coming faster. 'I can remember it all now. I wanted to go down to the hotel with her and wait, but she said no, it might take ages. I stayed at home, I thought she might telephone to let me know what had happened, but she didn't. I was really nervous for her – it would have been so good, both of us working at the same place. And then she appeared, she just walked in and I could tell she'd got it. There was a huge smile on her face. Yes, that's it, she just walked in with this smile, hugged me and sat me down, then she gave me the ring. It wasn't in a box or anything, she just brought it out of her pocket.' Terry seems puzzled. 'Is it important?'

'Tell me again what she said. When she said she was sorry it wasn't gold.'

He frowns. 'I'm not sure if they were her exact words. It was something like, "This is more valuable than gold because it comes with my love. Remember this." That's it, she made me repeat it.' He looks apologetic. 'I don't have a good memory,' he says, 'never did have. But I remember now. That's what she said.'

'Come over here,' I tell him, 'and look at this.' He shoe-horns himself into the space beside me. Jodie moves round behind the sofa; she doesn't want to miss anything. I hold the ring up to the light, turn it slightly. Its metallic sheen is deep, lustrous, not brash like gold, not reflective like silver. 'The first time you showed this to me, I thought it was cheap silver. But it's not. There's a hallmark on it. The hallmark says it's platinum. Far more expensive than gold.' I place the ring in the palm of Terry's hand. 'It's heavy because there's a lot of metal in it. It's probably worth over a thousand pounds.'

He looks at the ring. He looks at me. He looks back at the ring. He doesn't need to say anything. At least a thousand pounds. That's a lot of money, more money than he's ever had in his life. More money than Annabelle ought to have had as well. Yet she bought him the ring and only told him in the most oblique, incomprehensible way possible that it was worth a great deal of money. So he's thinking now, he's thinking why didn't she tell me. He's thinking where she might have got the money. He's thinking how she might have got the money. His mind is spinning, he's lost. Emotions slide across his face, merge into one another.

'Hold on,' I say, 'hold on. There's something else, something I hadn't thought of. We shouldn't jump to conclusions.

200

Perhaps the ring meant a lot to Annabelle because it was a present from her parents. Perhaps she thought so much of it because . . .'

'No,' Terry shakes his head, 'no, it can't be that. I showed it to them, said she'd given it to me. They said it was nice but they didn't say it was a present from them. She could have stolen it or someone bought it for her or gave her a lot of money. But what could she have done in return?' He sinks into a swamp of dark thoughts.

'Do we still need to go and see your friend?' Jodie whispers. I nod a reply, unwilling to take my gaze from Terry. 'In that case,' she continues, 'I think we'd better take Terry with us. I don't think we ought to leave him alone.' She reaches beyond me and takes the ring from Terry's hand, pushes it onto his finger again. He realises what she's doing, stiffens his finger to accept the offering. 'You're coming with us,' she says to him. 'We're getting close and you need to be there.' Terry can do nothing but comply.

Jodie's not strictly correct. First of all, her use of the first person plural implies that she's an integral part of the team. I'm not yet prepared to recognise that, for her own sake as well as my own. If we are indeed getting closer to a solution, then we're also getting closer to the physical violence I've already experienced, don't want to experience again, and don't want any of my friends to experience. And secondly, we aren't any closer than we were before. We know that Annabelle bought Terry an expensive ring when she had no money. She may have stolen the ring, she may have borrowed the money to buy it, she may have earned the money in some legitimate fashion, she may have been involved in some criminal activity, she may have won the money in a bet or in the lottery. There are simply too many alternatives; the ring isn't a path, it's a dead-end. All it does is tell me that Annabelle Wilder was a more complex character than I first believed, and that doesn't make my job any easier.

'Come on, then, let's go.' Jodie is organising us. She hurries round the sofa, helps me to my feet. 'Got any of those biscuits and cake left?' she asks Terry. 'We may need supplies. Looks as if it's going to be a long night.'

'Yeah,' he says, waking from his trance, 'in the kitchen.'

'Come on then, jump to it. Go get them.' She pushes him ahead of her. 'Anything else we need from here?' Her question's directed at me, over her shoulder. 'Apart from a glass of water to help your painkillers down. I'll get those, you keep thinking.'

I look around the room again. If Rak's house is going to be turned, albeit short term and temporarily, into an incident room, then I need to focus everyone's mind on the task. 'Terry,' I shout, 'I need these photographs of Annabelle. Can I take them off the wall?'

'Help yourself,' comes his reply, a monotone. And so, a few minutes later, we're once again on our way to Rak's, armed with biscuits and photographs. The fellowship of the ring never seemed less well prepared.

CHAPTER SEVENTEEN

This time I do ring ahead. It's almost eleven and Rak's alone. I explain what's been happening. She offers sympathy, accepts that we're on our way to commandeer her computer room and promises to spend a few minutes tidying up. She also castigates me for the thankless task of aimless internet research. The directors of Amalgam are also executive and non-executive directors of many other companies. She's visited many of their websites. 'It's a bloody circular journey, boss, everywhere I go I hear what I already know; I never find anything new. There's nothing personal about the companies or their directors. I've wasted hours. I need something specific to look for.'

I reassure her that I need that as well and ask her to send an email to Norm in London, he should report any findings direct to her. By the time we finish complaining to each other the taxi's almost at her door.

'Any time you need driving around,' the driver tells me as he passes my credit card through the reader, 'you just ring me direct. If there's a fare inside I'll just kick them out; it's far more interesting ferrying you lot about. And you know what? I've been listening to you on and off for two or three hours, and I still haven't the faintest idea what you're on about.'

I hurry him on his way as Rak lets us in. She's playing mother hen; the kettle's on and she even claims to have rinsed (she doesn't use the word 'washed') some mugs. She bustles us into her computer room, the room she calls her study and leaves us as she gathers teapot and milk-jug. Along one wall is a long settee she uses, when fatigue decrees and she's too lazy to leave the room, as a bed. Her main computer (she has an internal network, stations in kitchen and bedroom) is directly opposite, together with a library of reference books shelved above and to the sides of her desk. The window is hung with heavy curtains; daylight is frowned upon. Rak feels that natural light is debilitating.

On the third wall is a whiteboard on which various messages and rude drawings are scrawled. I wipe it clean and write the name 'Annabelle Wilder' at the top. I rest the photographs of Annabelle against the board, then start writing my basic information along the left edge of the board; there's very little of it. At the right edge I list the names of the directors of Amalgam, my suspects. At the bottom I add the name 'Rook'.

Jodie and Terry watch me helplessly. When Rak returns she glances in my direction. 'Make yourself at home,' she says, 'but watch out, the information on that board was invaluable, irreplaceable and not written down anywhere else in the whole world.'

'I can remember the important bits,' I tell her, 'something about potatoes, vodka and pot noodles.'

'My new diet.' She sets down the tray on a pile of books. 'I take it that you're Terry and Jodie; the boorish man in the corner did mention that you were coming. Milk and sugar?' Terry wordlessly offers Rak a plastic bag containing his cooking. Rak puts her nose to the bag and sniffs appreciatively. 'Thank you, let's hope that Mr Oliphant will learn from your generosity.'

'I'm always kind to you, Rak. If it wasn't for me and the little problems I bring you, how would you get the intellectual stimulus you crave?'

'I could watch old episodes of *Murder, She Wrote* on daytime television.' She pours out the tea, brings a cup to me. 'Weak,' she says with mock poison in her voice. 'Is that the way you like it or is it just your character?' Before I can think of a stinging reply she notices the black-and-white photograph at the bottom of the whiteboard. 'This is Anna again? Good model. Good photographer as well; looks like a professional job. You want me to trace him?'

'Trace him? You mean find the photographer? How's that possible?'

Rak adopts her declamatory pose, the one she takes up when she has to explain computers to me. 'You know how to use a search engine, I take it?' She goes straight on, sure that I do possess that small piece of knowledge. 'Well, when you type in the words "naked wife next door", you don't really imagine that the computer looks those words up in a big dictionary, do you? No, your computer converts them to a basic electronic language, and that's compared to a vast database and all similarities are flagged. The more specific you are with your criteria, the fewer options you get. If you link words together then the search criteria become more complex. Are you with me?'

'So far, yes,' I tell her. Terry and Jodie nod from their seats that they too can understand.

'Good. Now then, when you send an image from one computer to another, that's simply a sequence of electronic impulses as well. Yes? So the latest piece of software I've got – it's only on trial, not yet available to normal humans – encodes images and searches databases and websites for similar strings of impulses.'

'Similar,' I ask, 'not identical?'

'Similar,' Rak repeats, 'because that's all you need. You can specify the degree of similarity as well. You might want to look for all the Degas paintings on the net. One way would be to search for "Degas", but that would bring every article and essay ever written about him. Instead, you just encode any Degas painting and the software searches, in effect, for a Degas style. In theory it might find paintings only possibly attributed to Degas. So using this software I scan the photographs of Annabelle, specify "France" as a source, or "Paris",

205

and see if we can come up with the identity of the photographer. Good, eh?'

'Sounds wonderful. It would tell us what she was doing in Paris, exactly when she was there. That's if the photographer can remember the occasion. Are you sure it'll work?'

Rak basks in her glory. 'Of course it'll work. Well, it will if the photographer has his own website. And providing his style hasn't changed over the years. I suppose there's also the chance that other photographers might have a similar style, after all, it's a pretty standard pose.' She weighs the possibility of success in the balance. 'In short, the chances aren't good. But it's the best option we have at the moment.' She picks up the photograph, begins to bend back the retaining wires. 'That's assuming you've already done the sensible thing and taken the photo out of its frame to see if the photographer's name's on the back, yes?' I look across at Terry. He looks back at me. Rak catches both of us. 'You haven't looked. I don't believe it, you haven't looked! Bloody hell, Billy, you're meant to be the detective around here, not me.'

Jodie springs to my defence, 'He's had a lot on his mind.'

'Yes, honey, and he's a man as well. I suppose I should make allowances for that. Only able to focus on one thing at a time, and we all know what that is.'

'Just get on with it, Rak.' I try to make my impatience clear to all, though I'm more annoyed with myself than Rak. She's right, I should have thought about this before.

'Don't hurry me, Billy. I just need to get this final clip off and . . . Voilà!'

'Well? Is there anything?'

Rak hands me the photograph. 'How's your French?'

The rear of the photograph has been stamped with a name, address and telephone number. Rak moves to the computer. 'Read it to me,' she says. 'I'll search. If he's got a website there should be an email address; we can send him a copy, see if he can identify it, remember anything about it.'

'*David Olivier, Photographe, Rue de Varenne no. 77, Paris.*
Wouldn't it be easier just to ring? You can access an online
phone book, can't you?'

'Like I said before, Billy, how's your French? Mine's non-
existent.'

'Me too,' I tell her.

'I speak reasonable French,' Jodie says.

'Great! And this guy has a website. Let's have a look . . .
yeah, this is him. Black and white photographs, elegant
nudes. And an email address; everything's clicking into place
alright. Now then, if I scan this photograph in and . . .' she
places the photograph face down in her scanner, presses a
button, '. . . Jodie? Can you do an email?'

'What do you want me to say,' Jodie asks, rising from her
seat.

'Billy'll tell you. Now then . . .'

The phone rings. I'm closest to it so I pick it up and grunt
into the mouthpiece.

'That you, Billy?'

'Norm?'

'The very same. Car mechanic, chauffeur and house-
breaker, at your service.'

'You broke in? Christ, Norm, I didn't expect you to take
that sort of risk.'

'Well, I didn't exactly break in. Not in the sense of
breaking windows or picking locks or anything like that. But
I did find the flat, just like in the photograph. And I did get
in, but I used my brains, not like that overgrown hulk of
muscle Sly would've done. I tell you, Billy, you should use
me more often. I could get used to this type of thing.'

'Norm, just hold on a second, will you?' I'm aware that
Jodie has crouched in front of me, mouthing words at me,
words I can't understand. 'Yes,' I ask, 'did you want something?'

'The email? I can speak French quite well, but I'm not
that good at writing it. I'll need time to translate it, if you

tell me now I can be working on it while you're on the phone.'

'Billy?' The phone is squawking at me again. 'Billy? Are you there?'

'Yes, Norm, I'm still here. Can you . . . Just hold on, my mobile's ringing.' I take it from my pocket; it's flashing 'Sly' at me. 'Billy here,' I say, 'what's new?'

'Some good and some bad, boss. The security system's shot to hell but I still can't figure out how someone could've dragged a body . . .'

'Billy? The signal's cutting out, I'll have to find a phone box . . .'

'The email Billy?'

'This Olivier guy's charging a hell of a lot for his photographs; he must be pretty good, pretty hot . . .'

'Boss? You still there?'

It's too much. After a day of nothing, there's suddenly a surfeit of information, all at once, an incessant flow of voices. I take a deep breath. I'm about to shout extremely loudly when I notice the noise has subsided. Jodie has taken my mobile from my hand and whispered something to Sly, Rak has done the same for Norm. It's nothing I've done or said has caused this, and I can still hear something. It's a small voice, Terry's voice, and it's crying, 'Stop it, please stop it,' over and over again. His face is buried in his hands. I push myself to my feet, sit beside him, put my arm round his shoulder. 'It's OK,' I tell him, 'we're getting there, that's why it's so noisy. All these people, they just want to help. And you can help too, even more than you've helped already.'

He sniffs loudly. Jodie fishes a paper handkerchief from the depths of a hidden pocket, hands it to him. He wipes his eyes, blows his nose. 'How can I help?' he asks.

'By being there. You see, we get carried away. An investigation like this, it can be like a puzzle. You can't see a solution, then, like Rak said, things start falling into place. And we're so involved, we concentrate too much on the solution.

So when that happens, just remind us why we're here. You asked us, you and Charles and Emily. We're here because someone you loved was killed. We're here to find out why and how. We're dealing with a person here, not an abstract puzzle. Just remind us, Terry. Remind us. Be our conscience.'

'Like Jiminy Crickett, you mean?'

'Just whistle.'

It takes me a few minutes to calm things down. Sly has amended instructions, he's to come out to Rak's to tell us what's happened and bring with him all the plans and documents, everything he can find in my room. Norm's to make his way back to his hotel where Rak will set up a conferencing link. I'll write an email to the French photographer which Jodie will translate (she's proving invaluable; perhaps my subconscious is proving to be an excellent judge of character). Events are moving, though I'm still not sure where.

It takes a long time to write the email. I'm wary about what to say and how to say it. I need information and I need it quickly, but I don't have the clout of a police force. In the end I decide to tell as much of the truth as I have to and rely on David Olivier's goodwill and humanity. The next problem is that Jodie's secondary school written French isn't quite as good as her spoken, and she has to request changes when she can't think of the words I've specified. In the end we decide to send my original text as well as her translation, and to move matters along we decide to telephone him. This requires further discussion. It's almost midnight, and Jodie is uneasy about disturbing someone from their sleep and explaining the background to our investigations in her conversational French. *A quelle heure part le prochain train pour Paris?* is not the most useful phrase on which to build a discussion about murdered young women.

Rak points out that the telephone number is likely to be that of a shop or office and that there'll be an answerphone in operation. This cheers Jodie, she can cope with passing on a message to Monsieur Olivier asking him to read an email from a mad amateur detective in England. When Rak also mentions that the phone could be on divert to the photographer's home, Jodie becomes nervous again. Just as she's plucking up the courage to ring, Sly arrives to contribute to the confusion. Rak's study isn't large, and there are too many people trying to do too many things at once. It's time for more executive decisions. I send Terry into the kitchen, he's in charge of refreshments for our little party. Rak and Jodie make their phone call to an answerphone; both are pleased with the result until they realise that, since we're now approaching Sunday, it's unlikely that the message will be heard until Monday morning. I decide to leave that problem until we've discussed Sly's and Norm's findings. It's after midnight when we sit down, mugs of tea and coffee by our sides, to listen to Sly.

'First things first,' he says, and it's with difficulty that I stop myself pointing out that he can't do second things first because, by definition, they then automatically become first things. I'm getting tired, I'm aching, and Jodie won't let me have any more medication for another hour. I try to concentrate on what Sly's telling me.

'The security system is intact and it works. It just doesn't work in the way it was designed to work. It hasn't been built to specification. The sensors – cameras, movement detectors, microphones, contacts on entry-sensitive windows and doors – are all below the standards required by the bill of quantities.'

I have to interrupt. 'Hold on a sec, the cameras I saw were top quality, German, there's no way . . .'

'No, boss, the casings were top quality. The content was cheap, shoddy workmanship in construction and, I have to say, installation. But I'll go on to that in a minute.' It's a mild reprimand – Sly was going to mention the cameras anyway. I mouth 'sorry' at him.

'Everything looks impressive. The security guy I spoke to –' he looks at his notes '– name of Beechey, Mick Beechey

– he's been working late and night shifts since the place opened, he was actually on duty when Annabelle Wilder's body was discovered – has had experience in a few different organisations. He says the set-up is as good as anything he's seen before, and he's probably right. But it was designed to be far *superior* to anything currently available, not just "as good as".' Sly's drinking coffee; he takes a mouthful from a brew so strong the smell could keep me awake. He intends working long into the night.

'As you've probably gathered, what's been put in is a bit of a dog's breakfast. There are parts from different manufacturers, poor quality cabling and jointing. That's why there've been so many call-outs. This Beechey guy had been complaining about breakdowns; he was told it was because the system was state-of-the-art, there would obviously be teething problems. But it was breaking down because it was crap.' Sly consults his notes again. 'Right, I could go into more technical details but they'd just bore you. You get the idea, though?' We all nod. 'OK, then, it didn't take long to check that lot out, so I decided to go into some detail. I started up on the top floor of the car park, where you had your accident, boss.'

'You mean you wanted to treat the cause rather than the symptoms?'

'Got it in one. Find out why no-one could see what was happening up there. There are several reasons. One, the lighting.' Sly points to a plan of the hotel he's stuck to the whiteboard. 'The spec requires double floodlights on four separate stands, plus pairs on the liftshaft-staircase and the main hotel wall. I had a look. There are single lights on two stands plus singles on wall and staircase. I couldn't check the wattage, but the lights seem to be underpowered. They're angled to hit the largest possible area of the car park, that has to be the central portion. The result? The walls and corners are in comparative darkness.'

'And that's why . . .'

'I haven't finished yet, boss.'

'There's more?'

'There's more. And that's just in the car park. While I was up there, I had a look at the camera. The spec is quite detailed about the light rating . . .'

'Hang on a sec.' It's Rak's turn to interrupt. 'There are some people here who don't get turned on by security jargon, would you mind translating?'

Sly looks as if he's pleased to show off his knowledge. 'Sorry,' he says, 'all these cameras work by digital imaging. The more sensitive they are, the better the resolution of the image.'

'Like pixels in digital cameras?' Jodie asks.

'To a certain extent, yes. But we're not just talking about the quality of the image, it's how useful they are in a range of lighting conditions. The spec asked for high sensitivity, wide resolution and night-vision backup. In effect, the camera would be all-seeing under any conditions. Reasonable assumption, boss?'

'Spot on.' The thought behind the system wasn't just belt and braces. Normally a security consultant will adapt parts of the system to augment other parts; better lighting will reduce the need for high-quality cameras. Here the lighting has been designed for the most important person, the customer parking a car. And the camera system has been designed for the security officer. The only problem is that the installer has put in a system whose quality is way below that specified. If that's repeated throughout the hotel, not only in the security system but in the construction of the building itself, then it's a dangerous place.

'Aren't there meant to be checks?' Rak asks. 'Planning and building regulations and so on, the council? Don't they have to make sure everything's up to standard?'

I always have to play the cynic. 'Up to standard, yes. That's not the same as being up to specification.'

Sly knows about these things as well. 'The person who

212

does have to make sure everything's up to spec is the architect, employed by the client – in this case, I assume, Amalgam – to make sure the building on paper and the real thing are identical.'

'You mean,' says Jodie, 'that the architect was at fault?'

Sly's keen to continue. 'Looks that way. And there's more . . .'

'Can I just make one point?' I can sound authoritative when I try; all faces are turned in my direction. 'Who might know that the system isn't up to spec?'

'The installer,' Sly says quickly.

'The architect.' Rak isn't far behind.

'The person who attacked me was quite specific about where he wanted to meet me. He knew I wouldn't deliberately put myself in danger. He knew I'd check to make sure I could be seen by the hotel security systems. And he knew no-one would see me on the top floor of the car park.'

'And probably plenty of other places in the hotel,' Sly adds.

Rak rubs her hands together, eager to get started. 'So all we need do is find out who was the architect and who installed the security system?'

'That would be a good start,' I say. 'But that still doesn't get us nearer finding who killed Annabelle. Yes, there might be a connection, but there might not. Let's get the rest of the information first. Sly?'

'Thanks, boss. You've all got the general idea, I think. Specifics? There are several places on the top floor of the car park where a car could remain unseen by the cameras. It's possible that Annabelle could have been tied up in such a car, the exhaust led back inside by means of a hosepipe. Death would have been by carbon monoxide poisoning. It fits.'

Terry hasn't said anything. I've been watching him and he's barely moved. Sly has moved, however, from the general to the specific to the personal, and this is Terry's moment.

He clears his throat to speak. 'If Anna was killed . . .' The voice is a whisper, barely audible. He starts again, more loudly. 'If Anna was killed in the car park, how could her body have been brought down to the kitchen?'

'That's where we start to have problems,' Sly admits. 'There are three cameras at each of the lift entrances in the stairwell. That's the only way down from the car park roof. From there I could devise four or five different ways of getting to the kitchen. Even allowing for the dummy cameras – yes, there are quite a few of those – on all of those routes someone carrying a body would have to pass another three functioning cameras.'

'So Anna can't have been killed on the car park roof.'

'Sly didn't say that, Terry.' I need to go over the information carefully and talking about it is the best way I know. 'Any passage from roof to kitchen passes at least six cameras. But let's look at the obvious. What would you expect to see in a car park? Cars. An invisible car on the roof – and that would be the best place for carbon monoxide poisoning, the gas would soon disperse – could easily become a visible car on the ground floor. Or a van. Simply moving the vehicle avoids three cameras.'

Jodie's hand's in the air, waving madly. 'Go on,' I say; there'd be a mess in the room if she burst before her enthusiasm was released. 'What you said!' she shouts, 'What you said before! What would you expect to see? In a hotel? At night, when everybody's meant to be in bed, that's when you get cleaners and so on. No-one would say anything if they saw someone pushing a trolley round, a laundry trolley for example. Could that be it? Perhaps that's how they moved the body!'

Again I look at Terry. I'm sure Jodie's trying to help, but the body she's talking about is, to Terry, a person. He doesn't appear to be reacting, but he might do if there were any further outbursts of zeal. I raise my eyebrows at Sly, he knows more about the hotel's security than me. As he gathers himself to respond I touch Jodie gently on the shoulder. 'Watch you don't upset someone,' I whisper. Her mouth opens and she glances at Terry; she begins to blush.

'I did wonder,' Sly begins in his clinical, methodical voice, 'whether it would be possible to move a body hidden in some container, perhaps even disguised as, say, a drunk on someone's shoulder. I asked the security guard if it would be possible. He said the police had asked him the same question and he'd run the recordings from the camera at the entrance to the kitchen for the whole of the night of the murder. There was nothing. I asked if I could see them as well, so he ran them for me in fast time. There's nothing between Terry leaving and then coming back the next morning.'

'Shit!' Terry's comment sums up all our feelings.

'So that idea's out?' Rak says.

'Just put to one side,' I tell her. 'It might need further thought.' I turn back to Sly. 'Anything else?'

'If I had more time, if I could look at every camera and every sensor at every window and every door in the place, then I might be able to come up with something. But for the moment, that's it.' He seems apologetic. He's like me, he wants everything bundled and boxed, wrapped and tied with a ribbon. His information has been of great use, it's given us a lot to go on, but that's not enough for him.

'OK, then, let's hear what Norm's found out.' He certainly sounded as if he'd been successful when I spoke to him only an hour before, but Norm is generally inclined to optimism. No, that's not strictly true; Norm's optimistic viewpoint is aimed entirely at his own accomplishments, and is balanced by the nihilism with which he views the achievements of others, particularly Sly. He doesn't do this through malice. It's just that he likes to win, and if he can't do so by running fast, he'll do it by slowing everyone else down.

Rak has set up her link, so we gather round the computer and stare at the screen, oblivious to the cyclopean webcam staring back at us. 'OK,' Rak announces, 'Norm will be able to see and hear us; we'll be able to see and hear him. The only thing is, he's by himself sitting close to a camera and microphone, whereas to get all of us in, we're quite a distance away. So if you speak, identify yourself first and talk loudly and clearly.'

'As if we're talking to an idiot?' Sly suggests.

The computer speakers crackle into life. 'I heard that, you big black moron.' Norm's image is indistinct; he's sitting at a desk and the light appears to be coming from one side only. His face is half in shadow and his head moves in ripples. My memory provides him with his familiar bald head and grey hair, his sallow complexion and bags under his eyes. Those who don't know him, Terry and Jodie, see a poorly lit skull.

'I think we have a link,' Rak says to me. 'Do you want to do the introductions?'

'Norm,' I begin, 'this is Billy. Can you hear me? I'm sitting in the centre of the group.'

'Hear you and see you, Billy. Well, I say see you, but the image is a bit fuzzy. I can tell I'm looking at people, but they could be anyone.'

Rak holds her hands out. This is a limitation imposed by her equipment – she can't improve matters.

'Sorry, Norm, it's the best we can do. I'll tell you who's here, as I introduce each person they'll wave to show where they're sitting.' I tell Norm about Terry and Jodie and he greets each politely. He exchanges insults with Sly and is carefully neutral with Rak; although he's met her frequently and acknowledges her talents with computers, he feels that lesbians should only be tolerated if they're very good-looking, in pairs, and performing in soft-core pornography. Rak puts up with him because he doesn't charge her for servicing her succession of aged and decrepit cars.

'Tell us what you've found,' I say, 'and make it good.'

'Righto. Here we go. Like I said earlier, I found the flat

216

no problem. There's not that many street names in Westminster ending in "Place". He stops. 'That's irony, Billy. You'd better tell Sly what "irony" means. Anyway, I looked them up in the guide book. There's twenty-seven different "Places" 'n not a single one ends "-gon". I didn't fancy visiting them all, so I used me head. Luckily there was a barman in the hotel; got to know him quite well the previous night; bought him a drink or two. Local lad, about the same age as me. Matter of fact, he's invited me back to his place for a meal, to meet his wife. People say southerners aren't friendly, but let me tell you . . .'

'Norm? It's Billy speaking. Can you stick to the point, we've got a lot to do up here.'

'Sorry, Billy, thought a bit of background might help. Where was I? Oh yeah, I showed him the photograph and he recognised the building style, told me exactly where it was. Somebody'd been playing with the street sign – it was "Southampton Place". So I went round. Found the house straightaway, big, posh. Oh, something else, I borrowed a car. Thought it might be a bit suspicious, just wandering round this exclusive area with a jemmy and a mask and a sack marked "swag". This bloke I met at the conference, he's got a business renting out cars and chauffeurs. I used me head, asked if I could borrow a Roller and a uniform. He said yes, of course, a stroll round the corner to pick 'em up 'n I was set. So off I went. You with me up to here?'

'I think we're all following,' I tell him, hiding my impatience, 'what happened next?'

'Right, I'm in the Roller, all done up, peaked cap and the lot.' Norm's in present tense, he's living his adventure again. 'I drive along Southampton Place once, make sure where the house is. Then I drive back and park outside. I get out and look at the building. It's an end terrace but big, and there's a bit of garden round the side; I can see the top of a tree behind a tall wall. I sort of scratch me head, playing the part, not quite sure what's meant to be happening.'

'That shouldn't be too difficult,' Sly whispers.

'There's lights on in the first floor and second floor flats. I can almost see into the basement, but there's no light in the ground floor flat. Now, I know that doesn't mean no-one's at home, so I have to find out. There's some big stairs leading up to the front door, so I go up them, slowly; and there's a list on the wall, names beside little buttons to ring bells, and a little speaker so's people inside can ask who's calling. I press the one for the ground floor . . .'

'What name?' I ask loudly.

'Pardon? Did you say what name? Just a sec.' The figure on the screen looks down, examines something on the desk. 'The name on the plate was Corrigan, G and L Corrigan.'

'Familiar to anyone?' I ask. There's a chorus of shaking heads.

'Anyway,' Norm goes on, 'I ring the bell, but there's nothing, nothing at all. So I try the next one up, still nothing. There's no name on that one, just a blank. Perhaps they've got those lights that switch themselves on, make you think someone's at home when there's really no-one there. So I try the top one, name of Broome; this time there's a crackling sound and a woman's voice says, "Who is it?" I've got me talk all ready. "Executive Limousines," I say, "for Mrs Broome." Of course, she says "Sorry, you must have the wrong address," but I just say no, this is the address, look out the window and she'll see the Roller all lit up and waiting, engine turning.'

'I take it that no-one's heard of anyone called Broome?' There's no need for me to look round the room, the silence tells me the answer's 'no'.

'There's a wait, so I stand back 'n I can see the curtains twitch. Now then, this is the clever bit. If I'd come in any old car, even if it'd been a taxi, she'd just have ignored me. But not with a Roller. She comes back on. "Someone must have been hoaxing you, we certainly haven't ordered a car of any type. Especially not a Rolls Royce." So I follow it up straight away. "I'm sorry to disturb you," I say, cool as anything, "but could I borrow your phone? The Roller doesn't have a mobile or a radio and I need to ring my boss." Clever, eh? Of course they say yes, the buzzer sounds, the door opens. And I'm in!'

'Anything on the door of the ground floor flat?' Sly asks. 'Or outside, a clue about the people who lived there?'

'I recognise that voice. Sly, just shut up and listen. I'm the one with brains, not just brute strength. But to answer your question, there was nothing. Couple of potted plants either side of the door, that's your lot.'

I'm beginning to feel despondent. I don't know if I can stand any more of Norm's rambling. 'We're not doing too well here, Norm. Is there anything else? Anything important?'

Even the poor resolution of the webcam shows Norm's insulted. He sits back, his mouth opens; all this happens in jerky slow motion. 'Oh ye of little faith. William Oliphant Esquire, have I ever failed you in your time of need?'

The answer is yes. Not serious failure, but still yes. I decide not to remind Norm about the 'investments' he's encouraged me to make, the money he's lost me, and my glare closes Sly's protesting mouth. 'Sorry, Norm, it's just that we're a little pushed for time here.'

'In that case,' says Norm magnanimously, 'I forgive you. 'Cos I've got some good stuff for you. You listening? Well, I goes upstairs and this woman's waiting for me; she won't let me all the way in – she's not that daft – but she's got a phone in her hallway and she lets me use it. I ring my mobile and do a pretend conversation. I do the nodding shaking bit, tell her it was definitely this address. Could be a different flat, I suggest, and ask her if that's likely. She says no, the couple in the bottom flat are old, in their eighties, and wouldn't be going out this time of night. Then she asks where I was going, where I was meant to be taking my clients. Well, I just makes it up. West End, I says, some nightclub, I've got the details in the car. "Oh," says me new friend, "that would definitely have been the couple in the next flat down; they're into socialising. Nice couple. But they're away at the moment. As a matter of fact, I look after the place when they're gone. Water their plants. Feed the fish. Could you have the wrong date?" "Well," I say, "anything's possible."'

'Names, Norm, did you get their names?' I'm leaning closer to the computer screen, almost shouting.

'Their names? Now then, did I get their names? Let me see.'

'The bastard,' hisses Sly, 'he's doing this deliberately!'

Rak pats him on the shoulder. 'It's his moment of glory, let him enjoy it.'

Sly sits back. 'OK, OK! But only because I don't have any choice. And because the old git has so few of them anyway.'

Norm reads from his notepad. 'Their names are Sanderson and Worrall. Liam Sanderson and Ben Worrall. Pair of woofters by the sound of them.'

I clench my fists in triumph. Rak does a little dance. Sly shouts 'Yes!' Terry, who knows the names of everyone who was in the hotel on the night Annabelle was murdered, recognises the significance of the connection, puts his arm round Jodie's shoulders and squeezes. Jodie herself, less sure of what's going on, looks at me with puzzlement.

Norm's voice comes from the speakers. 'Is that important, Billy?'

'Very important,' I tell him. 'It establishes a connection between Annabelle, through her photograph, and Sanderson. A connection Sanderson denied. It's a tenuous connection. I'm still not sure why the photograph was taken and what Annabelle had to do with them, but it'll give us something to work on, something to think about. Well done, Norm.'

'You're welcome.'

'You can go to bed now, get some well-earned rest. I'm

220

sorry I've mucked you about, but it's valuable stuff. Thanks a lot.'

'You mean you don't want to know the rest?'

The noise and the motion cease immediately. We all sink back into our seats. 'There's more?' I say.

'When I said I got in, I didn't just mean into the building. Come on, you know me. When the old dear's talking, saying how she looks after the place when the bumboys are away, I notice some keys on the hall table. Now I ask you, where would you put the keys to your neighbours' flat if you had to go and water their fish and feed their plants? So I put me hat on top of them while I'm making the phone call, and when I finish, I pick them up. Easy, eh? Then I says me goodbyes and off I go. The keys are for the front door as well, so I park the Roller round the corner – she was watching from the window; I reckon I could've scored there if I'd had a mind to – then come back, let meself in. Easy-peasy.'

'And did you find anything interesting?' Even as I speak I'm waving to Rak, asking her to get me the original photograph. It was definitely of the ground floor flat, not the one above. Why would Annabelle take a snapshot of the flat below Sanderson's? It doesn't make sense.

'Interesting? Depends on what you call interesting, Billy. Remember, I'm working in the dark here and don't know half what you know. But listen, I'll tell you what I saw, then you can tell me what's interesting. First of all I go round and close all the curtains. Then I switch the lights on. It's a posh place, Billy, like in those magazines you read in dentists' waiting rooms. It's got style. I mean, these type of lads, give them their due, they're good with colours and furniture and wallpaper, that type of thing. There's a living room, it's right on the corner, got two balconies and French windows. Two bedrooms – one's a spare, you can tell – so I was right about this pair. They're definitely gayboys. The kitchen's all white units and stainless steel, and there's not a speck of dust anywhere. And the study's like an office, with one of them big tables that tilts and swivels. It would have been better if I'd known what I was looking for.'

'You've done well, Norm, better than I could have hoped for. Did you find anything relating to Annabelle Robertson? A photograph? An address book with her name in it?'

'There were plenty of photo albums, but not many girls in them. No, I gave that up for a bad job. I did find some more interesting stuff, though. Hey, I'm getting damn good at this. I might just consider setting up in business meself.'

'Beginner's luck,' Sly mutters.

'He's joking,' I say, 'trying to annoy you.'

'In that case, it's about the only thing he's always good at. Succeeds every bloody time.' Sly increases the volume so Norm can hear him. 'Come on then, Sherlock, let's hear what else you've got.'

'Here we go, big boy. One. In the freezer there was a plastic box with dried leaves and flowery things in it. I think it was cannabis.'

'You think?' If I sound doubtful, it's because I need facts, not opinions.

'I think,' Norm repeats. 'Come on, Billy, don't press me on this. If I say "I know", then the next question is "how do you know?" and I'm in trouble for knowing things I shouldn't know. If you know what I mean.'

There's a giggle from Jodie; Sly lifts one hand to his head and makes small circling motions. Rak shrugs.

'I know what you mean,' I tell Norm. 'Is there any more?'

'Oh yeah. In the bedroom, beside the bed, there's a small chest of drawers. In the drawers there's a tin box. And in the tin box there's some fag papers and matches, one of them bong-pipe things, but small. And a tobacco pouch. Now, I might not know cannabis when I see it, but I know tobacco, and this wasn't tobacco. If you get my drift.'

'I understand exactly what you're saying, Norm.'

Even as I finish speaking Rak's muttering in the background. 'So this Sanderson or his boyfriend's into weed. That

222

still doesn't help us. It's hardly major league stuff. What's the connection with Anna there?'

'She could have found out,' I suggest. 'After all, it's not quite the thing you want a responsible person, a company director, doing, is it?' I turn to Terry. 'Did Annabelle use cannabis?'

'A little,' he replies. 'She wasn't a dope fiend or anything like that. We'd smoke a joint together, that was all.'

'Hey!' shouts Norm's computer image, 'I haven't got all night, you know!'

'You mean you've got more? I'm impressed.'

'So you should be. This was in the drawer beside the tin.' He holds something up to the camera. 'I'm going to take it back as soon as I finish with you lot. It's a sort of address book. Except it hasn't got any addresses in it. Just names and telephone numbers and little squiggly marks. I wouldn't have thought anything about it, 'cept that I can't understand what it's about. That's why I thought it might be important. 'Cos I didn't understand it.'

'Somewhere,' says Sly, 'in that argument, he's either showing he's very clever or very stupid. But I can't work out which it is.'

'Is Annabelle's name in there,' I shout, 'Annabelle Robertson?'

'Nah, I already looked.'

'Shit! What about girls' surnames beginning with "R"?' I'm thinking back to Annabelle's pseudonym when she first left home, Stacey Richards.

We can see Norm flicking through the book. He adjusts his glasses, scratches his chin. 'About twenty names under R. About half of them women, Billy. You want me to give you the numbers? It won't take . . .'

'No,' Rak interrupts, 'there's bound to be a scanner there. You know how to use one?'

'Yeah,' Norm answers unconvincingly.

'I'll run you through it, you can copy the whole book.'

She turns to me. 'There might be other names in there that might make a connection. It won't take long.'

'Right, Norm, you do as Rak says. Anything else to tell us?'

'That's the lot,' Norm says, 'but if there's anything else you want me to look for, just say. I've still got the keys 'cos I've got to go back with the address book anyway.'

'I don't think there's anything,' I say, 'but get the address book scanned and I'll see what we can think of.'

'I still don't see how this helps,' Terry begins again. 'It's not as if Anna's name's in the book and, even if it was, it's a small connection. How does . . .'

'Do you always call her Anna?' My interruption silences him for a second.

'Well, yes. That's what she said her name was, the first time I met her. Only her mam and dad called her Annabelle. Why?'

'I don't know. Leastways, there's something tickling and I want to scratch it but . . . Did she have any other names? Did anyone call her Belle?'

'No. Someone tried to, once, as a joke. I'm not sure how he found out that she was called Annabelle, but he did and started calling her Belle and Bella. She said something about retaining the initials, she didn't mind Anne or Annie or even Arabella, but it had to begin with "A". Funny, that.'

Jodie's listening carefully, her eyes flicking from side to side, concentrating on something. Then she climbs to her feet, grabs a pen and a piece of paper from Rak's desk and begins writing.

My own mind is chasing reasons as well. 'Were there any other names she used?' I ask Terry. 'Or names she liked you to use for her? Pet names?'

'Billy,' Jodie squats beside me, 'what was the name she used when she worked in that bookshop?

'Stacey,' I say, 'Stacey Richards. But I need to think . . .'

'Who called her that?'

'What?'

'Who called her that? Was it Annabelle herself? Or the police? Or the owner of the shop?'

My impatience shows. 'I don't know, how could I know that? It was the shop owner, I think. She was the one Rak spoke to.'

'She was wrong.'

Everyone's listening to Jodie now. Terry and Rak and Sly are all looking at her.

'What do you mean?' I'm curious as well, wherever my thoughts were going they've lost their way and a diversion might be welcome.

'Someone I knew at school was called Stacey,' she says and writes the name down. 'Then another girl came; she was called Stacey as well. Except she wasn't. What's "Stacey" short for?'

We look at each other, and our faces wear similar expressions of double puzzlement – we know neither the answer nor the reason for asking the question.

'It's not short for anything,' Rak acts as spokesperson. 'It's like "Jodie".'

'Exactly! But the new girl's name was spelled like this!' Jodie writes out the letters carefully on her paper, S-T-A-S-I, then holds it up for us all to see. And to make sure we understand, she spells it out for us, 'S-T-A-S-I. Pronounced the same, "Stasi". But what's it short for? Anastasia.'

'Anastasia Richards. A-R. That might work. Rak, can you get onto the bookshop owner right away, ask her if . . .'

'Billy, it's after two in the morning!'

'So? We're all awake, why shouldn't she be? Tell her it's urgent. And has Norm finished scanning that address book yet?'

'Nearly there,' comes Norm's voice. 'Then I'll have to get back, put the book and the keys back, return the Roller. No bloody sleep for me tonight.' His face suddenly closes in on the camera, becomes a distorted, spoon-faced image on the screen. 'Come on, look closer, it's amazing what you can see if you look closely! I was a handsome youth when I first met you, Billy Oliphant. Now I've got bags and dark circles under me eyes. I'm a martyr for the cause.'

'Look closer?' The blurred face is surreal, an animal mask. 'Norm,' I say, 'back off, there are young people here who might be easily frightened.' But although the face retreats, what Norm says stays with me. Look closer. Sometimes, if you want to see something, you have to back off. You have to look at the whole picture, only then can you focus on the details. Then you might just see details you haven't noticed before, perhaps in a totally different place to the one you were first looking. Perhaps we need to look at things again.

'Sly? Did you bring the photographs, the ones from my hotel room?'

'In the folder, boss.' He slides a brown envelope across to me.

I open it, look through until I find Annabelle's snapshot of the London flat. Sly's already found information I didn't notice first time – the name of the street. And I was concentrating on the ground floor flat when Sanderson and his partner lived on the first floor. So once again I allow my eyes to scan the familiar scene. Two storeys visible. Shadows in the ground floor flat – are they important? Should I ignore them? And upstairs, nothing. No-one at the windows, just a high wall sheltering a garden and, barely visible, the end of a balcony. The balcony must overlook the garden. I look closer. 'Rak,' I say, not caring that she seems to be deeply involved in talking to Norm, 'do you have a magnifying glass?'

'No. But I've got one of those bookplate things that magnifies, works like a prism.' She begins fishing around beneath the detritus of her desktop filing system. 'Not that I need it. My eyes are perfectly good, most of the time. But in dim light . . . Yes, here we are.' She hands me the flat piece of plastic.

I place it over the photograph. 'Terry,' I say, 'Jodie. Would you mind having a look at this?' They wander over to sit beside me. 'Can you see anything on the balcony?'

Jodie squints at the photograph. 'There's some sort of plant in a mini-greenhouse.'

'What sort of plant?'

'Billy! I can barely see it's a plant, let alone identify it.'

It's Terry's turn. He nods, sighs. 'Cannabis?'

I have to agree. 'It does seem to have a rather particular shape of leaf.'

'On a balcony where everyone can see it? Surely not!' Jodie's doubts are logical, and I'm sharing them.

'But we didn't see it,' Terry points out, 'not until we were given a clue. And perhaps it wasn't usually there. Perhaps it was put outside because of the fine weather.'

'Or because it was being harvested,' I suggest, more of a question than a statement. 'I wonder what was behind the wall?'

'No,' Jodie says, 'I can't believe they were growing pot as a . . . a commercial crop! In the middle of London? It's impossible.'

'Unlikely,' I say, 'but not impossible. We need Norm to check when he goes back; he has to see what's behind the wall. If each flat has a garden, part of Sanderson's could be dedicated to growing cannabis. As long as it isn't overlooked.'

'We're getting the address book through,' Rak announces. 'Quite a good reproduction as well, all the names seem legible.'

'Good. Print it out, we can all take a section and look through. Norm, when you go back, I need you to check on the view from the balcony. Can you report back on your mobile?'

'If I can stay awake that long. OK, Billy, will do. Anything else?'

'No, you've done a great job. We couldn't have managed without you.'

'Thanks. It's always nice to have your skills and talents recognised by your peers. Eh Sly?'

'Sure, you old reprobate.' The praise is grudging but I know Sly means it. Insults are, for Norm and Sly, terms of affection.

'I'll be going, then. I'll ring you when I get into the flat.' He waves at the camera and puts his baseball cap back on.

'Watch you don't lose the tenner,' Sly calls, 'in your hat band.'

We see Norm reach up and remove a slip of paper from his hat. He laughs. 'No,' he says, 'not a tenner, I'd be so lucky. I picked it up in the flat – it's a calling card.' He holds it at arms length. '"Benjamin Worrall," it says, "RIBA". What's that, then?'

'It's what that cartoon bird says,' suggests Terry. 'You know, the roadrunner.'

'No,' I say, 'it's not. We're looking for a crooked architect. "RIBA" stands for the "Royal Institute of British Architects". We may just have found our missing link.' I'm aware that these are possibilities, not probabilities. If there is a link, it's certainly not fashioned from steel. It feels like tissue paper, the connections fragile, insubstantial and unsubstantiated. But it might provide us with something.

'OK, Norm, you're doing well, you're giving us lots of ammunition here.'

'We're just not sure if it's live rounds or blanks' Sly whispers, 'or even those things that explode in your face when you try to use them.' I motion to him for silence as he's too close to the microphone and Norm might hear him. He ignores me. 'And we don't know who to fire the damn things at anyway.'

'I'll see what else I can do,' Norm answers, a swagger in his voice. He salutes the screen. 'I'll be in touch. Over and out.' The monitor goes momentarily blank, then reverts to Rak's mildly pornographic wallpaper.

I turn to Terry who lowers his eyes as if he already knows

what I'm going to say. 'You seemed pretty sure that was a cannabis plant up in the balcony.'

'So did you,' he counters defensively.

'I'm an ex-cop. I know what LSD looks like, and cocaine. I've tasted them. I've come across them in the line of duty. What's your excuse?'

Jodie butts in before Terry can say anything. 'I've smoked pot,' she says, 'hasn't everyone?' I can see Sly shaking his head, though I'm not sure if he's announcing his silent disapproval or that he too has never inhaled. 'I didn't like it,' Jodie continues, 'it just made my nose numb and I felt thirsty and a bit woozy. But the point is, lots of people have tried it; it's nothing to be ashamed of these days.'

'I'm not suggesting . . .'

'Yes you were. You said "what's your excuse?" It's clear you don't approve. Shouldn't you be neutral? Your attitude might discourage Terry from talking, and that's not what you want, is it?'

'No, but . . .'

'So what do you say?'

I stare at Jodie, but she doesn't shrivel under my gaze. I turn to Terry, he's looking at Jodie as well, as if amazed that someone should defend him. I take a deep breath. 'My mam says I've to say I'm sorry if I've offended you. I'm sorry, Terry.'

'That's OK,' he mumbles.

'And you're not very good at the sarcasm,' Jodie flounces. She gets up to see if she can help Rak.

'Was Annabelle into drugs of any type?' I ask Terry softly.

'She smoked pot when I met her, quite a bit.' The words come out grudgingly. 'And she shared it with me. But after once or twice I had to tell her I didn't like it. Funny, it had the same effect on me it did on Jodie. Anyway, Anna kept using it for a while, then she stopped. We were going out together, saving for a place of our own; it didn't seem right.'

'Where did she get it?'

'I don't know. She had a supply, though. I think she used it till there was none left and that was it.'

I'm still chasing the connection, the tenuous link, and I don't know which direction I'm going. It looks as if Annabelle was a regular user of cannabis until she met Terry. She had a photograph of Sanderson and Worrall's flat. Why? What was she hoping to do with it? Norm's visit might help, might provide more information. But until then I need something to keep me occupied.

Rak and Jodie are plucking the address book pages from the printer, examining each in detail, highlighting the names and telephone numbers of those people – men and women – whose first name begins with A or whose surname begins with R. They're working at speed, no need for help there. Terry's back in his own world, looking at the photographs of Annabelle. He's analysing each in detail, memorising each curve and smile, each nuance of expression and gesture. There's no sadness in his face. Instead there's a sense of pride, the same look I've seen on parents' faces at nativity plays, a beatific unconditional love. I can't interrupt him.

The room's dark walls and ceiling, its air of busy-ness and untidy clutter, conspire to create a feeling of warmth and community. We're working together, working to solve a crime, to fight injustice. It feels right. Sly's poring over the hotel plans, the layout of sensors and alarms, cameras and cables as they should be. Pencilled over the top is his limited analysis of what's actually there. He's trying to figure out what alternative points of entry there are, how well they're watched. I raise myself gingerly to my feet (my aches and pains are returning) and wander across the room to see him. 'Any luck?' I ask.

'Too many possibilities, boss. I need a week, longer, to go over the whole system. I didn't even have time to finish the whole ground floor, but I did check every entrance and emergency exit. They're all alarmed, all cameras working.'

'So how did they get the body in?'

230

'Inside something?'

'It's a possibility.'

'There's a camera in the corridor outside the kitchen. I checked, it's working. I looked at the recordings, they show Terry leaving on the Saturday night, and Terry coming back on the Sunday morning, but nothing in between. Apparently the police checked as well. The clock on the digital record is accurate, no-one's been fiddling with it. There are no laundry trolleys, no-one hauling a big sack on their shoulders, nothing. No-one came into the kitchen.'

'Except someone with Annabelle's body.'

'Exactly. How the hell did they do it?'

'Through an emergency exit? Let in by someone inside the building? A conspiracy?'

'There'd still be video evidence, boss. Even if it was a conspiracy between everybody in the building, there'd still be evidence. But there's nothing.'

'No, there's always something, Sly. We just haven't found it yet.'

'I'll keep looking, then. Keep thinking.' Sly's tired, I can tell by the way he's holding himself, his shoulders slumped, his head dropping.

'No, I've a better idea. You know where Jen's flat is, so go upstairs, have a few hour's kip. Tomorrow . . . no, I mean today, of course, it's after two . . . later on today I'll have to go back to the hotel and I might need you to have another look at the system, see if there's anything specific needs investigating. You'll have to be on top form.'

Sly stretches and yawns. 'You mean you don't have to be on top form?'

'Yes. But the way things are going, I'll be live-wired on adrenaline. And pain-killers, if I can persuade nurse Jodie to let me overdose. Go on, bed.'

Sly goes out, waves to the rest of the room; they barely notice him. I tiptoe across to where Rak and Jodie have the address book labels laid out. 'How's . . .'

231

'Don't even ask,' Rak says, 'it's impossible.'

'Nothing's impossible, just . . .'

'This is impossible, Billy. In the first place, there are hundreds, thousands of names here. This bloke's social life must have been ring-a-ding-ding. First names beginning with A? Seventy-eight. Last names beginning with R? Eighty. A reasonable overall distribution, I believe. Number on both lists? None. So what do we do, ring them all? What do we say? We've stolen somebody's address book, you were in it, would you mind telling me why?'

'Hold on,' I say, 'let's think carefully. Come on, put the sheets down. Sit on the sofa, both of you.' I move round behind them like a crab, slipping sideways between the sofa and the Terry-filled armchair. I stretch out my hands to rest the fingers on Rak's neck, my thumbs push gently on the top of her back. I apply more pressure, only with my thumbs, move them in slow circles.

'Shit, that's good,' Rak says. 'With a touch like that you should have been a dyke. Mm, yes, down just a little bit.'

'Sh, relax. Let your mind work on autopilot. Think. What do we have?'

'An address book.'

'A full address book.' Jodie's keen to join in. 'Lots of names and telephone numbers.'

'And that's unusual in itself,' Rak drones.

'Why's that?' I ask.

'You're a Luddite, Billy Oliphant. Everyone – except for the technologically challenged – has a mobile phone these days. The best mobile phones, and this bloke will have the best, have a huge memory for names and numbers. Address books are redundant. Dinosaurs. Not long for this world.'

'She's right,' Jodie says, 'I keep all my friends' numbers on my phone, never write them down.'

Terry takes a sudden interest. 'I hate them,' he says. 'Always going off, interrupting you. We managed without them for years, why . . .'

'Why, then – ' I ignore him, interrupt him ' – would someone have so much important information in such an archaic retrieval system?' We might be onto something here. 'Neither Sanderson nor Worrall struck me as being techno-phobes.'

'Didn't trust phones?' Jodie suggests without any real enthusiasm.

'Changed them frequently.' It's Rak again, her voice low and purring. 'Smart young gays about Town, they want to be seen with the latest fashion accessories. Phone memories were difficult to transfer until recently, that could have meant a build-up of information in the address book. Then, once that information got past a certain level, it became just too laborious to transfer the information.'

'Perhaps the book was really important,' Jodie says.

'What do you mean by that?' I keep on digging my thumbs into Rak's back; it seems to help the clarity of her thinking. I wish someone would do the same for me.

'Well, if it was really important, the information might be on a mobile or on a computer, but this could be the backup. In case something went wrong. I mean, you can lose mobiles easily, can't you. And there's always something going wrong with computers.'

The muscles in Rak's neck tighten a little as she absorbs Jodie's calumny, but I tug at them and she relaxes again.

'It still doesn't help,' Terry bleats. 'It doesn't matter why there's an address book. Even if Anna's name was in there, which it isn't, unless it's a false name, and even then we can't find it . . .' He trails off, forgetting where he was going. 'What I mean is, it doesn't lead us anywhere. It doesn't tell us who killed her.'

I want to explain to him about following up leads without knowing where they might be going, about making con-nections, about curiosity, about sifting and filtering every possible piece of information you have in case it's important. I want to tell him I don't really know what we're doing. I want to tell him about desperation, about the impossibility of the task I've set for us. I want to tell him how much my arms and legs and body and head hurt, and that the reason I hurt is because I'm trying to help him. I want to stand up and grab him, haul him from his seat and point to the people all around him, all trying to find out who killed his wife. I want to remind him that they too are tired and under pressure. But I do none of this. Instead, I stop rubbing Rak's shoulders and pick up the sheets of paper that represent the address book.

'You don't like mobiles, Terry?'

'I told you, I hate them. Always going off when . . .'

'You've never had one?'

'No. I could never afford one anyway.'

'So why do you complain about them?'

'Anna's was always ringing. Day and night, phone calls and text messages; it never stopped. She used to run this party scheme selling make-up; she stopped just before she met me, but people kept on ringing her up. That's why she had to answer every call, "Sorry, I don't do that any more." It was really annoying.'

'When you say people rang up at night, do you mean early evening? Or later, nine, ten o'clock?'

'Late. And later than that, in the early hours of the morning as well. It went on for about a month after we met, then it gradually stopped.'

'Right. I can see why you don't like mobile phones, then. What happened to Annabelle's?'

'I don't know. It's probably in a drawer at home. Why?'

'Can you remember the number?'

'No.'

'You must have rung her on it at some time.'

'Yeah, but . . . Can you remember mobile numbers?' He's right, for some reason they don't stick in the mind the way landlines do.

'Have you finished the massage?' Rak sounds as if she's just woken from a deep sleep.

234

'Yes, sorry. My thumbs are dropping off.' I need something to lift me now, nothing's leading anywhere right now. I'd submit myself to Rak's stubby fingers, but I suspect that a mere man might suffer from her ministrations. She's overweight but she's also overstrong; there are muscles below the flesh.

'Is Anna's phone number important?' Terry asks sulkily.

'It might be.'

'Oh.' He fishes in his trouser pocket and brings out a battered wallet. He opens it and draws out what looks like a passport photograph. He hands it to me; there's a telephone number on the back. I read it aloud; Jodie's the one who writes it down and begins checking it against those in the address book. While she's doing this I turn the photograph over. It is, as I ought to have known, of Annabelle. She looks tired, bleary-eyed, as though the photograph was someone else's idea and she's going along with it because it would be too much bother to argue.

'It was taken on our first date,' Terry admits coyly, 'in King's Cross station about three in the morning.'

Jodie's shout prevents me from commenting. 'We've got a match!' she cries triumphantly. 'The number's here under the name "Anne Aaronsen".'

'And the first name initial matches too,' Rak says.

'Shit!' My swearing silences everyone else.

'Isn't it good, finding the match?' Jodie asks.

'We could have found it earlier, if we'd thought more carefully. Look at the name. It's written down incorrectly. It's not "Anne Aaronsen", or if it is, Annabelle's making fun of us. It's "Anna Ronson". Sanderson or Worrall must have misheard the name when she first told them, then it was too much trouble for her to correct it. That has to be it.'

There's no celebration, no cheering or clapping. The connection's been made, but it's simply a step towards another problem. None of us needs to voice the next questions. Why was Annabelle's telephone number in the book?

Why would Sanderson or Worrall have wanted to contact her?

'It's after three,' Rak says, 'I'm pooped and I'm going to bed. Anyone want to join me?' Jodie looks worriedly at me. 'I've a double bed,' Rak continues. 'I intend removing my outer clothing, rolling into my side, and going to sleep. If anyone else, male, female or any stop between, want the other half of the bed, they're welcome. Or there's the sofa; I've a spare quilt somewhere. Fourth person sleeps on a chair or on the floor. Sort it out yourself, that massage finished me off, goodnight.' She bends down and kisses me on the forehead, waddles out of the room.

'I'm staying here,' I say. 'I'm not sure I can manage the stairs, I need more painkillers and I want to be around when Norm rings. I'll take the armchair.'

Jodie's quick to occupy the silence. 'I'd better stay with Billy. I need to get him his medication and that French photographer might get back in touch.'

Terry accepts his fate gracefully. 'In that case, I'll share with Rak.' He forces an unconvincing smile to his pale lips. 'I'll be safe. I'm not her type.' He follows her out of the room, reappears a moment later with a quilt that Rak must have thrown down the stairs, drapes it over the sofa then leaves again. Jodie measures out my tablets and watches me take them with a swig of water. She takes the glass from me and, when I motion to her to help me out of the sofa and into the armchair, simply smiles and shakes her head.

'We can work in shifts,' she says. 'You sleep first.' She lays the quilt over me, despite my protestations that she should retain it for herself, places herself in the armchair close to the telephone. 'Sleep, Billy. I'll wake you up when Norm rings, don't worry.'

It's too difficult to fight a determined woman. I close my eyes and the world slips away from me.

CHAPTER EIGHTEEN

There's a dim light filtering round the rectangle of the heavy curtains. I'm halfway between awake and asleep, and I can't remember where I am. The shadows of bookcases and desk, computer, armchair, gather on the fringes of my consciousness. I'm neither sitting nor lying, slumped in one corner of the sofa. Then I recall, Rak's house.

I try to move my head and find that, at some time while I've been asleep, my neck has been replaced by a piece of rough-sawn timber. I send messages out into my body, but muscles everywhere respond by shouting at me not to bother. The only parts of me that seem to be operating with any degree of efficiency are my pain receptors.

The central part of my torso seems to be numbed, as if a heavy weight is pressing into me. When I let my head roll forward (the roll is painless, simply a relaxing of muscles; the halt is the opposite, a jarring buzz-saw of sharp teeth digging into the back of my neck) I find Jodie lying across me, asleep. Her head is supported by the nearest wing of the sofa, hair awry, curled and tangled. Her left arm is around my waist, her right, a knot in my spine tells me, somewhere behind my back. Her body is covered by the quilt, but I can feel her knees touching my right thigh as she lies curled in a foetal position. She's breathing gently, and I'm loath to wake her, except that I can remember now the events of the past night. I shake her shoulder gently, and her eyes open immediately. She blinks and smiles, says hello and uncurls herself from around me all in one movement.

Her shoes are on the floor. 'You must be aching all over,'

she says, sliding her feet into them. 'The day after an injury is always the worst. I'll get your medication sorted.'

I'm starting to regain feelings in my extremities. I've pins and needles in toes and fingers, nails and knife-blades everywhere else.

'Did Norm phone?' I croak. 'You said you'd wake me . . .'

Jodie's on her feet, smoothing her skirt down. 'You didn't wake up when he rang, so I just wrote down what he said. It didn't seem important that you should know straightaway. And there's been a reply from Monsieur Olivier, an email, in pretty good English. He'd been out last night, but checked his phone and his computer when he got in at just after four in the morning. He said he recognised the photographs, he'd check them in his files to find out exactly when they were taken and the names of the people involved, and he'd wait for you to ring him. I replied saying it would be about nine o'clock our time.' She looks at her watch. 'That gives you about fifteen minutes to get yourself sorted.'

I try to gather my thoughts. Norm's phone call and the photographer's information should help me piece together . . . what? I feel as if I'm making something without having been given the instructions or a sketch of what the finished object should look like.

'Instructions?' Jodie asks.

'Wake everyone. No, wake Sly first, tell him to come down here and help me get to the toilet. While I'm doing that you can get my tablets, see if you can raise Rak and Terry from the dead. And I have to know what Norm said. Everyone to meet back here in ten minutes.'

It takes less than that. Jodie tells everyone that we have more results, and as Rak sweeps aside the curtains and allows a bright morning to join us, there's an air of anticipation which (helped by a timely opened window) cloaks the odours of night and the as yet unwashed. I urge Jodie to begin.

'Norm rang from the house,' she says, scribbled notes in

her hand. 'He was whispering because he didn't want to wake the neighbours. He had a torch with him. He assumed that, because he managed to get into the flat, there was no alarm on the balcony doors. There was a key in them, they opened without a problem.' She looks at us all, aware of the responsibility she's taken on herself by not letting me talk to Norm. 'There's a flight of steps straight down from the balcony into the garden. Norm didn't want to go down because it was dark, but I said if he shone the torch down onto the steps no-one would see. He went down into the garden. He could see back up the stairs; the doors onto the balcony are the only opening in the gable wall. There's nothing above overlooks the garden at all, and from the street the view's blocked by that high brick wall, remember it from the photograph?' We all nod, trying to paint an image of the garden from Jodie's words.

'It's not a big garden, and the bit under the stairs, under the balcony, is a lean-to greenhouse. The glass has got plastic bubble-wrap stuff at every pane, I said I didn't know why, maybe so people couldn't see in properly, but Norm said it was to stop tender leaves being burned by the sun. The door was closed but it wasn't locked. He had a look inside. It was full of cannabis plants.'

'We may be getting somewhere,' I say.

Jodie's keen to continue. 'And that's not all. Against the wall there's a brick building; originally it must have been a potting shed or something like that. Now remember, this is a big house turned into flats, and a big garden turned into smaller gardens. And this shed must have been for the whole garden, it runs the whole length of the wall. The windows were all blacked out, but there was no key and the door wasn't locked again. Norm had a look inside. It was very warm, there was some type of heating in there, and hanging up from racks were hundreds of cannabis leaves. On the shelves there were little parcels. They were even labelled, I wrote down what Norm said was in them.' She refers to her notes. 'There was hashish, skunk, weed, something called "white widow" I think, but I'm not sure what it is. Oh, and super skunk as well. It's a little cannabis factory.'

Jodie lowers her paper and grins triumphantly. 'Any questions?'

'We've got a connection,' I say. 'Small-scale, high-quality, home-grown cannabis. By the looks of it, imported stuff as well. There'd have to be some imports for this number of buyers.' I hold up the sheets of paper, the address-book printout. 'The customers.'

'Could be, I suppose,' Rak says.

'Has to be,' adds Sly, 'there's no other explanation.'

'There's always another explanation,' I tell him, 'but this one works for the information we have.'

'Hold on,' says Terry, 'Anna gave up weed soon after she met me.'

'But before then,' Sly points out, 'she had to be getting it from somewhere. This is obviously the place.'

Terry is still puzzled. 'But where does the photograph fit in?'

It looks as if Sly's going to speak, but he realises he doesn't know the answer and deflects the question in my direction.

'Let's assume that Annabelle took the photograph. It could have been her attempt to record the plant on the balcony. Why? As a record of fact, to show that cannabis was being grown at the home of Sanderson and Worrall. My first and most obvious thought is that she was black-mailing them.'

'No!' shouts Terry, 'she wouldn't do that!'

'Or it may have been insurance. They threatened her with something, so she let them know that she had something against them as a counter. I'm just guessing, it could be anything. I'll find out later today.'

Rak is the first to ask. 'How? How will you find out later today?'

'When I go back to the hotel this afternoon and put all

our information in front of the directors of Amalgam. Make a few suggestions. Ask a few questions. Do a little insinuating, imply some undiscovered criminality. Try a little character assassination. All the things your friendly local private investigator does when he's pretending he knows more than he does know.'

'But it sounds as if you really do know what you're doing,' Jodie says, mystified.

'It sounds as if you know who killed Annabelle,' Terry adds, menace in his voice. It's clear that he wants to dispense justice in his own way.

'I can say a confident "no" on both counts. I don't know what I'm doing and I don't know who killed Annabelle. But we're a damn sight closer than we were yesterday.' I fix my gaze on each of my audience in turn. 'We're getting information, people, can't you see that? And information is valuable; it's a currency that's recognised in places where money's useless. We're going somewhere.'

'I should point out,' Sly explains to everyone, 'as one of the boss's longer-term companions, that the "somewhere" he's referring to here is usually prison, crown court, or the bad guy's dark and dingy basement.'

Sly's joking, I feel optimistic enough to recognise that. 'But before we set off to infinity and beyond, I've a call to make to a Monsieur David Olivier, photographer *extraordinaire*.'

The phone is answered quickly. David Olivier speaks excellent, if somewhat formal and stilted English, in a deep, warm voice. He seems pleased to be involved, albeit indirectly, in solving a murder case, especially one where the victim is, in his own words, 'such a beautiful young lady'. He's checked his records and his negatives, his contact prints and his invoices. The photographs were taken at his studios, not, he's quick to point out, rooms with a view of the Eiffel Tower, but a warehouse in St Denis.

'My gallery is small but in a good part of the city, close to the Rodin museum. I have a window display and, inside,

241

many albums of my work. I employ an *assistante* to work in the shop; she takes bookings and makes appointments for sittings in my studio. Now then, I make notes in my diary and I have checked through them. This was a particularly memorable session for several reasons. First, my *assistante* telephoned me at my studio early in the morning to ask if I could fit in an extra session; you see, she knew I was fully booked for weeks ahead. She told me there was an Englishwoman in the shop who had to leave Paris the next day but wanted some portraits done before she left. Now, I do not normally do extra work, I did not need to do so then and I do not need to do so now. So I said no, but the next thing I find is that the Englishwoman has taken the phone and is speaking to me. She did not threaten me, she did not plead with me. She just told me how impressed she was with my work and asked me, very politely, if I would agree to take some photographs. Nude photographs.

'I asked her to give the phone back to my *assistante*. I asked her to answer, either yes or no, several questions. I asked if the woman was good looking, and she was. I found out her age, how tall she was, the colour of her hair and skin. And she sounded interesting. So I arranged for her to come to my studio that evening at eight o'clock.

'I was surprised when the time came round, because there was not one Englishwoman, but two. One of them was clearly in charge – she was the one who was to pay for the sessions. She told me her name was Carol Parker. Her travelling companion, the young lady in your photograph, was called Abigail Rafferty, though she answered to Abby. I know this for certain – I asked Abby to write her name down because it was, to me, unusual. The arrangement was that I should photograph the two women separately and then together. Now I began to complain, I told them I did not have enough time for three sessions. I had thought that I was to photograph one woman, one session. But this Carol Parker would not listen; she told me they were both photogenic and would be easy to photograph. Somehow she managed to persuade me. I set up the studio and they went into my changing rooms to undress.

'She was almost right in what she said. They were both photogenic, easy to pose; they did not flinch when I had to touch them, to move their bodies. They did not complain when I had them standing or sitting or lying in unusual positions. But there was a difference.'

I can hear him laughing down the phone. It's not an unpleasant laugh; he's not laughing at some risible memory. No, it's a laugh of affection, the laugh old people perform when talking about long hot summers or their first kiss.

'It is strange, Monsieur Oliphant, just looking at the one photograph you sent brought back memories of all the others. I have taken thousands and thousands of photographs, but these ones have stayed with me. You see, the camera loved Abby. I suspected that was the case as I was photographing them, but it is not always easy to tell; the key moment is when the film is developed and the negative printed. So I went on photographing. I assumed they were lovers, they were certainly happy to be naked together when I photographed them as a pair. And they were an interesting contrast: Abby had pale skin and delicate features, she was not exceptionally tall but it seemed as if she could stretch herself and become long-limbed; Carol was shorter, round and curved, her body was more mature. But they were professional, they did not try to be sexy – that is not the way I take photographs – but . . . well, you have seen the photograph of Abby. Somehow the sexiness still comes through.

'That Parker woman, she drove a hard bargain. They were leaving the next day and, even though it was after eleven when we finished, she wanted finished prints the next morning. She said I could decide which negatives to print, she trusted my judgement. I will tell the truth, I was worried about the way the prints would come out, and I was right to be worried. The photographs of Carol Parker were good. She was a good model, photogenic, handsome. In isolation, I would not have been displeased with her photographs. I would have been pleased to have them on display or in my portfolio. But . . . but, Monsieur Oliphant, the photographs of Abby Rafferty were so much better. They were so good I wanted to photograph her again. I have not felt such excitement with a model since then because . . . because she was natural. She was untrained. I have photographed other women since then, models, professional models, who were undoubtedly better than her, but they had been trained. Abby had talent; she had the potential to be exceptional.

'I wrote her a letter telling her how impressed I was. I told her I'd pay her to pose for me, and that I would find other employment for her. She could have made a career from it, I was sure of that. I expected both women to come back, but it was only Carol Parker who came and I gave her the letter, asked her to pass it on to Abby. And I knew she would not.'

This time the photographer sighs, I can feel his loss.

'Carol Parker was an intelligent woman. She looked at the photographs I had printed, she could read what she was seeing and she saw the same as I did. She saw that the camera had told the truth; she was beautiful, but Abby was more beautiful. She thanked me politely, took the photographs and the letter, and left. I didn't see her again. I didn't hear anything from Abby Rafferty.'

David Olivier tells me he's printed copies of all his negatives and he'll send them as email attachments. I thank him profusely and promise to tell him the outcome of my investigations. I put down the phone.

Throughout the conversation I've said little, and my audience has been unable to hear what I've been told. But when I turn to face them no-one says anything. They wait for me to gather my thoughts.

'The best link yet,' I tell them. 'A connection with Carol Parker. Photographic evidence of them together. And, not that we need it, the initials of her name fit. Add evidence of jealousy, a definite motivation for malice. It's good.' I proceed to tell them the story.

When I finish there are no questions, there's no need. I give my instructions. Sly gathers together the security plans and sets off back to the hotel to check on the locations we've identified as being of interest. Terry and Rak are to remain behind to work on any other possible links they can find, though I've taken Rak to one side and explained her real purpose in life: she's to make sure that Terry Wilder comes nowhere near the hotel; the bewilderment he displayed yesterday has been replaced by a fixed grimace of determination to do something. I'm sure he doesn't intend asking the Amalgam directors polite questions.

Jodie is to come with me to the hotel where she's back on duty at eleven. She's not quite sure what to make of this. She says she wants to stay with me, she's sure I'll need help just to get around. I point out that she'll be of more use as an insider, and she goes off to have a shower and borrow some clean underwear a little happier. By ten-thirty, after compressing my aching body into a taxi, we're on our way.

CHAPTER NINETEEN

It's a normal Sunday morning. The placards outside
newsagents forget coach crash deaths and political intrigue,
ignore financial scandals and industrial unrest; the local team
won away the day before, and that's more important news.

Runners are spread at random along city pavements, prams
and pushchairs decorate park paths; dogs are walked, washing
hung, windows cleaned, bicycles spun, everyone is enjoying
the peaceful calm of a temperate day of rest. Children find
themselves surprisingly out of doors, yelling and scrabbling
through drifts of early autumn leaves. Cars on their way to
DIY warehouses and supermarkets, car boot sales and riverside markets, seem content to cruise rather than speed, staring
at the day. Somewhere, in the far distance, bells summon the
elderly to church. There's a sense of clean freshness in the
air, a promise of a few days stolen from summer and hidden
away somewhere dark, suddenly escaped and shouting their
freedom.

Or perhaps it's me. I'm watching the world from the warm
comfort of a taxi's back seat with a feeling of content. I'm
congratulating myself on the hard work of the previous day
and night, on some connections found and proved, on others
more tenuous. But this self-satisfaction won't last long.
Anxiety will come soon to regain its rightful place in my
mind. All I can prove is that some members of the board of
Amalgam are liars, or have very poor memories. Others are
probably criminals and fraudsters, and there'll be grounds
for a further police investigation when Kim Bryden hears
what we've found. But on the big task, finding Annabelle

Wilder's murderer, we've made little progress. I've made little progress. As the leader of this small, makeshift team, I have to accept responsibility. There are so many questions, so little time to find the answers.

Nervousness is creeping around me, its tendrils making their presence known by curling around my limbs, heading slowly but inexorably for my heart, my mind. I shift in my seat, as if believing that movement will break the fragile fibres, but it only serves to halt their motion for a second or two. Not only that, it reminds me of the pain I feel in every limb, in stomach and chest and head. I should be at home, in bed. I should have been woken by an early morning alarm and luxuriated in the delight of switching it off, ignoring it.

Jodie, alerted by my movement or the groan I thought was silent, opens her eyes. She looks around her. The taxi is dipping into the central motorway, the curves of two-storey concrete that hurry vehicles around the city centre into the bottleneck of the bridges over the river.

'I don't know if I can face a whole shift of being nice to people,' she says. 'All those grey-haired old women playing detective. It doesn't seem so much fun when you've been doing the real thing. When you know it isn't really glamorous. When you know it can be dangerous.'

'You mean you haven't enjoyed it?'

Her face normally moves easily from neutrality into a smile or a laugh, as if she has a mask she simply lifts into place. This time she smiles, but not straightaway. The mask has been hidden, she's had to search to find it. 'It's been interesting,' she says, nodding her head to show the word has been carefully chosen. 'Interesting, eye-opening. Lots of things. I mean – I'm a bit mixed up, so much has happened, I haven't had enough sleep – but I didn't know what it was like to do this, to try to find out things about other people. And I didn't know how unpleasant, how nasty, people could be. I feel sorry for Terry, and for Annabelle, of course. And

I'm pleased I met Sly and Rak, I'm pleased I could help you, even if it hasn't been much help . . .'

'It's been a lot,' I tell her. 'You probably saved my life.'

She ignores my compliment, 'No, let's be honest, that was an accident, and it would have been the same if anyone had been there. I've helped a bit, not much. But . . . I don't know. I wouldn't have missed it. I won't say it's been enjoyable. And I don't think I'll be able to stay working at the hotel for long, not now I've seen what they're like.'

'You could walk into another job any day, Jodie, with your talents . . .'

'No, not hotels. Something else, perhaps.' That's when she looks at me, really looks at me, looks deep into my eyes. 'I feel I could do more than just be a receptionist. I don't know, I might go back to college. It's like I've been allowed to look at something, then been told I can't look again. No, that's wrong; I've seen something dangerous, and then been told I can look at it again, but no-one's giving me any advice about what to do. It's all up to me, and I'm not sure I like having that responsibility for myself. Does that sound stupid? Does it make me seem mad?'

'Yes.' Jodie seems surprised by my conclusion; I go further. 'But that's a basic qualification for everyone else I know. Why should you be any different?' She subsides into her seat, satisfied with the judgement.

The taxi turns off the motorway and circles a huge roundabout with a tower block at its centre. It slides off the roundabout into the wide canyons of the old part of the city, the tall stone-faced offices built with the proceeds of commerce and capitalism, slavery and subjugation. We go left, down the hill towards the gentrified river, then along the waterfront.

'We'd better go in separately,' I suggest, 'just in case.' I turn my attention to the driver, ask him to drive past the hotel and stop further along the road.

Jodie's still in pensive mood. 'The trouble is, I'm not sure what I can be. What I want to be.'

248

I try to reassure her. 'In a day, a week, things will be back to normal. Don't do anything impulsive. I mean, I don't know what's going to happen today, let alone tomorrow. Take it as it comes, but don't do anything rash. That's the best advice I can give.'

Jodie takes a deep breath, leans across and kisses me gently on the cheek. 'The old me might have accepted your advice,' she says, 'but I'm not sure about the new one. Let me know what happens, will you?'

'I'll keep in touch.' I squeeze her hand, then she's away. I ask the driver to wait for five minutes, then he drops me at the main door. I pay him, hobble towards the main doors, then change my mind. I'm not ready for a confrontation yet. I walk along the side of the hotel, past the car park, heading for the river. I still need to think.

The riverside path is busy. People have decided that this is the day when they'll savour the air, exercise the limbs, find the sights and sounds to store away for the long winter's hibernation. Sometime in January conversations will begin with 'Remember that autumn day when we went for a walk beside the river and . . .' And what? What memories will the day bring them? What memories will it bring me?

I move slowly, trying to persuade myself that even this mild exercise will help ease my pain. My normal slouching, bear-like walk has become a rolling seadog's gait, this inefficient means of progress is the best I can manage to ease me round the corner of the hotel and onto the path parallel to the river. That's when I see Sly. He's in the yard where the waste bins are stored, where the delivery wagons unload, staring at the walls and doors around him. I force my muscles to change my direction; they complain, but I head towards him.

'Any news?' I ask. He doesn't turn to look at me, his eyes are squinting as if he's looking for a hidden entrance. Perhaps there is one, a door not on the plans. That would, I decide, make the job of finding a way in so much easier.

He looks down at the plans folded onto his clipboard. 'Could be.' He shoots a glance in my direction. 'God, you look rough, boss.'

'Really? Strange, that, I feel great.'

'Yeah, like I feel confident we can find out who killed Annabelle.' It's worrying when Sly sounds down; it takes a great deal to topple his tower of optimism. 'There's too much to look at, boss, and not enough of me to go round. I mean, take this as an example. There's a camera up on the wall there, and a floodlight. This area –' he gestures to show he means the whole yard ' – really needs four lights and two cameras, that's what's shown on the plans. But the camera itself has a semi-fisheye lens, so it does show the whole area, and the floodlight is brighter and has a more diffused illumination pattern than the four specified, so a fair amount of the yard is lit. But I won't know until tonight how effective the two are together, how much of the yard can be seen in the dark.'

'Why not . . .'

'And that's not all. Look, there are four doors. One is the entrance to the boiler room – it's a dead-end, no internal door to the hotel, so that doesn't really matter. But the other three are all potential entry points. One is the delivery door to the kitchen, all foodstuffs go through there; the second is the emergency exit – and yes, it's alarmed and I've tested the alarm, it works; third is the staff entrance, keypad operated from the outside, electric release from the inside. They all look secure, but we know there was a breach of security, so any of them could be a point of weakness.' He's as tired as me. 'So could any other door. There might as well be no bloody security system at all.'

'Got your chalk?'

He seems surprised, but produces from one of his pockets a piece of bright yellow waterproof crayon.

'Where's the light-switch?'

He points at a small green box on the wall, covered with

waterproof plastic. 'Ten-minute switch-off during the day, automatic switch-on at dusk. I can't really check that as the sensor's too high up the wall for me to cover it.'

'It doesn't matter. It's too busy a spot not to work. Just switch it on and walk from the middle of the yard out towards each door in turn. If you can see the bulb or its reflection in the mirror, don't do anything. As soon as you can't see them, mark the ground. Do that for a few places between the doors, that'll give you an approximate area of cover. Join up the marks, that's the edge of your lit area, the beginning of your shadow.'

Sly's walking the yard even as I finish talking; I'm jealous of his speed. I watch carefully as he switches on the light, retreats. He glances up at the light, moves, looks up again, moves again, then draws a mark on the ground. He repeats the actions, slowly and economically, walking the diagonals and radii of the yard. Then he steps back to admire his work. 'I could be wrong, boss, but it looks to me as if someone could walk round the perimeter of the yard, in the dark, and not be seen.'

'I don't think you're wrong, Sly. It's a way in.'

'So what do you want me to do now? Try the other entrances and exits in the same way?'

If we had time, or manpower, that would be the best way of proceeding. Work inwards, try all possible entrances, narrow down the possibilities. There are ways into the hotel through fire exits, the main entrance, the terrace bar overlooking the river, the car park. It would be tempting to concentrate on the last of these, but the route from the car park through the hotel to the freezer is long and definitely overlooked by working cameras. So I have to work on possibilities. I have to assume that someone chose the freezer as the final destination for the body (even if I don't yet know the reason). I have to assume that the murderer knew there were weaknesses in the security system, that there was a way round the outside of the yard where they wouldn't be seen carrying a body. Now, if that's all true, and even if that body was in a car in the car park, I'd drive the car round to the yard to make the job of transferring it easier. So the yard is the logical place for entry, and my decision is made easier. Sly's waiting patiently for a response – he can tell by the vacant expression on my face that I'm thinking. 'They got in through the yard, they must have done. So work backwards from the freezer; go from the final resting place outwards. Find the path.'

'OK, boss. But do you really mean "they"?'

I don't. I was using the word in its modern sense, meaning "he or she", but Sly's right. Why restrict myself to one murderer? Two people can carry a body where one would have problems. A third might open doors for them, check that no-one was coming. Why limit myself to two, or even three? All the directors could be involved. Would that thought be paranoia? 'Work on one, or more than one. Any possibility. But work outwards from the freezer, from the kitchen.'

Sly examines his watch. 'I'm not going to be very popular in there. The hotel's full and the kitchen'll be serving Sunday lunches to non-residents as well.'

'Good. Make yourself as obtrusive as possible. Get in their way. Make them impatient. They might be able to tell you something about the security that could help us.'

Sly's already on his way. He heads for the staff entrance, the door's held open by a small piece of wood. 'Can't they tell you the code to get in?' I call across the yard.

'I know it,' he shouts back. 'I didn't wedge it open, it was like that when I got here.' He disappears inside the building, leaving me alone with my thoughts. I turn, head for the yard gates. So much for security. As in so many other places, it's the people inside who help the outsiders get in. I take time to examine the gates themselves. They're nothing special, ferrous metal. I could climb over them (though I couldn't carry a body over them), and there's a significant padlock wedded to one of them. There's a pass gate for pedestrians, again with a padlock fitted. Are both locked at night? Who has a key? I turn back, look at the yard again before leaving. Then I head back into the yard. I can't afford to take anything for granted. Sly said that there was no way into the hotel from the boiler room; was that according to the plans, or had he checked in the room itself? It should take only a few minutes to find out.

The door isn't locked. Even if it had been, the impressive steel plate hides only a two-lever lock, I could get in by breathing heavily on it. I open the door gingerly, feel for the light switch, wait for the flickering tubes to show me the contents. And there's nothing unexpected. Four huge boilers are in a line along the wall to my right. They raise shiny steel exhausts to the ceiling before bending towards the outside wall. Pumps whine, pipes twist and turn around each other as if unwilling to begin their journeys into the hotel. I close the door behind me and the noise intensifies. At the far end of the room there's a brick wall, no sign of a door, but the last of the boilers prevents me seeing everything. I head for the wall.

Each of the boilers is flashing sequences of green and red lights, LEDs indicate temperature and pressure. On the wall to my left four separate indicators show the contents of the four oil tanks which feed the boilers. At least the hotel's heating system is efficient.

The room is built into, shares three walls with the hotel itself. I'm suspicious enough to run my fingers along the brickwork to see if there's a hidden door, but each tap and touch reveals solidity. I can't quite see into the furthest corner as the last boiler is in the way. There's a thin layer of dust on the floor, and I don't want to get my trousers dirty by kneeling down. There's also the problem of getting back up again. Although my muscles don't feel as sore as they did earlier, my lack of sleep is beginning to show; I feel incredibly tired. I tell myself I should be thorough – there might be a hidden exit in that corner, the key to solving the crime.

So, to keep my conscience happy, I lower my knees to the ground, allow my hands to join in the exercise, and peer round and below the last boiler into the corner. The brick wall is as solid as everywhere else in the room.

I stay where I am for a moment. It's surprisingly comfortable, spreading my weight and my aches amongst four limbs rather than two, and it's warm from the heat of the boilers. And I can see something in the dust, a small piece of what looks like grey material. I reach out, hook it towards me with a finger. It's dry to the touch; only when it's close to my head do I realise that it's a desiccated mouse. I try desperately to summon the energy to heave myself to my feet, and that's when I see something else. Disturbed by my dragging the mouse out, it must have lain hidden by dust. It's glinting, metallic. Probably a washer, I tell myself; just leave it there, it's not worth the effort. But since I'm down on the floor, since I don't really want to get up from this comfortable concrete, I decide that I might as well finish the task. I touch the piece of metal, manage to catch it in the pincer of finger and thumb. By now I'm lying stretched out on the floor, the dirt and dust forgotten. The metal isn't the flat disc I'd been expecting, it's fatter, crafted. It reminds me of something I've seen before. I don't have the strength or the will to sit up so I roll over onto my back, try to focus on the band of polished metal. What is it? Why is it familiar? My brain can't cope with such complex open questions. I can feel it shutting down. First my eyes close. Then the slow, smooth diminution of sound tells me that my ears are ceasing to function. I can feel my breathing begin to slow, the need to push air through nose and mouth into lungs isn't really important. I have the luxury of not worrying about anything, the most important thing in the world is to fall asleep. And so I do, not with the sudden rush of hospital anaesthetic, but with a gentle, smiling acknowledgement that life is both wonderful and fragile.

CHAPTER TWENTY

The passage from unconsciousness is swift and unpleasant. I feel a course mouth on my own, the back of my head is being pushed against hard ground. A spasm of pain ripples through my body, my eyes flash open to reveal Sly's head descending towards my own. I begin to cough and he stops, stares at me.

'Oh, thank God. Jesus Christ, boss, what would I have said to Jen! Are you OK? Can you speak?'

I contradict myself by nodding. His hand is around my wrist, feeling for my pulse.

'What happened? Did someone hit you? Who was it?'

This time I shake my head in a vain attempt to stop him asking questions. I need to concentrate on more basic functions like breathing. He seems to take the hint from my silence, but I have to close my eyes under the relentless pressure of his gaze. I can feel his knees pressing against my flank, one hand still at my wrist, the other on my shoulder as if he's protecting me with his presence. I take a deep breath, summon the energy for one short sentence. I open my eyes again. Sly bends his head closer.

'What happened?' It's a whisper, the best I can manage, but it's intelligible.

'You won't believe me,' Sly grins manically. 'The security system, that's what saved you.' He begins to laugh, a mixture of hysteria and relief. 'I was watching, on the monitors. I saw you go into the boiler room. I was doing other things, checking the cameras in the kitchen, but I kept one eye on the yard. You didn't come out. And you didn't come out. I began to get worried. I thought you must have left when I glanced away, but . . . well, I was worried someone might have attacked you. So I came down. I found you lying on the door, picked you up, carried you out.' His laughter stops. 'I couldn't feel you breathing, boss. I couldn't remember what to do. Recovery position, heart massage, ring for help, I just didn't know what to do. I panicked. Then I put you down, I tilted your head back, and . . .'

'No,' I manage to croak, 'please, no. Not the kiss of life.'

'Yeah, 'fraid so. But not with tongues.'

I manage to cough. It hurts my chest, my lungs, but it helps me breathe again. The air tastes good. 'Help me up,' I tell Sly, 'so I can sit.'

He pulls me up, one arm round my shoulders. With the other he feels around the back of my skull, trying to find out where I was hit.

'No-one attacked me.' I uncurl one fist as I talk. 'Look.' I still have the ring in my hand. I hold it out to him.

'You slipped it on your finger and the Nazgul came to get you?'

'It matches Terry's. It belonged to . . . Annabelle. Sly, she was in there.' Even through the hammer and flame of an approaching headache I can see the expression on his face change. 'But why?' he says. 'Why would she go in there?'

My tongue and voice are beginning to behave themselves. 'She didn't . . . go voluntarily, Sly. Someone . . . locked her in. Something wrong with the . . . ventilation, they haven't built it properly.' I can't gather my thoughts properly, can't control my brain. I start again, slowly, gasping the words into sentences. 'No-one hit me, Sly. No-one attacked me. Annabelle was locked . . . in the boiler room. Not in a car. Not a hosepipe on the exhaust. Fumes enough in the boiler room. Carbon monoxide fumes. Not enough ventilation. Someone knew. Sly, someone knew. They put her there . . . to die.'

*

Sly helps me into the hotel. The most convenient place to sit me down is in the entrance lobby where Jodie contrives to fuss about me until Sly points out that she's simply drawing attention to me. So she retreats to her place behind the reception desk and fights back the temptation to call an ambulance, the police, the fire brigade and the coastguard. Inactivity isn't in her dictionary. I send him away to check the levels of carbon monoxide in the boiler room, to find the body of the dead mouse. If the gas levels are high today and I can prove that the desiccated mouse died from CO poisoning, then that's probably enough to suggest that Annabelle Wilder died in that room. The ring will make a good court exhibit, but Police Forensics are bound to be able to find some other evidence of Annabelle's presence.

I can feel my strength – the little strength I had after the previous day's beating – return slowly. The cocktail of paracetamol, ibuprofen and iced water forced into me by Sly and Jodie attacks my headache and manages to keep it fenced in, if not entirely under control; small parties of skirmishers still manage sneak offensives against my eyes or temples.

To a stranger I look almost normal. Jodie has wiped down my jacket and trousers so that I no longer look as if I've been rolling on the floor. I'm breathing more easily. And if someone was to comment on the strange expression crossing my face, the occasional blink and frown of a distracted man, then I'd have a good excuse. Not pain, not worry, but an attempt to put into place all the new facts I have. I must make them fit smoothly with the old; I can't just hammer them into place to fit a pre-existing theory. So although I can place Annabelle in the hotel, in the boiler room, and I'm sure that's where she died, I still have to find out who locked her in there to die. Then I have to figure out why she was moved into the freezer. Of course, motivation also rears its head; that's awkward, too many of the Amalgam directors had a connection with Annabelle. But why would any of them want to kill her? There is a reason, of course. She had information,

information that might have been dangerous. But it would only be dangerous if she threatened to let the wrong people know. Did she have it in her to be a blackmailer?

'Mr Oliphant. I thought we'd got rid of you.' I realise that I've closed my eyes, haven't seen King's approach. He's standing over me, newspaper concertinaed under his arm. 'Unless you managed to find another bed to sleep in?' His voice is sneering; he's certain of himself and his power over me.

'I wasn't sure if I'd be safe in my room.' I can still barely speak, but he steps back. Damaged vocal cords make sarcasm sound like venom.

'The maid said your bed hadn't been slept in. There was no luggage.'

'I was too busy to sleep. Too busy finding out about you and your fellow directors.'

'You had a fruitless night, then,' he snorts. 'Still, you'll be glad to see us go. Just as we're pleased to see the back of you.' He raises the corners of his mouth, a gesture of dismissal that has nothing to do with smiling. 'Six o'clock flight to London. Doubt we'll ever want to come back to this Godforsaken place.'

I whisper, 'Four o'clock.' He must have good hearing to make it out though I put as much effort into it as I can. He turns round, unwilling to believe that I still have the potential to annoy him. 'What did you say?'

I motion him closer; he takes a step forward. I repeat the movement, keep on doing so until he's angled above me, bent at the waist.

'Four o'clock,' I say again, 'in your room. All of you. Be there.'

'You're joking, Mr Oliphant! You really do have the most exquisite sense of humour; there are times when I feel I could almost like you.' He straightens up again. 'Well, perhaps that's going a little too far.' He consults his mental thesaurus. 'Not quite "liking". Tolerating? Yes that's better. I could put

258

up with your company for, let us say, a short period of time. A few minutes. At the most.'

'Four o'clock,' I repeat, whispering doesn't hurt as much as speaking. 'You'll be there. Or else.'

'Or else? Threats now, Mr Oliphant?'

'Yes. I'm sure you want to know who killed Annabelle Wilder. That's when I'll tell you. All of you. Together.'

His laugh is false. He's worried. 'No, Mr Oliphant, not this time. You've had your fun. At four we'll be packing. And if you knew anything of any import you'd have told the police, and *they* haven't been knocking at my door. So let's just say goodbye now. I think it would be best if you left the premises immediately. You make the entrance lobby look so untidy.'

It's time to let him know a little of what I know, but he's already turning to leave. It costs me all my energy to throw myself to my feet, but I do so, grab his shoulder, spin him around. The anger on his face suggests he might just be about to hit me.

'Is there anything the matter?' Jodie's voice interrupts our face-out.

'No, it's alright,' King says, 'Mr Oliphant here is about to leave.'

I bend close to him, even though he shies away. 'I know,' I tell him. 'The same as I knew about Rawlings. I know about Carol Parker. I know about Sanderson and Worrall. I know about the Cooksons. I know about this place and its secrets. And I know about you, King, I know everything. Be there. All of you. Four o'clock.' I let myself fall back into the chair. King stares at me, then turns and strides away.

I motion to Jodie. She hurries round to me. 'Could you help an old man to somewhere a little more quiet? Somewhere an old man can ask a few questions? How about the security control room?'

The security guard doesn't seem too pleased to see me, he's already been interrupted today by Sly's repeated visits

259

and requests for information. He ushers me in the direction of a seat in the corner; I ask Jodie to leave me unsupported for a while so that she can bring the seat beside him. When I'm safely perched there, I tell him I want information; he replies that he's a busy man, that it's more than his job's worth to let himself be distracted again. I tell him he won't have a job unless he helps me, threaten him with King's name; he looks for help to Jodie who simply nods to signify that I can do this. He sighs, shakes his head, makes tutting noises in his throat, but he doesn't try to ring anyone.

My voice is returning; I sound like I've been gargling with smoke. 'OK,' I tell him, 'first of all, what's your name?'

'Huxley. George Huxley.'

'OK, George. My name's Billy. I'm looking into the murder that took place here a year ago, OK? I want you to bring up the kitchen camera images from the night before Annabelle Wilder's body was found, when the last person left, until the moment Terry Wilder opened the fridge door the following morning.'

'They'll be worn out by now.'

'You mean lots of people have been looking at them?'

'Too true. Your mate, the big black bloke. The police. The manager. The boss of the firm who put the security system in.'

'That's Arma-something, yeah?'

'Armaclad.'

'And what's his name, the bloke who's the Armaclad boss?'

'Jules Cooper.'

'That's right. I thought I knew him.' I scribble the words 'Rak – Search: Armaclad, Jules Cooper (owner, MD). Tie-in with Annabelle Wilder? Other info?' I fold it as if I'm going to put it in my pocket, instead hold it out for Jodie. She nods as she leaves.

'Let's go then, George. Saturday night to Sunday morning, one year ago.' At least my speech can be heard clearly now.

Huxley taps his computer keyboard and a menu appears. He enters a date and we wait. After a few seconds a series of small images appears across the screen. 'Different views from different cameras,' he explains. 'This is the one from the kitchen.' He positions the cursor above the image and clicks, the image grows larger. There's a time indicator at the bottom of the screen, he advances it to 22.00. Two figures dance across the screen in fast motion and, as they move, the file name at the top of the screen alters. It looks to me as if the images are stored in five-minute sections.

'Is this how the records are kept?' I ask.

'Digital images,' he replies, as if that tells me everything.

'Yes?' The question demands he explain further.

'We're only looking at a little bit of what's stored. I mean, I can show you it all in real time, but that'll take eight hours. Is that what you want?'

'No. What about the police, did they . . .'

'They copied it all, took it away. I assume they looked at it in real time.'

'And Jules?'

He looks at an exercise book on his desk. 'No, he just checked it here. According to this it was just before you were in here, yesterday evening. Me and Mick Beechey, we keep a record of who's in here and when. It must have been just before you went up onto the roof. Just before you were attacked.'

I'm pleased I asked for Cooper and his company to be investigated, I don't believe in coincidences. 'And which scenes was he looking at?'

'I'm not sure. He knows the system himself, doesn't need me to guide him round.'

'And would there be a record of what he looked at?'

Huxley thinks. He isn't a quick-witted man, so the process takes a while. His face goes blank. Eventually he delivers the answer. 'Yes.'

'So?'

'What?'

'So what part of the record did he check?'

'I don't know. That is, I know it's possible to find out. I'm just not sure how. I'm not much of an expert on computers, you see, not yet. I've been promised some training, but they haven't got round to doing it yet.'

I slide my chair across to his keyboard and look more closely at the screen. It's a standard Windows set-up. 'Is everything recorded automatically?'

'Yes.'

'So you don't have to do anything on that front?'

'No.'

'And when do you check what's been recorded on any particular camera?'

'When someone asks me.'

'OK. So most of the time you just watch the camera images as they come in?'

Huxley points at the monitors hung on the wall above his desk. 'They change at random, but I can choose which ones to watch.' He sniggers. 'A few weeks ago there was a couple in the car park, they were . . . you know. They were doing it. So I did a close-up of them. You want to . . .' He catches a glimpse of my face. 'No, I suppose not.'

I'm talking to myself now, even in my present confused state I get a better response than I would from Huxley. 'When someone opens a recorded image from a stored file, does it store that image as a separate file? What about . . . Huxley, is it possible to do close-ups of stored images?'

'Yes. I can show you how to do that. There isn't as much detail, but you can normally see what's happening.'

Rak doesn't like Microsoft. She says they're so big, they discourage experimentation amongst smaller companies. But at least, if you're familiar with their software, you're familiar with most operating systems. I'm no expert on computers, but I know that, if I've been working on a document, closed it, and want to open it again without going through 'My

Documents' and folders and sub-folders, there's a quick way. Go through 'Start' and 'Documents' and you're shown the most recent files opened. So I do.

At the top of the list is a document named 'Kitchen'. I click on it. The screen goes blank, then dark. At first I think there's something wrong, but then I realise that the time/date indicator has changed to show the night of Annabelle's death, and the clock is ticking in real time. The screen is dark because the room is dark. I try to remember the layout of the room as seen from the camera high up in the corner. The freezer door is over to the left; the entrance into the kitchen is immediately below the camera; and the emergency exit is slightly to the right of centre.

'Is there a light inside the kitchen freezer?'

'A what?'

I try to remain patient. 'When you open the freezer door, is there a light inside? Does it go on automatically?'

'I don't know. How would I know? I don't . . .'

'Well, go and look. Now, please.' There's no movement. I pick up the phone, dial 0 for reception. 'Hello, it's Billy Oliphant here. I've a problem in security, could you get Mr King on the line straight away? Thank you.'

'I'm going,' says Huxley. 'Keep your hair on, I'm going.'

I put the phone down. 'And bring me back a cup of tea,' I call after him, 'milk but no sugar. And two chocolate digestive biscuits.'

Even as I've been talking I've been watching the screen. My eyes seem to be accustoming themselves to the darkness. I'm sure I can make out the sheen of stainless-steel table tops, a faint glimmer from windows high in the wall. But there's nothing else, and the five-minute section soon comes to a close with a message asking me if I want to watch the next sequence. I click no, return to my original starting place and watch the sequence again, but still see nothing. The door is barged open and George Huxley backs into the room.

'Tea, milk, no sugar. Chocolate shortbread was all they had. And yes, there is a light, but it's operated by a switch on the outside of the door.'

'Thanks, George. Now, if you can jut sit down and be quiet, I need to think. In fact you can help. Watch this and tell me if you can see anything.' We watch the sequence again but still see nothing. This is curious. Why would Jules Cooper want to watch a sequence of film where nothing happens? To make sure nothing happens? To alter the record so it looks as if nothing happens?

'Is it possible to alter a file, once it's been recorded?'

'You mean delete a camera record?'

'Or part of it, yes, that's what I mean.'

Huxley is a man of few words. 'No.'

So why open that file? I go back again to the record of recently opened files. I was so keen that I didn't look at any others, but nestling below the top file is another named 'Kitchen'. I open it; its time record shows it was the previous five-minute section to the one I've just been examining. I try to imagine what I'd do if there was a video record – even a dim, barely visible record – of me on a database. In the first place, I wouldn't be sure exactly where it was. Then, when I found it, I might not be sure when my appearance finished. So I'd watch the section I appeared in, *and* the one after. Just to make sure. The one after was the most recent. So the record of Annabelle's body being moved is running on the screen, now. My finger hovers over the mouse button, the cursor positioned to pause the action. 'Watch closely, George,' I say. 'If you see anything move on here, and I mean anything at all, yell out.'

The sequence advances, reaches its close. There's nothing. 'Try altering the contrast,' Huxley suggests, 'you can make it lighter if you want. Easier to see if there's anything happening.'

'How do you do that?'

He moves the mouse and clicks on a drop-down menu.

I'm offered the choice of close-up, brightness and contrast. 'If you were moving a body into that room,' I ask him, 'you wouldn't switch the light on, would you?'

'Not if I didn't want to be seen.'

'So how would you do it?' I'm asking the question of myself. If Jules Cooper's company installed the system below standard, then he'd have known that the camera resolution wasn't up to detecting movement in a semi-darkened room. But to get in, the intruder must have either used the door beneath the camera or the emergency exit, having opened it first from the inside.

'A muffled torch,' Huxley says.

'Pardon?'

'A muffled torch. That's how I'd see. You wrap a piece of material, a woolly hat or something, round a torch. It gives off a dull glow, enough to see by, but the cameras don't pick it up.'

'How do you know that?' It seems a doubtful piece of science to me, not one I understand. I need evidence.

'I've tried it. To find out if a heat sensor works in some of the rooms, you have to go inside and move about. But the sensors also work off visible light, so if you go in with a torch, how do you know if it's you triggering the sensor, or the light? But if you don't have a light, how can you see where you're going? Mr Cooper said a muffled torch would give enough light to see by, but it wouldn't trigger the sensors.'

What Huxley's saying, translated from his layman's terms into something I can easily understand, is that the light sensors are so cheap, they're operating on a very narrow specification. It sounds as if the cameras aren't powerful enough to see a dim light. The question is . . . 'George, are there heat sensors in the kitchen?'

'Don't be silly. They'd go off all the time, wouldn't they! There's too much heat.'

I feel I know what's happening. I move the cursor around

the screen, click maximum contrast, but turn the brightness right down. Then I close up on the area immediately below the camera, where the kitchen entrance is situated. Either the body was brought into the room that way, or the emergency exit was opened from the inside. 'Watch,' I tell Huxley, 'if you see anything, yell.'

We don't have long to wait. He yells and my finger clicks the pause at exactly the same time. The glow is so minute, I'd swear I could pick out the individual pixels on the screen, and they number no more than nine or ten. But there's something there.

'A torch?' I ask.

'A muffled torch,' Huxley answers, triumphantly.

'Can you advance this a frame at a time, or a second at a time?'

'Yes. If you just move out of the way.' He takes control of computer and mouse. We follow the progress of the glow. At times it disappears entirely. Sometimes it reappears where we don't expect it, as a reflection from one of the polished surfaces or kitchen utensils. But its path is directed inexorably towards the emergency exit.

'Shouldn't there be an alarm on that door?' I'm not sure why I expect Huxley to know the answer, he knows little else about the hotel and its security. His muttered 'Yes' comes as a surprise, and I have to ask him to elaborate.

'It should be alarmed as it's a door opening direct to the outside. But it isn't. I know because the kitchen staff used to keep it open during the summer, it was so hot down there.'

Even as we speak we're still watching the screen. There's a rectangle of paler darkness as the door is opened. 'Now,' I say, 'can you keep the contrast high but adjust the brightness, find a level that lets us see what's going on.'

Huxley plays with the controls. The rectangle becomes lighter, but so does the background. When the difference between the two is as great as we can perceive, he runs the video on. And for a brief moment, silhouetted against the night, a figure appears. It's too short, too wide at the shoulder to be human. Unless that human is carrying a heavy load.

'That's the way in,' I say.

'Two people as well,' Huxley points out. 'See, there's still a glow from the torch. One to open the door, one to carry the body.' He's getting carried away now. 'But there's not enough light to see any faces. Shit!' He bends closer to the screen. He adjusts the contrast, the brightness, he zooms in and zooms out, but no more detail is revealed.

'Hold on,' I say, 'Think. Let's use our heads. Whoever opened the door had to get there from somewhere else in the hotel. But the only people in the hotel were upstairs in the penthouse suites. If it was one of them, they'd have to come down the stairs or in the lift and there'd be some video record of them doing that. Do you agree?'

'Seems right. The cameras in the corridors are all working.'

'But Sly's just shown that the perimeter of the outside yard was in darkness. Perhaps there were two murderers. One came in through the other door, the staff door, then along the corridor and into the kitchen. He opened the door for murderer two to carry the body in. Would it work?'

Huxley's already searching for the file showing the video footage from the corridor. He brings it up on the screen and we watch. Again there's a faint rectangle of light showing the door opening, the barely visible glow of the torch. But there's more. This door is in a different position to the emergency exit; the corridor is wide and high, but the camera is, for some reason, quite low down on the wall. Its unusual angle allows us to see something extra, something we only notice because we're looking at a certain place at a certain time with the resolution altered in a certain way. That night, as it is every night, the bridge just down-river from the hotel was floodlit. And that provided enough backlighting to make out, for a brief second as the door closed behind him, the silhouette of a man. Huxley freezes the frame.

'You can't see his face,' he says, 'no details at all. If there was a mirror to reflect . . .'

'Can you print that? As much detail as possible, different degrees of close-up, different contrasts? See what you can do.'

'Why? It won't help you; there's not enough detail.'

'We don't know that for certain, George. I mean, if there was time we could look at the photos in detail; we know the height of the camera and the angle, we could use that to work out the height of the man. Except we don't have time. And even if we did . . . Christ, George, call it clutching at straws, call it pandering to an old man's whims, call it desperation. There might be enough, there just might be enough.' I push myself slowly to my feet, then let my body sink back down. 'But first, would you mind asking Jodie if she'd come and help me? Preferably with a wheelchair.'

CHAPTER TWENTY-ONE

It's three o'clock. One hour to go until the showdown. Jodie wheels me into the dining room, now set for a multitude of afternoon teas for the amateur detectives. I could go to my room, but I'm not sure my key-card will open the door. Anyway, I feel safer in the company of a large crowd; the last time I was tempted into lonely seclusion someone tried to throw me off the top of the car park. Jodie commandeers a table close to the fire. 'Would you like me to get a blanket to cover your legs?' she asks. I hope she's joking. 'You need to keep warm.'

'If you say "someone in your state should take more care of himself," I'll . . .'

'Run your wheelchair over my toes? Come on, Billy, you need someone to look after you. Tea? Biscuits? There's some nice cake and pastries?'

'Jodie, you're beginning to sound like a hotel receptionist.'

She seems affronted. 'There's no need to insult me,' she pouts.

I can see Sly hurrying through the tables towards us; behind him the first cohorts of the grey brigade are surging into the room. He slumps into the seat beside me, crushes a biscuit into his mouth. 'Well, boss,' he splutters, 'they could employ someone to do a full survey of the security system here. It would take weeks, months even, cost a fortune. But I could tell you exactly what it would say. "The system is crap. Tear it out. Start again."'

'That good?'

'Flaws everywhere. Nothing's what it's meant to be, every

item's below specification. Nothing's where it's meant to be, and that includes lights, sensors and locks. What's the firm called that fitted this little lot, "Armaclad"? Their motto should be "Why fit two when one will do?"'

'And ways of getting in?'

'With a little help, virtually anywhere.'

'That's good. But I think we've got our point of entry.' I explain what I've seen on George Huxley's monitors and Sly nods his appreciation while demolishing the biscuits before him.

'But doesn't that mean the people who killed Annabelle were outsiders?' Jodie asks. 'I mean, if somebody came in from the service area and then opened the emergency exit, that means none of the directors were involved. Doesn't it?'

'Not necessarily,' I tell her. 'Their involvement may not have been in carrying the body, but there's still collusion and conspiracy to consider.'

'So what do we do now?' she asks.

'You go back to the desk,' I tell her, 'or people will start asking questions.' Jodie's hands are on her hips; she's getting good at playing the petulant teenager.

'People will start talking about you two,' Sly adds. He's dabbing at the plate with a moistened thumb, picking up biscuit crumbs. Because his attention is elsewhere, he doesn't see Jodie's blush.

'Did you get that message to Rak?' I don't want her to be upset. It's only when her face goes red or she stamps her feet that I remember how young she really is.

'Yes,' she says. I can't be sure if she's sulking or not.

'That's why I need you on reception. You're our eyes and ears. Yes, I know we've got mobiles, but if anything happens, if King or Rawlings or any of the other directors does something, the only way we hear about it is if you tell us. You're helping us, but no-one else knows.'

'Yes,' she says, 'I can see that. But, in comparison to everything else I've been doing this weekend, it is rather boring.

So I suppose I'd better go. We don't want people to start talking about us.' She flounces away, switches on a smile when she sees an occasional familiar face.

'Now what?' It's Sly's turn to demand answers.

'More connections, I hope. Rak's looking up Armaclad and their boss, Jules Cooper. They've managed to get away with sub-standard work. The question is, have they been paid according to the original spec? Has the architect, our friend Mr Worrall, colluded with Armaclad and split the excessive profits they've made? That's serious fraud.'

'Do you think it's getting out of our league, then?'

'Possibly. Do you think we should involve the police?'

'It would be the safe thing to do, boss. The logical thing. After all, we wouldn't want anything nasty to happen. I mean, what resources do we have? You in a wheelchair, a teenager with a detective fixation, and me.' He looks at his watch. 'And I need to be home by six, can't be late for Sunday tea.'

'Which means?'

'You tell the police over my dead body! Hell, boss, they gave up on this months ago, we're almost there in a weekend. Let's go for it. But from now on, I stay with you. Just so you can look after me.'

'And Sunday tea?'

'Oh, alright then. You can come as well.'

We're attacking our cakes when the phone rings and Rak assaults me. 'Thanks for the extra work,' she spits. 'Research and baby-sitting, what more do I need?'

'So you've found something?'

'"Sorry to spoil your weekend, Rak." "I owe you one, Rak" – well, actually you owe me three or four, but we'll let that go for the moment. "Sorry your love life is suffering" – yes, I turned down a pleasant afternoon out because of you, Billy Oliphant.'

There seems little alternative but to say the obvious, 'Sorry.'

'But you aren't! You go on doing the same thing over and

over again, and even when you say sorry, you never mean it. And you hardly even bother saying thank you. I'm getting really pissed off with this.'

Rak loses her temper easily and often. I've grown used to her mercurial nature and can recognise when flares of anger are imminent. These are generally impressive to see, hugely out of proportion to the cause, and rarely last longer than a few moments. If they occur when I'm in the same room as her, I usually shelter behind large items of furniture or surround myself with cushions and soft toys, protection from the missiles she sometimes throws. If – as now – she's on the other end of a phone, I tend to placate and ignore her in equal measures. But there's a tone in her voice I don't recognise, an edge which seems real and threatening. Stuffed teddy bears and soft furnishings would be of little use to me if I was within throwing distance of Rak's strong, though thankfully inaccurate, arms.

'What's the matter?' I ask. 'Whatever I've done to offend you . . .' I stop. There are strange sounds coming down the phone, as if Rak is crying. I've never heard her cry before. 'Rak, I'm sorry. Please don't cry. Rak . . .'

'GOTCHA!' the phone screams at me, 'Billy Oliphant, you fell for that one.' Rak's laughing, loud and hard. I wait for the sound to die down.

'So you did find something?'

'I did, you bet I did. And now you're wondering what it is, aren't you?'

'Yes.' Sometimes she can be very trying.

'Aren't you going to ask me, then? Politely?' She's still breathing heavily; it sounds as if she's on the verge of hysteria. Again.

'Rak. Please tell me what you've discovered.' I know I have to play her game.

'You'll have to be more polite than that.'

'Please. Pretty please. Please doubled and redoubled, please to the power ten, an infinity of pleases. Please tell me

272

what you've found, beautiful Rak, sexy Rak, with a skin so soft and hair . . .'

'Now you're taking the piss.'

'Tell me what you've found or I'll rip your long, over-used, manipulative tongue out of your mouth and stuff it so far up your . . .'

'Stop! Don't go any further, I might like it. OK, I'll tell you. Billy Oliphant, you won't believe how good I am.'

'Of course I won't, because you haven't told me anything I can be bloody well pleased about!'

We wait. Rak waits for me to calm down; I wait for her to gather her information together. We mutter soothing mantras. Then she begins. 'Armaclad has a website. It's a sizeable company, started here in the city fifteen years ago by your man Cooper. Chugged along at a steady, un-impressive rate – I'm paraphrasing here – until two or three years ago then suddenly started expanding, loads of work, loads of new depots. No reason given, but the site does list some of the projects they've been involved in. Mostly large, new-build hotels, some work in existing buildings. Of the ones I checked, half were controlled by Amalgam. There's a link and a half.'

'That's good,' I tell her, 'very good.'

'That's not all, my chubby little William. I looked at the other work, the other half. Four or five different companies, but still in the same field – hotels, leisure complexes, gyms and so on – and all fairly large companies, some based in the UK, some abroad. I checked on their owners. One name came up three times. A holding company called Hermes Investments.' She pauses, triumphant. 'Good, eh?'

I'm tired, my brain will accept only simple information. 'I was beaten up yesterday, Rak, poisoned today. Explain, please.'

'Poisoned? What's all this about being poisoned?'

'I'll tell you later. Your turn first – why is Hermes important?'

'It's a guess, boss, the type *you* usually boast about. "Amalgam" means a mixture of metals, usually silver or gold with mercury. Mercury is the Roman messenger of the gods. Greek equivalent? Hermes. A connection?'

I'll admit it's a connection, but is it a coincidence? It's tenuous, fragile, not something I'd care to use as a weapon in a fight against King. Rak is obviously aware of my silence and she can't resist speaking. 'If you'd found it, you'd say it was wonderful.'

'No, Rak, I wouldn't have been able to find it. You've done well.'

'I've done well but . . . There's a "but" there, isn't there, Billy. A silent "but". Oh well, I tried. I even went so far as to look up "Hermes" in the dictionary. He was more than just the messenger of the gods. He was a god in his own right. The god of commerce and cunning. The god of theft, travellers and rascals. Would any of the Amalgam directors have been able to resist owning a company with that name?'

The answer is yes. Most of them wouldn't care at all, they'd buy an off-the-shelf company with some silly name like 'Twinkledome' or 'Brandenbachman' and they'd keep it because it wasn't worth changing. But not all of them. I remember Kim Bryden telling me about the name "Amalgam", how appropriate it was. And she told me King came up with the idea. I can imagine him setting up another company and choosing a name, the time he'd spend on it. It would have to be just right. He'd think of what he was doing. Hermes, the god of theft and rascals; he'd like that. The word 'rascals' has a roguish, devil-may-care sound to it; it's not like 'criminal' or 'burglar' or even 'villain'. Hermes, the god of commerce and cunning; that would be King's vision of himself. It's a long shot, and I have no proof, but I'm sure Hermes is King's company. But why? He can't need the money, not if he owns that much property. Could it be the thrill of winning, of defeating the system, of not being found out? Perhaps it started with a mistake, an honest error.

274

Perhaps it started when some work was done in one of the hotels, below spec, and it was okayed and paid and King realised he could cheat the system. And then he did it deliberately, small scale, and found it worked. So he did it again, bigger, better, involving more people. And now he's in so deep it's not worth him turning round and wading out, he might as well keep going.

It's all conjecture, the product of a fevered, exhausted mind. But it's a possibility. 'You might just have something there,' I say to Rak, 'well done.'

'"Well done"? For you, Billy, that's praise indeed.' For once Rak isn't being sarcastic, she knows I'm pleased; I find it almost as difficult to offer compliments as I do to express my emotions.

'You've done well. Now if you can keep going, find something else linking Annabelle to Armaclad or Hermes, I'd be eternally grateful. Ring straight away if – no, when – you've got something for me.' I spend five minutes telling Rak what I've discovered, in case there's anything relevant to her search. Then I notice Sly pointing at his watch; it's almost four. I ring off, suddenly nervous.

'What's the plan?' Sly asks. He picks my briefcase off the floor, puts it in my lap and pushes me out of the dining room.

'I don't know yet. Start off with what I know for certain, bring in a little of what I suspect. Then I'll roll out the probable, the likely, the possible, all in that order. After that? The unlikely, finishing with the downright impossible. I still don't know how or why Annabelle was brought here, I don't know why she was killed. But by exploring every piece of information I have, in public, I might just get the lead I need. So keep your eyes open; there'll be some worried people with guilty consciences in that room.'

We trundle into the entrance hall. Huxley's standing at the door to his room; he gives an informal salute as we pass by. Jodie's watching from behind her desk; she smiles, winks, mouths 'good luck'. When the lift door opens I expect to hear stirring music, the type that accompanies cavalry galloping over the hill, the outnumbered hero facing up to his enemy, Luke Skywalker commencing his last torpedo attack on the Death Star guided only by the Force. Instead there's a sanitised synthesiser version of 'Yesterday'.

'That cake and biscuits were good,' Sly says to break the silence.

'The condemned man ate a hearty breakfast.'

CHAPTER TWENTY-ONE

When the lift door opens we find the atrium bathed in light and the door to the roof garden open. There's a warm breeze blowing, tossing the curtains in billowing swathes that any film director would love to capture. Sly pauses the wheel-chair by the door. It's not the first time he's been up here, but his previous visit was purely to check the presence and efficiency of security cameras. This time he can appreciate his surroundings. He looks out of the door, then steps through it. 'Wow, boss, there's a hell of a view out here.' I don't feel inclined to follow him; although the aches in my arms and legs seem to be diminishing, it's only in proportion to the pain in my chest. I don't think I could push myself to my feet, let alone walk. All I want to do is get through the next hour, then collapse.

Sly's voice is appreciative. 'It's a lovely day out here. You can see the bridges, you can see upriver. And the garden's absolutely beautiful. I wish I had a roof lawn.'

'Don't be stupid,' I say to myself, 'you live in a semi.'

He pokes his head back round the door. 'Have you seen this, boss? They've got everything out here, trees, shrubs, the lot. There's even a clock golf course with real grass.'

'I'm sure it's very pleasant, Sly, but we really ought to be getting on.'

'Oh. Yeah, sorry. I'm just not used to . . . It must have cost a fortune! The hotel's not a year old, but some of those plants are huge. And looking after it can't be cheap.'

'Money's no object for some people, Sly. Now if you don't mind?' I gesture towards the door, but he's already ahead of me. There's no need to ring the bell, the door's ajar; they're obviously ready, waiting.

I don't expect a friendly reception from the Amalgam directors. I've spent a weekend trying to prove there's a murderer in their midst, I've bullied their managing director, I'm keeping them from a leisurely flight home (most of them will be calculating the last moment at which they can leave to make sure they catch that plane). In short, I've been a troublesome and unwelcome addition to what ought to have been a pleasant weekend. I'm sure that Kim Bryden will have gone down in their estimation. I can imagine what they're saying about her: 'she wanted us to employ him!'; 'three hundred thousand pounds a year!'; 'needs her head examining!'

My strategy is simple. Let them think I know more than I know. Let them fill in the gaps through what they say and what they do. I rehearse the arguments, the information. There's not enough, but that often happens. I'll have to wing it, to improvise.

Sly pushes me along the hallway and parks me in the middle of the room. They're all there in front of me, gathered round the table. I feel as if they're going to ask me when I last saw my mother. They're smartly dressed, no casual clothes this time. The rule appears to be dark suits – women as well – white shirts and blouses. I'm not the snappiest of dressers, stylish clothes and designer labels mean nothing to me and I don't feel overawed by those who spend a great deal on clothing. But I'm aware that I've spent thirty-six hours in the same clothes, I've been beaten up and gassed in that time, and the little sleep I've stolen was a few hours sitting in a chair. I'm dirty, scruffy, and I don't give a shit.

King rises to his feet. 'Mr Oliphant, have you been hurt? I do hope you're alright.' There's no irony in his voice; it's as if he doesn't know the meaning of the word 'sarcasm'.

'No,' I tell him, 'Every part of my body hurts.'

'What happened?' Carol Parker asks. She seems genuinely concerned.

278

I could tell her. I could mention my suspicions that the person who attacked me was, directly or indirectly, in the employ of her company. But I have no proof, and I'd rather begin the events by stating facts rather than suppositions. 'Someone tried to drop me off a high building. But I always bounce back.'

As humour goes, it's bottom of the lowest league, but it brings a smile to her face. The rest of them try to echo it with various degrees of success; Rawlings manages to twitch the muscles at the corners of his mouth; Heather Cookson begins to laugh aloud until she realises how false she sounds, then brings her tittering to an abrupt halt.

King assumes control again. 'May I, on behalf of the board, offer my sincere sympathy for the condition in which you find yourself, and assure you that, despite the disagreements we recently experienced, any hurt you may have been done was without the knowledge of, and certainly the sanction of, the board.' He pauses for dramatic effect. 'I am so sorry, Mr Oliphant.' Speech finished, he sits down. I expect a round or applause, but none materialises. No-one says anything. It must be my turn.

'May I introduce . . .' I begin, but I have no chance to continue, it's beyond my ability to halt King's relentless interruption.

'Mr Oliphant, we're all aware of the time and energy you've expended – at great personal cost, it appears – in your relentless search to resolve the incident of the "body in the freezer".' He makes it sound as if the investigation has been part of the murder weekend. 'We also know that it would be impossible for us to offer – and probably for you to accept – the employment which was the original reason for you attending the hotel.' He brings the fingertips of right and left hands together, looks directly at me over the bridge of his glasses. 'We appreciate that in the eyes of the law our original meeting might constitute an offer of employment, and that compensation would be due if such a contract were to be terminated. We are also aware that your efforts this weekend could constitute "employment" by the company. We are therefore willing to make you an offer, a generous offer, in lieu of notice of employment and cancellation of contract.'

My brain is working particularly slowly, only now do I realise that he's trying to buy me off. 'And what would that offer be?' I ask.

'Before we talk cash, Mr Oliphant, I think I ought to mention the conditions under which this offer is made. First of all, you must acknowledge, in writing, that you have been working solely for Amalgam. You must deliver your findings to us in a private and confidential written report, and not divulge your findings to any other individual or body, public or private.'

'I take it that includes the police?'

'The agreement you will sign names no individual body. I can assure you, however, that the phrasing is such that you would be permitted to tell no-one. May I continue?'

'Please do.'

'In return, you will receive three years salary in lieu of notice, and a fee – including expenses, disbursements and any other payments – of one hundred thousand pounds. A grand total of one million pounds.'

I hear Sly swear under his breath, the wheelchair moves slightly as his grip on the handles intensifies. The money worries me. It means we're really onto something. King's not expecting refusal, but I'm sure he'll have some back-up plan to deal with me should I be particularly pig-headed. A million pounds. That's a great deal of money.

'I'd have to pay a hell of a lot of tax on that.'

King rubs his hands together in anticipation, as if the money's his. 'I'm sure I could persuade our accountants to assist you with plans to minimise the tax burden. And I do think you would be well advised to replace the future conditional with the future definite tense in your previous sentence.'

That's as near as King will get to a threat, but there's

malice in his voice. Someone told me that, when you're bitten by a cobra, despite the fact that the venom is injected directly into your bloodstream, the first unusual thing you notice is a sweet taste on your tongue. King's like the cobra – his poison's disguised with an overdose of sugar.

'It's tempting,' I say.

'It was designed to be so, Mr Oliphant. You see, we all wish to leave quickly, and negotiation can be so tiring. The sum is beyond negotiation. And it can be delivered to you in bonds, banker's drafts, cash, shares, or any combination you care to choose.' King glances at his watch. 'What do you say, then?'

There's only one possible answer. 'Very well. I agree.'

King tries not to let his relief show, but he's pleased. 'A wise decision, Mr Oliphant, a very wise decision.'

I look around the table; the other directors are glum-faced, none of them returning my gaze. 'I'm not sure your colleagues agree, King. Look at them. Not exactly celebrating, are they? I suspect they feel it's money poorly spent. After all, they don't actually know what they're going to get. They don't know what I've found out about them.'

'They will, Mr Oliphant, they will.'

'Yes, but think how miserable they'll feel if I haven't been able to finger them. All that money for nothing. Except for Rawlings, of course; he already knows he's guilty by association. He already knows that he contributed to Annabelle Wilder's death by his actions.'

Rawlings raises his head. He focuses with difficulty – he's been drinking. 'I have a clear conscience,' he says. The alcohol hasn't affected his speech. Either he hasn't drunk too much or his body is used to his indulgences. King motions to him for silence.

The rod's ready, the bait attached; all I have to do is cast it. 'I think we already know, Rawlings, from the evidence we've seen, that your conscience is dead. Or pickled in booze.'

He rises to his feet. He's a big man; his momentum, if he was allowed to build it, would carry him across the table. He'd hurt me just by landing on top of me. But he doesn't get the chance. Sly's ready – it's the moment he's been waiting for. There's a long slim pocket on the back of the wheelchair; it's meant to be used for a furled umbrella, but a single-hooked crowbar will fit there just as nicely. Sly brings it out, over his head and down onto the table-top in one smooth movement. The noise is shocking. The damage it does is impressive. It doesn't break the table in two, solid mahogany, cross-braced, doesn't split easily. But the wood splinters, the crowbar gouges a deep wound; if the blow was repeated in the same place, the table's back would be broken. All movement halts.

'Sit down, please,' I say politely. They do as they're told. 'Thank you. Oh, forgive me, that's why you all look so shocked. I'm forgetting the rules of politeness and courtesy. I didn't introduce you to my friend. This is Sly.'

Sly bows his head slightly. He rests the crowbar easily across his arms and bids the room, 'Afternoon.'

'I take it,' King glares at me, 'that you were joking when you said you wished to accept our monetary offer.'

'Looks that way, doesn't it. Damn, why do I have to be so incorruptible? Now where were we? Oh yes, we were just reminding ourselves that Rawlings here was, probably still is, a drunk who made false accusations of theft which resulted in a young girl of sixteen being imprisoned. And, when he was proved wrong, he didn't even bother to try apologising. The damage caused? Who can tell? Let's just say that, if the child is the father of the man, then by hurting this girl you probably did immense psychological damage to the woman she became.'

Rawlings stays in his seat but leans towards me; I can feel Sly's hand twitch behind me. 'No matter what you say,' Rawlings growls, 'you won't get me to agree with you. I refuse to accept that what I did had any part in this woman's death.'

282

'You've no regrets, then?'

'Damn it, I've done nothing to have regrets about! Yes, I made a mistake. But to say that I should be held in some way responsible for her death, years later . . . well, it's beyond belief. Sheer stupidity.'

Heather Cookson seems to be talking to herself. 'When I was young, my brother locked me in a room with a spider. I've been terrified of them ever since.'

'I hardly think that's relevant,' Rawlings retorts. 'Or helpful.'

I direct my question to Rawlings. 'So you don't believe that events, traumatic events, effect the way people behave in later years?'

'Certainly not in this case.'

'And you, Mrs Cookson, presumably disagree with Mr Rawlings?'

'Yes,' Heather Cookson says thoughtfully, 'I do. We all react to what happens to us. It's logical, really.' She looks at Rawlings. 'Sorry, Trevor, but I am allowed to have an opinion.'

Heather Cookson remains my target. 'So presumably you'd do everything possible to protect your loved ones – let's say your daughter – from any trauma.'

'Of course. That goes without saying.'

'But would that apply to anyone else? I mean, if anyone else was suffering from something you were doing, you'd stop doing it straightaway, wouldn't you?'

She's beginning to get suspicious. 'What are you getting at?'

'I'm just trying to find out where you stand on certain matters, Mrs Cookson. How much you'd take other people's feelings into consideration. Or whether your own needs, your own desires, come before everything else.'

Her suspicion is becoming annoyance. 'I don't see what it has to do with you or anyone else what my needs and desires are.'

283

'You can't have children, can you?' As I speak I look into her eyes. There's suddenly a terrible sadness there, and an absolute knowledge that I know something she doesn't want anyone else to know. Her husband, sitting beside her, touches her hand. I could stop then. That look, that touch, they combine to give Heather Cookson an appearance of fragility. It happens a lot; private detectives and hardened police officers feel sympathy for their suspects. It usually happens because they've worked hard, come to know the people they're accusing of serious crimes. Few people are entirely evil; every murderer can love his mother. I don't know Heather Cookson well enough to see the good in her, but I do recognise the look on her face. I've seen it before, in the mirror: when Sara, my ex-wife, told me she wanted a divorce; when Kirsty, my daughter, told me she hated me. It's a realisation that you've done some irreparable damage to someone. I have to banish my sympathy, however – Annabelle Wilder has no-one feeling sorry for her; her memory's need is greater.

'That is right,' I repeat, 'you can't have any children.'

'How . . .'

'Never mind how I know. But it's true, isn't it? It's common knowledge that you and your husband were trying for a child without success. You didn't hide it then, why hide it now?'

Gary Cookson decides to defend his wife. 'I don't see what it has to do with you . . .'

'Be quiet, Mr Cookson. Save your breath for answering you own questions.'

Heather Cookson's playing with her gold bracelet, turning it round on her wrist. She still says nothing.

'Very well,' I continue, 'let's say your silence is acceptance of the statement. Of course, it takes two to tango. When a couple tries for a child, it's necessary to test both for infertility. But there's no need to test your husband, is there Heather? He's already proved that he's capable of fathering a child. Your child. Again, it's common knowledge that she was adopted. What isn't so well known is that he's the father.'

'How did you find out?' she sobs. The truth is, of course, that I didn't find out, I only suspected it. But now she's confirmed it.

'What on earth are you trying to prove?' Carol Parker, sitting next to Heather Cookson, is comforting her. Gary Cookson is wondering how much I know. It's time to tell him.

'I'm sorry, some of you aren't aware of the full story here, so please, let me explain. The Cooksons adopted a child, you all know that. What you don't know is that Gary Cookson is the natural father of that child. And the mother? Unfortunately, she's dead. But you know her. Her name was Annabelle Wilder, though on the birth certificate she used her maiden name, Robertson. As for how it all happened . . . well, perhaps you're the best one to explain that, Mr Cookson. Or would you like me . . .'

'I have no intention of saying anything,' Gary Cookson announces.

'For Christ's sake, Gary,' his wife shouts, 'can't you see he knows? He knows everything. Tell them. Tell them how I found out you'd been screwing around. God knows, I relive it every day. Or would you rather I told them?'

Gary Cookson's caught between me and his wife, and he's not sure which is likely to cause him most damage. But he quickly realises that his best chance of spinning his story to his own benefit is to relate it in his own words. 'I'll tell you then,' he blusters, 'but I'm not ashamed. I've done nothing wrong.'

'Like hell you've done nothing wrong!' his wife yells, 'you bastard!'

'Heather, you're just making it worse. Shut up and let me speak.' His wife glares at him, but remains silent. Gary Cookson's eyes wander round the table, greeting everyone except me. Then he begins. 'You all know how desperately Heather and I wanted a child . . .'

'*I* wanted a child, Gary, you didn't care . . .'

'OK, OK! You wanted a child, I . . . I didn't mind. If you became pregnant, great. If not? Yes, I'll admit it, it didn't matter too much to me. But after a while I got the feeling that I wasn't a husband, I wasn't a lover, I was a means of you having children.' He's talking directly to her now; the rest of us aren't important. 'I mattered less than your need for a child. We didn't make love because we felt like it, we made love because it was the right time of the month, or because your temperature suggested you'd just ovulated. There was no spontaneity, sex was planned, even down to . . . yes, even down to you having to lie on your back afterwards with your legs waving in the air!' He's jabbing his finger at her like a sword. 'I felt unwanted. Unloved.'

He pauses to gather the threads of his story around him, to weave them into a garment strong enough to deflect any blows I or his wife might aim at him. When he talks, he's talking to us all, but his face is staring at the table. 'Heather was working a lot, late hours, days and sometimes weeks away from home. I didn't have a job at the time. Good God, I had to make an appointment just to have lunch with her. One day I went to see her at the office and she'd been delayed in a meeting, so I went for a cup of coffee across the road from her office. I got talking to a girl there. No, that's not right, she got talking to me. She said she'd seen me coming out of the building and asked if I worked there. I explained that I didn't, my wife did. She asked me questions; I was honest with my answers. I told her what I've just told you. She was good company, I suppose, because she listened. I didn't ask her any questions about her background, I was too busy talking about myself. She was . . . yes, she was pretty. Not beautiful. She looked damaged. Hurt. Her eyes were wide; she looked as if she wanted to cry.'

He considers how much he ought to say then moves on. 'Then Heather rang me on my mobile, said something had come up so she wouldn't be able to come for lunch. I had time to kill so I told the girl I was going for a walk in the park and asked her if she wanted to come with me. She said yes. We walked, I talked. We fed the ducks. I took her for a row on the lake.'

He stops. It's as if he's reliving the story.

'Go on, then,' his wife prompts, 'tell them the rest.'

'There's not that much to tell. I had to go home. She had to go home as well, get changed, get to work.'

'Where did she work?' The interruption is mine – a thought has occurred.

'Where did she . . . She did say. The office block near where I met her; she was a cleaner or something. But it didn't matter. It started to rain so I flagged down a taxi, said I'd take her home. When we got there, some horrible flats, she said thank you. I smiled at her. We kissed, not passionately, not a long kiss, just a touch of lips. But she smiled back and asked if I'd like to come in. And I said yes.'

'Ah, how touching.' Heather Cookson's fangs are dripping poison.

'The staircase stank of piss. Her room was tiny, a bedsit. Shared toilet on the next floor down. Damp on the walls. The railway ran at the back of the place, it was noisy, there were people shouting and babies crying. When we got in she closed the door and smiled again. She began to undress, not a striptease, she just took her clothes off; she seemed awkward. I can remember her saying, "Will I do?" And then we had sex.'

'But that was just the start, wasn't it, dear. Tell them what else you did for your little nymphet.'

Gary Cookson's voice is steady – he's involved in his story now, his wife's barbed interruptions don't affect him. 'I felt sorry for her. We arranged to meet again. And again. She never asked for anything. Then, about two weeks later, she said we'd have to stop seeing each other. She'd fallen behind with her rent and was being evicted; she was going to go back to stay with her mother, somewhere in the Midlands. I realised I didn't want her to go. So I found her a flat, said I'd pay for it. Heather was earning a lot then, huge bonuses; we had more money than we knew what to do with.'

'You quickly found a way of dealing with that, didn't you, my love.'

Gary Cookson nods, not in agreement with his wife, more as if confirming that his story's on course. 'She refused at first, said she didn't want to cause me any trouble. But I insisted and she eventually agreed. I said she could pay me back sometime. I used to go round to see her every day. When Heather was away, I'd spend the night with her. She never came back to our house. Then one day she told me she was pregnant.'

A few moments before they'd been touching hands; now Heather Cookson's hurling insults. 'That would have cheered you up, lover boy. I can just see the look on your face. But don't let me stop you; go on, tell them what you did.'

'She said she'd always been irregular, she was too far gone to have an abortion. I offered to marry her. Said I'd tell Heather, ask for a divorce. She said no, she didn't want to break us up . . .'

'And if you believe that, you'll believe anything!' Heather Cookson's on her feet, her finger's a sword now, a rapier, she's attacking her husband with it. It points, it thrusts without making contact, and he retreats before her. 'He didn't give a damn about her. Divorce me? How the hell would he live? He's unemployable, he's a parasite, he lives off me. And look at him, look at the way he dresses, look at his rings, his watch, his jewellery; he's not exactly low maintenance.'

That's enough for Gary Cookson. It's his turn to rise to his feet, his turn to shout. 'Heather, you stupid bitch, can't you keep your bloody mouth shut! Can't you see, this is just what he wants to hear!'

I take it that I'm the vague, indeterminate third person pronoun he's referring to. And, of course, Gary Cookson's right, this is exactly what I do want to hear. But I can't let them know that. I shake my head, adopt a severe tone. 'If your wife hadn't interrupted you, Cookson, I would have done. I know about you, Cookson, I know about you. Do you want me to continue with this rather sorry story? Or will you tell the truth?'

'Of course he won't tell the truth,' Heather Cookson interrupts, 'he can't tell the truth, not if it puts him in a bad light.' Carol Parker pulls her back to her seat but can't stop her talking. 'I'll tell you all what happened. While I was working hard to support him, and yes, all the time desperately wanting a baby, he was screwing every tart he could find. This Annabelle wasn't the first one and she wasn't the only one. But then, when she got caught, he dropped her. So what did she do? She came to see me. Not to say she was sorry, not even to plead for help. No, she wanted to do a deal.'

I'm scribbling notes as she talks. My pen hovers over the page, waiting for her to start again, but she doesn't, not straightaway. I look at her, head low, as if she's gathering her thoughts, perhaps she's preparing for the big lie. I'll have to judge her words as they come.

'She stopped me on the way out of the office one lunchtime, said she was pregnant and Gary was the father.' Her voice is calm now, controlled. 'I was shocked, of course, I didn't know whether to believe her or not. Then she started telling me about Gary, about me. She knew how much I wanted a baby, Gary had told her everything. I was amazed how much she did know. She said she hadn't been sleeping with anyone else and was willing to take a DNA test to prove the child was Gary's. She was businesslike, matter-of-fact. She said she wanted money while she was pregnant and a lump sum when the baby was born. In return she'd give up the baby.' At the mention of the word 'baby' a smile creases her face. 'I told the office I wouldn't be back until the next morning. I took the girl home, we confronted Gary, he confessed. And then we sat down and talked about what we were going to do. It was quite easy, really. They didn't love each other, though they did have a love of money in common. Gary wanted to stay with me – he knew when he was on to a good thing. I wanted a baby. And it would be far easier to arrange it because Gary was the natural father. The downside, of course, was that I needed him. He was the glue holding the whole thing together. I could put up with that.

'Next day I had the documents drawn up, signed. Money was handed over. Part of the agreement was that Annabelle could stay in the flat. She had to have regular blood tests, she had to keep off the dope and the booze and the cigarettes. I was sent a doctor's report every week. Everything was going well.'

I pick up on the last sentence, get my point in quickly. 'But it didn't keep on going well, did it?'

She shakes her head. 'She disappeared just before the baby was due. That's where having money comes in handy – I hired a team of detectives. She was used to luxury by then, she wouldn't consider going through childbirth alone. So they found her in a private hospital in Manchester, a day after she'd given birth. We took all the paperwork with us, twenty thousand pounds in cash – that was the final payment due – and we took the baby away. She pleaded with us not to, said she'd changed her mind, we could keep the cash, she wanted her baby. But of course, it wasn't her baby. It was mine.'

The room is silent. I have a picture in my mind of the scene in the hospital room, of Annabelle screaming to be allowed to keep her child, of it being taken away forcibly. There will have been a bailiff there, someone from social services perhaps, a police officer. Would there have been a nurse as well, a doctor, all crowded into a small room with the Cooksons and Annabelle? The documentation will have been perfect, precise. There would have been no way back for Annabelle. The baby was no longer hers.

'Is there anything else you have to say?'

'No. Should there be?'

'Well, I've just listened to you describing how you took a baby away from her mother. I was wondering if you felt any remorse. If you had any regrets. If, perhaps, you felt that Annabelle Wilder reappearing in your lives might be a worry, a concern.'

'You forget, Mr Oliphant, we weren't here on the night Annabelle Wilder was killed.'

'No, Mrs Wilder, I hadn't forgotten. Just as I haven't forgotten you saying earlier, "Money comes in handy". It lets you buy babies. It lets you hire detectives. It could let you hire other, more unsavoury characters, to do anything you wanted, without you being anywhere near.'

She's angry with me now, 'Are you suggesting that . . .'

'I'm suggesting nothing, Mrs Cookson. I'm actually being very polite.' I direct my attention to everyone ranged around the table. 'You see, I'm not even reminding you that you all denied any connection with Annabelle Wilder. Yesterday you didn't know her. Today? You, Rawlings, had her locked up for a theft she didn't commit. You, Mr and Mrs Cookson, contrived to take her baby away from her without her ultimate consent. None of you say you feel guilty in any way, yet the re-appearance of this young lady could be very embarrassing for you. That leads me to ask some simple questions, questions I can't answer, but I'd like you to think about them. Mr and Mrs Cookson, does your daughter know she was adopted? Have you told her what you've just told me about her removal from her natural mother? And you, Rawlings, would you care for the details of your drunken behaviour years ago to be made public? How would this affect your standing amongst your friends, neighbours, colleagues in the business community? Would the police consider your potential vexation, your inevitable distress, to be sufficient motivation for murder?'

The murmur of dissent becomes a mutinous rumble – it's one thing to force them to confess to their bad behaviour in the past, quite another to accuse them of murder. King hushes them, his smooth hands promise to speak on their behalf.

291

'Forgive me, Mr Oliphant,' he says politely, 'I may not be as well versed with criminal law as you are, but I feel confident in saying that Trevor, Gary and Heather have committed no crime. They may have, individually, been foolish or impetuous, they may have behaved childishly or recklessly, yet – I repeat – they have committed no crime.'

'And yet, ladies and gentlemen, a crime has been committed. Simply because none of you has yet admitted it, simply because I haven't yet specifically mentioned it, doesn't mean that I don't know that one of you, perhaps more, was directly involved in Annabelle Wilder's death.'

'So tell us.' Carol Parker's statement is brief, to the point. It's what I would have said if I'd been in their place. 'Don't keep us in suspense. If you know who killed the girl, tell us.'

'I have a slight problem there,' I tell her. 'You all seem to believe that what I'm doing here is simply investigating Annabelle Wilder's death. That's not the case. Yes, I'm keen to find out how she died. But the more I find out, the more I believe that you've all, in some way, affected her life for the worse. And you may therefore have contributed, directly or indirectly, to her death. And this is despite you all dissociating yourself from any connection with her whatsoever. In a court of law, a counsel may justifiably try to convince a jury that witnesses or defendants are disreputable, shouldn't be trusted, because they're liars. Putting it frankly, I've already demonstrated that with three of you. And I can do so with the rest of you as well.'

Glances are exchanged. There are looks of disbelief, suspicion, what could be fear, nervousness. There's even relief from those who have already been accused and dealt with. But none of them try to get up, none try to leave. I've heard about rabbits, mesmerised by the sight of a weasel twisting and spiralling in front of them, unable to flee. The weasel dances closer and closer until, sure of his prey, he pounces. Have I become the weasel? The directors, the rabbits? If so, who will be the prey? Whose turn will it be next? They're waiting for me.

'Ms Parker, have you ever been to Paris?'

'Many times, Mr Oliphant. It's one of my favourite cities. And my job with Amalgam means I have to travel a great deal, particularly in Europe. I try to visit Paris whenever I can, usually four or five times a year.'

'And do you normally travel alone?'

'Most of the time, yes. Sometimes I take a friend or colleague, particularly if I'm actually on holiday.'

'And in which of those categories was Abigail Rafferty? Do you remember her?'

Carol Parker is quick. 'Oh yes, I remember Abby. I definitely remember Abby.'

'So would you care to tell us about her?'

She looks puzzled. 'Why?'

'So the rest of us can also know about her.'

She looks at King; he shrugs. Rawlings is beyond making a comment, head in hands; I'm not even sure he's listening. Liam Sanderson, silent until now, is about to speak.

'We already know about her,' he says. 'We should do, after what she did to us.'

I don't know what they're talking about. How did they know about her? What did they know about her? I have to mark time. I return to Carol. 'And that time in Paris, what, ten years ago? She was with you. Was that a private trip, a holiday? Was it work? And what about the photographs you had taken?'

This time her smile is a grin. 'Those photographs? I see. And Abby was really Annabelle? The same girl who had Gary's child, the same girl Trevor had the police arrest? My my, she got around.'

I have nothing to add. I content myself with nodding sagely.

'You don't know me very well, Mr Oliphant. If you did, you wouldn't have wasted your time chasing for information on this little episode. Abby was . . . Just a minute. Abby Rafferty? Annabelle, what was her real name, Robertson? Yes, I see now, she always used the same initials. But why come to work for us at all, if she really hated Trevor that much? Unless she was planning revenge.'

I hope I can hide the relief I'm feeling. She worked for Amalgam; Annabelle worked for Amalgam! So there's a direct connection with everyone in the room now.

'Just a second,' King says, 'are you saying that this girl Annabelle Wilder actually worked for us? In London? At our offices?'

Rawlings growls an excuse. 'I didn't recognise her.'

'She was my personal secretary for a while,' Sanderson explains, 'before that she was a pool secretary. But I wouldn't have known she was the same girl in the photographs the police showed me. She wore glasses sometimes, and quite a lot of make-up. Her hair was a different colour as well.' He thinks to himself. 'She was quite good at her job, if I remember correctly.'

'I needed a PA,' Carol explains, 'I'd seen her around, liked the look of her.'

'Wanted to get into her pants, more like,' Sanderson complains. 'You offered her the job before you even mentioned it to me. Took me ages to find anyone good enough to replace her. She was good, wasn't she.'

'Definitely. Quite a good PA as well.' She grins again, Cheshire cat wide, and Sanderson leers back at her.

'Oh,' King says, '*that* young girl. The one on the wall. Yes, I do remember her after all. Not that I had that much to do with her. Pretty little thing, certainly in her photograph.'

This time I can't avoid looking puzzled. Carol Parker quickly puts me out of my misery. 'Abby, Annabelle, whatever her name was, came to France with me. She was my PA at the time, but I'd just begun to sleep with her as well. This isn't news to my colleagues; they're aware of my bisexuality; I've never tried to hide it. Did you find a copy of the photographs of her? They're good, aren't they. I was really pleased with them when they came out. My colleagues are also aware of the photographs, as is everyone who visits my office. I have some of them on display, Mr Oliphant, together with some the photographer took of me. I must say, however, that she took to the camera far better than I did. I remember picking the prints up; I was quite jealous. I'd tried so hard to look sexy and knowing, but I looked as if I was acting. She looked . . . perfect.'

'So what happened to her? When you got back from the holiday?'

Carol sucks her bottom lip into her mouth, then releases it. Her face shrugs, eyebrows rise into her forehead. 'I have a very low boredom threshold,' she says. 'I find it difficult, almost impossible, to sustain a sexual relationship with anyone for more than a few months. I really do hate it when the excitement of a new lover is gradually replaced by the *tristesse* of repetition, of knowing what your partner's going to do, when he or she is going to do it. I always explain, right from the start, what I'm like. Isn't that right, Liam?'

The question was pointed, directed at Sanderson but for my benefit. Sanderson's knowing 'That's right, Carol,' confirms to me what the rest of them already know, that the two of them were, at some time, lovers.

'I did the same with Abby, told her I'd end up not wanting her. I usually remain on good terms with my ex-lovers, but Abby was an exception. She accused me of introducing her to the perversities of lesbianism. I told her she seemed to enjoy them at the time we were practising them. When I put the photographs on my wall everyone admired them except her. She ripped them down, broke all the glass. I quickly realised I couldn't work with her.'

'So you fired her?'

'Good grief, no! We offered her alternative work in the office, but she refused. We tried to find her a job with one of our subsidiaries, but she refused that as well. In the end she just disappeared. Didn't come in to work, didn't reply to our letters. I went round to her flat but there was no answer. We got in touch with her landlord but he didn't have a forwarding address. We paid her what was due, and a bonus, I seem to remember, at the end of the financial year. We did everything we could, Mr Oliphant.'

'And looking back, thinking about what she was like, was she in any way disturbed? Distracted?'

Carol Parker does take time to think, but eventually shakes her head. 'Who isn't, in some way, a little strange. She had her strange habits, but nothing to make me think she was unusual. In the light of what happened before with Rawlings, and what happened afterwards with Heather and Gary, I suppose she was, well, a bit fragile. She was always asking me if I thought she was good looking when it was obvious that she was. She needed reassurance.'

'So you ending your relationship with her would have damaged her self-confidence?'

Again she takes time to think. 'Yes, I suppose it would have done. I didn't think of it that way. I assumed, because I told her at the beginning that I wasn't any good with relationships, that she'd be ready for it to end. I mean, it was obvious she didn't cope. But by the time I realised that, it was too late.'

King's looking at his watch. It must be time to go, time to catch the plane south, time to leave this all behind. But I haven't finished yet. Nor has Carol Parker.

'I believe that I'm the person I am because of everything that has happened to me in the past. So that has to be the case for everyone else as well, including Abby. If I hurt her in some way, then that's something I have to cope with. I don't actually believe that I contributed to her death, but if I did . . . Well, I suppose you'll be able to tell me more about that.'

I can't admit that, at the moment, I can't tell her a great deal more than she already knows. And my supposition that there was some evil intent on the part of those who knew Annabelle has been, if not destroyed, then at least weakened by Carol Parker's admissions. I can see further difficulties as well. The Annabelle I know, the one described by Terry, by Charles and Emily Robertson, isn't the same woman who tried to sell her baby. The question I'm asking myself is, how much did her trials affect her mind. She was prone to acute depression. After her affair with Carol Parker, did she deliberately set out to ensnare Gary Cookson? She must have recognised Rawlings in the time she spent working for Amalgam, even if she'd changed enough for him not to recognise her. Why didn't she say anything?

More and more it's coming down to the state of Annabelle's mind. It's as if she's been a stalker, but her victim wasn't an individual, it was a company. So how does that alter the way I have to approach the next item on the agenda? This is the most difficult. Even if Carol Parker has acknowledged that she may have been at fault in the way she treated Annabelle, King was right when he said that his colleagues had committed no criminal act, even if they did lack humanity. But I'm about to suggest that someone in the firm has committed fraud. That's a criminal offence, and it may have been carried out on a huge scale. Then there's the matter of the cannabis plants. Yet my accusations will be based on slim evidence gathered on behalf of a dead woman who may have been mentally ill. I need to be right. And at that crucial moment, just as I'm preparing to come to the central point of my case, my mobile rings. I move out into the corridor and answer it. Rak sounds worried.

'Good and bad news, Billy.'

'Go on then, tell me both.'

'Good first. Armaclad aren't that hot as a security company, especially not on the high-tec stuff. Their office does their own computer maintenance, updates and so on, at weekends, so their system's left live. Their email and website have a direct live link into that system, and I managed to find my way in. They have various levels of passwords; it's almost impossible to alter any information or to access current information. But I could read some of their purchase ledger from last year. They made regular payments to a company called A R Holdings. A R? Familiar initials? I checked the payment information, credit transfer. Terry was helping me and he thinks he recognised the account number. It was Annabelle's account. Total amount, thirty thousand pounds.'

'Christ! Any idea why the payments were made?'

'It was analysed into sundry payments. But we know she didn't do any real work for him; she didn't even live up here then. So what could it be? Services rendered? Information? I'd be guessing.'

'OK. And the bad news?'

'Terry's gone. He said he was going to sort this out once and for all. I couldn't stop him. I think he's on his way down there.'

'I'll deal with it when it happens. Thanks.' I disconnect, come quickly back into the room. How does this fit in with what I already know? Does it help me? At the moment I feel it does nothing but confuse me. King is suffering no such anxieties; he's focused on leaving. He gathers his papers together, stacks them neatly, peers at me.

'I'm sorry, Mr Oliphant, but you've run out of time. We've been most patient with you, but we must leave now if we're going to catch the plane back to London. Your investigations have been interesting, but they've unearthed no criminal activity and no evidence that would lead to any of us being accused of Annabelle Wilder's murder. Now if you'll call off your friend, we must go.'

He's making a very good job of being assertive. If I was faced with Sly holding a crowbar, I don't know if I'd be able to summon the same bravado King is demonstrating. Perhaps he believes right is on his side. The rest of the directors are taking their lead from their boss, they too are rising to their feet, though they're watching Sly carefully.

'I think you'd better cancel your flight,' I say, not loudly, not overbearingly, but with as much authority as I can muster. They all pause, except for King. 'Now why should that be?' he asks politely. 'Why would we possibly want to do that?'

'Because I haven't finished yet. And those of you who are innocent might want to find out which of you was involved in Annabelle Wilder's murder.'

'And if we don't want to stay?' This time it's Sanderson asking the question.

'Then I'll speak to those remaining.'

'And you won't try to stop us?' King's seeking reassurance. 'No.'

Again, no-one moves. Glances are exchanged. Throats are cleared. I've implied that the innocent will want to remain, and none of them is willing to make the first move towards leaving. They're sheep.

'I think I'll stay,' Gary Cookson announces. This is help from an unexpected quarter.

'Why on earth would you want to do that?' his wife asks, clearly surprised.

'Because I know I'm innocent. And I'll be honest, I've been put through the mill, I want to see others suffering. But most of all because, as a group of people, you're a bunch of self-centred, sanctimonious pricks. All that crap, Carol, "I'm so sorry if anything I did hurt poor ickle Annabelle," God, it made me puke. You were only after one thing, you got it, you threw her away. You're as bad as the rest of them.'

He sits down again. Heather Cookson lowers herself into the seat beside him. 'You've got balls after all, Gary.' She looks up at me. 'I'll stay as well. That's an audience of two. What about the rest of you? Have you got the nerve to stay?'

Carol Parker joins them. 'I've got nothing to hide. And there's always the chance that Gary's true colours might be revealed again. Yellow, that is.'

Rawlings sits down without saying anything, pulls his wife into the seat beside him. Sanderson, a little more reluctantly, subsides into his seat; Worrall, silent as ever, joins him, but whispers in his ear. King and his wife are the only ones left standing. He looks at his watch. 'We'd probably be too late now. Very well, we'll stay for the final adventure. But can I suggest a break for the toilet and something to drink. And I'd like to ring my housekeeper in London to tell her we'll be back late. Ten minutes?'

I nod. Ten minutes. The way I feel at the moment I may not last that long.

CHAPTER TWENTY-TWO

Sly wheels me into a corner, finds a glass of water to wash my next batch of painkillers down me. 'You look terrible,' he says.

'Good, I feel terrible. I'd be really disappointed if I felt this bad but looked fit and healthy. Would you mind turning me round so I can see what's happening?'

King's gone out, presumably into his bedroom, to make his telephone call. The Cooksons are talking to each other, but their arms are crossed over their chests, they aren't looking at each other's eyes, it's clear that they haven't made up yet. The others have gone out onto the roof to stretch their legs.

'Anything you want me to watch out for?' Sly asks.

'Terry's escaped Rak's clutches, so he's probably heading down here. He might burst in, he might try to hurt someone. If he does, restrain him. He's no fighter; just pick him up and stuff him in your pocket.'

'Will do. And what about Sanderson and Worrall? How do you think they'll react?'

'God knows. I'm almost past caring, Sly. I just want to get this finished and go home.'

Sly's worried about me. He rests his hand, hard and cool, on my forehead. His fingers find the pulse in my neck. He squats in front of me, looks into my eyes. 'You ought to see a doctor, boss. In a hospital. Now. And if I was the friend I think I am, I should be carrying you out of here, even if you yell and scream and kick and bite.'

'I wouldn't have the strength to do that, Sly. And it's

301

because you're an even better friend than you think you are that you're staying here with me. Thank you.'

He pretends to punch me on the chest. 'Aw shucks, I bet you say that to all the handsome black guys carrying crow-bars.' He pushes me back across the room. On the way I motion him to stop beside one of the windows. I twitch aside the net curtains. It's getting dark, the sun's setting through a canopy of tree-shaped clouds touched, fittingly, with autumnal reds and yellows and golds. The roof garden lights are on, delicate blooms of colour grow on lawn, shrub and flower bed. Three silhouettes are strolling back towards the doors. There's a glow from Carol Parker's cigarette, a faint double-edged reflection from Worrall's diamond earrings, Sanderson's knife-edged nose in sudden relief against the pale blue western sky. And then it hits me. Evidence. 'Sly,' I say, 'back to the table.' When we get there I shuffle through the clumsily filed photographs, the sheets of scribbled notes, until I find what I want.

'I think we're ready to start,' King interrupts my thoughts. 'I've booked us all seats on the late train to London; it leaves just after ten. We *will* have finished by then, I take it.'

He's ridiculously polite. He's hiding something. Just like me. I take as deep a breath as I can, my lungs feel shallow, their muscles wasted. 'I'd hate you to have to stay a moment longer than is absolutely necessary. Are you sitting comfort-ably? Then I'll begin. I've already had initial discussions with three of you, so the fickle finger of fate moves on to . . . you, Mr Sanderson. I take it you now admit that you knew Annabelle Wilder?'

'I think that's obvious. Except that I didn't know her by that name.'

'And you didn't recognise the photograph the police showed you?'

'No, and nor did anyone else. It's very difficult comparing the face of a dead body with someone who was young, who's changed with the passage of years, who had a different hairstyle and colour when I last saw her.' He's sitting with his hands flat on the table, as if he's decided that's a pose which radiates truth and sanctity.

'Thank you. And did you meet Annabelle at any time since she left Amalgam?'

'Not knowingly.'

'Could you explain that term? It sounds as if you're not quite certain.'

'I mean exactly what I said. If I met her, it was without knowing that it was her. She seems to have changed her name, her appearance, her identity, with great frequency. She also seems to have had a fixation with the company. So she may have talked to me in some guise where I didn't recognise her. But to my knowledge, I haven't seen her since she worked for Carol.'

'Thank you for clarifying that matter. I'd like to move on, so I suppose this question is aimed at both you and Mr Worrall. Why do you have a significant amount of cannabis stored at your home?' I'm watching Worrall, but the reply comes immediately from Sanderson.

'I assume you're guessing this, but I'll be honest with you anyway. You could pose the same question to anyone under forty and, if they were being honest, half of them would answer the same way. Yes, I have cannabis at home. But I'd hardly call it significant, Mr Oliphant. After all, doesn't everyone indulge a little these days?' His face hasn't changed. If I didn't know anything to the contrary I'd swear he was telling the truth. But then . . . I decide to change tack.

'Are you a keen gardener, Mr Sanderson?'

This time he does look at Worrall. 'I don't see what it has to do with anything, but no, as a matter of fact, I hate it.'

'Liam,' Worrall says, 'I think you'd better not say anything else.' It's the first time he's spoken during the session; it might even be the first time I've heard him say anything at all. His voice is deeper than I thought it would be.

'It's alright, Ben, there's no problem.'

'Yes there is, Liam. You've heard the way he's found things out. He knows lots of things; he just wants us to incriminate ourselves.'

'Ben, you're being silly, It's alright, we've nothing to hide.'

I manage to interject my next question. 'Do you have a large garden?'

Sanderson seems pleased at the ease with which he can answer my questions. Worrall puts his head in his hands as his partner begins to speak. 'No, our garden isn't big really. We have a first-floor flat with a balcony, steps lead down to the garden. There's a greenhouse. Ben tries to grow tomatoes and pot plants in there, but he doesn't have much success. The lawn, such as it is, is all yellow moss. There's a high wall, so the garden gets very little sunlight. I sometimes sit on the balcony in summer, but I rarely go down into the garden.' He sniffs ostentatiously. 'I get hay fever, sinusitis, I'm allergic to pollen. You've probably seen me with my inhaler some time during the weekend, and that's in autumn.'

I can see why Worrall didn't want his partner to go on. If Liam Sanderson is telling the truth – and I've no reason to doubt him – then by freeing himself of suspicion, he's incriminating Worrall. The questions are asking themselves now – I just have to make sure they come out of my mouth in the right order. 'Did you ever have a cannabis plant in the house?'

'Yes. It was a present; Ben grew it from a seed; he used to . . .'

'One seed? Someone gave him one seed as a present?'

'I think so. There might have been more, two or three in the same pot, but Ben said that was always the best way of growing things. Put three seeds in a pot, see which one is the strongest, let that one grow and pull the other shoots out.' He looks at Worrall. 'That's right, isn't it Ben?' Like me, he can only see the top of Worrall's head. He gets no response. 'Ben, are you okay?'

'He's suffering premonitions,' I tell Sanderson. 'Everything he sees has the shadows of bars in front of it. Did you ever move the plant out of the house?'

'What the hell are you on about? Ben, what's the matter, why . . .'

'Mr Sanderson!' I have to shout to assert my authority. Sly takes a step forward, Sanderson's eyes widen. 'I asked a question! Now answer it. The cannabis plant, you moved it outside, didn't you. Put it on the balcony. Because it affected your hay fever.'

'I . . . I don't remember. In fact, I'm not even sure there was a plant. I might have been mistaken; it could have been something else. Yes, that's it, there was a plant, not a cannabis plant, and I had to . . .'

I flick the photograph of the flat across the table to him. Even that small motion hurts my arm. He picks it up.

'Don't piss me about, Sanderson, you'll only make it worse for yourself and for Worrall. Look at the photograph. I have the negative.' I've always believed that lies in the pursuit of justice are forgivable, but I've told so many in my time that absolution may not be forthcoming; thank God I'm not religious. 'It's your flat, your balcony, your cannabis plant. It also allowed us to trace the property. A colleague in London managed to gain entry. Your greenhouse has been used to grow cannabis plants. Your potting shed has been used to store the product. Unfortunately, there's rather more there than can be accounted for by the small-scale production your greenhouse would allow. It's measured, packaged, labelled, ready for sale. You seem to have a substantial amount of hashish, skunk, weed, white widow and super skunk. Now, in my book, this classifies you or Worrall, or perhaps both of you, as mainstream dealers. My colleague is, even now, informing the police of his findings. There are witnesses all around you. Please think before you answer the next question. Are you now, or have you ever been, involved in the production or sale of any marijuana product?'

He doesn't even have the opportunity to reply.

'Of course he wasn't, never has been,' Worrall says, 'but you already know that. You know everything.'

'I'm sure he doesn't,' King's smooth voice glides easily into the pause, 'though I'm also sure Mr Oliphant is very perceptive.' He turns his attention to me. 'If what you say is true, Mr Oliphant, then Ben here is in trouble. But it is possible for evidence to be planted, and none of us are sure of the bona fides of your London colleague.' He looks back at Worrall. 'You are, however, a young man who has always been a friend of the company, and the company will not deny you in your hour of need. We'll do everything we can to assist you, Ben. Perhaps we'd better summon a lawyer. I'd advise you to say nothing until one arrives.'

'Yes,' I say to Worrall, 'say nothing. Demonstrate your innocence. Give yourself time to think of an excuse. Perhaps share the blame a little. How could Liam Sanderson not have known you were dealing? After all, you were supplying direct from the flat, even if it was to smaller dealers. And we know who they are as well.' I bring the copy of his address book from my folder, don't bother handing it to him. Instead I begin to read the names out.

'Stop!' Worrall shouts, and Sly twitches by my side. His nervousness is unnecessary, Worrall isn't the type to run or fight. His words are apologetic, aimed at King and Sanderson. 'I might as well tell him, because I'm not telling him anything he doesn't know. In fact, it's not telling, it's confirming. Yes, I've been dealing. It's been going on for quite a while now; I didn't mean to do it. It just started. Liam was right when he said someone gave me seeds, but it was more than that . . .'

'I'm not interested in that much detail, Worrall, you can tell it to the police.' I have to tease out the connection with Annabelle before Worrall's attitude changes, before he hardens up. 'What does interest me is a name on your list of customers. Someone by the name of Aaronson. Tell me about Aaronson.'

Worrall begins to laugh. He stares at me as if I'm a fool, and he begins to laugh. His mania alarms those around him; even Liam Sanderson flinches, moves a little in his seat. I can't recall saying anything strange, anything humorous, anything silly. So I wait for the laughter to die down. Worrall reaches into his pocket, brings out a silk handkerchief and dabs at his eyes. He regains control. 'So you don't know everything after all, Oliphant. Thank God for that!' He wheezes again once or twice and fills his lungs with air.

'The name,' I repeat, 'Aaronson. Tell me about it.'

'But you said you didn't want to know,' Worrall crows in triumph. 'They all heard you. You said you didn't want any detail about how I came to start dealing.' Despite his apparent reluctance to talk, he wants to tell his story. He just needs coaxing.

'Aaronson has something to do with why you started dealing?' I hope it's the right question.

'Something to do with . . .' He laughs again, but this time it's forced, easily brought back under his control. 'Something to do with me starting dealing,' he whispers. 'Oh yes, it's that alright.' Suspicion returns. 'But you knew that all along, didn't you! You're just playing with me.'

'No, Ben, I'm not playing with you.' I leave the statement open. It doesn't matter whether he believes me or not; what's important is that he keeps talking.

'Aaronson was . . .' He comes to a quick halt, screws up his eyes as if he's trying to remember something. 'No, let's call her by her first name. We knew each other quite well. I met Anne a long time ago, when she was working as a waitress in a cocktail bar – no, it's true! – and I was out celebrating some contract and . . . Yeah, I remember, the drinks were flowing and we were giving out tips like madmen. I said I fancied a smoke and she gave me one. I thought she was coming on to me. I was drunk, getting high. I told her I was gay. But we got talking and suddenly I was the only one left. When the bar closed she put me in a taxi, dropped me at home. She left me a spliff in my pocket, and her number. No name, mind you. Just a mobile number. When I came round – next day, next week, next year – I rang her. It was the start of a business relationship. But she wasn't a customer, Oliphant, she was dealing. She sold me cannabis.'

'Worrall, there's no way she could have supplied you with all the drugs you have in your shed. If you lie . . .'

'No, honest. She supplied me, but only with stuff for me to use. And then . . . She gave me some seeds, not just three, quite a few. I grew them, got some good results. I started selling to friends. Then I started buying wholesale. Trouble was, doing that cut Anne out of the equation. She got upset. She came round a few times, each time high or drunk, but I think by then she was doing other stuff as well. She threatened me.'

'With what?'

'Nothing specific. Just threats. Said she'd get me. But it got tiresome after a while, so I told her to stop coming or I'd do something to her.'

'And did she stop?'

Worrall says nothing.

'Let's look at it a different way, Worrall. If you start dealing in London, you tread on some big toes. So what do you do? You cut them in. Anne Aaronson threatens you, so you tell your protector. And what does he do. He leans on her.'

'I swear to God I don't know what happened! I told her, I said get out while she had the chance. She didn't come back, I thought she'd just taken my advice.'

'Conspiracy to cause GBH as well as dealing? You're in a bad way, Worrall.'

'Jesus Christ, she was only a poxy drug dealer!'

Carol Parker touches him on the shoulder. 'Ben, listen. What was her name?'

'I've already told you. Anne Aaronson.'

'Anne Aaronson?' She pauses for effect. 'Or did you mishear it? Could it have been Anna Ronson? Look at the initials, A-R.'

'Are you suggesting,' King asks, 'that it's the same girl?'

'The same one. Perhaps she was playing with names by then, perhaps Ben didn't get the name wrong. But it doesn't really matter, does it. Mr Oliphant wouldn't be asking questions if it wasn't the same girl.'

King purses his lips. 'It seems we have a problem here,' he announces gravely. 'You have indeed proved a connection between Annabelle Wilder – in one of her various guises and pseudonyms – and several directors of the company. But the only alleged criminal connection is with Mr Worrall here, who is not a director. And there's still nothing to link any of us with the death of Annabelle Wilder. Indeed, given her apparent fixation with the company and its directors, it would be surprising if more of us haven't come across her in some form or another during her brief life.' He allows the fingers of both hands to meet, to ripple against each other. 'So the question is, do you have anything else to offer as evidence that one of us was involved in the girl's alleged murder?'

I do. But it's not proof. It's a story with holes, and someone at the table can fill in the holes. The question is, which one has his or her finger in the dyke? And if I can threaten, cajole or persuade that person to take out that solitary finger, will that release the flood of information I need? How can I find out who to attack?

It's dark outside now, the evening's taken over. The lighting in the room is dim, but no-one seems to have noticed the encroaching darkness. My eyes seem to prefer the gloom. I'm becoming crepuscular – brightness equals pain. It would be easy to close my eyes entirely, to let sleep wash over me, but I force them open. Across the table my suspects look tired, apprehensive. How must I appear to them? I've been lucky; everything has fallen into place so far. Are they seeing omniscience, someone who knows exactly what happened a year ago? I don't feel that I know everything. On the contrary, there are many things I don't know, and probably some things I don't even know I don't know. Even the thought of my own personal Rumsfeldt moment can't bring a smile to my face. I have to go on; I have to do so quickly before my body shuts down.

'Mr Worrall, do you always wear earrings? In both ears?'

He looks surprised at the question, worried where such an admission might lead. After a pause for thought he nods.

'You've already said that you weren't staying at the hotel a year ago. Can you confirm that?'

'Yes, that's right.'

'And where were you?'

'I'm not quite sure. I'd have to check my movements. I travel quite a lot, at home and abroad. I might have been . . .'

'Think carefully, Mr Worrall. Did you have a meeting with a client in or near the city? Or were you at a conference somewhere nearby? Perhaps you had a free weekend and wanted to spend it in our beautiful city? I suppose you could have finished your business in London and decided you wanted to surprise Liam Sanderson? You see, I don't know the reason you came here, but I do know you were here. Not just in the city. But here, in the hotel.'

'Ben?' Liam Sanderson can't hide his surprise. 'What is he on about? Tell him he's wrong, you weren't here – you would have come to see me. Tell him.'

I can afford to be calm, gentle even. My physical state prevents me being anything other than quiet. 'Mr Sanderson, you weren't aware that your lover was a drugs dealer. He didn't tell you. Why should he tell you about his other criminal activities?'

King intervenes again. 'Really, Mr Oliphant, your allegations about Ben are precisely that, allegations. You're not a policeman; you have no judicial authority. And yet you're about to start maligning Ben further, when he has no-one to advise him on his rights, his defence. I really do think that he should . . .'

The droning voice, the clipped tones, the air of self-importance, they're too much for me. 'King,' I say softly, but the very act of me speaking causes him to listen, 'shut up. Stop interrupting me. Worrall is guilty, guilty as hell, and I can prove it. Let me have my say. I'll call the police, they can arrest him, then we can all go home.'

The silence doesn't last long, but no words destroy it. Instead there's the high-pitched rise and fall of a siren. I can't hide my irritation. 'What the hell is that?'

'Fire?' Sly asks. Faces look at each other, but no-one moves. The siren continues to wail.

'I think we'd better leave,' King says, 'I don't think it's a drill.' There's still no movement.

I motion to Sly. 'Would you mind having a look out of the window?' He slips out of the room and into the lobby where a viewpoint beside the lift will allow him to see the road in front of the building. He's back in a few seconds. 'Lots of people on the front lawn,' he announces, 'and I'm sure I can smell smoke. I think we'd better leave.'

For some reason everyone looks at me. 'OK. Worrall, you stay beside me. Sly, keep your eyes on him. If he tries to run away, break his legs. I'd suggest that the rest of you leave. I'll be right behind you, I won't be in the way.'

They leave in an orderly fashion, the Cooksons at the front, Carol – shrugging herself into a coat – close behind. Trevor Rawlings and his silent wife grumble in their wake; King is beside a confused-looking Liam Sanderson, arm around his shoulder. Sanderson looks back at Worrall, mouths 'It'll be alright.' Sly trundles me along in their wake.

Outside in the lobby they're ignoring the lift, heading for the stairs. Sly disregards them, presses the lift button.

'You aren't meant to use lifts if there's a fire,' Worrall says fearfully, watching his colleagues' descent; he's expecting to be greeted by a jet of flame when the lift doors open in front of him.

'That,' Sly explains, hefting the crowbar into his left hand and pushing me closer, 'is a myth put about by security consultants who want to reserve the lifts for their wheelchair-bound friends. Anyway, if there was a fire in the lift shaft, there'd be smoke coming out of the doors.'

We wait. The lift, according to the red electronic numbers above the doors, is on the ground floor. Two minutes later it's still there.

'Boss, d'you think there might be a real fault?' Sly asks. 'Perhaps the noise we heard wasn't the fire alarm; perhaps it was the lift alarm.'

'Could be. But that shouldn't sound in the rooms.'

'Perhaps it's the lift that's on fire?' Worrall suggests. 'Perhaps there's no smoke yet.'

None of us wants to imagine the effects of a fire starting in the lift shaft itself. The shaft would act like a chimney, encouraging the flames at its base. Most lift shafts have a sprinkler system installed within the shaft, but given the quality of the emergency equipment we've seen in the hotel, it's possible the sprinkler system has been missed out completely.

I put my hands against the door. 'There's no heat there. But that doesn't help us get down. Sly, I can probably manage the stairs if I go very slowly.'

'Yeah, might be for the better. But I can carry you, if I get you onto my back.'

'Don't be silly, Sly, there's no need for that.'

'We're wasting time, boss. Remember, there might be a fire? Big red flamey things? Very hot; they burn you?'

'OK, OK. You win. But only if you promise I can carry you back up again when I'm feeling better.'

He clicks the wheelchair's brakes on, squats down in front of me. Before I can even try to rise to my feet, the chair's pushed over. As I fall I see a black-clad figure, his face obscured by a balaclava helmet, standing over Sly; a truncheon rises and falls and Sly collapses forward. The truncheon is lifted again, and again it descends. Sly doesn't move, but I can hear the sound of something hard hitting flesh, the truncated slap of meat being tenderised, of a body being bruised and hurt. I can barely move and my voice is a whisper, my cries unheard. But Worrall acts as my mouthpiece. 'Stop it!' he screams, 'you'll kill him!'

The blows cease. The dark-clad figure straightens up, peels off his headgear, uses it to wipe his face. He looks at Worrall, looks down again at Sly. 'I'll kill him? Strange, I always thought that was the idea.'

Before he can begin to hit Sly again I find I can draw a gasp of painful air into my lungs, expel it over harsh vocal cords, and what comes out of my mouth is a reasonable approximation of words. 'Rook,' I hiss, 'good to see you again.'

He looks down at me as if he's aware of my presence for the first time. He motions to Worrall. 'Pick him up,' he commands. Worrall does so, rights the chair first, drags me into it.

'Check Sly,' I tell him, 'make sure he's OK.'

Worrall seeks permission from Rook; Rook shrugs; Worrall takes this as a sign that he may go ahead. He bends down, puts his head to Sly's face, feels his pulse. 'He's breathing,' Worrall reports, 'his heart's beating. He's bleeding from a cut in the back of his head.' He wrinkles up his nose in distaste. 'Looks as if he'll need stitches.'

'Did you start the fire?' I ask Rook. 'Or is it an imaginary one, just you over-riding the alarms?'

The reply is swift, the voice familiar 'No, it's a real fire. But the damage will be localised. It'll be blamed on a short circuit in the lift. Trouble is, all the security cabling runs inside the lift shaft, so everything's shut down. The alarms are working, but all the cameras and sensors are down. Such an inconvenience.'

'You should know all about the cameras and sensors in this place, it was your company installed them. You are Jules Cooper, aren't you?'

The man facing me nods, mouth turned up in what I take to be appreciation of my deductions. 'That's me,' he says.

'Why are you telling him?' Worrall squeaks.

'I'm not telling him anything he doesn't know,' Cooper replies scornfully, 'and anyway, he's not going to tell anyone else, is he.'

'What do you mean by that?'

Cooper can't be bothered to respond.

'Think, Ben, think.' It's obvious I'll have to explain. 'Matters are serious; that's why Cooper's been drafted in. I'm too near to the truth. You said yourself, I know what happened a year ago . . .'

Cooper snorts his disbelief.

'I know most of what happened. So I'm being disposed of. I'm not quite sure how, and I don't know what Cooper intends doing with Sly, but I'm sure he'll have thought of something believable.'

Worrall seems shocked. 'Is that right? Are you going to kill them both?'

''Fraid so, pretty boy. After all, someone has to cover your rear; no insult intended. I mean you're already going down for dealing; we don't want you to spend any longer in prison than you have to. All those big hairy men. They'd eat you up and spit you out. Though I can see you might actually enjoy that. Still, we need to get going. Come on, give me a hand to move this big bastard.'

Worrall doesn't move. 'What are you going to do?'

Cooper sighs, looks at his watch. 'The fire brigade should be here very soon.' He holds up his finger. 'Ah yes, the sound of sirens.' He looks at me, says, 'Simon and Garfunkel?' and waits for me to react, but I'm in no mood to appreciate bad puns. Cooper turns his attention back to Worrall. 'Listen carefully. In a couple of minutes, all the lift doors on every floor are going to open. I know this because I've programmed them to do so. There's a fire in the base of the lift shaft; it'll be burning rather well by now, especially since the cabling and ducting is, how should I put it, a little more flammable than it ought to be. But you should know about that, shouldn't you. Anyway, when the doors open there'll be a lot of smoke and flames billowing about. In the confusion, Oliphant and his friend here are going to stumble into the lift shaft. You will be a witness to this, as will Mr King who should be heading bravely back upstairs at this very moment to see what's happening to you. He'll help you back down again and stay with you to make sure your story isn't forgotten. OK?'

From the stairs there comes the sound of panting and King duly appears. 'What's happened?' he gasps, 'I thought the doors . . .'

'One minute,' Cooper says, 'trust me.'

'But why?' Worrall asks Cooper, 'why are you doing this? She was already dead when we put her in the freezer, that's . . . oh, I don't know, conspiracy or something, but it's not murder. We haven't killed anyone. So why start now.'

If I weren't in such a predicament I'd be congratulating myself. An admission from Worrall that the three of them were involved in putting Annabelle's body in the freezer. I'd already suspected him, the reflections from his earrings were the clue. But now he's incriminated the others. It's a pity I'm unlikely to live to see them pay for their crimes.

'It's still murder,' I explain. 'You put her into the boiler room, didn't you? You knew there was carbon monoxide gas. Therefore you murdered her.'

'That's not true!' Worrall shouts at me. 'I wasn't even there. It was King who called me, said I had to come down and help out because there'd been an accident. But I didn't know.'

'You won't get away with this,' I say.

'Down to clichés now, Oliphant?' King's regaining his breath, his composure and his smugness.

'Thirty seconds.' Cooper's looking at his watch.

I'm staring at Sly, his foot twitched a moment before and no-one saw it. He could be returning to consciousness; he could yet rescue us. And although I'm in agony, I've no intention of going without a fight. But there are three of them.

'So you didn't put her in the boiler room? And you didn't know there was a leak of carbon monoxide gas? Surely you don't expect me to believe that.'

'It's true,' King says. 'If only you'd believed me when we said we weren't involved in killing her. She wasn't murdered at all. It was all an accident. Oh, for Christ's sake, tell him, Cooper.'

'Twenty seconds and counting, so I'll have to be brief. Here we go then. This girl, Annabelle, sells pot to Worrall here, and to quite a few of his bumboy mates. He stops buying from her, decides to deal himself. She gets annoyed, goes round to see him. While she's there she sees the plans of a hotel, this hotel, and faggo Worrall's notes about how they can save money. Unfortunately he's done a little memo to King, pointing out that it's dangerous and illegal – ten seconds to go – to change the spec. She thinks nothing of it till she comes up here with her little boyfriend, applies for a job and gets it, then realises that the hotel's the same as the one on the plans. She puts two and two together, makes five beans and Jack's your beanstalk. So she comes to see me, tells me she wants some money or she'll go public. I does what any honest businessman would do – I pays up.' He stops, shakes his watch.

'Don't tell me,' I say, 'you bought the timing mechanisms to open the doors from the same place you bought the rest of the stuff for this hotel. It's all cheap rubbish.'

'Torching hotels isn't an exact science, Billy. It'll happen.' He doesn't seem worried. 'Now where was I? Oh yes, little Miss Wilder. I pay her the money, she wants more. So I arrange to meet her, down by the river, at the back of the hotel.'

'To throw her in?'

'Oliphant, please, would I? No, I just wanted to threaten her. But she got frightened. She ran away, I chased her. She hid in the boiler room. She died in the boiler room. Bit like a canary down a mine, actually, she did us a favour. We didn't

316

know there was a problem with the boiler room.' He giggles. 'I would have left her there, but King said no, we had to move her. And we couldn't carry her out to the riverside. But I knew about the system's blind spots; I knew where we could hide her and interest would be, how should I say, diverted from the boiler room, from the hotel itself, to the body. I knew her bonzo boyfriend worked here as well. That's why we stripped her and tied her up. Apart from confusing the fuzz we thought it might incriminate him.'

'I can see now,' I say, 'you couldn't afford to leave her there because the police would find out that the building was badly designed and built. They'd close the hotel down, there'd be an investigation, and they might find that . . .'

King interrupts, '. . . that we'd done it deliberately. That Ben drew up an over-the-top spec, Jules here tendered for the work and got it because he knew he wouldn't have to do the work properly, then Ben signed it off.'

'And you?'

'Me? Ah yes, what's my role? Well, I just like to be involved.'

'I can believe that. You make profits with Amalgam because you peddle an overpriced product and promise luxury, but what your customers get is all flash and no substance. You make profits with Armaclad – yes, I know about your interests there as well – because their income is grossly inflated, they buy in cheap and sell at a huge profit. I assume you've got the same scam going with your other hotel groups as well. You make your profits by cheating the customers and by cheating the shareholders. No wonder you didn't want anyone to find out.'

Behind me the doors begin to open, then jam when they're only a few inches apart. Black smoke curls out and drifts across the landing.

'Shit!' Cooper swears. He reaches to pick up Sly's crowbar.

'You'll leave marks on the door,' I tell him, 'as evidence. They'll be suspicious.'

317

He stops, drops the crowbar, tries with his hands to open the doors further.

'You'll be found out,' I tell Worrall and King. 'What about the payments to Annabelle Wilder? They're traceable, straight out of Armaclad's accounts into hers. You see! I know, I know it all. And I'm not stupid enough to keep it to myself. Even if you kill me, others know. You won't get away with it.'

'Shut the fuck up!' Cooper's having some success – the doors are inching open, the smoke is thickening.

King becomes spokesman. 'We've investigated you thoroughly, Oliphant. We know who's been helping you. The information you mention was gained by your friend "Rak".' He rolls the letter 'R' as if he's savouring the bad tastes it leaves in his mouth. 'She too can be dealt with. You see, we have money. Money counts for everything.'

The doors are opening further, certainly wide enough to get a wheelchair through. Black smoke is flooding the landing, descending from the ceiling.

'It looks as if we'll be saying goodbye in a moment, Oliphant. Such a pity, you could have done so well with us. And why did you give everything up? For a two-timing tart, a blackmailer, a smack-head, a little whore. Was it worth it, Oliphant?' His eyes are streaming, he's beginning to cough.

Cooper has put down his crowbar; he steps around my wheelchair. I push myself to my feet. He won't get rid of me easily; there'll be a struggle. But he's swinging his truncheon in the air; he'll knock me out easily. He stops in front of me. 'I really do feel sorry for Annabelle,' he says. 'It was an accident, believe me. And I was getting to know her quite well. Our little arrangement didn't just involve money. She was quite a demon in bed. It might even have been me who got her up the stick.' He grins. 'But now? Time to die, Ollie.'

I back away, if he wants to hit me he'll have to come after me. He swings and the blow hits me on the forearm. The pain is excruciating, I fall to the ground. He steps closer.

He's closer to the lift door than I am. I lunge for him but my movement is slow, my aim poor. He easily avoids me, jumps and steps away. I'm prostrate in front of him; now he can't miss. I raise my head. That's when I hear the howl of anger, that's when we all hear it. It comes from Terry Wilder's mouth as he appears out of the smoke like a demon and hurls himself at Cooper. Cooper tumbles backwards towards the door. He'd have had no problem if he could stay on his feet, but Sly's awake, though barely capable of movement. What he does is enough – he raises his leg so Cooper falls over it. His fall is complete, straight through the open lift doors. He doesn't even scream.

Terry's eyes are wild, red and filled with tears, and not just from the smoke. He picks up both the crowbar and the truncheon. 'Now you!' he says, advancing on King. 'Either you jump down the shaft, or I kick you down it!'

King's backing away, but he has nowhere to go to. He can barely breathe, he can hardly see the blackened, grimy figure approaching him.

'No Terry!' I shout. 'It won't help. He didn't kill her.'

'He built the hotel,' Terry growls. 'He cut costs. He was responsible.'

'Help me,' King pleads, down on his knees. He's looking at me. Behind him Worrall is pressed against the wall, terrified that he'll be next. Terry moves between them as King tries to twist round to face him.

'Crawl,' Terry says.

King shakes his head. 'I can't,' he whimpers.

'Crawl!' Terry swings the truncheon lazily; it catches King on the thigh and he spins around. Terry repeats the blow, this time on his backside. 'Crawl,' he repeats.

I can hear the rattle of flames far down the lift shaft, desperate to reach us. They're urging waves of heat upwards, heat that's forcing the acrid smoke out of the open doors. I roll towards Sly. 'You alright?'

'What the hell d'you think!'

'We need to get downstairs. Can you walk?'

'Do I have any choice?'

'No.'

'I can walk.' He pushes himself to his feet.

'Don't try to stop me!' Terry warns, brandishing the crowbar. At the same time he hits King again, this time on the back.

'Please don't make me,' King cries again, but he's forced to move inexorably closer to the doors and the smoke and the fire.

It's my turn to make the attempt to stand up. Remember those films where the hero's in a fight and he's all bleeding and battered, but he still manages to overcome huge obstacles and rescue the heroine. Don't believe them. I need the wall and Sly's arm to raise me to a crouch. I'm trying to keep the smoke above me. I don't think my lungs are working at all. But still I manage to move. I lurch forward like Quasimodo to stand between Terry and King.

'I meant it,' Terry hisses. 'I could just push you aside. He needs to die.'

'I agree,' I say, 'but if you kill him, you kill me and you kill Sly. Look at us. We can barely stand up, let alone walk. We need help to get downstairs, and quickly, before the whole place goes up in flames. We need you, Worrall and King to help us. We need all of you, not just two of you. We need you now.'

He shakes his head. 'He needs to die.'

'Go on then!' It takes all my strength to yell those three words, then I'm down on my knees again. 'But if you make him go one inch further, you're as bad as he was. Is that what Annabelle would want?'

Terry considers. He smiles at the thought of his wife. 'Yes,' he says softly, 'that's what she'd want. She'd want him to die. She'd want them all to die. I knew, Billy, I knew how she felt. She didn't tell me why, but she hated them. She didn't tell me everything about herself, but she didn't have to. They'd all done something to her, something wrong. And if she was here instead of me, if it was the other way round, she'd kick his arse down that lift shaft and laugh as he bloody well fell!' He tries to draw breath, coughs. It would take a kick, nothing more, to push King over the edge. Terry eyes the gap, measures himself for the effort. Then he stops.

'Anna would have killed him. But I'm me, Billy. I'm different.' He pokes King with the end of the truncheon. 'Come on, you bastard, on your feet. Give us a hand. You and Worrall help Sly, I'll take Billy. Come on, before I change me mind!'

It takes only a little organising. Sly and I allow ourselves to be dragged down the stairs through layers of smoke until we hurl ourselves against a pair of fire doors on the ground floor. They give way and deposit us on a water-soaked pavement. Hands grab us, push us onto stretchers and cover us with blankets, hurry us away. I'm lying on my back, staring up at a building wreathed in smoke and flames. There are dozens of fire-tenders.

We pass a fire officer talking to a colleague; he wipes the back of his hand across a dirt-flecked, sweaty forehead. 'It shouldn't have gone up like that,' he says. 'The sprinklers weren't working; there's something in the fabric of the building that's just feeding the flames; we'll have to pull back. The whole thing's going to come down . . .'

I want to look round to see if Sly's OK, to find Terry and say thank you, but the effort of moving my head is too great. Instead I close my eyes.

CHAPTER TWENTY-THREE

There are several endings to this story. They don't resolve matters. Some of them merely ask questions. But here they are, in the order of them happening.

In the first ending, I feel better before Sly does – it'll be another week before he leaves hospital. After a night of oxygen therapy I can at least breathe. Walking without the aid of a zimmer frame takes another day. The hospital needs beds, so they discharge me into the immediate, though temporary, care of Kim Bryden. We talk in the hospital canteen amidst the smell of boiled cabbage and gravy.

Kim is keen to hear about attempted murder, arson, blackmail and sundry lesser crimes. Few of the accusations appear to be aimed at me, save the usual ones of not telling her when I get into trouble. She gives me her standard lecture, the one reminding me that I'm an ex-policeman, that I shouldn't take the law into my own hands, that I might have got myself killed (not necessarily a bad thing) or even got someone else killed (unforgivable). When she switches from oppressor to confidante I find out that Ben Worrall has confessed to dealing and has explained his part in moving Annabelle Wilder's body into the freezer. King is revealing the extent of his criminality a little at a time, in the company of a very expensive London lawyer.

After she's finished scolding me, Kim is almost unstinting in her approval. 'Not a bad weekend's work,' she tells me. That is praise indeed from Kim Bryden. 'You seem to have tied up quite a few loose ends.'

My encounters with Kim in the past have rarely been as

amicable. It sounds to me as if something's wrong. 'Where's the "but"?'

'What are you talking about?'

'There's always a "but" when you say something pleasant about me. Where is it?'

'There isn't one, Billy. You've solved several crimes and a problem.'

This is infuriating. I prefer Kim when she's confirming that she has no sense of humour. 'OK, the references to crimes I can understand, but who's the one with the problem? Come on then, tell me.'

Kim's enjoying her moment of superiority. 'No, Billy, you tell me. Remember Friday, when we had dinner together and I told you about me going to work for Amalgam?'

'How could I forget? You got me into this.'

'Did you ever intend working for Amalgam?'

The question catches me unaware. The snappy response would have been to suggest that we went together like petrol and matches, the mixture would have been too explosive. But she doesn't want the witty reply, she wants honesty. So, for once, I use it. 'No, Kim. I never intended working for Amalgam.'

'Of course not. And why?'

Again, she's surprising me, and I find that, once again, I have to be honest. I don't like being honest with Kim, it breaks the habits of a lifetime. 'It's against my principles. And before you ask, I don't know what they are. Something to do with public service, not private enterprise. Power to the people. Down with big business but up with small businesses, especially if they're to do with installing security systems and they're run by balding middle-aged ex-cops. But most of all because the whole thing smelled, Kim. There was obviously something wrong.'

'I agree with all that, Billy. Given that, given what you know about me, I've got a question for you. Do you think I could ever have intended working for Amalgam?'

The penny doesn't so much drop as creep into my head and ricochet round my otherwise empty skull. It's not that I can't see the wood for the trees, more that my head has become a piece of solid timber. 'No. Please don't say that. Please don't tell me it was all a set-up. Because if it was, I'll be knocking on someone's door pointing out that I was almost killed and asking for a penny or two in compensation.'

'That's already being dealt with,' says Kim apologetically. 'I'm not sure how much, but it'll be substantial. You see, we suspected the directors had some involvement in Annabelle's death, but we couldn't figure out what or why. After six months with no leads the case was being wound down. It was suggested I become more involved.'

'Undercover?'

'Undercover. So why were you there? Well, several reasons. First of all, you were a sort of test. If you believed me, and the Amalgam directors believed me, and they offered you a job, I was safe. Then there was the possibility that you might even be able to help, but that was in the medium term, and by then I would have told you what was going on. But then you went and stuck your silly little nose into someone else's business.'

I can't believe I didn't see through her, see the game she was playing. 'So there was never going to be a big payday? Not for you, not for me?'

Kim shakes her head. 'Not really.'

'Do the rest of the Amalgam directors know about this yet? Do they know you were planning a sting?'

She snorts. 'No, not yet. But they will, eventually. There's already a DTI enquiry planned into the company. They'll find out who knows what. But they won't be able to claim entrapment, will they, because I wasn't actually involved in the case at the end? So stay safe, Billy. You'll be needed at the trial.' She gets to her feet, a sign that the discussion is over. She graciously helps me up and offers me a lift to Rak's where I'm to recuperate. I accept, but during the journey I'm silent. I can't help feeling I've been used, and it's a medicine I'm more used to dispensing than swallowing. And when I close my eyes I see an image of a woman's body, pale, lifeless, ice-cold.

There's a second ending.

I fly down to London, take an expensive taxi to middle-class suburbia where I've arranged to meet Charles and Emily Robertson.

Their drawing room is precisely that; it's full of chintz and politeness, Betjeman would have loved it. There's tea in porcelain cups, sugar in a matching bowl with tongs, a three-layer cake and biscuit stand. We sit on comfortable chairs with billowing cushions, the arms covered by white linen protectors. I've a napkin spread on my lap. There's a walnut grandfather clock in the corner, its tick-tock hypnotises the room into obedient somnolence. I can see why Annabelle rebelled.

I've come to explain what I've discovered. There will, eventually, be a trial. Worrall and King will be found guilty. These are only predictions, but I've enough experience to know when evidence will stick. I also know that there'll be a great deal of accusation and counter-accusation, and that Annabelle's name and character will be a target for the defending counsels. She'll have no-one speaking for her. It'll take a while, six months to a year, before the matter comes to court, but I feel Charles and Emily ought to be prepared for the worst.

It's difficult explaining to an elderly couple that their daughter was a drug dealer. That she was an unmarried mother who agreed to sell her baby. That she was a blackmailer. I try to explain that the path she chose to take was the wrong one, but that the choices she had were limited. I tell them that if I'd been Annabelle I would probably have done exactly what she did, because I too am weak, and lonely and human. And I tell them how, at the end, she was deeply in love with a man who loved her in return, that she was happy.

I don't think it's enough. I fear that, if Charles lasts that long, the trial will probably kill him. Emily has no daughter to care for her in her old age. There are no other relatives. We agree to keep in touch, but I suspect we won't.

I leave, pleased to have done my duty, waving at two frail figures holding each other upright beneath a bower of late roses. But when I close my eyes I see an image of a woman's body, pale, lifeless, ice-cold.

There's a third ending.

I like airports. I also like motorway service areas, cheap transport cafes, shopping malls, city centres late at night. I like to watch people there, to see them eating and drinking, touching or not touching. I like to wonder about their lives, where they live, what they do. I like to wonder why they're there, at that particular moment. But today, as Jen walks towards me, I wonder what other people see when they watch us.

I know how I feel. I feel a sense of utter relief that she's smiling at me, and I can't stop myself smiling at her. I feel I want to cry with happiness. I feel silly and boyish. I feel that the seconds until we can touch are too long. But what about the others around me, the others who also like watching people? Do they see a middle-aged man trying to break into a shambling run and wincing as he does so? Do they wonder why the attractive young girl has abandoned her trolley laden with cases and is running towards him? Do they try to reconcile the relationship? Are we father and step-child, uncle and niece? Are we lovers? If so, how have I tempted her? With money? It certainly isn't good looks.

We don't kiss, not to begin with. We hug, not a polite hug using the arms and the cheeks. Our bodies touch from head to toe, press against each other. I can smell her perfume, feel the softness of her hair. I can hear her crying.

'I'm not going again,' she says.

'You're not going again,' I tell her.

'Not unless you come with me.'

'Not unless I come with you.'

She laughs. Bells ring, klaxons sound. She pushes me away from her, just a little. 'Do you think people are watching us?' she asks.

'Yes. They're wondering which famous film star you are.'

'Flatterer. I've got something for you.'

'From Canada? Don't tell me, an inflatable moose.'

'Damn, you guessed! No, that's in the luggage.' She puts her hand into her pocket and holds out her fist towards me, knuckles upward. She turns it over, opens it slowly. It's a ring-pull from a soft drink can.

'Is it the one that wins you a prize?' I ask.

'That depends. I've been thinking, Billy, thinking a lot. And then, when I saw you . . . Anyway, the prize depends on whether you answer the question properly or not.'

'And the question is?'

She drops down on one knee. 'Billy Oliphant, will you marry me?'

Payback

Alan Dunn

Security consultant, ex-cop and some-time detective Billy
Oliphant is suffering from more than just winter blues. His
girlfriend is on a year's sabbatical in North America and his
ex-wife is honeymooning with her new husband, leaving
Billy with their sixteen-year-old daughter. Sly, Billy's friend,
thinks that a weekend at the Forestcrag Moorland Holiday
Village will cheer him up. But having battled the worsening
weather to get to Forestcrag, they discover things are far
from idyllic. The park manager believes someone is
poisoning his staff. Billy is reluctant to get involved, but soon
has little choice when the Village is snowed in and the body
of Eric Salkeld is discovered.

It looks like a straightforward suicide. Left nominally in
charge of the investigation by police unable to get to the
crime scene, Billy feels that the suicide looks a little too
staged. Amongst the guests trapped at the Village, there could
be a killer. And, if the police are right that a recently escaped
prisoner is heading for Forestcrag, perhaps more than one...

Praise for Alan Dunn's previous book, *Die Cast*:

'Enough twists and hairpin turns to have your head spinning.
Terrific storytelling' CAMPBELL ARMSTRONG

'A dark thriller that trumpets an emerging talent' *Time Out*

'good tight prose...' *Literary Review*

'this excellent novel is both a delight and a surprise...it will
be a pleasure to see Dunn's next book' *Newcastle Journal*

A SELECTION OF NOVELS AVAILABLE FROM PIATKUS BOOKS

THE PRICES BELOW WERE CORRECT AT THE TIME OF
GOING TO PRESS. HOWEVER PIATKUS BOOKS RESERVE
THE RIGHT TO SHOW NEW RETAIL PRICES ON COVERS
WHICH MAY DIFFER FROM THOSE PREVIOUSLY
ADVERTISED IN THE TEXT OR ELSEWHERE.

0 7499 3335 6	Payback	Alan Dunn	£6.99
0 7499 3254 6	Die Cast	Alan Dunn	£6.99
0 7499 3303 8	Making a Killing	Iain McDowall	£6.99
0 7499 3393 3	Perfectly Dead	Iain McDowall	£6.99
0 7499 3629 0	Blood of the Innocents	Chris Collett	£6.99
0 7499 3603 7	Cold Blood	Denise Ryan	£6.99

ALL PIATKUS TITLES ARE AVAILABLE FROM:
PIATKUS BOOKS C/O BOOKPOST
PO Box 29, Douglas, Isle Of Man, IM99 1BQ
Telephone (+44) 01624 677237
Fax (+44) 01624 670923
Email; bookshop@enterprise.net
Free Postage and Packing in the United Kingdom.
Credit Cards accepted. All Cheques payable to Bookpost.
(Prices and availability subject to change without prior notice. Allow 14 days for delivery. When
placing orders please state if you do not wish to receive any additional information.)

OR ORDER ONLINE FROM:
www.piatkus.co.uk
Free postage and packing in the UK (on orders of two books or more)